06- DOB-176

THIS IS THE NOVEL
THAT TOPS THEM ALL!
THE BIGGEST BESTSELLER
OF THE YEAR!

FREDERICK FORSYTH'S
THE ODESSA FILE

is a stunning successor to
The Day of the Jackal—
shocking, explosive, suspenseful—
a superb documentary thriller!

"A BRILLIANT ENTERTAINMENT!"
—*The Guardian*

A WORLD OF PRAISE

the
odessa
file

frederick forsyth

BANTAM BOOKS
TORONTO · NEW YORK · LONDON

THE ODESSA FILE

A Bantam Book / published by arrangement with
THE VIKING PRESS, INC.

PRINTING HISTORY
Viking edition published November 1972
Bantam edition published January 1974

To all press reporters

AUTHOR'S NOTE

IT IS CUSTOMARY for authors to thank those who have helped them to compile a book, particularly on a difficult subject, and in doing so to name them. All those who helped me, in however small a way, by assisting me to get the information I needed to write *The Odessa File* are entitled to my heartfelt thanks, and if I do not name them it is for three reasons.

Some, being former members of the SS, were not aware at the time either whom they were talking to, or that what they said would end up in a book. Others have specifically asked that their names never be mentioned as sources of information about the SS. In the case of others still, the decision not to mention their names is mine alone, and taken, I hope, for their sakes rather than for mine.

Throughout the book there occur the names of places and organizations and the titles and ranks of various people, most of which in the original language would be in German. To assist those who do not read German and find the longer words unpronounceable, I have taken the liberty of translating the majority into English. Those with a knowledge of German, who will no doubt recognize the original form, are asked to forgive the translations.

F. F.

FOREWORD

THE ODESSA of the title is neither the city in southern Russia nor the smaller city in Texas. It is a word composed of six initial letters, which in German stand for *Organisation der ehemaligen SS-Angehörigen.* In English this means "Organization of Former Members of the SS."

The SS, as most readers will know, was the army within an army, the state within a state, devised by Adolf Hitler, commanded by Heinrich Himmler, and charged with special tasks under the Nazis who ruled Germany from 1933 to 1945. These tasks were supposedly concerned with the security of the Third Reich; in effect they included the carrying out of Hitler's ambition to rid Germany and Europe of all elements he considered to be "unworthy of life," to enslave in perpetuity the "subhuman races of the Slavic lands," and to exterminate every Jew, man, woman, and child, on the face of the Continent.

In carrying out these tasks the SS organized and executed the murder of some fourteen million human beings, comprising roughly six million Jews, five million Russians, two million Poles, half a million gypsies, and half a million mixed others, including, though it is seldom mentioned, close to two hundred thousand non-Jewish Germans and Austrians. These were either mentally or physically handicapped unfortunates, or so-called enemies of the Reich, such as Communists, Social Democrats, liberals, editors, reporters, and priests who spoke out too inconveniently, men of conscience and courage, and later Army officers suspected of lack of loyalty to Hitler.

Before it had been destroyed the SS had made the

two initials of its name, and the twin-lightning symbol of its standard, synonymous with inhumanity in a way that no other organization before or since has been able to do.

Before the end of the war its most senior members, quite aware the war was lost and under no illusions as to how civilized men would regard their actions when the reckoning came, made secret provision to disappear to a new life, leaving the entire German people to carry and share the blame for the vanished culprits. To this end vast sums of SS gold were smuggled out and deposited in numbered bank accounts, false identity papers were prepared, escape channels opened up. When the Allies finally conquered Germany, the bulk of the mass-murderers had gone.

The organization which they formed to effect their escape was the Odessa. When the first talk of ensuring the escape of the killers to more hospitable climes had been achieved, the ambitions of these men developed. Many never left Germany at all, preferring to remain under cover with false names and papers while the Allies ruled; others came back, suitably protected by a new identity. The few very top men remained abroad to manipulate the organization from the safety of a comfortable exile.

The aim of the Odessa was and remains fivefold: to rehabilitate former SS men *into the professions of* the new Federal Republic created in 1949 by the Allies, to infiltrate at least the lower echelons of political party activity, to pay for the very best legal defense for any SS killer hauled before a court and in every way possible to stultify the course of justice in West Germany when it operates against a former *Kamerad,* to see that former SS men established themselves in commerce and industry in time to take advantage of the economic miracle that has rebuilt the country since 1945, and finally to propagandize the German people to the viewpoint that the SS killers were in fact none other than ordinary patriotic soldiers doing their duty to the Fatherland, and in no way deserving of the persecution to which justice and conscience have ineffectually subjected them.

In all these tasks, backed by its considerable funds, it has been measurably successful, and in none more so than in reducing official retribution through the West German courts to a mockery. Changing its name several times, the Odessa has sought to deny its own existence as an organization, with the result that many Germans are inclined to say the Odessa does not exist. The short answer is: it exists, and the *Kameraden* of the Death's Head insignia are still linked within it.

Despite its successes in almost all its objectives, the Odessa does occasionally take a defeat. The worst it ever suffered occurred in the early spring of 1964, when a package of documents arrived unannounced and anonymously at the Ministry of Justice in Bonn. To the very few officials who ever saw the list of names on these sheets, the package became known as "The Odessa File."

PUBLISHERS' NOTE

As in the case of Mr. Forsyth's first novel, *The Day of the Jackal*, many characters in *The Odessa File* are real people. Some will be immediately recognized by the reader; others may puzzle the reader as to whether they are true or fictional, and the publishers do not wish to elucidate further because it is in this ability to perplex the reader as to how much is true and how much false that much of the grip of the story lies.

Nevertheless, the publishers feel the reader may be interested or assisted to know that the story of former SS Captain Eduard Roschmann, the commandant of the concentration camp at Riga from 1941 to 1944, from his birth in Graz, Austria, in 1908 to his present exile in South America, is completely factual and drawn from SS and West German records.

New York

1972

1

THERE WAS a thin robin's-egg-blue dawn coming up over Tel Aviv when the intelligence analyst finished typing his report. He stretched the cramped muscles of his shoulders, lit another filter-tipped Time, and read the concluding paragraphs.

The man on whose debriefing the report was based stood at the same hour in prayer fifty miles to the east at a place called Yad Vashem, but the analyst did not know this. He did not know precisely how the information in his report had been obtained, or how many men had died before it reached him. He did not need to know. All he needed was to be assured the information was accurate and that his forward-analysis was soundly and logically arrived at.

Corroborative details arriving in this office indicate the substantial accuracy of the named agent's claim with regard to the location of the factory. If the appropriate action is taken, it may safely be assumed the West German authorities will concern themselves with its dismantlement.

It is recommended that the substantial record of the facts be placed soon in the hands of these authorities. It is felt by this agency that this would be the best way of ensuring an attitude at the highest level in Bonn that will ensure the continuance of the Waldorf deal.

To all intents and purposes therefore the Right Honourable members of the Committee may be assured the project known as Vulkan is in the process of being dismantled. Consequent on this, our best authorities assure us the rockets can never fly in time. Finally, that being so, it may be concluded that if and when war with Egypt comes, that war will be fought and won by conventional weapons, which is to say by the Republic of Israel.

The analyst signed the foot of the document and dated it: February 23, 1964. Then he pressed a bell to summon a dispatch rider who would take it to the office of the Prime Minister.

Everyone seems to remember with great clarity what he was doing on November 22, 1963, at the precise moment he heard President Kennedy was dead. Kennedy was hit at twelve-thirty in the afternoon, Dallas time, and the announcement that he was dead came at about half past one in the same time zone. It was two-thirty in New York, seven-thirty in the evening in London, and eight-thirty on a chilly, sleet-swept night in Hamburg.

Peter Miller was driving back into the town center after visiting his mother at her home in Osdorf, one of the outer suburbs of the city. He always visited her on Friday evenings, partly to see if she had everything she needed for the weekend and partly because he felt he had to visit her once a week. He would have telephoned her if she had a telephone, but as she had none, he drove out to see her. That was why she refused to have a telephone.

As usual, he had the radio on, and was listening to a music show being broadcast by Northwest German Radio. At half past eight he was in the Osdorf Way, ten minutes from his mother's flat, when the music stopped in the middle of a bar and the voice of the announcer came through, taut with tension.

"*Achtung, Achtung.* Here is an announcement. President Kennedy is dead. I repeat, President Kennedy is dead."

Miller took his eyes off the road and stared at the dimly illuminated band of frequencies along the upper edge of the radio, as if his eyes would be able to deny what his ears had heard, assure him he was tuned in to the wrong radio station, the one that broadcast nonsense.

"Jesus," he breathed quietly, eased down on the brake pedal, and swung to the right-hand side of the road. He glanced up. Right down the long, broad, straight highway through Altona toward the center of Hamburg, other drivers had heard the same broadcast and were pulling in to the side of the road as if driving and listening to the radio had suddenly become mutually exclusive, which in a way they had.

Along his own side he could see the brake lights glowing on as the drivers ahead swung to the right to park at the curb and listen to the supplementary information pouring from their radios. On the left the headlights of the cars heading out of town wavered wildly as they too swung away toward the pavement. Two cars overtook him, the first hooting angrily, and he caught a glimpse of the driver tapping his forehead in Miller's direction in the usual rude sign, indicating lunacy, that one German driver makes to another who has annoyed him.

He'll learn soon enough, thought Miller.

The light music on the radio had stopped, replaced by the "Funeral March," which was evidently all the disk jockey had on hand. At intervals he read snippets of further information straight off the teleprinter, as they were brought in from the newsroom. The details began to fill in: the open-car ride into Dallas, the rifleman in the window of the School Book Depository. No mention of an arrest.

The driver of the car ahead of Miller climbed out and walked back towards him. He approached the lefthand window, then realized that the driver's seat was inexplicably on the right and came round the car. He wore a nylon-fur-collared jacket. Miller wound down his window.

"You heard it?" asked the man, bending down to the window.

"Yeah," said Miller.

"Absolutely fantastic," said the man. All over Hamburg, Europe, the world, people were walking up to complete strangers to discuss the event.

"You reckon it was the Communists?" asked the man.

"I don't know."

"It could mean war, you know, if it was them," said the man.

"Maybe," said Miller. He wished the man would go away. As a reporter he could imagine the chaos sweeping across the newspaper offices of the country as every staff man was called back to help put out a crash edition for the morning breakfast tables. There would be obituaries to prepare, the thousands of instant tributes to correlate and typeset, the telephone lines jammed with yelling men seeking more and ever more details because a man with his head shattered lay dead in a city in Texas.

He wished in a way he were back on the staff of a daily newspaper, but since he had become a freelance three years earlier he had specialized in news features inside Germany, mainly connected with crime, the police, the underworld. His mother hated the job, accusing him of mixing with "nasty people," and his arguments that he was becoming one of the most sought-after reporter-investigators in the country availed nothing in persuading her that a reporter's job was worthy of her only son.

As the reports from the radio came through, his mind was racing, trying to think of another "angle" that could be chased up inside Germany and might make a sidebar story to the main event. The reaction of the Bonn government would be covered out of Bonn by the staff men; the memories of Kennedy's visit to Berlin the previous June would be covered from there. There didn't seem to be a good pictorial feature he could ferret out to sell to any of the score of German picture magazines that were the best customers of his kind of journalism.

The man leaning on the window sensed that Miller's attention was elsewhere and assumed it was out of grief for the dead President. Quickly he dropped his talk of world war and adopted the same grave demeanor. *"Ja, ja, ja,"* he murmured with sagacity, as if he had seen it coming all along. "Violent people, these Ameri-

cans, mark my words, violent people. There's a streak
of violence in them that we over here will never understand."

"Sure," said Miller, his mind still miles away.

The man took the hint at last. "Well, I must be getting
home," he said, straightening up. *"Grüss Gott."* He
started to walk back to his own car.

Miller became aware he was going. *"Ja, gute Nacht,"*
he called out of the open window, then wound it up
against the sleet whipping in off the Elbe River. The
music on the radio continued in funereal vein, and
the announcer said there would be no more light music
that night, just news bulletins interspersed with suitable
music.

Miller leaned back on the comfortable leather upholstery of his Jaguar and lit up a Roth-Händl, a filter-
less black-tobacco cigarette with a foul smell, another
thing that his mother complained about in her disap-
pointing son.

It is always tempting to wonder what would have happened if . . . or if not. Usually it is a futile exercise,
for what might have been is the greatest of all the
mysteries. But it is probably accurate to say that if
Miller had not had his radio on that night he would not
have pulled in to the side of the road for half an hour.
He would not have seen the ambulance, or heard of
Salomon Tauber or Eduard Roschmann, and forty
months later the republic of Israel would probably
have ceased to exist.

He finished his cigarette, still listening to the radio,
wound down the window, and threw the stub away. At
a touch of the button the 3.8-liter engine beneath the
long sloping bonnet of the Jaguar XK 150 S thundered
once and settled down to its habitual and comforting
rumble, like an angry animal trying to get out of a
cage. Miller flicked on the two headlights, checked
behind, and swung out into the growing traffic stream
along Osdorf Way.

He had got as far as the traffic lights on Stresemann-
strasse, and they were standing at red, when he heard

the clamor of the ambulance behind him. It came past him on the left, the wail of the siren rising and falling, slowed slightly before heading into the road junction against the red light, then swung across Miller's nose and down to the right into Daimlerstrasse. Miller reacted on reflexes alone. He let in the clutch, and the Jaguar surged after the ambulance, twenty meters behind it.

As soon as he had done it he wished he had gone straight home. It was probably nothing, but one never knew. Ambulances meant trouble, and trouble could mean a story, particularly if one were first on the scene and the whole thing had been cleared up before the staff reporters arrived. It could be a major crash on the road, or a big wharf fire, a tenement building ablaze, with children trapped inside. It could be anything. Miller always carried a small Yashica with flash attachment in the glove compartment of his car because one never knew what was going to happen right in front of one's eyes.

He knew a man who had been waiting for a plane at Munich airport on February 6, 1958, and the plane carrying the Manchester United football team had crashed a few hundred meters from where he stood. The man was not even a professional photographer, but he had unslung the camera he was taking on a skiing holiday and snapped the first exclusive pictures of the burning aircraft. The pictorial magazines had paid more than 50,000 marks for them.

The ambulance twisted into the maze of small and mean streets of Altona, leaving the Altona railway station on the left and heading down toward the river. Whoever was driving the flat-snouted, high-roofed Mercedes ambulance knew his Hamburg and knew how to drive. Even with his greater acceleration and hard suspension, Miller could feel the back wheels of the Jaguar skidding across the cobbles slick with rain.

Miller watched Menck's auto-parts warehouse rush by, and two streets later his original question was answered. The ambulance drew up in a poor and sleazy street, ill lit and gloomy in the slanting sleet, bordered by crumbling tenements and rooming-houses. It stopped in front of one of these, where a police car already stood, its blue roof light twirling, the beam sending a ghostly glow across the faces of a knot of bystanders grouped round the door.

A burly police sergeant in a rain cape roared at the crowd to stand back and make a gap in front of the door for the ambulance. Into this the Mercedes slid. Its driver and attendant climbed down, ran round to the back, and eased out an empty stretcher. After a brief word with the sergeant, the pair hastened upstairs.

Miller pulled the Jaguar to the opposite curb twenty yards down the road and raised his eyebrows. No crash, no fire, no trapped children. Probably just a heart attack. He climbed out and strolled over to the crowd, which the sergeant was holding back in a semi-circle around the door of the rooming-house.

"Mind if I go up?" asked Miller.

"Certainly do. It's nothing to do with you."

"I'm press," said Miller, proffering his Hamburg city press card.

"And I'm police," said the sergeant. "Nobody goes up. Those stairs are narrow enough as it is, and none too safe. The ambulance men will be down right away."

He was a big man, standing six feet three, and in his rain cape, with his arms spread wide to hold back the crowd, he looked as immovable as a barn door.

"What's up, then?" asked Miller.

"Can't make statements. Check at the station later on."

A man in civilian clothes came down the stairs and emerged onto the pavement. The turning light on top of the Volkswagen patrol car swung across his face, and Miller recognized him. They had been at school together at Hamburg Central High. The man was now a junior detective inspector in the Hamburg police, stationed at Altona Central.

"Hey, Karl."

The young inspector turned at the call of his name

and scanned the crowd behind the sergeant. In the next swirl of the police-car light he caught sight of Miller and his raised right hand. His face broke into a grin, part of pleasure, part of exasperation. He nodded to the sergeant.

"It's all right, Sergeant. He's more or less harmless."

The sergeant lowered his arm, and Miller darted past. He shook hands with Karl Brandt.

"What are you doing here?"

"Followed the ambulance."

"Damned vulture. What are you up to these days?"

"Same as usual. Freelancing."

"Making quite a bundle out of it by the look of it. I keep seeing your name in the picture magazines."

"It's a living. Hear about Kennedy?"

"Yes. Hell of a thing. They must be turning Dallas inside out tonight. Glad it wasn't on my turf."

Miller nodded toward the dimly lit hallway of the rooming-house, where a low-watt naked bulb cast a yellow glare over peeling wallpaper.

"A suicide. Gas. Neighbors smelled it coming under the door and called us. Just as well no one struck a match; the place was reeking with it."

"Not a film star by any chance?" asked Miller.

"Yeah. Sure. They always live in places like this. No, it was an old man. Looked as if he had been dead for years anyway. Someone does it every night."

"Well, wherever he's gone now, it can't be worse than this."

The inspector gave a fleeting smile and turned as the two ambulance men negotiated the last seven steps of the creaking stairs and came down the hallway with their burden. Brandt turned around. "Make some room. Let them through."

The sergeant promptly took up the cry and pushed the crowd back even farther. The two ambulance men walked out onto the pavement and around to the open doors of the Mercedes. Brandt followed them, with Miller at his heels. Not that Miller wanted to look at the dead man, or even intended to. He was just following

Brandt. As the ambulance men reached the door of the vehicle, the first one hitched his end of the stretcher into the runners and the second prepared to shove it inside.

"Hold it," said Brandt and flicked back the corner of the blanket above the dead man's face. He remarked over his shoulder, "Just a formality. My report has to say I accompanied the body to the ambulance and back to the morgue."

The interior lights of the Mercedes ambulance were bright, and Miller caught a single two-second look at the face of the suicide. His first and only impression was that he had never seen anything so old and ugly. Even given the effects of gassing, the dull mottling of the skin, the bluish tinge at the lips, the man in life could have been no beauty. A few strands of lank hair were plastered over the otherwise naked scalp. The eyes were closed. The face was hollowed out to the point of emaciation, and with the man's false teeth missing, each cheek seemed to be sucked inward till they almost touched inside the mouth, giving the effect of a ghoul in a horror film. The lips hardly existed, and both upper and lower were lined with vertical creases, reminding Miller of the shrunken skull from the Amazon basin he had once seen, whose lips had been sewn together by the natives. To cap the effect, the man seemed to have two pale and jagged scars running down his face, each from the temple or upper ear to the corner of the mouth.

After a quick glance, Brandt pulled the blanket back and nodded to the ambulance attendant behind him. He stepped back as the man rammed the stretcher into its berth, locked the doors, and went around to the cab to join his partner. The ambulance surged away. The crowd started to disperse accompanied by the sergeant's muted growls: "Come on, it's all over. There's nothing more to see. Haven't you got homes to go to?"

Miller looked at Brandt and raised his eyebrows. "Charming."

"Yes. Poor old guy. Nothing in it for you, though?"

Miller looked pained. "Not a chance. Like you say,

there's one a night. People are dying all over the world tonight, and nobody's taking a bit of notice. Not with Kennedy dead."

Inspector Brandt laughed mockingly. "You lousy journalists."

"Let's face it. Kennedy's what people want to read about. They buy the newspapers."

"Yeah. Well, I must get back to the station. See you, Peter."

They shook hands again and parted. Miller drove back toward Altona station, picked up the main road back into the city center, and twenty minutes later swung the Jaguar into the underground garage off the Hansa Square, two hundred yards from the house where he had his penthouse apartment.

Keeping the car in an underground garage all winter was costly, but it was one of the extravagances he permitted himself. He liked his fairly expensive apartment because it was high and he could look down on the bustling boulevard of the Steindamm. Of his clothes and food he thought nothing, and at twenty-nine, just under six feet, with the rumpled brown hair and brown eyes that women go for, he didn't need expensive clothes. An envious friend had once told him, "You could pull broads in a monastery," and he had laughed but been pleased at the same time because he knew it was true.

The real passions of his life were sports cars, reporting, and Sigrid, though he sometimes shamefacedly admitted that if it came to a choice between Sigi and the Jaguar, Sigi would have to find her loving somewhere else.

He stood and looked at the Jaguar in the lights of the garage after he had parked it. He could seldom get enough of looking at that car. Even approaching it in the street, he would stop and admire it, occasionally joined by a passer-by who, not realizing it was Miller's, would stop also and remark, "Some motor, that."

Normally a young freelance reporter does not drive a Jaguar XK 150 S. Spare parts were almost impossible to come by in Hamburg, the more so as the XK series, of which the S model was the last ever made, had gone out of production in 1960. He maintained it himself, spending hours on Sunday in overalls beneath the chassis or half buried in the engine. The gas it used, with its three SU carburetors, was a major strain on his pocket, the more so because of the price of gas in Germany, but he paid it willingly. The reward was to hear the berserk snarl of the blown exhausts when he hit the accelerator on the open autobahn, to feel the thrust as it rocketed out of a turn on a mountain road. He had even hardened up the independent suspension on the two front wheels, and as the car had stiff suspension at the back, it took corners steady as a rock, leaving other drivers rolling wildly on their cushion springs if they tried to keep up with him. Just after buying it, he had had it resprayed black with a long wasp-yellow streak down each side. As it had been made in Coventry, England, and not as an export car, the driver's wheel was on the right, which caused an occasional problem in passing but allowed him to change gear with the left hand and hold the shuddering steering wheel in the right hand, which he had come to prefer.

Even now he wondered at the lucky stroke that had enabled him to buy it. Earlier that summer he had idly opened a pop magazine while waiting in a barber shop to have his hair cut. Normally he never read the gossip about pop stars, but there was nothing else to read. The center-page spread had been about the meteoric rise to fame and international stardom of four tousel-headed English youths. The face on the extreme right of the picture, the one with the big nose, meant nothing to him, but the other three faces rang a bell in his filing cabinet of a memory.

The names of the two disks that had brought the quartet to stardom, "Please, Please Me" and "Love Me, Do," meant nothing either, but three of the faces puzzled him for two days. Then he remembered them, more than a year earlier, in 1962, singing way down on the program at a small cabaret off the Reeperbahn. It took him another day to recall the name, for he had only once popped in for a drink to talk to an underworld figure from whom he needed information about the Sankt Pauli gang. The Star Club. He went down there and checked through the billings for 1962 and found them. They had been five then, the three he recognized and two others, Pete Best and Stuart Sutliffe.

From there he went to the photographer who had done the publicity photographs for the impresario Bert Kämpfert, and had bought right and title to every one he had. His story "How Hamburg Discovered the Beatles" had made almost every pop-music and picture magazine in Germany and a lot abroad. On the proceeds he had bought the Jaguar, which he had been eyeing in a car showroom, where it had been sold by a British Army officer whose wife had grown too pregnant to fit into it. He even bought some Beatles records out of gratitude, but Sigi was the only one who ever played them.

He left the car and walked up the ramp to the street and back to his flat. It was nearly midnight, and although his mother had fed him at six that evening with the usual enormous meal, he was hungry again. He made a plate of scrambled eggs and listened to the late-night news. It was all about Kennedy and heavily accented on the German angles, since there was little more news coming through from Dallas. The police were still searching for the killer. The announcer went to great lengths about Kennedy's love of Germany, his visit to Berlin the previous summer, and his statement in German, *"Ich bin ein Berliner."*

There was then a recorded tribute from the Governing Mayor of West Berlin, Willy Brandt, his voice choked with emotion, and other tributes were read from Chancellor Ludwig Erhard and the former Chancellor Konrad Adenauer, who had retired the previous October 15.

Peter Miller switched off and went to bed. He wished Sigi was home because he always wanted to snuggle up to her when he felt depressed, and then he got hard and then they made love, after which he fell into a dreamless sleep, much to her annoyance because it was after lovemaking that she always wanted to talk about marriage and children. But the cabaret at which she danced did not close till nearly four in the morning, often later on Friday nights, when the provincials and tourists were thick down the Reeperbahn, prepared to buy champagne at ten times its restaurant price for a girl with big tits and a low-cut dress, and Sigi had the biggest and the lowest.

So he smoked another cigarette and fell asleep alone at quarter to two to dream of the hideous face of the old gassed man in the slums of Altona.

While Peter Miller was eating his scrambled eggs at midnight in Hamburg, five men were sitting drinking in the comfortable lounge of a house attached to a riding school near the pyramids outside Cairo. The time there was one in the morning. The five men had dined well and were in a jovial mood, the cause being the news from Dallas they had heard almost four hours earlier.

Three of the men were Germans, the other two Egyptians. The wife of the host and proprietor of the riding school, a favorite meeting place of the cream of Cairo society and the several-thousand-strong German colony, had gone to bed, leaving the five men to talk into the small hours.

Sitting in the leather-backed easy chair by the shuttered window was Hans Appler, formerly a Jewish expert in the Nazi Propaganda Ministry of Dr. Josef Goebbels. Having lived in Egypt since shortly after the end of the war, where he had been spirited by the Odessa, Appler had taken the Egyptian name of Salah Chaffar and worked as an expert on Jews in the Egyptian Ministry of Orientation. He held a glass of whisky. On his left was another former expert from Goebbels' staff, Ludwig Heiden, also working in the Orientation Ministry. He had in the meantime adopted the Moslem faith, made a trip to Mecca, and was called El Hadj. In deference to his new religion he held a glass of orange juice. Both men were still fanatical Nazis.

The two Egyptians were Colonel Shamseddin Badran,

personal aide to Marshal Abdel Hakim Amer, later to
become Vice-President of Egypt before being accused
of treason after the Six-Day War of 1967 and later committing suicide. The other was Colonel Ali Samir, head
of the Moukhabarat, the Egyptian Secret Intelligence
Service.

There had been a sixth guest at dinner, the guest of
honor, who had rushed back to Cairo when the news
came through at nine-thirty, Cairo time, that President
Kennedy was dead. He was the Speaker of the Egyptian
National Asesmbly, Anwar el Sadàt, a close collaborator
of President Nasser and later to become his successor.

Hans Appler raised his glass toward the ceiling. "So
Kennedy the Jew-lover is dead. Gentlemen, I give you a
toast."

"But our glasses are empty," protested Colonel Samir.

Their host hastened to remedy the matter, filling the
empty glasses from a bottle of Scotch from the sideboard.

The reference to Kennedy as a Jew-lover baffled none
of the five men in the room. On March 14, 1960, while
Dwight Eisenhower was still President of the United
States, the Premier of Israel, David Ben-Gurion, and
the Chancellor of Germany, Konrad Adenauer, had met
secretly at the Waldorf-Astoria hotel in New York, a
meeting that ten years earlier would have been deemed
impossible. What was deemed impossible even in 1960
was what happened at that meeting, which was why
details of it took years to leak out and why even at the
end of 1963 President Nasser refused to take seriously
the information that the Odessa and the Moukhabarat
of Colonel Samir placed on his desk.

The two statesmen had signed an agreement whereby
West Germany agreed to open a credit account for
Israel to the tune of fifty million dollars a year, without
any strings attached. Ben-Gurion, however, soon discovered that to have money was one thing, to have a
secure and certain source of arms was quite another. Six
months later the Waldorf agreement was topped off with
another, signed by the Defense Ministers of Germany

and Israel, Franz-Josef Strauss and Shimon Peres. Under its terms, Israel would be able to use the money from Germany to buy weapons in Germany.

Adenauer, aware of the vastly more controversial nature of the second agreement, delayed for months, until in 1961 he was in New York to meet the new President, John Fitzgerald Kennedy. Kennedy put the pressure on. He did not wish to have arms delivered directly from the United States to Israel, but he wanted them to arrive somehow. Israel needed fighters, transport planes, Howitzer 105-mm. artillery pieces, armored cars, armored personnel carriers, and tanks, but above all tanks.

Germany had all of them, mainly of American make, either bought from America to offset the cost of keeping American troops in Germany under the NATO agreement, or made under license in Germany.

Under Kennedy's pressure the Strauss-Peres deal was pushed through.

The first German tanks started to arrive at Haifa in late June 1963. It was difficult to keep the news secret for long; too many people were involved. The Odessa had found out in late 1962 and promptly informed the Egyptians, with whom its agents in Cairo had the closest links.

In late 1963 things started to change. On October 15, Konrad Adenauer, the Fox of Bonn, the Granite Chancellor, resigned and went into retirement. Adenauer's place was taken by Ludwig Erhard, a good vote-catcher as the father of the German economic miracle, but in matters of foreign policy weak and vacillating.

Even while Adenauer was in power there had been a vociferous group inside the West German cabinet in favor of shelving the Israeli arms deal and halting the supplies before they had begun. The old Chancellor had silenced them with a few terse sentences, and such was his power that they stayed silenced.

Erhard was quite a different man and already had earned himself the nickname of the Rubber Lion. As soon as he took the chair the anti-arms-deal group, based in the Foreign Ministry, ever mindful of its excellent and improving relations with the Arab world, opened up again. Erhard dithered. But behind them all was the determination of John Kennedy that Israel should get her arms via Germany.

And then he was shot. The big question in the small hours of the morning of November 23 was simply: would President Lyndon Johnson take the American pressure off Germany and let the indecisive Chancellor in Bonn renege on the deal? In fact he did not, but there were high hopes in Cairo that he would.

The host at the convivial meeting outside Cairo that night, having filled his guests' glasses, turned back to the sideboard to top up his own. His name was Wolfgang Lutz, born at Mannheim in 1921, a former major in the German Army, a fanatical Jew-hater, who had emigrated to Cairo in 1961 and started his riding academy. Blond, blue-eyed, hawk-faced, he was a top favorite among both the influential political figures of Cairo and the expatriate German and mainly Nazi community along the banks of the Nile.

He turned to face the room and gave a broad smile. If there was anything false about that smile, no one noticed it. But it was false. He had been born a Jew in Mannheim but had emigrated to Palestine in 1933 at the age of twelve. His name was Ze'ev, and he held the rank of *rav-seren* (major) in the Israeli Army. He was also the top agent of Israeli Intelligence in Egypt at that time. On February 28, 1965, after a raid on his home in which a radio transmitter was discovered in the bathroom scales, he was arrested. Tried on June 26, 1965, he was sentenced to hard labor in perpetuity. Released after the end of the 1967 war as part of an exchange against thousands of Egyptian prisoners of war, he and his wife stepped back onto the soil of home at Lod Airport on February 4, 1968.

But the night Kennedy died this was all in the future: the arrest, the tortures, the multiple rape of his wife. He raised his glass to the four smiling faces in front of him.

In fact, he could hardly wait for his guests to depart,

for something one of them had said over dinner was of vital importance to his country, and he desperately wished to be alone, to go up to his bathroom, get the transmitter out of the bathroom scales, and send a message to Tel Aviv. But he forced himself to keep smiling.

"Death to the Jew-lovers," he toasted. *"Sieg Heil."*

Peter Miller woke the next morning just before nine and shifted luxuriously under the enormous feather cushion that covered the double bed. Even half awake, he could feel the warmth of the sleeping figure of Sigi seeping across the bed to him, and by reflex he snuggled closer so that her buttocks pushed into the base of his stomach. Automatically he began to erect.

Sigi, still fast asleep after only four hours in bed, grunted in annoyance and shifted away toward the edge of the bed. "Go away," she muttered without waking up.

Miller sighed, turned onto his back, and held up his watch, squinting at the face of it in the half-light. Then he slipped out of bed on the other side, pulled a toweling bathrobe around him, and padded through into the living room to pull back the curtains. The steely November light washed across the room, making him blink. He focused his eyes and looked down into the Steindamm. It was a Saturday morning, and traffic was light down the wet black tarmac. He yawned and went into the kitchen to brew the first of innumerable cups of coffee. Both his mother and Sigi reproached him with living almost entirely on coffee and cigarettes.

Drinking his coffee and smoking the first cigarette of the day in the kitchen, he considered whether there was anything particular he ought to do that day and decided there was not. For one thing, all the newspapers and the next issues of the magazines would be about President Kennedy, probably for days or weeks to come. And for another, there was no particular story he was chasing at the time. Besides which, Saturday and Sunday are bad days to get hold of people in their offices, and they seldom like being disturbed at home. He had re-

cently finished a well-received series on the steady infiltration of Austrian, Parisian, and Italian gangsters into
the gold mine of the Reeperbahn, Hamburg's half-mile
of nightclubs, brothels, and vice, and had not yet been
paid for it. He thought he might contact the magazine
to which he had sold the series, then decided against it.
It would pay in time, and he was not short of money
for the moment. Indeed his bank statement, which had
arrived three days earlier, showed he had more than
5000 marks to his credit, which he thought would keep
him going for a while.

"The trouble with you, pal," he told his reflection in
one of Sigi's brilliantly polished saucepans as he rinsed
out the cup with his forefinger, "is that you are lazy."

He had been asked by a civilian-careers officer, at
the end of his military service ten years earlier, what
he wanted to be in life. He had replied, "An idle rich
man," and at twenty-nine, although he had not achieved
it and probably never would, he still thought it a perfectly reasonable ambition.

He carried the portable transistor radio into the
bathroom, closed the door so Sigi would not hear it,
and listened to the news while he showered and shaved.
The main item was that a man had been arrested for
the murder of President Kennedy. As he had supposed,
there were no other items of news on the entire program
but those connected with the Kennedy assassination.

After drying off he went back to the kitchen and made
more coffee, this time two cups. He took them into the
bedroom, placed them on the bedside table, slipped off his
robe, and clambered back under the cushion beside Sigi,
whose fluffy blond head was protruding onto the pillow.

She was twenty-two and at school had been a cham-
pion gymnast who, so she said, could have gone on to
Olympic standing if her bust had not developed to the
point where it got in the way and no leotard could safely
contain it. On leaving school she became a teacher of
physical training at a girls' school. The change to striptease dancer in Hamburg came a year later and for

the very best and most simple of economic reasons. It earned her five times more than a teacher's salary.

Despite her willingness to take her clothes off to the buff in a nightclub, she was remarkably embarrassed by any lewd remarks made about her body by anyone whom she could see when the remarks were made.

"The point is," she once told an amused Peter Miller with great seriousness, "when I'm on the stage I can't see anything behind the lights, so I don't get embarrassed. If I could see them, I think I'd run offstage."

This did not stop her from later taking her place at one of the tables in the club when she was dressed again, and waiting to be invited for a drink by one of the customers. The only drink allowed was champagne, in half-bottles or preferably whole bottles. On these she collected a fifteen-per-cent commission. Although almost without exception the customers who invited her to drink champagne with them hoped to get much more than an hour of gazing in stunned admiration at the canyon between her breasts, they never did. She was a kindly and understanding girl, and her attitude to the pawing attentions of the customers was one of gentle regret rather than the contemptuous loathing that the other girls hid behind their neon smiles.

"Poor little men," she once said to Miller, "they ought to have a nice woman to go home to."

"What do you mean, poor little men?" protested Miller. "They're dirty old creeps with a pocketful of cash to spend."

"Well, they wouldn't be if they had someone to take care of them," retorted Sigi, and on this her feminine logic was unshakable.

Miller had seen her by chance on a visit to Madame Kokett's bar just below the Café Keese on the Reeperbahn, when he had gone to have a chat and a drink with the owner, an old friend and contact. She was a big girl, five feet, nine inches tall and with a figure to match, which, on a shorter girl, would have been out of proportion. She stripped to the music with the habitual supposedly sensual gestures, her face set in the usual bedroom pout of strippers. Miller had seen it all before and sipped his drink without batting an eyelid.

But when her brassière came off even he had to stop and stare, glass half-raised to his mouth. His host eyed him sardonically. "She's stacked, eh?" he said.

Miller had to admit she made *Playboy*'s Playmates of the Month look like severe cases of undernourishment. But she was so firmly muscled that her bosom stood outward and upward without a vestige of support.

At the end of her turn, when the applause started, the girl had dropped the bored poise of the professional dancer, bobbed a shy, half-embarrassed little bow to the audience, and given a big sloppy grin like a half-trained bird dog which against all the betting has just brought back a downed partridge. It was the grin that got Miller, not the dance routine or the figure. He asked if she would like a drink, and she was sent for.

As Miller was in the company of the boss, she avoided a bottle of champagne and asked for a gin fizz. To his surprise, Miller found she was a very nice person to be around and asked if he might take her home after the show. With obvious reservations, she agreed. Playing his cards coolly, Miller made no pass at her that night. It was early spring, and she emerged from the cabaret, when it closed, clad in a most unglamorous duffel coat, which he presumed was intentional.

They just had coffee together and talked, during which she unwound from her previous tension and chatted gaily. He learned she liked pop music, art, walking along the banks of the Alster, keeping house, and children. After that they started going out on her one free night a week, taking in a dinner or a show, but not sleeping together.

After three months Miller took her to his bed and later suggested she might like to move in. With her single-minded attitude toward the important things of life, Sigi had already decided she wanted to marry Peter Miller, and the only problem was whether she should try to get him by not sleeping in his bed or the other way around. Sensing his ability to fill the other half of his mattress with other girls if the need arose, she decided to move in and make his life so comfortable that he would want to marry her. They had been together for six months by the end of November.

Even Miller, who was hardly house-trained, had to admit she kept a beautiful home, and she made love with a healthy and bouncing enjoyment. She never mentioned marriage directly but tried to get the message across in other ways. Miller feigned not to notice. Strolling in the sun by the Alster lake, she would sometimes make friends with a toddler under the benevolent eyes of its parent.

"Oh, Peter, isn't he an angel?"

Miller would grunt. "Yeah. Marvelous."

After that she would freeze him for an hour for having failed to take the hint. But they were happy together, especially Peter Miller, who was suited down to the ground by this arrangement of all the comforts of marriage, the delights of regular loving, without the ties of marriage.

After drinking half his coffee, Miller slithered down into the bed and put his arms around her from behind, gently caressing her crotch, which he knew would wake her up. After a few minutes she muttered with pleasure and rolled over onto her back. Still massaging, he leaned over and started to kiss her breasts. Still half asleep, she gave vent to a series of long mmmms, and her hands started to move drowsily over his back and buttocks. Ten minutes later they made love, squealing and shuddering with pleasure.

"That's a hell of a way to wake me up," she grumbled afterward.

"There are worse ways," said Miller.

"What's the time?"

"Nearly twelve," Miller lied, knowing she would throw something at him if she learned it was half past ten and she had had only five hours' sleep. "Never mind, you go back to sleep if you feel like it."

"Mmmm. Thank you, darling, you are good to me," said Sigi and fell asleep again.

Miller was halfway to the bathroom after drinking the rest of his coffee and Sigi's as well, when the phone rang. He diverted into the sitting room and answered it.

"Peter?"

"Yes, who's that?"

"Karl."

His mind was still fuzzed, and he did not recognize the voice. "Karl?"

The voice was impatient. "Karl Brandt. What's the matter? Are you still asleep?"

Miller recovered. "Oh, yes. Sure, Karl. Sorry, I just got up. What's the matter?"

"Look, it's about this dead Jew. I want to talk to you."

Miller was baffled. "What dead Jew?"

"The one who gassed himself last night in Altona. Can't you even remember that far back?"

"Yes, of course I remember last night," said Miller. "I didn't know he was Jewish. What about him?"

"I want to talk to you," said the police inspector. "But not on the phone. Can we meet?"

Miller's reporter's mind clicked into gear immediately. Anyone who has got something to say but does not wish to say it over the phone must think it important. In the case of Brandt, Miller could hardly suspect a police detective would be so cagy about something ridiculous.

"Sure," he said. "Are you free for lunch?"

"I can be," said Brandt.

"Good. I'll buy it if you think it's something worth while." He named a small restaurant on the Goose Market for one o'clock and replaced the receiver. He was still puzzled, for he couldn't see a story in the suicide of an old man, Jewish or not, in a slum tenement in Altona.

Throughout the lunch the young detective seemed to wish to avoid the subject about which he had asked for the meeting, but when the coffee came he said simply, "The man last night."

"Yes," said Miller. "What about him?"

"You must have heard, as we all have, about what the Nazis did to the Jews during the war and even before it?"

"Of course. They rammed it down our throats at school, didn't they?" Miller was puzzled and embarrassed. Like most young Germans, he had been told at school when he was twelve or so that he and the rest of his countrymen had been guilty of massive war crimes. At the time he had accepted it without even knowing what was being talked about.

Later it had been difficult to find out what the teachers had meant in the immediate postwar period. There was nobody to ask, nobody who wanted to talk—not the teachers, not the parents. Only with coming manhood had he been able to read a little about it, and although what he read disgusted him, he could not feel it concerned him. It was another time, another place, a long way away. He had not been there when it happened, his father had not been there, his mother had not been there. Something inside him had persuaded him it was nothing to do with Peter Miller, so he had asked for no names, dates, details. He wondered why Brandt should be bringing the subject up.

Brandt stirred his coffee, himself embarrassed, not knowing how to go on.

"That old man last night," he said at length. "He was a German Jew. He was in a concentration camp."

Miller thought back to the death's head on the stretcher the previous evening. Was that what they ended up like? It was ridiculous. The man must have been liberated by the Allies eighteen years earlier and had lived on to die of old age. But the face kept coming back. He had never seen anyone who had been in a camp before—at least, not knowingly. For that matter he had never met one of the SS mass-killers, he was sure of that. One would notice, after all.

His mind strayed back to the publicity surrounding the Eichmann trial in Jerusalem two years earlier. The papers had been full of it for weeks on end. He thought of the face in the glass booth and remembered that his impression at the time had been how ordinary that face was, so depressingly ordinary. It was in reading the press coverage of the trial that for the first time he had gained an inkling of how the SS had done it, how they had got away with it. But these had all been about things in Poland, Russia, Hungary, Czechoslovakia, far away and a long time back. He could not make them personal.

He brought his thoughts back to the present and the sense of unease Brandt's line of talk aroused in him.

"What about it?" he asked the detective.

For answer Brandt took a brown-paper-wrapped parcel out of his attaché case and pushed it across the table. "The old man left a diary. Actually, he wasn't so old. Fifty-six. It seems he wrote notes at the time and stored them in his foot-wrappings. After the war he transcribed them all. They make up the diary."

Miller looked at the parcel with scant interest. "Where did you find it?"

"It was lying next to the body. I picked it up and took it home. I read it last night."

Miller looked at his former friend quizzically. "It was bad?"

"Horrible. I had no idea it was that bad—the things they did to them."

"Why bring it to me?"

Now Brandt was embarrassed. He shrugged. "I thought it might make a story for you."

"Who does it belong to now?"

"Technically, Tauber's heirs. But we'll never find them. So I suppose it belongs to the Police Department. But they'd just file it. You can have it, if you want it. Just don't let on that I gave it to you. I don't need any trouble in the department."

Miller paid the bill, and the pair walked outside.

"All right, I'll read it. But I don't promise to get steamed up about it. It might make an article for a magazine."

Brandt turned to him with a half-smile. "You're a cynical bastard," he said.

"No," said Miller, "it's just that, like most people, I'm concerned with the here and now. What about you? After ten years in the police I'd have thought you'd be a tough cop. This thing really upset you, didn't it?"

Brandt was serious again. He looked at the parcel under Miller's arm and nodded slowly. "Yes. Yes, it did. I just never thought it was that bad. And by the way, it's not all past history. That story ended here in Hamburg last night. Good-by, Peter."

The detective turned and walked away, not knowing how wrong he was.

2

PETER MILLER took the brown-paper parcel home and arrived there just after three. He threw the package onto the living-room table and went to make a large pot of coffee before sitting down to read it.

Settled in his favorite armchair with a cup of coffee at his elbow and a cigarette going, he opened it. The diary was in the form of a looseleaf folder with stiff covers of cardboard bound in a dull black vinyl, and a series of clips down the spine so that the leaves of the book could be extracted, or further leaves inserted, if necessary.

The contents consisted of a hundred and fifty pages of typewritten script, apparently banged out on an old machine, for some of the letters were above the line, others below it, and some either distorted or faint. The bulk of the pages seemed to have been written years before, or over a period of years, for most of them, although neat and clean, bore the unmistakable tint of white paper several years old. But at the front and back were a number of fresh sheets, evidently written barely a few days previously. There was a preface of some new pages at the front of the typescript, and there was a sort of epilogue at the back. A check of the dates on the preface and the epilogue showed both to have been written on November 21, two days previously. Miller supposed the dead man had written them after he had made the decision to end his life.

A quick glance at some of the paragraphs on the first page surprised him, for the language was clear and precise German, the writing of a well-educated and cultured man. On the outside of the front cover a square of white paper had been pasted, and over it a larger square of cellophane to keep it clean. On the square of paper had been written in large block capitals in black ink: THE DIARY OF SALOMON TAUBER.

Miller settled himself deeper in his chair, turned to the first page, and began to read.

TAUBER'S DIARY: PREFACE

My name is Salomon Tauber, I am a Jew and about to die. I have decided to end my own life because it has no more value, nor is there anything left for me to do. Those things that I have tried to do with my life have come to nothing, and my efforts have been unavailing. For the evil that I have seen has survived and flourished, and only the good has departed in dust and mockery. The friends that I have known, the sufferers and the victims, are all dead, and only the persecutors are all around me. I see their faces on the streets in the daytime, and in the night I see the face of my wife, Esther, who died long ago. I have stayed alive this long only because there was one more thing I wished to do, one thing I wanted to see, and now I know I never shall.

I bear no hatred or bitterness toward the German people, for they are a good people. Peoples are not evil; only individuals are evil. The English philosopher Burke was right when he said, "I do not know the means for drawing up the indictment of an entire nation." There is no collective guilt, for the Bible relates how the Lord wished to destroy Sodom and Gomorrah

for the evil of the men who lived in
them, with their women and children,
but how there was living among them one
righteous man, and because he was
righteous he was spared. Therefore guilt
is individual, like salvation.

When I came out of the concentration
camps of Riga and Stutthof, when I
survived the Death March to Magdeburg,
when the British soldiers liberated my
body there in April 1945, leaving only
my soul in chains, I hated the world. I
hated the people, and the trees and the
rocks, for they had conspired against me
and made me suffer. And above all I
hated the Germans. I asked then, as I
had asked many times over the previous
four years, why the Lord did not strike
them down, every last man, woman, and
child, destroying their cities and their
houses forever from the face of the
earth. And when He did not, I hated Him
too, crying that He had deserted me and
my people, whom He had led to believe
they were His chosen people, and even
saying that He did not exist.

But with the passing of the years I
have learned again to love; to love the
rocks and the trees, the sky above and
the river flowing past the city, the
stray dogs and the cats, the weeds
growing between the cobblestones, and
the children who run away from me in
the street because I am so ugly. They
are not to blame. There is a French
adage, "To understand everything is to
forgive everything." When one can
understand the people, their gullibility
and their fear, their greed and their

lust for power, their ignorance and their
docility to the man who shouts the
loudest, one can forgive. Yes, one can
forgive even what they did. But one can
never forget.

There are some men whose crimes
surpass comprehension and therefore
forgiveness, and here is the real
failure. For they are still among us,
walking through the cities, working in
the offices, lunching in the canteens,
smiling and shaking hands and calling
decent men Kamerad. That they should
live on, not as outcasts but as
cherished citizens, to smear a whole
nation in perpetuity with their individual evil, this is the true failure.
And in this we have failed, you and
I, we have all failed, and failed
miserably.

Lastly, as time passed, I came again
to love the Lord, and to ask His forgiveness for the things I have done
against His Laws, and they are many.

Shema Yisroel, Adonai elohenu, Adonai
ehad.

[The diary began with twenty pages during which
Tauber described his birth and boyhood in Hamburg, his working-class war-hero father, and the
death of his parents shortly after Hitler came to
power in 1933. By the late thirties he was married
to a girl called Esther and was working as an architect. He was spared being rounded up before 1941
owing to the intervention of his employer. Finally
he was taken, in Berlin, on a journey to see a client.
After a period in a transit camp he was packed with
other Jews into a boxcar on a cattle train bound
for the east.]

I cannot really remember the date the train finally rumbled to a halt in a railway station. I think it was six days and seven nights after we were shut up in the car in Berlin. Suddenly the train was stationary, the slits of white light told me it was daytime outside, and my head reeled and swam from exhaustion and the stench.

There were shouts outside, the sound of bolts being drawn back, and the doors were flung open. It was just as well I could not see myself, who had once been dressed in a white shirt and well-pressed trousers. (The tie and jacket had long since been dropped to the floor.) The sight of the others was bad enough.

As brilliant daylight rushed into the car, men threw arms over their eyes and screamed with the pain. Seeing the doors opening, I had squeezed my eyes shut to protect them. Under the pressure of bodies half the car emptied itself onto the platform in a tumbling mass of stinking humanity. As I had been standing at the rear of the car, to one side of the centrally placed doors, I avoided this and, risking a half-open eye despite the glare, I stepped down upright to the platform.

The SS guards who had opened the gates, mean-faced, brutal men who jabbered and roared in a language I could not understand, stood back with expressions of disgust. Inside the boxcar thirty-one men lay huddled and trampled on the floor. They would never get up again. The remainder, starved,

half-blind, steaming and reeking from
head to foot in their rags, struggled
upright on the platform. From thirst,
our tongues were gummed to the roofs of
our mouths, blackened and swollen, and
our lips were split and parched.

Down the platform forty other cars
from Berlin and eighteen from Vienna
were disgorging their occupants, about
half of them women and children. Many
of the women and most of the children
were naked, smeared with excrement,
and in much as bad shape as we were.
Some women carried the lifeless bodies
of their children in their arms as they
stumbled out into the light.

The guards ran up and down the platform, clubbing the deportees into a sort
of column, prior to marching us into the
town. But what town? And what was the
language these men were speaking? Later
I was to discover that this town was
Riga and the SS guards were locally
recruited Latvians, as fiercely anti-
Semitic as the SS from Germany, but of a
much lower intelligence, virtually
animals in human form.

Standing behind the guards was a cowed
group in soiled shirts and slacks, each
bearing a black square patch with a big
J on the chest and back. This was a
special command from the ghetto,
brought down to empty the cattle cars
of the dead and bury them outside the
town. They too were guarded by half a
dozen men who also had the J on their
chests and backs, but who wore armbands
and carried pickax handles. These were
Jewish Kapos, who got better food than

the other internees for doing the job
they did.

There were a few German SS officers
standing in the shade of the station
awning, distinguishable only when my
eyes were accustomed to the light. One
stood aloof on a packing crate, sur-
veying the several thousand human
skeletons who emptied themselves from
the train with a thin but satisfied
smile. He tapped a black riding quirt
of plaited leather against one jackboot.
He wore the green uniform with black
and silver flashes of the SS as if it
were designed for him and carried the
twin-lightning strikes of the Waffen SS
on the right collar. On the left his
rank was indicated as captain.

He was tall and lanky, with pale blond
hair and washed-out blue eyes. Later I
was to learn he was a dedicated sadist,
already known by the name that the
Allies would also later use for him—
the Butcher of Riga. It was my first
sight of SS Captain Eduard Roschmann.

[At 5 a.m. on the morning of June 22, 1941,
Hitler's 130 divisions, divided into three army
groups, had rolled across the border to invade
Russia. Behind each army group came the swarms
of SS extermination squads, charged by Hitler,
Himmler, and Heydrich with wiping out the Communist commissars and the rural-dwelling Jewish
communities of the vast tracts of land the Army
overran, and penning the large urban Jewish communities into the ghettos of each major town for
later "special treatment."

The Army took Riga, capital of Latvia, on July
1, 1941, and in the middle of that month the first

SS commandos moved in. The first onsite unit of
the SD and SP sections of the SS established themselves in Riga on August 1, 1941, and began the
extermination program that would make Ostland
(as the three occupied Baltic states were renamed)
Jew-free.

Then it was decided in Berlin to use Riga as the
transit camp to death for the Jews of Germany and
Austria. In 1938 there were 320,000 German Jews
and 180,000 Austrian Jews, a round half-million.
By July 1941 tens of thousands had been dealt with,
mainly in the concentration camps within Germany
and Austria, notably Sachsenhausen, Mauthausen,
Ravensbrück, Dachau, Buchenwald, Belsen, and
Theresienstadt in Bohemia. But they were getting
overcrowded, and the obscure lands of the east
seemed an excellent place to finish off the rest.
Work was begun to expand or begin the six extermination camps of Auschwitz, Treblinka, Belzec,
Sobibor, Chelmno, and Maidanek. Until they were
ready, however, a place had to be found to exterminate as many as possible and "store" the rest.
Riga was chosen.

Between August 1, 1941, and October 14, 1944,
almost 200,000 exclusively German and Austrian
Jews were shipped to Riga. Eighty thousand stayed
there, dead; 120,000 were shipped onward to the
six extermination camps of southern Poland already
mentioned; and 400 came out alive, half of them to
die at Stutthof or on the Death March back to
Magdeburg. Tauber's transport was the first into
Riga from the German Reich, and reached there at
3:45 in the afternoon of August 18, 1941.]

The Riga ghetto was an integral part
of the city and had formerly been the
home of the Jews of Riga, of whom only a
few hundred existed by the time I got
there. In less than three weeks Rosch-

mann and his deputy, Krause, had over-
seen the extermination of most of them,
as per orders.

The ghetto lay at the northern edge
of the city, with open countryside to
the north. There was a wall along the
south face; the other three were sealed
off with rows of barbed wire. There was
one gate, on the northern face, through
which all exits and entries had to be
made. It was guarded by two watchtowers
manned by Latvian SS. From this gate,
running clear down the center of the
ghetto to the south wall, was Mase
Kalnu Iela, or Little Hill Street. To
the right-hand side of this (looking
from south to north toward the main
gate) was the Blech Platz, or Tin
Square, where selections for execution
took place, along with roll call,
selection of slave-labor parties,
floggings, and hangings. The gallows
with its eight steel hooks and permanent
nooses swinging in the wind stood in
the center of this. It was occupied
every night by at least six unfortunates, and frequently several shifts
had to be processed by the eight hanging
hooks before Roschmann was satisfied
with his day's work.

The whole ghetto must have been just
under two square miles, a township that
had once housed 12,000 to 15,000 people.
Before our arrival the Riga Jews, at
least the 2000 of them left, had done
the bricking-off work, so the area left
to our transport of just over 5000 men,
women, and children was spacious. But
after we arrived transports continued to

come day after day until the population
of our part of the ghetto soared to
30,000 to 40,000, and with the arrival
of each new transport a number of the
existing inhabitants equal to the number
of the surviving new arrivals had to be
executed to make room for the newcomers.
Otherwise the overcrowding would have
become a menace to the health of the
workers among us, and that Roschmann
would not have.

So on that first evening we settled
ourselves in, taking the best-con-
structed houses, one room per person,
using curtains and coats for blankets
and sleeping on real beds. After drinking his fill from a water butt, my room
neighbor remarked that perhaps it would
not be too bad after all. We had not yet
met Roschmann.

As summer merged into autumn and
autumn into winter, the conditions in
the ghetto grew worse. Each morning the
entire population—mainly men, for the
women and children were exterminated on
arrival in far greater percentages
than the work-fit males—was assembled
on Tin Square, pushed and shoved by the
rifle butts of the Latvians, and roll
call took place. No names were called;
we were counted and divided into work
groups. Almost the whole population,
men, women, and children, left the
ghetto each day in columns to work
twelve hours at forced labor in the
growing host of workshops nearby.

I had said earlier that I was a car-
penter, which was not true, but as an

architect I had seen carpenters at work
and knew enough to get by. I guessed,
correctly, that there would always be a
need for carpenters, and I was sent to
work in a nearby lumber mill where the
local pines were sawed up and made into
pre-fabricated hutments for the troops.

The work was backbreaking, enough to
ruin the constitution of a healthy man,
for we worked, summer and winter, mainly
outside in the cold and damp of the
low-lying regions near the coast of
Latvia.

Our food rations were a half-liter
apiece of so-called soup, mainly tinted
water, sometimes with a knob of potato
in it, before marching to work in the
mornings, and another half-liter, with
a slice of black bread and a moldy
potato, on return to the ghetto at
night.

Bringing food into the ghetto was
punishable by immediate hanging before
the assembled population at evening roll
call on Tin Square. Nevertheless, to
take that risk was the only way to stay
alive.

As the columns trudged back through
the main gate each evening, Roschmann
and a few of his cronies used to stand
by the entrance, doing spot checks on
those passing through. They would call
to a man or a woman or a child at
random, ordering the person out of the
column to strip by the side of the gate.
If a potato or a piece of bread was
found, the person would wait behind
while the others marched through toward

Tin Square for evening roll call.

When they were all assembled, Roschmann would stalk down the road, followed
by the other SS guards and the dozen
or so condemned people. The males among
them would mount the gallows platform
and wait with the ropes around their
necks while roll call was completed.
Then Roschmann would walk along the
line, grinning up at the faces above
him and kicking the chairs out from
under, one by one. He liked to do this
from the front, so the person about to
die would see him. Sometimes he would
pretend to kick the chair away, only to
pull his foot back in time. He would
laugh uproariously to see the man on
the chair tremble, thinking he was
already swinging at the rope's end,
only to realize the chair was still
beneath him.

Sometimes the condemned men would
pray to the Lord; sometimes they would
cry for mercy. Roschmann liked to hear
this. He would pretend he was slightly
deaf, cocking an ear and asking, "Can
you speak up a little? What was that
you said?"

When he had kicked the chair away—
it was more like a wooden box, really—
he would turn to his cronies and say,
"Dear me, I really must get a hearing
aid."

Within a few months Eduard Roschmann
had become the Devil incarnate to us
prisoners. There was little that he did
not succeed in devising.

When a woman was caught bringing food

into the camp, she was made to watch
the hangings of the men first, especially if one was her husband or
brother. Then Roschmann made her kneel
in front of the rest of us, drawn up
around three sides of the square, while
the camp barber shaved her bald.

After roll call she would be taken to
the cemetery outside the wire and made
to dig a shallow grave, then kneel
beside it while Roschmann or one of the
others fired a bullet from his Luger
point-blank into the base of the skull.
No one was allowed to watch these
executions, but word seeped through
from the Latvian guards that he would
often fire past the ear of the woman to
make her fall into the grave with shock,
then climb out again and kneel in the
same position. Other times he would
fire from an empty chamber, so there
was just a click when the woman thought
she was about to die. The Latvians were
brutes, but Roschmann managed to amaze
them for all that.

There was one certain girl at Riga who
helped the prisoners at her own risk.
She was Olli Adler—from Munich, I
believe. Her sister Gerda had already
been shot in the cemetery for bringing
in food. Olli was a girl of surpassing
beauty and took Roschmann's fancy. He
made her his concubine—the official
term was housemaid, because relations
between an SS man and a Jewish girl
were banned. She used to smuggle medi-
cines into the ghetto when she was
allowed to visit it, having stolen them

from the SS stores. This, of course, was
punishable by death. The last I saw of
her was when we boarded the ship at
Riga docks.

By the end of that first winter I was
certain I could not survive much longer.
The hunger, the cold, the damp, the
overwork, and the constant brutalities
had whittled my formerly strong frame
down to a mass of skin and bones. Looking in the mirror, I saw staring back
at me a haggard, stubbled old man with
red-rimmed eyes and hollow cheeks. I
had just turned thirty-five, and I
looked double that. But so did everyone
else.

I had witnessed the departure of tens
of thousands to the forest of the mass
graves, the deaths of hundreds from
cold, exposure, and overwork, and of
scores from hanging, shooting, flogging,
and clubbing. Even after surviving five
months, I had outlived my time. The
will to live that I had begun to show
in the train had dissipated, leaving
nothing but a mechanical routine of
going on living that sooner or later had
to break. And then something happened
in March that gave me another year of
will power.

I remember the date even now. It was
March 3, 1942, the day of the second
Dünamünde convoy. About a month earlier
we had seen for the first time the
arrival of a strange van. It was about
the size of a long single-decker bus,
painted steel-gray, and without windows.
It parked just outside the ghetto gates,

and at morning roll call Roschmann said
he had an announcement to make. He said
there was a new fish-pickling factory
just started at the town of Dünamünde,
situated on the Düna River, about eighty
miles from Riga. It offered light work,
he said, good food, and good living
conditions. Because the work was so
light the opportunity was open only to
old men and women, the frail, the sick,
and the small children.

Naturally, many were eager to go to
such a comfortable kind of labor.
Roschmann walked down the lines, select-
ing those to go, and this time, instead
of the old and sick hiding themselves
at the back to be dragged screaming and
protesting forward to join the forced
marches to Execution Hill, they seemed
eager to show themselves. Finally more
than a hundred were selected, and all
climbed into the van. Then the doors
were slammed shut, and the watchers
noticed how tight they fitted together.
The van rolled away, emitting no exhaust
fumes. Later, word filtered back what
the van was. There was no fish-pickling
factory at Dünamünde; the van was a
gassing van. In the parlance of the
ghetto the expression "Dünamünde convoy" henceforward came to mean death
by gassing.

On March 3 the whisper went around
the ghetto that there was to be another
Dünamünde convoy, and sure enough, at
morning roll call Roschmann announced
it. But there was no pressing forward
to volunteer, so with a wide grin
Roschmann began to stroll along the

ranks, tapping on the chest with his
quirt hose who were to go. Astutely,
he started at the fourth and rear rank,
where he expected to find the weak,
the old, and the unfit-for-work.

There was one old woman who had foreseen this and stood in the front rank.
She must have been close to sixty-five,
but in an effort to stay alive she had
put on high-heeled shoes, a pair of
black silk stockings, a short skirt
even above her knees, and a saucy hat.
She had rouged her cheeks, powdered her
face, and painted her lips carmine. In
fact she would have stood out among any
group of ghetto prisoners, but she
thought she might be able to pass for a
young girl.

Reaching her as he walked by, Roschmann stopped, stared, and looked again.
Then a grin of joy spread over his face.

"Well, what have we here?" he cried,
pointing to her with his quirt to draw
the attention of his comrades in the
center of the square guarding the
hundred already chosen. "Don't you want
a nice little ride to Dünamünde, young
lady?"

Trembling with fear, the old woman
whispered, "No, sir."

"And how old are you, then?" boomed
Roschmann as his SS friends began to
giggle. "Seventeen? Twenty?"

The old woman's knobbly knees began
to tremble. "Yes, sir," she whispered.

"How marvelous," cried Roschmann.
"Well, I always like a pretty girl.
Come out into the center so we can all
admire your youth and beauty."

So saying, he grabbed her by the arm and hustled her toward the center of Tin Square. Once there, he stood her out in the open and said, "Well now, little lady, since you're so young and pretty, perhaps you'd like to dance for us, eh?"

She stood there, shivering in the bitter wind, shaking with fear as well. She whispered something we could not hear.

"What's that?" shouted Roschmann. "You can't dance? Oh, I'm sure a nice young thing like you can dance, can't you?"

His cronies of the German SS were laughing to bust. The Latvians could not understand but started to grin. The old woman shook her head.

Roschmann's smile vanished. "Dance," he snarled.

She made a few little shuffling movements, then stopped. Roschmann drew his Luger, eased back the hammer, and fired it into the sand an inch from her feet. She jumped a foot in the air from fright.

"Dance . . . dance . . . dance for us you hideous Jewish bitch," he shouted, firing a bullet into the sand benath her feet each time he said, "Dance."

Smacking in one spare magazine after another until he had used up the three in his pouch, he made her dance for half an hour, leaping even higher and higher, her skirts flying round her hips with each jump, until at last she fell to the sand unable to rise whether she lived or died. Roschmann fired his last three slugs into the sand in front of her face, blasting the sand up into her eyes. Between the crash of each shot came the old woman's rattling wheeze that could be heard across the parade square.

When he had no more ammunition left he shouted, "Dance," again and slammed his jackboot into her belly. All this had happened in complete silence from us, until the man next to me started to pray. He was a Hasid, small and bearded, still wearing the rags of his long black coat; despite the cold which forced most of us to wear ear-muffs on our caps, he had the broad-brimmed hat of his sect. He began to recite the <u>Shema,</u> over and over again, in a quavering voice that grew steadily louder. Knowing that Roschmann was in his most vicious mood, I too began to pray silently that the Hasid would be quiet. But he would not.

"<u>Shema Yisroel</u> . . ." (Hear, O Israel . . .)

"Shut up," I hissed out of the corner of my mouth.

"<u>Adonai elohenu</u> . . ." (the Lord is our God . . .)

"Will you be quiet! You'll get us all killed."

"<u>Adonai eha-a-a-ad.</u>" (The Lord is One.)

Like a cantor, he drew out the last syllable in the traditional way, as Rabbi Akiba had done as he died in the amphitheater at Caesarea on the orders of Tinius Rufus. It was just at that moment that Roschmann stopped screaming

at the old woman. He lifted his head
like an animal scenting the wind and
turned toward us. As I stood a head
taller than the Hasid, he looked at me.

"Who was that talking?" he screamed,
striding toward me across the sand.
"You—step out of line." There was no
doubt he was pointing at me. I thought:
This is the end, then. So what? It
doesn't matter; it had to happen, now or
some other time. I stepped forward as he
arrived in front of me.

He did not say anything, but his face
was twitching like a maniac's. Then it
relaxed and he gave his quiet, wolfish
smile that struck terror into everyone
in the ghetto, even the Latvian SS men.

His hand moved so quickly no one could
see it. I felt only a sort of thump
down the left side of my face, simul-
taneous with a tremendous bang as if a
bomb had gone off next to my eardrum.
Then the quite distinct but detached
feeling of my own skin splitting like
rotten calico from temple to mouth.
Even before it had started to bleed,
Roschmann's hand moved again, the other
way this time, and his quirt ripped
open the other side of my face with the
same loud bang in the ear and the feeling of something tearing. It was a two-
foot quirt, sprung with whippy steel
core at the handle end, the remaining
foot-length being of plaited leather
thongs without the core, and when drawn
across and down human skin at the same
time, the plaiting could split the hide
like tissue paper. I had seen it done.

Within a matter of seconds I felt the

trickle of warm blood beginning to flow
down the front of my jacket, dripping
off my chin in two little red fountains.
Roschmann swung away from me, then back,
pointing to the old woman still sobbing
in the center of the square.

"Pick up that old hag and take her
to the van," he barked.

And so, a few minutes ahead of the
arrival of the other hundred victims, I
picked up the old woman and carried her
down Little Hill Street to the gate
and the waiting van, pouring blood onto
her from my chin. I set her down in the
back of the van and made to leave her
there. As I did so, she gripped my wrist
in withered fingers with a strength I
would not have thought she still
possessed. She pulled me down toward
her, squatting on the floor of the death
van, and with a small cambric handker-
chief that must have come from better
days stanched some of the still flowing
blood.

She looked up at me from a face
streaked with mascara, rouge, tears, and
sand, but with dark eyes bright as
stars.

"Jew, my son," she whispered, "you
must live. Swear to me that you will
live. Swear to me you will get out of
this place alive. You must live, so
that you can tell them, them outside in
the other world, what happened to our
people here. Promise me, swear it by
the Torah."

And so I swore that I would live, somehow, no matter what the cost. Then she
let me go. I stumbled back down the

road into the ghetto, and halfway down I fainted.

Shortly after returning to work I made two decisions. One was to keep a secret diary, nightly tattooing words and dates with a pin and black ink into the skin of my feet and legs, so that one day I would be able to transcribe all that had happened in Riga and give precise evidence against those responsible.

The second decision was to become a Kapo, a member of the Jewish police.

The decision was hard, for these were men who herded their fellow Jews to work and back, and often to the place of execution. Moreover, they carried pickax handles and occasionally, when under the eye of a German SS officer, used them liberally to beat their fellow Jews so they would work harder. Nevertheless, on April 1, 1942, I went to the chief of the Kapos and volunteered, thus becoming an outcast from the company of my fellow Jews. There was always room for an extra Kapo, for despite the better rations, living conditions, and release from slave labor, very few agreed to become Kapos.

I should here describe the method of execution of those unfit for labor, for in this manner between 70,000 and 80,000 Jews were exterminated under the orders of Eduard Roschmann at Riga. When the cattle train arrived at the station with a new consignment of prisoners, usually about 5000 strong, there were always close to a thousand

already dead from the journey. Only
occasionally was the number as low as a
few hundred, scattered among fifty cars.

When the new arrivals were lined up
in Tin Square, the selections for
extermination took place, not merely
among the new arrivals but among us all.
That was the point of the head-count
each morning and evening. Among the new
arrivals, those weak or frail, old or
diseased, most of the women, and almost
all the children, were singled out as
being unfit for work. These were set to
one side. The remainder were then
counted. If they totaled 2000, then
2000 of the existing inmates were also
picked out, so that 5000 had arrived and
5000 went to Execution Hill. That way
there was no overcrowding. A man might
survive six months of slave labor,
seldom more; then, when his health was
reduced to ruins, Roschmann's quirt
would tap him on the chest one day, and
he would go to join the ranks of the
dead.

At first these victims were marched in
column to a forest outside the town.
The Latvians called it Bickernicker
Forest, and the Germans renamed it the
Hochwald or High Forest. Here, in clear-
ings between the pines, enormous open
ditches had been dug by the Riga Jews
before they died. And here the Latvian
SS guards, under the eye and orders of
Eduard Roschmann, mowed them down so
that they fell into the ditches. The
remaining Riga Jews then filled in
enough earth to cover the bodies, adding

one more layer of corpses to those
underneath until the ditch was full.
Then a new one was started.

From the ghetto we could hear the
chattering of the machine guns when
each new consignment was liquidated,
and watch Roschmann riding back down the
hill and through the ghetto gates in his
open car when it was over.

After I became a Kapo all social contact between me and the other internees
ceased. There was no point in explaining
why I had done it, that one Kapo more
or less would make no difference, not
increasing the death toll by a single
digit, but that one single surviving
witness might make all the difference,
not to save the Jews of Germany, but to
avenge them. This at least was the
argument I repeated to myself, but was
it the real reason? Or was I just afraid
to die? Whatever it was, fear soon
ceased to be a factor, for in August
that year something happened that caused
my soul to die inside my body, leaving
only the husk struggling to survive.

In July 1942 a big new transport of
Austrian Jews came through from Vienna.
Apparently they were marked without
exception for "special treatment," for
the entire shipment never came to the
ghetto. We did not see them, for they
were all marched from the station to
High Forest and machine-gunned. Later
that evening, down the hill rolled four
trucks full of clothes, which were
brought to the Tin Square for sorting.

They made a mound as big as a house
until they were sorted out into piles of
shoes, socks, underpants, trousers,
dresses, jackets, shaving brushes,
spectacles, dentures, wedding rings,
signet rings, caps, and so forth.

Of course this was standard procedure
for executed deportees. All those killed
on Execution Hill were stripped at the
graveside and their effects brought
down later. These were then sorted and
sent back to the Reich. The gold,
silver, and jewelry were taken in
charge by Roschmann personally.

In August 1942 there was another
transport, from Theresienstadt, a camp
in Bohemia where tens of thousands of
German and Austrian Jews were held
before being sent eastward to extermination. I was standing at one side
of the Tin Square, watching Roschmann as
he went around making his selections.
The new arrivals were already shaved
bald, which had been done at their
previous camp, and it was not easy to
tell the men from the women, except for
the shift dresses the woman mainly wore.
There was one woman across on the other
side of the square who caught my attention. There was something about her
cast of features that rang a bell in
my mind, although she was emaciated,
thin as a rake, and coughing con-
tinuously.

Arriving opposite her, Roschmann
tapped her on the chest and passed on.
The Latvians following him at once
seized her arms and pushed her out of

line to join the others in the center of
the square. There were many from that
transport who were not work-fit, and
the list of selections was long. That
meant fewer of us would be selected to
make up the numbers, though for me the
question was academic. As a Kapo I wore
an armband and carried a club, and the
extra food rations had increased my
strength a little. Although Roschmann
had seen my face, he did not seem to
remember it. He had slashed so many
across the face that one more or less
would not attract his attention.

Most of those selected that summer
evening were formed into a column and
marched to the ghetto gates by the
Kapos. The column was then taken over
by the Latvians for the last four miles
to High Forest and death.

But as there was a gassing van standing by also at the gates, a group of
about a hundred of the frailest of the
selected ones was detached from the
crowd. I was about to escort the other
condemned men and women to the gates
when SS Lieutenant Krause pointed to
five of us Kapos. "You," he shouted,
"take these to the Dünamünde convoy."

After the others had left, we five
escorted the last hundred, most of
them limping, crawling, or coughing, to
the gates where the van waited. The thin
woman was among them, her chest racked
by tuberculosis. She knew where she was
going—they all did—but like the rest
she stumbled with resigned obedience to
the rear of the van. She was too weak
to get up, for the tailboard was high

off the ground, so she turned to me for
help. We stood and looked at each other
in stunned amazement.

I heard somebody approach behind me,
and the other Kapos at the tailboard
straightened to attention, scraping
their caps off. Realizing it must be
an SS officer, I did the same. The
woman just stared at me, unblinking. The
man behind me came forward. It was
Captain Roschmann. He nodded to the
other Kapos to carry on, and stared at
me with those pale blue eyes. I thought
he could only mean I would be flogged
that evening for being slow to take my
cap off.

"What's your name?" he asked softly.

"Tauber, Herr Kapitän," I said, still
ramrod at attention.

"Well, Tauber, you seem to be a little
slow. Do you think we ought to liven
you up a little this evening?"

There was no point in saying anything.
The sentence was passed. Roschmann's
eyes flickered to the woman and narrowed
as if he were suspecting something;
then his slow, wolfish smile spread
across his face.

"Do you know this woman?" he asked.

"Yes, Herr Kapitän," I answered.

"Who is she?" he asked. I could not
reply. My mouth was gummed together as
if by glue.

"Is she your wife?" he went on.

I nodded dumbly.

He grinned even more widely. "Well,
now, my dear Tauber, where are your
manners? Help the lady up into the van."

I still stood there, unable to move.
He put his face closer to mine and
whispered, "You have ten seconds to
pack her in, or you will go yourself."

Slowly I held out my arm and Esther
leaned upon it. With this assistance she
climbed into the van. The other Kapos
waited to slam the doors shut. When she
was up, she looked down at me, and two
tears came, one from each eye, and
rolled down her cheeks. She did not say
anything to me; we never spoke throughout. Then the doors were slammed shut
and the van rolled away. The last thing
I saw was her eyes looking at me.

I have spent twenty years trying to
understand the look in her eyes. Was it
love or hatred, contempt or pity,
bewilderment or understanding? I shall
never know.

When the van had gone, Roschmann
turned to me, still grinning. "You may
go on living until it suits us to finish
you off, Tauber," he said. "But you are
dead as of now."

And he was right. That was the day
my soul died inside me. It was August
29, 1942.

After August that year I became a
robot. Nothing mattered any more. There
was no feeling of cold or of pain, no
sensation of any kind at all. I watched
the brutalities of Roschmann and his
fellow SS men without batting an eyelid.
I was inured to everything that can
touch the human spirit and most things
that can touch the body. I just noted
everything, each tiny detail, filing
them away in my mind or pricking the

dates into the skin of my legs. The
transports came, their occupants marched
to Execution Hill or to the vans, died,
and were buried. Sometimes I looked into
their eyes as they went, walking beside
them to the gates of the ghetto with my
armband and club. It reminded me of a
poem I had once read by an English poet,
which described how an ancient mariner,
condemned to live, had looked into the
eyes of his crewmates as they died of
thirst, and read the curse in them. But
for me there was no curse, for I was
immune even to the feeling of guilt.
That was to come years later. There was
only the emptiness of a dead man still
walking upright . . .

[Peter Miller read on late into the night. The effect of the narration of the atrocities on him was at
once monotonous and mesmerizing. Several times
he sat back in his chair and breathed deeply for a
few minutes to regain his calm. Then he read on.

Once, close to midnight, he laid the book down
and made more coffee. He stood at the window
before drawing the curtains, looking down into the
street. Farther down the road the brilliant neon
light of the Café Chérie blazed across the Steindamm, and he saw one of the part-time girls who
frequent it to supplement their incomes emerge on
the arm of a businessman. They disappeared into a
pension a little farther down, where the businessman would be relieved of 100 marks for half an
hour of copulation.

Miller pulled the curtains across, finished his
coffee, and returned to Salomon Tauber's diary.]

In the autumn of 1943 the order came
through from Berlin to dig up the tens

of thousands of corpses in the High
Forest and destroy them more permanently,
with either fire or quicklime. The
job was easier said than done, with
winter coming on and the ground about
to freeze hard. It put Roschmann in a
foul temper for days, but the administrative details of carrying out the
order kept him busy enough to stay away
from us.

Day after day the newly formed labor
squads were seen marching up the hill
into the forest with their pickaxes and
shovels, and day after day the columns
of black smoke rose above the forest.
For fuel they used the pines of the
forest, but largely decomposed bodies
do not burn easily, so the job was slow.
Eventually they switched to quicklime,
covered each layer of corpses with it,
and in the spring of 1944, when the
earth softened, filled them in.*

The gangs who did the work were not
from the ghetto. They were totally
isolated from all other human contact.
They were Jewish, but were kept imprisoned in one of the worst camps in
the neighborhood, Salas Pils, where
they were later exterminated by being
given no food at all until they died of
starvation, despite the cannibalism to
which many resorted.

When the work was more or less completed in the spring of 1944, the ghetto

------

* This procedure badly burned the corpses but did not
destroy the bones. The Russians later uncovered these 80,000
skeletons.

was finally liquidated. Most of its
30,000 inhabitants were marched toward
the forest to become the last victims
that pinewood was destined to receive.
About 5000 of us were transferred to
the camp of Kaiserwald, while behind us
the ghetto was fired and then the ashes
were bulldozed. Of what had once been
there, nothing was left but an area of
flattened ashes covering hundreds of
acres.*

[For a further twenty pages of typescript Tauber's diary described the struggle to survive in
Kaiserwald concentration camp against the on-
slaught of starvation, disease, overwork, and the
brutality of the camp's guards. During this time no
sign was seen of SS Captain Eduard Roschmann.
But apparently he was still in Riga. Tauber described how in early October of 1944 the SS officers, by now panic-stricken at the thought they
might be taken alive by the vengeful Russians, prepared for a desperate evacuation of Riga by sea,
taking along a handful of the last surviving prisoners as their passage ticket back to the Reich in the
west. This became fairly common practice for the
SS staff of the concentration camps as the Russian

---

* The Russian spring offensive of 1944 carried the tide of
war so far westward that the Soviet troops pushed south of the
Baltic States and through to the Baltic Sea to the west of them.
This cut off the whole of Ostand from the Reich and led to a
blazing quarrel between Hitler and his generals. They had seen
it coming and had pleaded with Hitler to pull back the forty-
five divisions inside the enclave. He had refused, reiterating his
parrot-cry, "Death or Victory." All he offered those 500,000
soldiers inside the enclave was death. Cut off from resupply,
they fought with dwindling ammunition to delay a certain
fate, and eventually surrendered. Of the majority, made prisoners and transported in the winter of 1944–1945 to Russia, few
returned ten years later to Germany.

advance swept on. So long as they could still claim
they had a task to perform, important to the Reich,
they could continue to outrank the Wehrmacht and
avoid the terrible prospect of being required to face
Stalin's divisions in combat. This "task," which
they allotted to themselves, was the escorting back
into the still safe heart of Germany of the few remaining wretches from the camps they had run.
Sometimes the charade became ridiculous, as when
the SS guards outnumbered their tottering charges
by as many as ten to one.]

It was in the afternoon of October 11
that we arrived, by now barely 4000
strong, at the town of Riga, and the
column went straight down to the docks.
In the distance we could hear a strange
crump, as if of thunder, along the
horizon. For a while it puzzled us, for
we had never heard the sound of shells
or bombs. Then it filtered through to
our minds, dazed by hunger and cold—
there were Russian mortar shells landing
in the suburbs of Riga.
When we arrived at the dock area it
was crawling with officers and men of
the SS. I had never seen so many in one
place at the same time. There must have
been more of them than there were of us.
We were lined up in rows against one
of the warehouses, and again most of us
thought that this was where we would die
under the machine guns. But this was not
to be.
Apparently the SS troops were going
to use us, the last remainder of the
hundreds of thousands of Jews who had
passed through Riga, as their alibi to
escape from the Russian advance, their

passage back to the Reich. The means of
travel was berthed alongside Quay Six—
a freighter, the last one out of the
encircled enclave. As we watched, the
loading began of some of the hundreds of
German Army wounded who were lying on
stretchers in two of the warehouses
farther along the quay.

It was almost dark when Captain
Roschmann arrived, and he stopped short
when he saw how the ship was being
loaded. When he had taken in the sight
of the German Army wounded being put
onto the ship he turned around and
shouted to the medical orderlies bearing
the stretchers, "Stop that."

He strode toward them across the quay
and slapped one of the orderlies in the
face. He whirled around on the ranks of
us prisoners and roared, "You scum. Get
up on that ship and get these men off.
Bring them back down here. That ship is
ours."

Under the prodding of the gun barrels
of the SS men who had come down with us,
we started to move toward the gang-
plank. Hundreds of other SS men,
privates and NCOs, who till then had
been standing back watching the loading, surged forward and followed the
prisoners up onto the ship. When the
first got on the deck, they began picking up the stretchers and carrying them
back to the quay. Rather, they were
about to, when another shout stopped us.

I had reached the foot of the gangway and was about to start up, when I

heard the shout and turned to see what was happening.

An Army captain was running down the quay, and he came to a stop quite close to me by the gangway. Staring up at the men above, bearing stretchers they were about to unload, the captain shouted "Who ordered these men to be offloaded?"

Roschmann walked up behind him and said, "I did. This boat is ours." The captain spun around. He delved in his pocket and produced a piece of paper. "This ship was sent to pick up Army wounded," he said. "And Army wounded is what it will take."

With that he turned to the Army orderlies and shouted to them to resume the loading. I looked across at Roschmann. He was standing trembling, I thought with anger. Then I saw he was scared. He was frightened of being left to face the Russians. Unlike us, they were armed.

He began to scream at the orderlies, "Leave them alone! I have commandeered this ship in the name of the Reich." The orderlies ignored him and obeyed the Wehrmacht captain. I noticed his face, as he was only two meters away from me. It was gray with exhaustion, with dark smudges under the eyes. There were lines down each side of the nose and several weeks of stubble on his chin. Seeing the loading work begin again, he made to march past Roschmann to supervise his orderlies. From among the crowded stretchers in the snow of the quay I heard a voice shout in the

Hamburg dialect, "Good for you, Captain.
You tell the swine."

As the Wehrmacht captain was abreast
of Roschmann, the SS officer grabbed his
arm, swung him around, and slapped him
across the face with his gloved hand. I
had seen him slap men a thousand times,
but never with the same result. The
captain took the blow, shook his head,
bunched his fist, and landed a haymaker
of a right-fisted punch on Roschmann's
jaw. Roschmann flew back several feet
and went flat on his back in the snow,
a small trickle of blood coming from his
mouth. The captain moved toward his
orderlies.

As I watched, Roschmann drew his SS
officer's Luger from its holster, took
careful aim, and fired between the
captain's shoulders. Everything stopped
at the crash from the pistol. The Army
captain staggered and turned. Roschmann
fired again, and the bullet caught the
captain in the throat. He spun over
backward and was dead before he hit the
quay. Something he had been wearing
around his neck flew off as the bullet
struck, and when I passed it, after
being ordered to carry the body and
throw it into the water, I saw that the
object was a medal on a ribbon. I never
knew the captain's name, but the medal
was the Knight's Cross with Oak Leaf
Cluster.

[Miller read this page of the diary with growing
astonishment gradually turning to disbelief, doubt,
belief again, and finally a deep anger. He read the

page a dozen times to make sure there was no
doubt, then resumed reading the diary.]

After this we were ordered to start
unloading the Wehrmacht wounded and told
to lay them back in the gathering snow
on the quayside. I found myself helping
one young soldier back down the gang-
plank onto the quay. He had been
blinded, and around his eyes was wrapped
a dirty bandage torn from a shirttail.
He was half delirious and kept asking
for his mother. I suppose he must have
been about eighteen.

Finally they were all taken off, and
we prisoners were ordered on board. We
were all taken down into the two holds,
one forward and one aft, until we were
so cramped we could hardly move. Then
the hatches were battened down and the
SS began to come aboard. We sailed just
before midnight, the captain evidently
wishing to be well out into the Gulf of
Latvia before dawn came, to avoid the
chance of being spotted and bombed by
the patrolling Russian Stormoviks.

It took three days to reach Danzig,
well behind German lines. Three days in
a pitching, tossing hell below decks,
without food or water, during which a
quarter of the four thousand prisoners
died. There was no food to vomit, and
yet everyone was retching dry from
seasickness. Many died from the exhaustion of vomiting, others from hunger or
cold, others from suffocation, others
because they simply lost the will to
live, lay back, and surrendered to

death. And then the ship was berthed
again, the hatches were opened, and
gusts of ice-cold winter air came
rushing into the fetid, stinking holds.

When we were unloaded onto the quay
at Danzig, the dead bodies were laid
out in rows alongside the living, so
that the numbers should tally with those
that had been taken on board at Riga.
The SS was always very precise about
numbers.

We learned later that Riga had fallen
to the Russians on October 14, while we
were still at sea.

[Tauber's pain-wracked Odyssey was reaching
its end. From Danzig the surviving inmates were
taken by barge to the concentration camp of Stutthof, outside Danzig, and until the first weeks of
1945 he worked daily in the submarine works of
Burggraben by day and lived in the camp by night.
Thousands more at Stutthof died of malnutrition.
He watched them all die, but somehow stayed alive.

In January 1945, as the advancing Russians
closed on Danzig, the survivors of Stutthof camp
were driven westward on the notorious Death
March through the winter snow toward Berlin. All
across eastern Germany these columns of wraiths,
used as a ticket to safety in Western hands by their
SS guards, were being herded westward. Along the
route, in snow and frost, they died like flies.

Tauber survived even this, and finally the rem-
nant of his column reached Magdeburg, west of
Berlin, where the SS men finally abandoned them
and sought their own safety. Tauber's group was
lodged in Magdeburg prison, in the charge of the
bewildered and helpless old men of the local Home
Guard. Unable to feed their prisoners, terrified of
what the advancing Allies would say when they

found them, the Home Guard permitted the fittest
of them to go scrounging for food in the surrounding countryside.]

The last time I had seen Eduard Roschmann was when we were being counted on
Danzig quayside. Warmly wrapped against
the winter cold, he was climbing into a
car. I thought it would be my last
glimpse of him, but I was to see him
one last time. It was April 3, 1945.

I had been out that day toward Garde-
legen, a village east of the city, and
had gathered a small sackful of potatoes
with three others. We were trudging back
with our booty when a car came up behind
us, heading west. It paused to negotiate
a horse and cart on the road, and I
glanced around with no particular
interest to see the car pass. Inside
were four SS officers, evidently making
their escape toward the west. Sitting
beside the driver, pulling on the
uniform jacket of an Army corporal, was
Eduard Roschmann.

He did not see me, for my head was
largely covered by a hood cut from an
old potato sack, a protection against
the cold spring wind. But I saw him.
There was no doubt about it.

All four men in the car were apparently changing their uniforms even as
the vehicle headed west. As it disappeared down the road a garment was
thrown from one window and fluttered
into the dust. We reached the spot where
it lay a few minutes later and stooped
to examine it. It was the jacket of an
SS officer, bearing the silver twin-

lightning symbols of the Waffen SS and
the rank of captain. Roschmann of the SS
had disappeared.

Twenty-four days after this came the
liberation. We had ceased to go out at
all, preferring to stay hungry in the
prison than venture along the streets,
where complete anarchy was loose. Then
on the morning of April 27 all was quiet
in the town. Toward midmorning I was in
the courtyard of the prison, talking to
one of the old guards, who seemed terrified and spent nearly an hour explaining
that he and his colleagues had nothing
to do with Adolf Hitler and certainly
nothing to do with the persecution of
the Jews.
I heard a vehicle drive up outside
the locked gates, and there was a
hammering on them. The old Home Guard
man went to open them. The man who
stepped through, cautiously, with a
revolver in his hand, was a soldier in
full battle uniform, one that I had
never seen before.
He was evidently an officer, for he
was accompanied by a soldier in a flat
round tin hat who carried a rifle. They
just stood there in silence, looking
around at the courtyard of the prison.
In one corner were stacked about fifty
corpses, those who had died in the past
two weeks and whom no one had the
strength to bury. Others, half alive,
lay around the walls, trying to soak up
a little of the spring sunshine, their
sores festering and stinking.
The two men looked at each other,

then at the seventy-year-old Home Guard.
He looked back, embarrassed. Then he
said something he must have learned in
the First World War. He said, "Hello,
Tommy."

The officer looked back at him, looked
again around the courtyard, and said
quite clearly in English, "You fucking
Kraut pig."

And suddenly I began to cry.

I do not really know how I made it
back to Hamburg, but I did. I think I
wanted to see if there was anything left
of the old life. There wasn't. The
streets where I was born and grew up
had vanished in the great firestorm of
the Allied bombing raids; the office
where I had worked was gone, my apartment, everything.

The English put me in the hospital in
Magdeburg for a while, but I left of my
own accord and hitchhiked back home.
But when I got there and saw there was
nothing left, I finally, belatedly collapsed completely. I spent a year in the
hospital as a patient, along with
others, who had come out of a place
called Bergen-Belsen, and then another
year working in the hospital as an
orderly, looking after those who were
worse than I had been.

When I left there, I went to find a
room in Hamburg, the place of my birth,
to spend the rest of my days.

[The book ended with two more clean, white
sheets of paper, evidently recently typed, which
formed the epilogue.]

I have lived in this little room in Altona since 1947. Shortly after I came out of the hospital I began to write the story of what happened to me and to the others at Riga.

But long before I had finished it, it became clear that others had also survived the holocaust. My original intent —believing, as others had done elsewhere in their isolation, that I might be the only survivor—had been to bear witness, to tell the world what had happened. It is clear now that this has already been done. So I did not submit my diary for publication. I kept it and the notes in the hope that one day I might at least bear witness to what happened in the small arena of Riga. I never even let anyone else read it.

Looking back, it was all a waste of time and energy, the battle to survive and to be able to write down the evidence, when others have already done it so much better. I wish now I had died in Riga with Esther.

Even the last wish, to see Eduard Roschmann stand before a court, and to give evidence to that court about what he did, will never be fulfilled. I know this now.

I walk through the streets sometimes and remember the old days here, but it can never be the same. The children laugh at me and run away when I try to be friends. Once I got talking to a little girl who did not run away, but her mother came up screaming and dragged her away. So I do not talk to many people.

Once a woman came to see me. She said she was from the Reparations Office and that I was entitled to money. I said I did not want any money. She was very put out, insisting that it was my right to be recompensed for what was done. I kept on refusing. They sent someone else to see me, and I refused again. He said it was very irregular to refuse to be recompensed. I sensed he meant it would upset their books. But I only take from them what is due to me.

When I was in the British hospital one of the doctors asked me why I did not emigrate to Israel, which was soon to have its independence. How could I explain to him? I could not tell him that I can never go up to the Land, not after what I did to Esther, my wife. I think about it often and dream about what it must be like, but I am not worthy to go.

But if ever these lines should be read in the Land of Israel, which I shall never see, will someone there please say Kaddish for me?

Salomon Tauber,
Altona, Hamburg,
November 21, 1963

Peter Miller put the diary down and lay back in his chair for a long time, staring at the ceiling and smoking. Just before five in the morning he heard the flat door open, and Sigi came in from work. She was startled to find him still awake.

"What are you doing up so late?" she asked.

"Been reading," said Miller.

Later they lay in bed as the first glint of dawn picked

out the spire of Sankt Michaelis, Sigi drowsy and contented, like a young woman who has just been loved, Miller staring up at the ceiling silent and preoccupied.

"Penny for them," said Sigi after a while.

"Just thinking."

"I know. I can tell that. What about?"

"The next story I'm going to cover."

She shifted and looked across at him. "What are you going to do?" she asked.

Miller leaned over and stubbed out his cigarette. "I'm going to track a man down," he said.

3

WHILE PETER MILLER and Sigi were asleep in each other's arms in Hamburg, a giant Argentine Coronado airliner swung over the darkened hills of Castile and entered final approach for a landing at Barajas Airport, Madrid.

Sitting in a window seat in the third row of the first-class passenger section was a man in his early sixties with iron-gray hair and a trim mustache.

Only one photograph had ever existed of the man, in his early forties, showing him with close-cropped hair, no mustache to cover the rattrap mouth, and a razor-straight parting along the left side of his head. Hardly any one of the small group of men who had ever seen that photograph would recognize the man in the airliner, his hair now growing thickly back from the forehead, without a parting. The photograph in his passport matched his new appearance.

The name in that same passport identified him as Señor Ricardo Suertes, citizen of Argentina, and the name itself was his own grim joke against the world. For *suerte* in Spanish means "luck," and "luck" in German is *Glück*. The airline passenger that January night had been born Richard Glücks, later to become full general of the SS, head of the Reich Economic Administration Main Office, and Hitler's Inspector General of Concentration Camps. On the wanted lists of West Germany and Israel, he was number three after Martin Bormann and the former chief of the Gestapo, Heinrich Müller. He ranked higher even than Dr. Josef Mengele, the Devil Doctor of Auschwitz. In the Odessa he ranked number two—direct deputy of Martin Bormann, on whom the mantle of the Führer had fallen after 1945.

The role Richard Glücks had played in the crimes of the SS was unique and matched only by the manner in which he managed to effect his own complete disappearance in May 1945. Glücks had surpassed even Adolf Eichmann as one of the master minds of the holocaust, and yet he had never pulled a trigger.

Had an uninformed passenger been told who the man sitting next to him was, he might well have wondered why the former head of an economic administration office should be so high on the wanted list.

Had he asked, he would have learned that of the crimes against humanity committed on the German side between 1933 and 1945, probably 95 per cent can accurately be laid at the door of the SS. Of these, probably 80 to 90 per cent can be attributed to two departments within the SS. These were the Reich Security Main Office and the Reich Economic Administration Main Office.

If the idea of an economic bureau being involved in mass murder strikes a strange note, one must understand how it was intended that the job should be done. Not only was it intended to exterminate every Jew on the face of Europe, and most of the Slavic races also, but it was intended that the victims should pay for the privilege. Before the gas chambers opened, the SS had already carried out the biggest robbery in history.

In the case of the Jews, the payment was in three stages. First they were robbed of their businesses, houses, factories, bank accounts, furniture, cars, and clothes. They were shipped eastward to the slave-labor camps and the death camps, assured they were destined for resettlement and mainly believing it, with what they could carry, usually two suitcases. On the camp square these were also taken from them, along with the clothes they wore.

Out of this baggage of six million people millions of dollars' worth of booty was extracted, for the European Jews of the time habitually traveled with their wealth upon them, particularly those from Poland and the eastern lands. From the camps entire trainloads of gold trinkets, diamonds, sapphires, rubies, silver ingots, louis d'or, gold dollars, and banknotes of every kind and description were shipped back to the SS headquarters inside Germany. Throughout its history the SS made a profit on its operations. A part of this profit, in the form of gold bars stamped with the eagle of the Reich and the twin-lightning symbol of the SS, was deposited toward the end of the war in the banks of Switzerland, Liechtenstein, Tangier, and Beirut to form the fortune on which the Odessa was later based. Much of this gold still lies beneath the streets of Zurich, guarded by the complacent and self-righteous bankers of that city.

The second stage of the exploitation lay in the living bodies of the victims. They had calories of energy in them, and these could profitably be used. At this point the Jews came onto the same level as the Russians and the Poles, who had been captured penniless in the first place. Those in all categories unfit for work were exterminated as useless. Those able to work were hired out, either to the SS's own factories or to German industrial concerns such as Krupp, Thyssen, von Opel, and others at three marks a day for unskilled workers, four marks for artisans. The phrase "per day" meant as much work as could be extracted from the living body for as little food as possible during a twenty-four-hour period. Hundreds of thousands died at their places of work in this manner.

The SS was a state within a state. It had its own factories, workshops, engineering division, construction section, repair and maintenance shops, and clothing department. It made for itself almost everything it could ever need, and used the slave laborers, which by Hitler's decree were the property of the SS, to do the work.

The third stage of the exploitation lay in the corpses of the dead. These went naked to death, leaving behind wagonloads of shoes, socks, shaving brushes, spectacles, jackets, and trousers. They also left their hair, which was shipped back to the Reich to be turned into felt boots for the winter fighting, and their gold teeth-fillings, which were yanked out of the corpses with pliers and later melted down to be deposited as gold bars in Zurich. Attempts were made to use the bones for fertilizer and render the body fats down for soap, but these were found to be uneconomical.

In charge of the entire economic or profit-making side of the extermination of fourteen million people was the Reich Economic Administration Main Office of the SS, headed by the man in seat 3-B on the airliner that night.

Glücks was one who preferred not to risk his neck, or his life-long liberty, by returning to Germany after his escape. He had no need to. Handsomely provided for out of the secret funds, he could live out his days comfortably in South America, and still does. His dedication to the Nazi ideal remained unshaken by the events of 1945, and this, coupled with his former eminence, secured him a high and honored place among the fugitive Nazis of Argentina, from whence the Odessa was ruled.

The plane landed uneventfully, and the passengers cleared customs with no problems. The fluent Spanish of the first-class passenger from row 3 had long enabled him to pass for a South American.

Outside the terminal building he took a cab and from long habit gave an address a block away from the Zurburán Hotel. After paying off the cab in the center of Madrid, he took his grip and walked the remaining two hundred yards to the hotel.

His reservation assured by Telex, he checked in and went up to his room to shower and shave. It was at nine o'clock on the dot that three soft knocks, followed by a pause and two more, sounded at his door. He opened it himself and stood back when he recognized the visitor.

The new arrival closed the door behind him, snapped to attention, and flashed up his right arm, palm downward, in the old salute.

"*Seig Heil*," said the man.

General Glücks gave the younger man an approving nod and raised his own right hand. *"Sieg Heil,"* he said more softly. He waved his visitor to a seat.

The man facing him was another German, a former officer of the SS and at that time the chief of the Odessa network inside West Germany. He felt very keenly the honor of being summoned to Madrid for a personal conference with a senior officer of such eminence, and suspected it had something to do with the death of President Kennedy thirty-six hours earlier. He was not wrong.

General Glücks poured himself and his visitor cups of coffee from the breakfast tray on the table beside him and carefully lit a large Corona.

"You have probably guessed the reason for this sudden and somewhat hazardous visit by me to Europe," he said. "As I dislike remaining on this continent longer than necessary, I will get to the point and be brief."

The subordinate from Germany sat forward expectantly.

"Kennedy is now dead, for us a remarkable stroke of good fortune," the general went on. "There must be no failure to extract the utmost advantage from this event. Do you follow me?"

"Certainly, in principle, General," the younger man replied eagerly, "but in what specific form?"

"I am referring to the secret arms deal between the rabble of traitors in Bonn and the pigs in Tel Aviv. You know about the arms deal? The tanks, guns, and other weaponry even now flowing from Germany to Israel?"

"Yes, of course."

"And you know also that our organization is doing everything in its power to assist the Egyptian cause so that it may one day prove completely victorious in the coming struggle?"

"Certainly. We have already organized the recruiting of numerous German scientists to that end."

General Glücks nodded. "I'll return to that later. What I was referring to was our policy of keeping our

Arab friends as closely informed as possible about the details of this treacherous deal, so that they may make the strongest representations to Bonn through diplomatic channels. These Arab protests have led to the formation of a group in Germany strongly opposed to the arms deal on political grounds, because the deal upsets the Arabs. This group, mainly unwittingly, is playing our game for us, bringing pressure on the fool Erhard, even as high as cabinet level, to call off the arms deal."

"Yes. I follow you, General."

"Good. So far Erhard has not called off the arms shipments, but he has wavered several times. For those who wish to see the German-Israeli arms deal completed, the main argument to date has been that the deal is supported by Kennedy, and what Kennedy wants, Erhard gives him."

"Yes. That's true."

"But Kennedy is now dead."

The younger man from Germany sat back, his eyes alight with enthusiasm, as the new state of affairs opened up its perspectives to his mind. The SS general flicked an inch of ash from the cigar into the coffee cup and jabbed the glowing tip at his subordinate.

"For the rest of this year, therefore, the main plank of political action within Germany that our friends and supporters must undertake will be to whip up public opinion on as wide a scale as possible against this arms deal and in favor of Germany's true and traditional friends, the Arabs."

"Yes, yes, that can be done." The younger man was smiling broadly.

"Certain contacts we have in the government in Cairo will ensure a constant stream of diplomatic protests through their own and other embassies," the general continued. "Other Arab friends will ensure demonstrations by Arab students and German friends of the Arabs. Your job will be to coordinate press publicity through the various pamphlets and magazines we secretly support, advertisements taken in major newspapers and magazines, lobbying of civil servants close to government and politicians who must be persuaded to join the growing weight of opinion against the arms deal."

The younger man's brow furrowed. "It's very difficult to promote feelings against Israel in Germany today," he murmured.

"There need be no question of that," said the other tartly. "The angle is simple: for practical reasons Germany must not alienate eighty million Arabs with these foolish, supposedly secret arms shipments. Many Germans will listen to that argument, particularly diplomats. Known friends of ours in the Foreign Office can be enlisted. Such a practical viewpoint is wholly permissible. Funds, of course, will be made available. The main thing is, with Kennedy dead and Johnson unlikely to adopt the same internationalist, pro-Jewish outlook, Erhard must be subjected to constant pressure at every level, including his own cabinet, to shelve this arms deal. If we can show the Egyptians that we have caused foreign policy in Bonn to change course, our stock in Cairo must inevitably rise sharply."

The man from Germany nodded several times, already seeing his plan of campaign taking shape before him. "It shall be done," he said.

"Excellent," replied General Glücks.

The man in front of him looked up. "General, you mentioned the German scientists now working in Egypt. . . ."

"Ah yes, I said I would return to them later. They represent the second prong in our plan to destroy the Jews once and for all. You know about the rockets of Helwan, of course?"

"Yes, sir. At least, the broad details."

"But not what they are really for?"

"Well, I assumed, of course—"

"That they would be used to throw a few tons of high explosive onto Israel?" General Glücks smiled broadly. "You could not be more wrong. However, I

think the time is ripe to tell you why these rockets and
the men who build them are in truth so vitally important."

General Glücks leaned back, gazed at the ceiling, and
told his subordinate the *real* story behind the rockets
of Helwan.

In the aftermath of the war, when King Farouk still
ruled Egypt, thousands of Nazis and former members of
the SS had fled from Europe and found a sure refuge
along the sands of the Nile. Among those who came
were a number of scientists. Even before the *coup d'état*
that dislodged Farouk, two German scientists had been
charged by Farouk with the first studies for the eventual
setting up of a factory to manufacture rockets. This was
in 1952, and the two professors were Paul Görke and
Rolf Engel.

The project went into abeyance for a few years after
Naguil and then Nasser took power, but after the military defeat of the Egyptian forces in the 1956 Sinai
campaign, the new dictator of Egypt swore an oath. He
vowed that one day Israel would be totally destroyed.

In 1961, when he got Moscow's final "No" to his
requests for heavy rockets, the Görke-Engel project for
an Egyptian rocket factory was revitalized with a vengeance, and during this year, working against the clock
and without rein on their expenditure of money, the
German professors and the Egyptians built and opened
Factory 333, at Helwan, north of Cairo.

To open a factory is one thing; to design and build
rockets is another. Long since, the senior supporters of
Nasser, mostly with pro-Nazi backgrounds stretching
back to the Second World War, had been in close contact with the Odessa representatives in Egypt. From
these came the answer to the Egyptians' main problem
—that of acquiring the scientists necessary to make the
rockets.

Neither Russia, America, Britain, nor France would

supply a single man to help. But the Odessa pointed out that the kind of rockets Nasser needed were remarkably similar in size and range to the V-2 rockets that Wernher von Braun and his team had once built at Peenemünde to pulverize London. And many of his former team were still available.

In late 1961 the recruiting of German scientists started. Many of these were employed at the West German Institute for Aerospace Research at Stuttgart. But they were frustrated because the Paris Treaty of 1954 forbade Germany to indulge in research or manufacture in certain realms, notably nuclear physics and rocketry. They were also chronically short of research funds. To many of these scientists the offer of a place in the sun, plenty of research money, and the chance to design real rockets was too tempting.

The Odessa appointed as chief recruiting officer in Germany a former major of the SS, Dr. Ferdinand Brandner, and he in turn employed as his legman a former SS sergeant, Heinz Krug. Together they scoured Germany, looking for men prepared to go to Egypt and build Nasser's rockets for him.

With the salaries they could offer, they were not short of choice recruits. Notable among them were Professor Wolfgang Pilz, who had been recruited from postwar Germany by the French and had later become the father of the French Véronique rocket, itself the foundation of De Gaulle's aerospace program. Professor Pilz left for Egypt in early 1962. Dr. Eugen Sänger and his wife Irene, both formerly on the Von Braun V-2 team, also went along, as did Dr. Josef Eisig and Dr. Kirmayer, all experts in propulsion fuels and techniques.

The world saw the first results of their labors at a parade through the streets of Cairo on July 23, 1962, to mark the eighth anniversary of the Egyptian republic. Two rockets, the El Kahira and the El Zafira, respectively with ranges of 500 and 300 kilometers, were trundled past the screaming crowds. Although these rockets were only the casings, without warheads or fuel, they were destined to be the first of four hundred such weapons that would one day be launched against Israel.

General Glücks paused, drew on his cigar, and returned to the present.

"The problem is that, although we solved the matter of making the casings, the warheads, and the fuel, the key to a guided missile lies in the teleguidance system." He stabbed his cigar in the direction of the West German. "And *that* was what we were unable to furnish to the Egyptians," he went on.

"By ill luck, although there were scientists and experts in guidance systems working at Stuttgart and elsewhere, we could not persuade one of them of any value to emigrate to Egypt. All the experts sent out there were specialists in aerodynamics, propulsion, and the design of warheads.

"But we had promised Egypt that she would have her rockets, and have them she will. President Nasser is determined there will one day be another war between Egypt and Israel, and war there will be. He believes his tanks and soldiers alone will win for him. Our information is not so optimistic. They might not, despite their numerical superiority. But just think what our position would be if, when all the Soviet weaponry, bought at a cost of billions of dollars, had failed, it turned out to be the rockets, provided by the scientists recruited through our network, which won the war. Our position would be unassailable. We would have achieved the double *coup* of ensuring an eternally grateful Middle East, a safe and sure home for our people for all time, and of achieving the final and utter destruction of the Jew-pig state, thus fulfilling the last wish of the dying Führer. It is a mighty challenge, and one in which we must not and will not fail."

The subordinate watched his senior officer pacing the room, with awe and some puzzlement. "Forgive me, General, but will four hundred medium warheads really finish off the Jews once and for all? A massive amount of damage, yes, but total destruction?"

Glücks spun around and gazed down at the younger man with a triumphant smile.

"But what warheads!" he exclaimed. "You do not think we are going to waste mere high explosive on these swine? We have proposed to President Nasser, and he has accepted with alacrity, that these warheads on the Kahiras and Zafiras be of a different type. Some will contain concentrated cultures of bubonic plague, and the others will explode high above the ground, showering the entire territory of Israel with irradiated cobalt-sixty. Within hours they will all be dying of the pest or of gamma-ray sickness. *That* is what we have in store for them."

The other gazed at him, open-mouthed. "Fantastic," he breathed. "Now I recall reading something about a trial in Switzerland last summer—just rumors, so much of the evidence was *in camera*. Then it's true. But, General, it's brilliant."

"Brilliant, yes, and inevitable, provided we of the Odessa can equip those rockets with the teleguidance systems necessary to direct them not merely in the right direction but to the exact locations where they must explode. The man who controls the entire research operation aimed at devising a teleguidance system for those rockets is now working in West Germany. His code name is Vulkan. You may recall that in Greek mythology Vulkan was the smith who made the thunderbolts of the gods."

"He is a scientist?" asked the West German in bewilderment.

"No, certainly not. When he was forced to disappear in 1955 he would normally have returned to Argentina. But your predecessor was required by us to provide him immediately with a false passport to enable him to stay in Germany. He was then funded out of Zurich with one million American dollars with which to start a factory in Germany. The original purpose was to use the factory as a front for another type of research in which we were interested at the time, but which has now been shelved in favor of the guidance systems for the rockets of Helwan.

"The factory Vulkan now runs manufactures transistor radios. But this is a front. In the research department of the factory a group of scientists is even now in the process of devising the teleguidance systems that will one day be fitted to the rockets of Helwan."

"Why don't they simply go to Egypt?" asked the other.

Glücks smiled again and continued pacing. "That is the stroke of genius behind the whole operation. I told you that there were men in Germany capable of producing such rocket-guidance systems, but none could be persuaded to emigrate. The group of them who now work in the research department of Vulkan's factory actually believe they are working on a contract, in conditions of top secrecy, of course, for the Defense Ministry in Bonn."

This time the subordinate got out of his chair, his coffee spilling on the carpet. "God in Heaven. How on earth was that arranged?"

"Basically quite simple. The Paris Treaty forbids Germany to do research into rockets. The men under Vulkan were sworn to secrecy by a genuine official of the Defense Ministry in Bonn, who also happens to be one of us. He was accompanied by a general whose face the scientists could recognize from the last war. They are all men prepared to work for Germany, even against the terms of the Paris Treaty, but not necessarily prepared to work for Egypt. Now they believe they *are* working for Germany.

"Of course, the cost is stupendous. Normally, re-. search of this nature can only be undertaken by a major power. This entire program has made enormous inroads into our secret funds. Now do you understand the importance of Vulkan?"

"Of course," replied the Odessa chief from Germany.

"But if anything happened to him, could not the program go on?"

"No. The factory and the company are owned and run by him alone. He is chairman and managing director, sole shareholder and paymaster. He alone can continue to pay the salaries of the scientists and the enormous research costs involved. None of the scientists ever has anything to do with anyone else in the firm, and no one else in the firm knows the true nature of the overlarge research section. The other workers believe the men in the closed-off section are working on microwave circuits with a view to making a breakthrough in the transistor market. The secrecy is explained as a precaution against industrial espionage. The only link man between the two sections is Vulkan. If he went, the entire project would collapse."

"Can you tell me the name of the factory?"

General Glücks considered for a moment, then mentioned a name.

The other man stared at him in astonishment. "But I know those radios," he protested.

"Of course. It's a bona fide firm and makes bona fide radios."

"And the managing director—he is . . . ?"

"Yes. He is Vulkan. Now you see the importance of this man and what he is doing. For that reason there is one other instruction to you. Here." General Glücks took a photograph from his breast pocket and handed it to the man from Germany.

After a long, perplexed gaze at the face, he turned it over and read the name on the back. "Good God, I thought he was in South America."

Glücks shook his head. "On the contrary. He is Vulkan. At the present time his work has reached a most crucial stage. If by any chance, therefore, you should get a whisper of anyone asking inconvenient questions about this man, that person should be—discouraged. One warning, and then a permanent solution. Do you follow me, *Kamerad?* No one, repeat, no one is to get anywhere near exposing Vulkan for who he really is."

The SS general rose. His visitor did likewise.

"That will be all," said Glücks. "You have your instructions."

4

"BUT YOU don't even know if he's alive."

Peter Miller and Karl Brandt were sitting side by side in Miller's car outside the house of the detective inspector, where Miller had found him over Sunday lunch on his day off.

"No, I don't. So that's the first thing I have to find out. If Roschmann's dead, obviously that's the end of it. Can you help me?"

Brandt considered the request, then slowly shook his head. "No, sorry, I can't."

"Why not?"

"Look, I gave you that diary as a favor. Just between us. Because it shocked me, because I thought it might make a story for you. But I never thought you were going to try and track Roschmann down. Why can't you just make a story out of the finding of the diary?"

"Because there's no story in it," said Miller. "What am I supposed to say? 'Surprise, surprise, I've found a looseleaf folder in which an old man who just gassed himself describes what he went through during the war'? You think any editor's going to buy that? I happen to think it's a horrifying document, but that's just my opinion. There have been hundreds of memoirs written since the war. The world's getting tired of them. Just the diary alone won't sell to any editor in Germany."

"So what are you going on about?" asked Brandt.

"Simply this. Get a major police hunt started for Roschmann on the basis of the diary, and I've got a story."

Brandt tapped his ash slowly into the dashboard tray. "There won't be a major police hunt," he said. "Look, Peter, you may know journalism, but I know the Hamburg police. Our job is to keep Hamburg crime-free now, in nineteen sixty-three. Nobody's going to start detaching overworked detectives to hunt a man for what he did in Riga twenty years ago. It's not going to happen."

"But you could at least raise the matter?" asked Miller.

Brandt shook his head. "No. Not me."

"Why not? What's the matter?"

"Because I don't want to get involved. You're all right. You're single, unattached. You can go off chasing will-o'-the-wisps if you want to. I've got a wife and two kids and a good career, and I don't intend to jeopardize that career."

"Why should this jeopardize your career with the police? Roschmann's a criminal, isn't he? Police forces are supposed to hunt criminals. Where's the problem?"

Brandt crushed out his stub. "It's difficult to put your finger on. But there's a sort of attitude in the police, nothing concrete, just a feeling. And that feeling is that to start probing too energetically into the war crimes of the SS can do a young policeman's career no good. Nothing comes of it anyway. The request would simply be denied. But the fact that it was made goes into a file. Then bang goes your chance of promotion. Nobody mentions it, but everyone knows it. So if you want to make a big issue out of this, you're on your own. Count me out."

Miller sat and stared through the windshield. "All right. If that's the way it is," he said at length. "But I've got to start somewhere. Did Tauber leave anything else behind when he died?"

"Well, there was a brief note. I had to take it and include it in my report on the suicide. By now it will have been filed away. And the file's closed."

"What did he say in it?" asked Miller.

"Not much," said Brandt. "He just said he was committing suicide. Oh, there was one thing; he said he left his effects to a friend of his, a Herr Marx."

"Well, that's a start. Where's this Marx?"

"How the hell should I know?" said Brandt.

"You mean to say that's all the note said? Just Herr Marx? No address?"

"Nothing," said Brandt. "Just Marx. No indication where he lives."

"Well, he must be around somewhere. Didn't you look for him?"

Brandt sighed. "Will you get this through your head? We are very busy in the police force. Have you any idea how many Marxes there are in Hamburg? Hundreds in the telephone directory alone. We can't spend weeks looking for this particular Marx. Anyway, what the old man left wasn't worth ten pfennigs."

"That's all, then?" asked Miller. "Nothing else?"

"Not a thing. If you want to find Marx, you're welcome to try."

"Thanks. I will," said Miller. The two men shook hands, and Brandt returned to his family lunch table.

Miller started the next morning by visiting the house where Tauber had lived. The door was opened by a middle-aged man wearing a pair of stained trousers supported by string, a collarless shirt open at the neck, and three days' stubble around his chin.

"Morning. Are you the landlord?"

The man looked Miller up and down and nodded. He smelled of cabbage.

"There was a man gassed himself here a few nights back," said Miller.

"Are you from the police?"

"No. The press." Miller showed the man his press card.

"I ain't got nothing to say."

Miller eased a ten-mark note without too much trouble into the man's hand. "I only want to look at his room."

"I've rented it."

"What did you do with his stuff?"

"It's in the back yard. Nothing else I could do with it."

The pile of junk was lying in a heap under the thin rain. It still smelled of gas. There were a battered old typewriter, two scuffed pairs of shoes, an assortment of clothes, a pile of books, and a fringed white silk scarf that Miller assumed must be something to do with the Jewish religion. He went through everything in the pile, but there was no indication of an address book and nothing addressed to Marx.

"Is that all?" he asked.

"That's all," said the man, regarding him sourly from the shelter of the back door.

"Do you have any tenant by the name of Marx?"

"Nope."

"Do you know of any Marx?"

"Nope."

"Did old Tauber have any friends?"

"Not that I knew of. Kept himself to himself. Came and went at all hours, shuffling about up there. Crazy, if you ask me. But he paid his rent regular. Didn't cause no trouble."

"Ever see him with anybody? Out in the street, I mean."

"No, never. Didn't seem to have any friends. Not surprised, the way he kept mumbling to himself. Crazy."

Miller left and started asking up and down the street. Most people remembered seeing the old man shuffling along, head down, wrapped in an ankle-length overcoat, head covered by a woolen cap, hands in woolen gloves, from which the fingertips protruded.

For three days he quartered the area of streets where Tauber lived, checking through the dairy, the grocer, the butcher, the hardware store, the bar, the tobacconist, intercepting the milkman and the postman. It was Wednesday afternoon when he found the group of urchins playing football up against the warehouse wall.

"What, that old Jew? Mad Solly?" said the leader of

the group in answer to his question. The rest gathered around.

"That's the one," said Miller. "Mad Solly."

"He was crazy," said one of the crowd. "He used to walk like this."

The boy hunched his head into his shoulders, hands clutching his jacket around him, and shuffled forward a few paces, muttering to himself and casting his eyes about. The others dissolved in laughter, and one gave the impersonator a hefty shove which sent him sprawling.

"Anyone ever see him with anyone else?" asked Miller. "Talking with anyone else? Another man?"

"Whatcher want to know for?" asked the leader suspiciously. "We didn't do him no harm."

Miller flicked a five-mark coin idly up and down in one hand. Eight pairs of eyes watched the silver glitter of the spinning coin. Eight heads shook slowly. Miller turned and walked away.

"Mister."

He stopped and turned around. The smallest of the group had caught up with him.

"I seen him once with a man. Talking, they was. Sitting and talking."

"Where was that?"

"Down by the river. On the grass bank along the river. There are some benches there. They was sitting on a bench, talking."

"How old was he, the other one?"

"Very old. Lot of white hair."

Miller tossed him the coin, convinced it had been a wasted gesture. But he walked to the river and stared down the length of the grass bank in both directions. There were a dozen benches along the bank, all of them empty. In summer there would be plenty of people sitting along the Elbe Chaussee watching the great liners come in and out, but not at the end of November.

To his left along the near bank lay the fishing port, with half a dozen North Sea trawlers drawn up at the wharfs, discharging their loads of fresh-caught herring and mackerel or preparing for the sea again.

As a boy, Peter had returned to the shattered city from a farm in the country where he had been evacuated during the bombing, and had grown up amid the rubble and the ruins. His favorite playing place had been this fishing port along the river at Altona.

He liked the fishermen, gruff, kindly men who smelled of tar and salt and shag tobacco. He thought of Eduard Roschmann in Riga and wondered how the same country could have produced them both.

His mind came back to Tauber and went over the problem again. Where could he possibly have met his friend Marx? Miller knew there was something missing but could not put his finger on it. It was not until he was back in his car and had stopped for gas close to Altona railway station that the answer came. As so often, it was a chance remark. The pump attendant pointed out there had been a price increase in top-grade gasoline and added, just to make conversation with his customer, that money went less and less far these days. He went to get the change and left Miller staring at the open wallet in his hand.

Money. Where did Tauber get his money? He didn't work. He refused to accept any compensation from the German state. Yet he paid his rent regularly and must have had something left over with which to eat. He was fifty-six years old, so he could not have had an old-age pension, but he could well have had a disability pension. Probably did.

Miller pocketed his change, gunned the Jaguar to life, and drove to the Altona post office. He approached the window marked PENSIONS.

"Can you tell me when the pensioners collect their money?" he asked the fat lady behind the grille.

"Last day of the month, of course," she said.

"That will be Saturday, then?"

"Except on weekends. This month it will be Friday, the day after tomorrow."

"Does that include those with disability pensions?" he asked.

"Everyone who's entitled to a pension collects it on the last day of the month."

"Here, at this window?"

"If the person lives in Altona, yes," replied the woman.

"At what time?"

"From opening time onward."

"Thank you."

Miller was back on Friday morning, watching the queue of old men and women begin to filter through the doors of the post office when it opened. He positioned himself against the wall opposite, watching the directions they took as they departed. Many had white hair, but most wore hats against the cold. The weather had turned dry again, sunny but chill. Just before eleven an old man with a shock of white hair like candy floss came out of the post office, counted his money to make sure it was all there, put it in his inside pocket, and looked around as if searching for someone. After a few minutes he turned and began to walk slowly away. At the corner he looked up and down again, then turned down Museum Street in the direction of the riverbank. Miller eased himself off the wall and followed him.

It took the old man twenty minutes to get the half-mile to the Elbe Chaussee; then he turned up the bank, crossed the grass, and settled himself on a bench. Miller approached slowly from behind.

"Herr Marx?"

The old man turned as Miller came around the end of the bench. He showed no surprise, as though he were often recognized by complete strangers.

"Yes," he said gravely, "I am Marx."

"My name is Miller."

Marx inclined his head gravely in acceptance of this news.

"Are you—er—waiting for Herr Tauber?"

"Yes, I am," said the old man without surprise.

"May I sit down?"

"Please."

Miller sat beside him, so they both faced toward the Elbe River. A giant dry-cargo ship, the *Kota Maru* out of Yokohama, was easing downriver on the tide.

"I'm afraid Herr Tauber is dead."

The old man stared at the passing ship. He showed neither grief nor surprise, as if such news was brought frequently. Perhaps it was.

"I see," he said.

Miller told him briefly about the events of the previous Friday night. "You don't seem surprised. That he killed himself."

"No," said Marx, "he was a very unhappy man."

"He left a diary, you know."

"Yes, he told me once about that."

"Did you ever read it?" asked Miller.

"No, he never let anybody read it. But he told me about it."

"It described the time he spent in Riga during the war."

"Yes, he told me he was in Riga."

"Were you in Riga too?"

The man turned and looked at him with sad old eyes. "No, I was in Dachau."

"Look, Herr Marx, I need your help. In his diary your friend mentioned a man, an SS officer, called Roschmann. Captain Eduard Roschmann. Did he ever mention him to you?"

"Oh, yes. He told me about Roschmann. That was really what kept him alive. Hoping one day to give evidence against Roschmann."

"That's what he said in his diary. I read it after his death. I'm a press reporter. I want to try and find Roschmann. Bring him to trial. Do you understand?"

"Yes."

"But there's no point if Roschmann is already dead.

Can you remember if Herr Tauber ever learned whether Roschmann was still alive and free?"

Marx stared out at the disappearing stern of the *Kota Maru* for several minutes.

"Captain Roschmann is alive," he said simply, "and free."

Miller leaned forward earnestly. "How do you know?"

"Because Tauber saw him."

"Yes I read that. It was in early April nineteen forty-five."

Marx shook his head slowly. "No, it was last month."

For several more minutes there was silence as Miller stared at the old man and Marx stared out at the water.

"Last month?" repeated Miller at length. "Did he say how he saw him?"

Marx sighed, then turned to Miller. "Yes. He was walking late at night, as he often used to do when he could not sleep. He was walking back home past the State Opera House just as a crowd of people started to come out. He stopped as they came to the pavement. He said they were wealthy people, the men in dinner jackets, the women in furs and jewels. There were three taxis lined up at the curb waiting for them. The doorman held the passers-by back so they could climb in. And then he saw Roschmann."

"In the crowd of opera-goers?"

"Yes. He climbed into a taxi with two others, and they drove off."

"Now listen, Herr Marx, this is very important. Was he absolutely sure it was Roschmann?"

"Yes, he said he was."

"But it was almost nineteen years since he last saw him. He must have changed a lot. How could he be so sure?"

"He said he smiled."

"He what?"

"He smiled. Roschmann smiled."

"That is significant?"

Marx nodded several times. "He said once you had seen Roschmann smile that way, you never forgot it. He could not describe the smile but just said he would recognize it among a million others, anywhere in the world."

"I see. Do you believe him?"

"Yes. Yes, I believe he saw Roschmann."

"All right. Let's accept that I do too. Did he get the number of the taxi?"

"No. He said his mind was so stunned he just watched it drive away."

"Damn," said Miller. "It probably drove to a hotel. If I had the number I could ask the driver where he took that party. When did Herr Tauber tell you all this?"

"Last month, when we picked up our pensions. Here, on this bench."

Miller stood up and sighed. "You must realize that nobody would ever believe his story?"

Marx shifted his gaze off the river and looked up at the reporter. "Oh yes," he said softly. "He knew that. You see, that was why he killed himself."

That evening Peter Miller paid his usual weekend visit to his mother, and as usual she fussed over whether he was eating enough, the number of cigarettes he smoked in a day, and the state of his laundry. She was a short, plump, matronly person in her early fifties who had never quite resigned herself to the idea that all her only son wanted to be was a reporter.

During the course of the evening she asked him what he was doing at the moment. Briefly he told her, mentioning his intention to try to track down the missing Eduard Roschmann. She was aghast.

Peter ate away stolidly, letting the tide of reproach and recrimination flow over his head.

"It's bad enough that you always have to go around covering the doings of those nasty criminals and people," she was saying, "without going and getting mixed up with those Nazi people. I don't know what your dear father would have thought, I really don't."

A thought struck him. "Mother."

"Yes, dear?"

"During the war——those things that the SS did to people . . . in the camps. Did you ever suspect—did you ever think that it was going on?"

She busied herself furiously, tidying up the table. After a few seconds she spoke. "Horrible things. Terrible things. The British made us look at the films after the war. I don't want to hear any more about it."

She bustled out. Peter rose and followed her into the kitchen. "You remember in nineteen fifty when I was sixteen and I went to Paris with a school party?"

She paused, filling the sink for the dishwashing. "Yes, I remember."

"And we were taken to see a church called the Sacré Coeur. And there was a service just finishing, a memorial service for a man called Jean Moulin. Some people came out, and they heard me speaking German to another boy. One of the group turned and spat at me. I remember the spittle running down my jacket. I remember I came home later and told you about it. Do you remember what you said?"

Mrs. Miller was furiously scouring a dinner plate.

"You said the French were like that. Dirty habits, you said."

"Well, they have. I never did like them."

"Look, Mother, do you know what we did to Jean Moulin before he died? Not you, not Father, not me. But us, the Germans, or rather the Gestapo, which for millions of foreigners seems to be the same thing."

"I don't want to hear. Now, that's enough of that."

"Well, I can't tell you, because I don't know. Doubtless it's recorded somewhere. But the point is, I was spat on not because I was in the Gestapo, but because I'm a German."

"And you should be proud of it."

"Oh, I am, believe me, I am. But that doesn't mean

I've got to be proud of the Nazis and the SS and the Gestapo."

"Well, nobody is, but there's no point in keeping talking about it."

She was flustered, as always when he argued with her, drying her hands on the dishtowel before bustling back into the living room. He trailed after her.

"Look, Mother, try to understand. Until I read that diary I never even asked precisely what it was we were all supposed to have done. Now at least I'm beginning to understand. That's why I want to find this man, this monster, if he's still around. It's right that he should be brought to trial."

She sat on the settee, close to tears. "Please, Peterkin, leave them alone. Just don't keep probing into the past. It won't do any good. It's over now, over and done with. It's best forgotten."

Peter Miller was facing the mantelpiece, which was dominated by the clock and the photograph of his dead father, who was wearing his Army captain's uniform, staring out of the frame with the kind, rather sad smile that Miller remembered. It was taken before he returned to the front after his last leave.

Peter remembered his father with startling clarity, looking at his photograph nineteen years later as his mother asked him to drop the Roschmann inquiry. He could remember before the war, when he was five years old, and his father had taken him to Hagenbeck's zoo and pointed out all the animals to him, one by one, patiently reading the details off the little tin plaques in front of each cage to reply to the endless flow of questions from the boy.

He could remember how his father came home after enlisting in 1940, and how his mother had cried and how he had thought how stupid women are to cry over such a wonderful thing as having a father in uniform. He recalled the day in 1944 when he was ten years old, and an Army officer had come to the door to tell his mother that her war-hero husband had been killed on the Eastern Front.

"Besides, nobody wants these awful exposés any more. Nor these terrible trials that we keep having, with everything dragged out into the open again. Nobody's going to thank you for it, even if you do find him. They'll just point to you in the street; I mean, they don't want any more trials. Not now, it's too late. Just drop it, Peter, please, for my sake."

He remembered the black-edged column of names in the newspaper, the same length as every day, but different that day in late October, for halfway down was the entry: "Fallen for Führer and Fatherland. Miller, Erwin, Captain, on October 11. In Ostland."

And that was it. Nothing else. No hint of where, or when, or why. Just one of tens of thousands of names pouring back from the east to fill the ever-lengthening black-edged columns, until the government had ceased to print them because they destroyed morale.

"I mean," said his mother behind him, "you might at least think of your father's memory. You think he'd want his son digging around into the past, trying to drag up another war-crimes trial? Do you think that's what he'd want?"

Miller spun around and walked across the room to his mother, placed both hands on her shoulders, and looked down into her frightened china-blue eyes. He stooped and kissed her lightly on the forehead.

"Yes, Mutti," he said. "I think that's exactly what he'd want."

He let himself out, climbed into his car, and headed back into Hamburg, his anger seething inside him.

Everyone who knew him and many who did not agreed Hans Hoffmann looked the part. He was in his late forties, boyishly handsome with carefully styled graying hair cut in the latest trendy fashion, and manicured fingers. His medium-gray suit was from Savile Row, his heavy silk tie was from Cardin. There was an air of expensive good taste of the kind money can buy about him.

If looks had been his only asset he would not have been one of West Germany's wealthiest and most successful magazine-publishers. Starting after the war with a hand-operated press, turning out handbills for the British Occupation authorities, he had founded in 1949 one of the first weekly picture magazines. His formula was simple—tell it in words and make it shocking, then back it up with pictures that make all competitors look like novices with their first box brownies. It worked. His chain of eight magazines ranging from love stories for teenagers to the glossy chronicle of the doings of the rich and sexy had made him a multimillionaire. But *Komet,* the news and current-affairs magazine, was still his favorite, his baby.

The money had brought him a luxurious ranch-style house at Othmarschen, a chalet in the mountains, a villa by the sea, a Rolls-Royce, and a Ferrari. Along the way he had picked up a beautiful wife, whom he dressed from Paris, and two handsome children he seldom saw. The only millionaire in Germany whose succession of young mistresses, discreetly maintained and frequently exchanged, were never photographed in his gossip magazine was Hans Hoffmann. He was also very astute.

That Wednesday afternoon he closed the cover of the diary of Salomon Tauber after reading the beginning, leaned back, and looked at the young reporter opposite.

"All right. I can guess the rest. What do you want?"

"I think that's a great document," said Miller. "There's a man mentioned throughout the diary called Eduard Roschmann. Captain in the SS. Commandant of Riga ghetto throughout. Killed eighty thousand men, women, and children. I believe he's alive and here in West Germany. I want to find him."

"How do you know he's alive?"

Miller told him briefly.

Hoffmann pursed his lips. "Pretty thin evidence."

"True. But worth a second look. I've brought home stories that started on less."

Hoffmann grinned, recalling Miller's talent for ferreting out stories that hurt the Establishment. Hoffmann had been happy to print them, once they were checked out as accurate. They sent circulation soaring.

"Then presumably this man—what do you call him, Roschmann? Presumably he's already on the wanted list. If the police can't find him, what makes you think you can?"

"Are the police really looking?" asked Miller.

Hoffmann shrugged. "They're supposed to. That's what we pay them for."

"It wouldn't hurt to help a little, would it? Just check out whether he's really alive, whether he was ever picked up; if so, what happened to him?"

"So what do you want from me?" asked Hoffmann.

"A commission to give it a try. If nothing comes of it, I drop it."

Hoffmann swung in his chair, spinning around to face the picture windows looking out over the sprawling docks, mile after mile of cranes and wharfs spread out twenty floors below and a mile away.

"It's a bit out of your line, Miller. Why the sudden interest?"

Miller thought hard. Trying to sell an idea was always the hardest part. A freelance reporter has to sell the story, or the idea of the story, to the publisher or the editor first. The public comes much later.

"It's a good human-interest story. If *Komet* could find the man where the police forces of the country had failed, it would be a scoop. Something people want to know about."

Hoffmann gazed out at the December skyline and slowly shook his head. "You're wrong. That's why I'm not giving you a commission for it. I should think it's the last thing people want to know about."

"But look, Herr Hoffmann, this is different. These people Roschmann killed—they weren't Poles and Russians. These were Germans—all right, German Jews, but they *were* Germans. Why wouldn't people want to know about it?"

Hoffmann spun back from the window, put his elbows on the desk, and rested his chin on his knuckles. "Miller, you're a good reporter. I like the way you cover a story; you've got style. And you're a ferret. I can hire twenty, fifty, a hundred men in this city by picking up the phone, and they'll all do what they're told, cover the stories they're sent to cover. But they can't dig out a story for themselves. You can. That's why you get a lot of work from me and will get a lot more in the future. But not this one."

"But why? It's a good story."

"Listen, you're young. I'll tell you something about journalism. Half of journalism is about writing good stories. The other half is about selling them. You can do the first bit, but I can do the second. That's why I'm here and you're there. You think this is a story everyone will want to read because the victims of Riga were German Jews. I'm telling you that's exactly why *no one* will want to read the story. It's the last story in the world they'll want to read. And until there's a law in this country forcing people to buy magazines and read what's good for them, they'll go on buying magazines to read what they want to read. And that's what I give them. What they want to read."

"Then why not about Roschmann?"

"You still don't get it? Then I'll tell you. Before the war just about everyone in Germany knew at least one Jew. The fact is, before Hitler started, nobody hated the Jews in Germany. We had the best record of treatment of our Jewish minority of any country in Europe. Better than France, better than Spain, infinitely better than Poland and Russia, where the pogroms were fiendish.

"Then Hitler started. Telling people the Jews were to blame for the First War, the unemployment, the poverty, and everything else that was wrong. People didn't know what to believe. Almost everyone knew one Jew who was a nice guy. Or just harmless. People had Jewish friends, good friends; Jewish employers, good employers;

Jewish employees, hard workers. They obeyed the laws; they didn't hurt anyone. And here was Hitler saying they were to blame for everything.

"So when the vans came and took them away, people didn't do anything. They stayed out of the way, they kept quiet. They even got to believing the voice that shouted the loudest. Because that's the way people are, particularly the Germans. We're a very obedient people. It's our greatest strength and our greatest weakness. It enables us to build an economic miracle while the British are on strike, and it enables us to follow a man like Hitler into a great big mass grave.

"For years people haven't asked what happened to the Jews of Germany. They just disappeared—nothing else. It's bad enough to read at every war-crimes trial what happened to the faceless, anonymous Jews of Warsaw, Lublin, Bialystok—nameless, unknown Jews from Poland and Russia. Now you want to tell them, chapter and verse, what happened to their next-door neighbors. Now can you understand it? These Jews"—he tapped the diary—"these people they knew, they greeted them in the street, they bought in their shops, and they stood around while they were taken away for your Herr Roschmann to deal with. You think they want to read about that? You couldn't have picked a story that people in Germany want to read about less."

Having finished, Hans Hoffmann leaned back, selected a fine panatela from a humidor on the desk, and lit it from a rolled-gold Dupont. Miller sat and digested what he had not been able to work out for himself.

"That must have been what my mother meant," he said at length.

Hoffmann grunted. "Probably."

"I still want to find that bastard."

"Leave it alone, Miller. Drop it. No one will thank you."

"That's not the only reason, is it? The public reaction. There's another reason, isn't there?"

Hoffmann eyed him keenly through the cigar smoke. "Yes," he said shortly.

"Are you afraid of them—still?" asked Miller.

Hoffmann shook his head. "No. I just don't go look-ing for trouble, that's all."

"What kind of trouble?"

"Have you ever heard of a man called Hans Habe?" asked Hoffmann.

"The novelist? Yes, what about him?"

"He used to run a magazine in Munich once. Back in the early fifties. A good one too—he was a damn good reporter, like you. *Echo of the Week,* it was called. He hated the Nazis, so he ran a series of exposés of former SS men living in freedom in Munich."

"What happened to him?"

"To him, nothing. One day he got more mail than usual. Half the letters were from his advertisers, with-drawing their custom. Another was from his bank, asking him to drop around. When he did, he was told the bank was foreclosing on the overdraft, as of that minute. Within a week the magazine was out of business. Now he writes novels, good ones too. But he doesn't run a magazine any more."

"So what do the rest of us do? Keep running scared?"

Hoffmann jerked his cigar out of his mouth. "I don't have to take that from you, Miller," he said, his eyes snapping. "I hated the bastards then and I hate them now. But I know my readers. And they don't want to know about Eduard Roschmann."

"All right. I'm sorry. But I'm still going to cover it."

"You know, Miller, if I didn't know you, I'd think there was something personal behind it. Never let jour-nalism get personal. It's bad for reporting, and it's bad for the reporter. Anyway, how are you going to finance yourself?"

"I've got some savings," Miller rose to go.

"Best of luck," said Hoffmann, rising and coming around the desk. "I tell you what I'll do. The day Roschmann is arrested and imprisoned by the West German police, I'll commission you to cover the story. That's straight news, so it's public property. If I decide not to print, I'll buy it out of my pocket. That's as far as I'll go. But while you're digging for him, you're not carrying the letterhead of my magazine around as your authority."

Miller nodded. "I'll be back," he said.

5

WEDNESDAY MORNING was also the time of the week when the heads of the five branches of the Israeli Intelligence apparat met for their informal weekly discussion.

In most countries the rivalry between the various separate Intelligence services is legendary. In Russia the KGB hates the guts of the GRU; in America the FBI will not cooperate with the CIA. The British Security Service regards Scotland Yard's Special Branch as a crowd of flat-footed coppers, and there are so many crooks in the French SDECE that experts wonder whether the French Intelligence service is part of the government or the underworld.

But Israel is fortunate. Once a week the chiefs of the five branches meet for a friendly chat without inter-departmental friction. It is one of the dividends of being a nation surrounded by enemies. At these meetings coffee and soft drinks are passed around, those present use first names to each other, the atmosphere is relaxed, and more work gets done than could be effected by a torrent of written memoranda.

It was to this meeting that the Controller of the Mossad and chief of the joint five branches of Israeli Intelligence, General Meir Amit, was traveling on the morning of December 4. Beyond the windows of his long black chauffeur-driven limousine a fine dawn was beaming down on the whitewashed sprawl of Tel Aviv. But the general's mood failed to match it. He was a deeply worried man.

The cause of his worry was a piece of information that had reached him in the small hours of the morning. A small fragment of knowledge to be added to the immense file in the archives, but vital, for the file into

which that dispatch from one of his agents in Cairo
would be added was the file on the rockets of Helwan.

The forty-two-year-old general's poker face betrayed
nothing of his feelings as the car swung around the Zina
Circus and headed toward the northern suburbs of the
capital. He leaned back on the upholstery of his seat
and considered the long history of those rockets being
built north of Cairo, which had already cost several men
their lives and had cost his predecessor, General Issar
Harel, his job. . . .

During the course of 1961, long before Nasser's two
rockets went on public display in the streets of Cairo,
the Israeli Mossad had learned of their existence. From
the moment the first dispatch came through from Egypt,
it had kept Factory 333 under constant surveillance.

It was perfectly well aware of the large-scale recruitment by the Egyptians, through the good offices of the
Odessa, of German scientists to work on the rockets of
Helwan. It was a serious matter then; it became infinitely
more serious in the spring of 1962.

In May that year Heinz Krug, the German recruiter
of the scientists, first made approaches to the Austrian
physicist Dr. Otto Yoklek in Vienna. Instead of allow-
ing himself to be recruited, the Austrian professor made
contact with the Israelis. What he had to say electrified
Tel Aviv. He told the agent of the Mossad who was
sent to interview him that the Egyptians intended to arm
their rockets with warheads containing irradiated nuclear
waste and cultures of bubonic plague.

So important was the news that the Controller of the
Mossad, General Issar Harel, the man who had personally escorted the kidnaped Adolf Eichmann back
from Buenos Aires to Tel Aviv, flew to Vienna to talk
to Yoklek himself. He was convinced the professor was
right, a conviction corroborated by the news that the
Cairo government had just purchased through a firm in
Zurich a quantity of radioactive cobalt equivalent to
twenty-five times Egypt's possible requirement for
medical purposes.

On his return from Vienna, Issar Harel went to see Premier David Ben-Gurion and urged that he be allowed to begin a campaign of reprisals against the German scientists who were either working in Egypt or about to go there. The old Premier was in a quandary. On the one hand he realized the hideous danger the new rockets and their genocidal warheads presented to his people; on the other, he recognized the value of the German tanks and guns due to arrive at any moment. Israeli reprisals on the streets of Germany might just be enough to persuade Chancellor Adenauer to listen to his Foreign Ministry faction and shut off the arms deal.

Inside the Tel Aviv cabinet there was a split developing similar to the split inside the Bonn cabinet over the arms sales. Issar Harel and the Foreign Minister, Madame Golda Meir, were in favor of a tough policy against the German scientists; Shimon Peres and the Army were terrified by the thought they might lose their precious German tanks. Ben-Gurion was torn between the two.

He hit on a compromise; he authorized Harel to undertake a muted, discreet campaign to discourage German scientists from going to Cairo to help Nasser build his rockets. But Harel, with his burning gut-hatred of Germany and all things German, went beyond his brief.

On September 11, 1962, Heinz Krug disappeared. He had dined the previous evening with Dr. Kleinwachter, the rocket-propulsion expert he was trying to recruit, and an unidentified Egyptian. On the morning of the eleventh, Krug's car was found abandoned close to his home in a suburb of Munich. His wife immediately claimed he had been kidnaped by Israeli agents, but the Munich police found not a trace of Krug or of evidence as to his kidnapers. In fact, he had been abducted by a group of men led by a shadowy figure called Leon, and his body dumped in the Starnberg lake, assisted to the weedbed by a corset of heavy-link chain.

The campaign then turned against the Germans in Egypt already. On November 27 a registered package, mailed in Hamburg and addressed to Professor Wolf-gang Pilz, the rocket scientist who had worked for the French, arrived in Cairo. It was opened by his secretary, Miss Hannelore Wenda. In the ensuing explosion the girl was maimed and blinded for life.

On November 28 another package, also mailed in Hamburg, arrived at Factory 333. By this time the Egyptians had set up a security screen for arriving parcels. It was an Egyptian official in the mail room who cut the cord. Five dead and ten wounded. On November 29 a third package was defused without an explosion.

By February 20, 1963, Harel's agents had turned their attention once again to Germany. Dr. Heinz Kleinwachter, still undecided whether to go to Cairo or not, was driving back home from his laboratory at Lörrach, near the Swiss frontier, when a black Mercedes barred his route. He threw himself to the floor as a man emptied his automatic through the windshield. Police subsequently discovered the black Mercedes abandoned. It had been stolen earlier in the day. In the glove compartment was an identity card in the name of Colonel Ali Samir. Inquiries revealed this was the name of the chief of the Egyptian Secret Service. Issar Harel's agents had got their message across, with a touch of black humor for good measure.

By now the reprisal campaign was making headlines in Germany. It became a scandal with the Ben-Gal affair. On March 2, young Heidi Görke, daughter of Professor Paul Görke, pioneer of Nasser's rockets, received a telephone call at her home in Freiburg, Germany. A voice suggested she meet the caller at the Three Kings Hotel in Basel, Switzerland, just over the border.

Heidi informed the German police, who tipped off the Swiss. They planted a bugging device in the room that had been reserved for the meeting. During the meeting, two men in dark glasses warned Heidi Görke and her young brother to persuade their father to get out of Egypt if he valued his life. Tailed to Zurich and arrested the same night, the two men went on trial at Basel on June 10, 1963. It was an international scandal.

The chief of the two agents was Yosef Ben-Gal, Israeli citizen.

The trial went well. Professor Yoklek testified as to the warheads of plague and radioactive waste, and the judges were scandalized. Making the best of a bad job, the Israeli government used the trial to expose the Egyptian intent to commit genocide. Shocked, the judges acquitted the two accused.

But back in Israel there was a reckoning. Although the German Chancellor Adenauer had personally promised Ben-Gurion he would try to stop German scientists from taking part in the Helwan rocket-building, Ben-Gurion was humiliated by the scandal. In a rage, he rebuked General Issar Harel for the lengths to which he had gone in his campaign of intimidation. Harel responded with vigor and handed in his resignation. To his surprise, Ben-Gurion accepted it, proving the point that no one in Israel is indispensable, not even the Chief of Intelligence.

That night, June 20, 1963, Issar Harel had a long talk with his close friend, General Meir Amit, then the head of Military Intelligence. General Amit could remember the conversation clearly, the taut, angry face of the Russian-born fighter, nicknamed Issar the Terrible.

"I have to inform you, my dear Meir, that as from now Israel is no longer in the retribution business. The politicians have taken over. I have tendered my resignation, and it has been accepted. I have asked that you be named my successor, and I believe they will agree."

The ministerial committee that in Israel presides over the activities of the Intelligence networks agreed. At the end of June, General Meir Amit became Chief of Intelligence.

The knell had also sounded, however, for Ben-Gurion. The hawks of his cabinet, headed by Levi Eshkol and his own Foreign Minister, Golda Meir, forced his resignation, and on June 26, 1963, Levi Eshkol was named Prime Minister. Ben-Gurion, shaking his snowy head in anger, went down to his kibbutz in the Negev in disgust. But he remained a member of the Knesset.

Although the new government had ousted David Ben-Gurion, it did not reinstate Isaar Harel. Perhaps it felt that Meir Amit was a general more likely to obey orders than the choleric Harel, who had become a legend in his own lifetime among the Israeli people and relished it.

Nor were Ben-Gurion's last orders rescinded. General Amit's instructions remained the same—to avoid any more scandals in Germany over the rocket scientists. With no alternative, he turned the terror campaign against the scientists already inside Egypt.

These Germans lived in the suburb of Meadi, seven miles south of Cairo on the bank of the Nile—a pleasant suburb, except that it was ringed by Egyptian security troops and its German inhabitants were almost prisoners in a gilded cage. To get at them, Meir Amit used his top agent inside Egypt, the riding-school-owner Wolfgang Lutz, who found himself from September 1963 onward forced to take suicidal risks, which sixteen months later would lead to his undoing.

For the German scientists, already shaken badly by the series of bomb parcels sent from Germany, the autumn of 1963 became a nightmare. In the heart of Meadi, ringed by Egyptian security guards, they began to get letters threatening their lives, mailed from Cairo.

Dr. Josef Eisig received one which described his wife, his two children, and the type of work he was engaged in with remarkable precision, then told him to get out of Egypt and go back to Germany. All the other scientists got the same kind of letter. On September 27 a letter blew up in the face of Dr. Kirmayer. For some of the scientists this was the last straw. At the end of September, Dr. Pilz left Cairo for Germany, taking the unfortunate Fräulein Wenda with him.

Others followed, and the furious Egyptians were unable to stop them, for they could not protect them from the threatening letters.

The man in the back of the limousine that bright

winter morning in 1963 knew that his own agent, the supposedly pro-Nazi German Lutz, was the writer of the letters and the sender of the explosives.

But he also knew the rocket program was not being halted. The information he had just received proved it. He flicked his eye over the decoded message once again. It confirmed simply that a virulent strain of bubonic bacillus had been isolated in the contagious-diseases laboratory of Cairo Medical Institute, and that the budget of the department involved had been increased tenfold. The information left no doubt that, despite the adverse publicity Egypt had received over the Ben-Gal trial in Basel the previous summer, the government was going ahead with the genocide program.

Had Hoffmann been watching, he would have been forced to give Miller full marks for cheek. After leaving the penthouse office, he took the elevator down to the fifth floor and dropped in to see Max Dorn, the magazine's legal-affairs correspondent.

"I've just been up to see Herr Hoffmann," he said, dropping into a chair in front of Dorn's desk. "Now I need some background. Mind if I pick your brains?"

"Go ahead," said Dorn, assuming Miller had been commissioned to do a story for *Komet*.

"Who investigates war crimes in Germany?"

The question took Dorn aback. "War crimes?"

"Yes. War crimes. Which authorities are responsible for investigating what happened in all the various countries we overran during the war, and finding and prosecuting the individuals guilty of mass murder?"

"Oh, I see what you mean. Well, basically it's the various attorney generals' offices of the provinces of West Germany."

"You mean they *all* do it?"

Dorn leaned back in his chair, at home in his own field of expertise. "There are sixteen provinces in West Germany. Each has a state capital and a state attorney general. Inside each SAG's office there is a department responsible for investigation into what are called 'crimes of violence committed during the Nazi era.' Each state capital is allocated an area of the former Reich or of the occupied territories as its special responsibility."

"Such as?" asked Miller.

"Well, for example, all crimes committed by the Nazis and the SS in Italy, Greece, and Polish Galicia are investigated by Stuttgart. The biggest extermination camp of all, Auschwitz, comes under Frankfurt. You may have heard there's a big trial coming up in Frankfurt next May of twenty-two former guards from Auschwitz. Then the extermination camps of Treblinka, Chelmno, Sobibor, and Maidanek are investigated by Düsseldorf-Cologne. Munich is responsible for Belzec, Dachau, Buchenwald, and Flossenburg. Most crimes in the Soviet Ukraine and the Lódz area of former Poland come under Hanover. And so on."

Miller noted the information, nodding. "Who is supposed to investigate what happened in the three Baltic States?" he asked.

"Hamburg," said Dorn promptly, "along with crimes in the areas of Danzig and the Warsaw sector of Poland."

"Hamburg?" said Miller. "You mean it's right here in Hamburg?"

"Yes. Why?"

"Well, it's Riga I'm interested in."

Dorn grimaced. "Oh, I see. The German Jews. Well, that's the pigeon of the SAG's office right here."

"If there had ever been a trial, or even an arrest, of anyone who had been guilty of crimes in Riga, it would have been here in Hamburg?"

"The trial would have been," said Dorn. "The arrest could have been made anywhere."

"What's the procedure with arrests?"

"Well, there's a book called the Wanted Book. In it is the name of every wanted war criminal, with surname, first names, and date of birth. Usually the SAG's office covering the area where the man committed the crimes spends years preparing the case against him before arrest. Then, when it's ready, it requests the police of the state in which the man is living to arrest him. A couple of detectives go there and bring him back. If a very much wanted man is discovered, he can be arrested wherever he's discovered, and the appropriate SAG's office informed that he's being held. Then they go and bring him back. The trouble is, most of the big SS men are not living under their own names."

"Right," said Miller. "Has there ever been a trial in Hamburg of anyone guilty of crimes committed in Riga?"

"Not that I remember," said Dorn.

"Would it be in the clippings library?"

"Sure. If it happened since 1950, when we started the clippings library, it'll be there."

"Mind if we look?" asked Miller.

"No problem."

The library was in the basement, tended by five archivists in gray smocks. It was almost half an acre in size, filled by row upon row of gray steel shelves on which reposed reference books of every kind and description. Around the walls, from floor to ceiling, were steel filing cabinets, the doors of each drawer indicating the contents of the files within.

"What do you want?" asked Dorn as the chief librarian approached.

"Roschmann, Eduard," said Miller.

"Personal index section, this way," said the librarian and led the way along onc wall. He opened a cabinet door labeled ROA-ROZ, and flicked through it.

"Nothing on Roschmann, Eduard," he said.

Miller thought. "Do you have anything on war crimes?" he asked.

"Yes," said the librarian. "War crimes and war trials section, this way."

They went along another hundred yards of cabinets.

"Look under Riga," said Miller.

The librarian mounted a stepladder and foraged. He came back with a red folder. It bore the label RIGA— WAR CRIMES TRIAL. Miller opened it. Two pieces of newsprint the size of large postage stamps fluttered out. Miller picked them up. Both were from the summer of

1950. One recorded that three SS privates had gone on trial for brutalities committed at Riga between 1941 and 1944. The other recorded that they had all three been sentenced to long terms of imprisonment. Not long enough: they would all be free by late 1963.

"Is that it?" asked Miller.

"That's it," said the librarian.

"Do you mean to say," said Miller, turning to Dorn, "that a section of the State Attorney General's office has been beavering away for fifteen years on my tax money, and all it's got to show for it is two postage stamps?"

Dorn was a rather Establishment figure. "I'm sure they're doing their best," he said huffily.

"I wonder," said Miller.

They parted in the main hall two floors up, and Miller went out into the rain.

The building in the northern suburbs of Tel Aviv that houses the headquarters of the Mossad excites no attention, even from its nearest neighbors. The entrance to the underground garage of the office building is flanked by quite ordinary shops. On the ground floor is a bank, and in the entrance hall, before the plate-glass doors that lead into the bank, are an elevator, a board stating the business of the firms on the floors above, and a porter's desk for inquiries.

The board reveals that in the building are the offices of several trading companies, two insurance firms, an architect, an engineering consultant, and an import-export company on the top floor. Inquiries for any of the firms below the top floor will be met courteously. Questions asked about the top-floor company are politely refused an answer. The company on the top floor is the front for the Mossad.

The room where the chiefs of Israeli Intelligence meet is bare and cool, white-painted, with a long table and chairs around the walls. At the table sit the five men who control the branches of Intelligence. Behind them on the chairs sit clerks and stenographers. Other nonmembers can be invited for a hearing if required, but this is seldom done. The meetings are classified top secret, for all confidences may be aired.

At the head of the table sits the Controller of the Mossad. Founded in 1937, its full name Mossad Aliyah Beth, or Organization for the Second Immigration, the Mossad was the first Israeli Intelligence organ. Its first job was to get Jews from Europe to a safe berth in Palestine.

After the founding of the state of Israel in 1948, it became the senior of all Intelligence organs, its controller automatically the head of all the five.

To the Controller's right sits the Chief of the Aman, the Military Intelligence unit whose job is to keep Israel informed of the state of war-readiness of her enemies. The man who held the job at that time was General Aharon Yaariv.

To the left sits the Chief of the Shabak, sometimes wrongly referred to as the Shin Beth. These letters stand for Sherut Bitachon, the Hebrew for "Security Service." The full title of the organ that watches over Israel's internal security, and *only* internal security, is Sherut Bitachon Klali, and it is from these three words that the abbreviation Shabak is taken.

Beyond these two men sit the last two of the five. One is the Director General of the research division of the Foreign Ministry, charged specifically with the evaluation of the political situation in Arab capitals, a matter of vital importance to the security of Israel. The other is the director of a service solely occupied with the fate of Jews in the "countries of persecution." These countries include all the Arab countries and all the Communist countries. So that there shall be no overlapping of activities, the weekly meetings enable each chief to know what the other departments are doing.

Two other men are present as observers, the Inspector General of police, and the head of the Special Branch, the executive arms of the Shabak in the fight against terrorism inside the country.

The meeting on that day was quite normal. Meir Amit took his place at the head of the table, and the discussion began. He saved his bombshell until last. When he had made his statement, there was silence as the men present, including the aides scattered around the walls, had a mental vision of their country dying as the radioactive and plague warheads slammed home.

"The point surely is," said the head of the Shabak at last, "that those rockets must never fly. If we cannot prevent them from making warheads, we have to prevent the warheads from ever taking off."

"Agreed," said Amit, taciturn as ever, "but how?"

"Hit them," growled Yaariv. "Hit them with everything we've got. Ezer Weizmann's jets can take out Factory 333 in one raid."

"And start a war with nothing to fight with," replied Amit. "We need more planes, more tanks, more guns before we can take Egypt. I think we all know, gentlemen, that war is inevitable. Nasser is determined on it, but he will not fight until he is ready. But if we force it on him now, the simple answer is that he, with his Russian weaponry, is more ready than we are."

There was silence again. The head of the Foreign Ministry Arab section spoke.

"Our information from Cairo is that they think they will be ready in early nineteen sixty-seven, rockets and all."

"We will have our tanks and guns by then, and our new French jets," replied Yaariv.

"Yes, and they will have those rockets from Helwan. Four hundred of them. Gentlemen, there is only one answer. By the time we are ready for Nasser, those rockets will be in silos all over Egypt. They'll be unreachable. For, once they are in their silos and ready to fire, we must not simply take out ninety per cent of them but all of them. And not even Ezer Weizmann's fighter pilots can take them all, without exception."

"Then we have to take them in the factory at Helwan," said Yaariv with finality.

"Agreed," said Amit, "but without a military attack. We shall just have to try to force the German scientists to resign before they have finished their work. Remember, the research stage is almost at an end. We have six months. After that the Germans won't matter any more. The Egyptians can build the rockets, once they are designed down to the last nut and bolt. Therefore I shall step up the campaign against the scientists in Egypt and keep you informed."

For several seconds there was silence again as the unspoken question ran through the minds of all those present. It was one of the men from the Foreign Ministry who finally voiced it.

"Couldn't we discourage them inside Germany again?"

General Amit shook his head. "No. That remains out of the question in the prevailing political climate. The orders from our superiors remain the same: no more muscle tactics inside Germany. For us from henceforth the key to the rockets of Helwan lies inside Egypt."

General Meir Amit, Controller of the Mossad, was not often wrong. But he was wrong that time. For the key to the rockets of Helwan lay in a factory inside West Germany.

6

IT TOOK MILLER a week before he could get an interview with the chief of section in the department of the Hamburg Attorney General's office responsible for investigation into war crimes. He suspected Dorn had found out he was not working at Hoffmann's behest and had reacted accordingly.

The man he confronted was nervous, ill at ease. "You must understand I have only agreed to see you as a result of your persistent inquiries," he began.

"That's nice of you all the same," said Miller ingratiatingly. "I want to inquire about a man whom I assume your department must have under permanent investigation, called Eduard Roschmann."

"Roschmann?" said the lawyer.

"Roschmann," repeated Miller. "Captain of the SS. Commandant of Riga ghetto from nineteen forty-one to nineteen forty-four. I want to know if he's alive; if not, where he's buried. If you have found him, if he has ever been arrested, and if he has ever been on trial. If not, where he is now."

The lawyer was shaken. "Good Lord, I can't tell you that," he said.

"Why not? It's a matter of public interest. Enormous public interest."

The lawyer had recovered his poise. "I hardly think so," he said smoothly. "Otherwise we would be receiving constant inquiries of this nature. Actually, so far as I can recall, yours is the first inquiry we've ever had from . . . a member of the public."

"Actually, I'm a member of the press," said Miller.

"Yes, that may be. But I'm afraid as regards this kind of information that only means you are entitled to as much as one would give a member of the public."

"How much is that?" asked Miller.

"I'm afraid we are not empowered to give information regarding the progress of our inquiries."

"Well, that's not right, to start with," said Miller.

"Oh, come now, Herr Miller, you would hardly expect the police to give you information about the progress of *their* inquiries in a criminal case."

"I would. In fact, that's just what I do. The police are customarily very helpful in issuing bulletins on whether an early arrest may be expected. Certainly they'd tell a journalist if their main suspect was, to their knowledge, alive or dead. It helps their relations with the public."

The lawyer smiled thinly. "I'm sure you perform a very valuable function in that regard," he said. "But from this department no information may be issued on the state of progress of our work." He seemed to hit on a point of argument. "Let's face it: if wanted criminals knew how close we were to completing the case against them, they'd disappear."

"That may be so," answered Miller. "But the records show your department has only put on trial three privates who were guards in Riga. And that was in nineteen fifty, so the men were probably in pretrial detention when the British handed them over to your department. So the wanted criminals don't seem to be in much danger of being forced to disappear."

"Really, that's a most unwarranted suggestion."

"All right. So your inquiries are progressing. It still wouldn't harm your case if you were to tell me quite simply whether Eduard Roschmann is under investigation, and where he now is."

"All I can say is that all matters concerning the area of responsibility of my department are under constant inquiry. I repeat, constant inquiry. And now I really think, Herr Miller, there is nothing more I can do to help you."

He rose, and Miller followed suit. "Don't bust a gut," he said as he walked out.

It was another week before Miller was ready to move.

He spent it mainly at home, reading six books concerned in whole or in part with the war along the Eastern Front and the things that had been done in the camps in the occupied eastern territories. It was the librarian at his local library who mentioned the Z Commission.

"It's in Ludwigsburg," he told Miller. "I read about it in a magazine. Its full name is the Central Federal Agency for the Elucidation of Crimes of Violence Committed during the Nazi Era. That's a bit of a mouthful, so people call it the Zentrale Stelle for short. Even shorter, the Z Commission. It's the only organization in the country that hunts Nazis on a nationwide, even an international level."

"Thanks," said Miller as he left. "I'll see if they can help me."

Miller went to his bank the next morning, made out a check to his landlord for three months' rent to cover January through March, and drew the rest of his bank balance in cash, leaving a 10-mark note to keep the account open.

He kissed Sigi before she went off to work at the club, telling her he would be gone for a week, maybe more. Then he took the Jaguar from its underground home and headed south toward the Rhineland.

The first snows had started, whistling in off the North Sea, slicing in flurries across the wide stretches of the autobahn as it swept south of Bremen and into the flat plain of Lower Saxony.

He paused once for coffee after two hours, then pressed on across North Rhine–Westphalia. Despite the wind and the descending darkness, he enjoyed driving down the autobahn in bad weather. Inside the XK 150 S he had the impression of being in the cockpit of a fast plane, the dashboard lights glowing dully under the facia, and outside the descending darkness of a winter's night, the icy cold, the slanting flurries of snow caught for a moment in the harsh beam of the headlights, whipping past the windshield and back into nothingness again.

He stuck to the fast lane as always, pushing the Jag

to close to 100 miles an hour, watching the growling hulks of the heavy trucks swish past to his right as he passed them.

By six in the evening he was beyond the Hamm Junction, and the glowing lights of the Ruhr began to be dimly discernible to his right through the darkness. He never ceased to be amazed by the Ruhr, mile after mile after mile of factories and chimneys, towns and cities so close as to be in effect one gigantic city a hundred miles long and fifty broad. When the autobahn went into an overpass he could look down to the right and see it stretching away into the December night, thousands of hectares of lights and mills, aglow from a thousand furnaces churning out the wealth of the economic miracle. Fourteen years ago, as he traveled through it by train toward his school holiday in Paris, it had been rubble, and the industrial heart of Germany was hardly even beating. Impossible not to feel proud of what his people had done since then.

Just so long as I don't have to live in it, he thought as the giant signs of the Cologne Ring began to come up in the light of the headlights. From Cologne he ran southeast, past Wiesbaden and Frankfurt, Mannheim and Heilbronn, and it was late that evening when he cruised to a halt in front of a hotel in Stuttgart, the nearest city to Ludwigsburg, where he spent the night.

Ludwigsburg is a quiet and inoffensive little market town set in the rolling pleasant hills of Württemberg, fifteen miles north of the state capital of Stuttgart. Set in a quiet road off the High Street, to the extreme embarrassment of the town's upright inhabitants, is the home of the Z Commission, a small understaffed, underpaid, overworked group of men whose job and dedication in life is to hunt down the Nazis and the SS guilty during the war of the crimes of mass murder. Before the Statute of Limitations eliminated all SS crimes with the exception of murder and mass murder, those being sought might have been guilty only of extortion, robbery, grievous bodily harm including torture, and a variety of other forms of unpleasantness.

Even with murder as the only remaining charge able
to be brought, the Z Commission still had 170,000
names in its files. Not unnaturally, the main effort had
been and still is to track down the worst few thousand
of the mass-murderers, if and where possible.

Deprived of any powers of arrest, able only to request
the police of the various states of Germany to make an
arrest when positive identification has already been
made, unable to squeeze more than a pittance each year
out of the federal government in Bonn, the men of
Ludwigsburg worked solely because they were dedicated
to the task.

There were eighty detectives on the staff, and fifty
investigating attorneys. Of the former group, all were
young, below the age of thirty-five, so that none could
possibly have had any implication in the matters under
examination. The lawyers were mainly older, but vetted
to ensure they too were uninvolved with events prior to
1945.

The lawyers were mainly taken from private practice,
to which they would one day return. The detectives
knew their careers were finished. No police force in
Germany wanted to see on its staff a detective who had
once served a term at Ludwigsburg. For detectives prepared to hunt the SS in West Germany, promotion was
finished in any other police force in the country.

Quite accustomed to seeing their requests for cooperation ignored in over half the states, to seeing their
loaned files unaccountably become missing, to see the
quarry suddenly disappear after an anonymous tip-off,
the Z men worked on as best they might at a task they
realized was not in accordance with the wishes of the
majority of their fellow countrymen.

Even on the streets of the smiling town of Ludwigsburg, the men on the staff of the Z Commission went
ungreeted and unacknowledged by the citizens, to whom
their presence brought an undesired notoriety.

Peter Miller found the commission at 58 Schorndorf-
erstrasse, a large former private house set inside an
eight-foot-high wall. Two massive steel gates barred the

way to the drive. At one side was a bell handle, which he pulled. A steel shutter slid back, and a face appeared. The inevitable gatekeeper.

"Please?"

"I would like to speak to one of your investigating attorneys," said Miller.

"Which one?" said the face.

"I don't know any names," said Miller. "Anyone will do. Here is my card."

He thrust his press card through the aperture, forcing the man to take it. Then at least he knew it would go inside the building. The man shut the hatch and went away. When he came back, it was to open the gate. Miller was shown up the five stone steps to the front door, which was closed against the clear but icy winter air.

Inside, it was stuffily hot from the central heating. Another porter emerged from a glass-fronted booth to his right and showed him into a small waiting room. "Someone will be with you right away," he said and shut the door.

The man who came three minutes later was in his early fifties, mild-mannered and courteous. He handed Miller back his press card and asked, "What can I do for you?"

Miller started at the beginning, explaining briefly about Tauber, the diary, his inquiries into what had happened to Eduard Roschmann.

The lawyer listened intently. "Fascinating," he said at last.

"The point is, can you help me?"

"I wish I could," said the man, and for the first time since he had started asking questions about Roschmann in Hamburg, Miller believed he had met an official who genuinely would like to help him. "But the point is, although I am prepared to accept your inquiries as completely sincere, I am bound hand and foot by the rules that govern our continued existence here. Which are in effect that no information may be given out about any wanted SS criminal to anyone other than a person supported by the official backing of one of a specific number of authorities."

"In other words, you can tell me nothing?" said Miller.

"Please understand," said the lawyer, "this office is under constant attack. Not openly—no one would dare. But privately, within the corridors of power, we are incessantly being sniped at—our budget, such powers as we have, our terms of reference. We are allowed no latitude where the rules are concerned. Personally, I would like to engage the alliance of the press of Germany to help, but it's forbidden."

"I see," said Miller. "Do you then have any newspaper-clippings reference library?"

"No, we don't."

"Is there in Germany at all a newspaper-clippings reference library that is open to an inquiry by a member of the public?"

"No. The only newspaper-clippings libraries in the country are compiled and held by the various newspapers and magazines. The most comprehensive is reputed to be that of *Der Spiegel* magazine. After that, *Komet* has a very good one."

"I find this rather odd," said Miller. "Where in Germany today does a citizen inquire about the progress of investigation into war crimes, and for background material on wanted SS criminals?"

The lawyer looked slightly uncomfortable. "I'm afraid the ordinary citizen can't do that," he said.

"All right," said Miller. "Where are the archives in Germany that refer to the men of the SS?"

"There's one set here, in the basement," said the lawyer. "And ours is all composed of photostats. The originals of the entire card index of the SS were captured in nineteen forty-five by an American unit. At the last minute a small group of the SS stayed behind at the castle where they were stored in Bavaria and tried to burn the records. They got through about ten per cent before the American soldiers rushed in and stopped them. The rest were all mixed up. It took the Americans, with some German help, two years to sort out the rest.

"During those two years a number of the worst SS men escaped after being temporarily in Allied custody. Their dossiers could not be found in the mess. Since the final classification the entire SS index has remained in Berlin, still under American ownership and direction. Even we have to apply to them if we want something more. Mind you, they're very good about it; no complaints at all about cooperation from that quarter."

"And that's it?" asked Miller. "Just two sets in the whole country?"

"That's it," said the lawyer. "I repeat, I wish I could help you. Incidentally, if you should get anything on Roschmann, we'd be delighted to have it."

Miller thought. "If I find anything, there are only two authorities that can do anything with it. The Attorney General's office in Hamburg, and you. Right?"

"Yes, that's all," said the lawyer.

"And you're more likely to do something positive with it than Hamburg." Miller made it a flat statement.

The lawyer gazed fixedly at the ceiling. "Nothing that comes here that is of real value gathers dust on a shelf," he observed.

"Okay. Point taken," said Miller and rose. "One thing, between ourselves, are you still looking for Eduard Roschmann?"

"Between ourselves, yes, very much."

"And if he were caught, there'd be no problems about getting a conviction?"

"None at all," said the lawyer. "The case against him is tied up solid. He'd get hard labor for life without the option."

"Give me your phone number," said Miller.

The lawyer wrote it down and handed Miller the piece of paper. "There's my name and two phone numbers. Home and office. You can get me any time, day or night. If you get anything new, just call me from any phone box on direct-dial. In every state police force there are men I can call and know I'll get action if necessary. There are others to avoid. So call me first, right?"

Miller pocketed the paper. "I'll remember that," he said as he left.

"Good luck," said the lawyer.

It's a long drive from Stuttgart to Berlin, and it took Miller most of the following day. Fortunately it was dry and crisp and the tuned Jaguar ate the miles northward past the sprawling carpet of Frankfurt, past Kassel and Göttingen to Hanover. Here he followed the branchoff to the right from autobahn E4 to E8 and the border with East Germany.

There was an hour's delay at the Marienborn Checkpoint while he filled out the inevitable currency-declaration forms and transit visas to travel though 110 miles of East Germany to West Berlin; and while the blue-uniformed customs man and the green-coated People's Police, fur-hatted against the cold, poked around in and under the Jaguar. The customs man seemed torn between the frosty courtesy required of a servant of the German Democratic Republic towards a national of revanchist West Germany, and one young man's desire to examine another's sports car.

Twenty miles beyond the border, the great motorway bridge reared up to cross the Elbe, where in 1945 the British, honorably obeying the rules laid down at Yalta, had halted their advance on Berlin. To his right, Miller looked down at the sprawl of Magdeburg and wondered if the old prison still stood. There was a further delay at the entry into West Berlin, where again the car was searched, his overnight case emptied onto the customs bench, and his wallet opened to see he had not given all his Westmarks away to the people of the worker's paradise on his progress down the road. Eventually he was through and the Jaguar roared past the Avus circuit toward the glittering ribbon of the Kurfürstendamm, brilliant with Christmas decorations. It was the evening of December 17.

He decided not to go blundering into the American Document Center the same way he had into the Attorney General's office in Hamburg or the Z Commission in Ludwigsburg. Without official backing, he had come to realize, no one got anywhere with Nazi files in Germany.

The following morning he called Karl Brandt from the main post office.

Brandt was aghast at his request. "I can't," he said into the phone. "I don't know anyone in Berlin."

"Well, think. You must have come across someone from the West Berlin force at one of the colleges you attended. I need him to vouch for me when I get there," shouted Miller back.

"I told you I didn't want to get involved."

"Well, you are involved." Miller waited a few seconds before putting in the body blow. "Either I get a look at that archive officially, or I breeze in and say you sent me."

"You wouldn't do that," said Brandt.

"I damn well would. I'm fed up with being pushed from pillar to post around this lousy country. So find somebody who'll get me in there officially. Let's face it, the request will be forgotten within the hour, once I've seen those files."

"I'll have to think," said Brandt, stalling for time.

"I'll give you an hour," said Miller. "Then I'm calling back."

He slammed down the receiver. An hour later Brandt was as angry as ever and more than a little frightened. He heartily wished he had kept the diary to himself and thrown it away.

"There's a man I was at detective college with," he said into the phone. "I didn't know him well, but he's now with Bureau One of the West Berlin force. That deals with the same subject."

"What's his name?"

"Schiller. Volkmar Schiller, detective inspector."

"I'll get in touch with him," said Miller.

"No, leave him to me. I'll call him today and introduce you to him. Then you can go and see him. If he doesn't agree to get you in, don't blame me. He's the only one I know in Berlin."

Two hours later Miller called Brandt back. Brandt sounded relieved. "He's away on leave," he said. "They tell me he's doing Christmas duty, so he's away until Monday."

"But it's only Wednesday," said Miller. "That gives me four days to kill."

"I can't help it. He'll be back on Monday morning. I'll ring him then."

Miller spent four boring days hanging around West Berlin, waiting for Schiller to come back from leave. Berlin was completely involved, as the Christmas of 1963 approached, with the issue by the East Berlin authorities, for the first time since the Wall had been built in August 1961, of passes enabling West Berliners to go through the Wall and visit relatives living in the eastern sector. The progress of the negotiations between the two sides of the city had held the headlines for days. Miller spent one of his days that weekend by going through the Heinestrasse Checkpoint into the eastern half of the city (as a West German citizen was able to do on the strength of his passport alone) and dropped in on a slight acquaintance, the Reuters correspondent in East Berlin. But the man was up to his neck in work on the Wall-passes story, so after a cup of coffee he left and returned to the west.

On Monday morning he went to see Detective Inspector Volkmar Schiller. To his great relief the man was about his own age and seemed, unusually for an official of any kind in Germany, to have his own cavalier attitude to red tape. Doubtless he would not get far, thought Miller, but that was his problem. He explained briefly what he wanted.

"I don't see why not," said Schiller. "The Americans are pretty helpful to us in Bureau One. Because we're charged by Willy Brandt with investigating Nazi crimes, we're in there almost every day."

They took Miller's Jaguar and drove out to the suburbs of the city, to the forests and the lakes, and at the bank of one of the lakes arrived at Number 1,

Wasserkäferstieg, in the suburb of Zehlendorf, Berlin 37.

The building was a long, low, single-story affair set amid the trees.

"Is that it?" said Miller incredulously.

"That's it," said Schiller. "Not much, is it? The point is, there are eight floors below ground level. That's where the archives are stored, in fireproof vaults."

They went through the front door to find a small waiting room with the inevitable porter's lodge on the right. The detective approached it and proffered his police card. He was handed a form, and the two of them repaired to a table and filled it out.

The detective filled in his name and rank, then asked, "What was the chap's name again?"

"Roschmann," said Miller. "Eduard Roschmann."

The detective filled it in and handed the form back to the clerk in the front office.

"It takes about ten minutes," said the detective. They went into the larger room set out with rows of tables and chairs. After a quarter of an hour another clerk quietly brought them a file and laid it on the desk. It was about an inch thick, stamped with the single title: ROSCHMANN, EDUARD.

Volkmar Schiller rose. "If you don't mind, I'll be on my way," he said. "I'll find my own way back. Mustn't stay away too long after a week's leave. If you want anything photostated, ask the clerk." He gestured to a clerk sitting on a dais at the other end of the reading room, no doubt to ensure that no visitors tried to remove pages from the files.

Miller rose and shook hands. "Many thanks."

"Not at all."

Ignoring the other three or four readers hunched over their desks, Miller put his head between his hands and started to peruse the SS's own dossier on Eduard Roschmann.

It was all there. Nazi Party number, SS number, application form for each, filled out and signed by the man himself, result of his medical check, evaluation of him after his training period, self-written curriculum vitae, transfer papers, officer's commission, promotion certificates, right up to April 1945. There were also two photographs, taken for the SS records, one full-face, one profile. They showed a man of six feet, one inch, hair shorn close to the head with a parting on the left, staring at the camera with a grim expression, a pointed nose, and a lipless slit of a mouth. Miller began to read. . . .

Eduard Roschmann was born on August 25, 1908, in the Austrian town of Graz, a citizen of Austria, son of a highly respectable brewery worker. He attended kindergarten, school, and high school in Graz. He attended college to try to become a lawyer, but failed. In 1931, at the age of twenty-three, he began work in the brewery where his father had a job and in 1937 was transferred to the administrative department from the brewery floor. The same year he joined the Austrian Nazi Party and the SS, both at that time banned organizations in neutral Austria. A year later Hitler annexed Austria and rewarded the Austrian Nazis with swift promotions all around.

In 1939, at the outbreak of war, he volunteered for the Waffen SS, was sent to Germany, trained during the winter of 1939 and the spring of 1940, and served in a Waffen SS unit in the overrunning of France. In December 1940 he was transferred back from France to Berlin —here somebody had handwritten in the margin the word "Cowardice?"—and in January 1941 was assigned to the SD, Amt Three of the RSHA.

In July 1941 he set up the first SD post in Riga, and the following month became commandant of Riga ghetto. He returned to Germany by ship in October 1944 and, after handing over the remainder of the Jews of Riga to the SD of Danzig, returned to Berlin to report. He returned to his desk in Berlin headquarters of the SS and remained there awaiting reassignment.

The last SS document in the file was evidently never completed, presumably because the meticulous little clerk in Berlin SS headquarters reassigned himself rather quickly in May 1945.

Attached to the back of the bunch of documents was one last one apparently affixed by an American hand since the end of the war. It was a single sheet bearing the typewritten words: "Inquiry made about this file by the British Occupation authorities in December 1947."

Beneath this was the scrawled signature of some GI clerk long since forgotten, and the date December 21, 1947.

Miller gathered the file and eased out of it the self-written life story, the two photographs, and the last sheet. With these he approached the clerk at the end of the room.

"Could I have these photocopied please?"

"Certainly." The man took the file back and placed it on his desk to await the return of the three missing sheets after copying. Another man also tendered a file and two sheets of its contents for copying. The clerk took these also and placed them all in a tray behind him, whence the sheets were whisked away through an aperture by an unseen hand.

"Please wait. It will take about ten minutes," the clerk told Miller and the other man. The pair retook their seats and waited, Miller wishing he could smoke a cigarette, which was forbidden; the other man, neat and gray in a charcoal winter coat, sitting with hands folded in his lap.

Ten minutes later there was a rustle behind the clerk, and two envelopes slid through the aperture. He held them up. Both Miller and the middle-aged man rose and went forward to collect.

The clerk glanced quickly inside one of the envelopes. "The file on Eduard Roschmann?" he queried.

"For me," said Miller and extended his hand.

"These must be for you," the clerk said to the other man, who was glancing sideways at Miller.

The gray-coated man took his own envelope, and side by side they walked to the door. Outside, Miller ran down the steps and climbed into the Jaguar, slipped away from the curb, and headed back toward the center of the city.

An hour later he rang Sigi. "I'm coming home for Christmas," he told her.

Two hours later he was on his way out of West Berlin. As his car headed toward the first checkpoint at Drei Linden, the man with the gray coat was sitting in his neat and tidy flat off Savigny Platz, dialing a number in West Germany. He introduced himself briefly to the man who answered.

"I was in the Document Center today. Just normal research, you know the sort I do. There was another man in there. He was reading through the file of Eduard Roschmann. Then he had three sheets photocopied. After the message that went around recently, I thought I'd better tell you."

There was a burst of questions from the other end.

"No, I couldn't get his name. He drove away afterward in a long black sports car. Yes, yes, I did. It was a Hamburg number plate."

He recited it slowly while the man at the other end took it down.

"Well, I thought I'd better. I mean, one never knows with these snoopers. Yes, thank you, very kind of you. . . . Very well, I'll leave it with you. . . . Merry Christmas, *Kamerad*."

7

CHRISTMAS DAY was on the Wednesday of that week, and it was not until after the Christmas period that the man in West Germany who had received the news from Berlin about Miller passed it on. When he did so, it was to his ultimate superior.

The man who took the call thanked his informant, put the office phone down, leaned back in his comfortable leather-padded executive chair, and gazed out of the window at the snow-covered rooftops of the Old Town.

"*Verdammt* and once again *verdammt*," he whispered. "Why now, of all times? Why now?"

To all the citizens of his city who knew him, he was a clever and brilliantly succesful lawyer in private practice. To the score of his senior executive officers scattered across West Germany and West Berlin, he was the chief executive inside Germany of the Odessa. His telephone number was unlisted, and his code name was the Werwolf.

Unlike the monster-figure of the mythology of Hollywood and the horror films of Britain and America, the German *Werwolf* is not an odd man who grows hairs on the backs of his hands during the full moon. In old Germanic mythology the *Werwolf* is a patriotic figure who stays behind in the homeland when the Teuton warrior-heroes have been forced to flee into exile by the invading foreigner, and who leads the resistance against the invader from the shadows of the great forests, striking by night and disappearing, leaving only the spoor of the wolf in the snow.

At the end of the war a group of SS officers, convinced that the destruction of the invading Allies was merely a matter of months, trained and briefed a score of groups of ultrafanatical teenage boys to remain behind and sabotage the Allied occupiers. They were formed in Bavaria, then being overrun by the Americans. These were the original Werwolves. Fortunately for them, they never put their training into practice, for after discovering Dachau the GIs were just waiting for someone to start something.

When the Odessa began in the late forties to reinfiltrate West Germany, its first chief executive had been one of those who had trained the teenage Werwolves of 1945. He took the title. It had the advantage of being anonymous, symbolic, and sufficiently melodramatic to satisfy the eternal German lust for play-acting. But there was nothing theatrical about the ruthlessness with which the Odessa dealt with those who crossed its plans.

The Werwolf of late 1963 was the third to hold the title and position. Fanatic and astute, constantly in touch with his superiors in Argentina, the man watched over the interests of all former members of the SS inside West Germany, but particularly those formerly of high rank or those high on the wanted list.

He stared out of his office window and thought back to the image of SS General Glücks facing him in a Madrid hotel room more than thirty days earlier, and to the general's warning about the vital importance of maintaining at all costs the anonymity and security of the radio-factory-owner now preparing, under the code name Vulkan, the guidance systems for the Egyptian rockets. Alone in Germany, he also knew that in an earlier part of his life Vulkan had been better known under his real name of Eduard Roschmann.

He glanced down at the jotting pad on which he had scribbled the number of Miller's car and pressed a buzzer on his desk. His secretary's voice came through from the next room.

"Hilda, what was the name of that private investigator we employed last month on the divorce case?"

"One moment." There was a sound of rustling papers as she looked up the file. "It was Memmers, Heinz Memmers."

"Give me the telephone number, will you? No, don't call him, just give me the number."

He noted it down beneath the number of Miller's car, then took his finger off the intercom key.

He rose and crossed the room to a wall-safe set in a block of concrete, a part of the wall of the office. From the safe he took a thick, heavy book and went back to his desk. Flicking through the pages, he came to the entry he wanted. There were only two Memmers listed, Heinrich and Walter. He ran his finger along the page opposite Heinrich, usually shortened to Heinz. He noted the date of birth, worked out the age of the man in late 1963, and recalled the face of the private investigator. The ages fitted. He jotted down two other numbers listed against Heinz Memmers, picked up the telephone, and asked Hilda for an outside line.

When the dialing tone came through, he dialed the number she had given him. The telephone at the other end was picked up after a dozen rings. It was a woman's voice. "Memmers Private Inquiries."

"Give me Herr Memmers personally," said the lawyer.

"May I say who's calling?" asked the secretary brightly.

"No, just put him on the line. And hurry."

There was a pause. The tone of voice took its effect. "Yes, sir," she said.

A minute later a gruff voice said, "Memmers."

"Is that Herr Heinz Memmers?"

"Yes, who is that speaking?"

"Never mind my name. It is not important. Just tell me, does the number 245.718 mean anything to you?"

There was dead silence on the phone, broken only by a heavy sigh as Memmers digested the fact that his SS number had just been quoted to him. The book now lying open on the Werwolf's desk was a list of every former member of the SS.

Memmers' voice came back, harsh with suspicion. "Should it?"

"Would it mean anything to you if I said that my

own corresponding number had only five figures in it—
Kamerad?"

The change was electric. Five figures meant a very
senior officer.

"Yes, sir," said Memmers down the line.

"Good," said the Werwolf. "There's a small job I
want you to do. Some snooper has been inquiring into
one of the *Kameraden*. I need to find out who he is."

"*Zu Befehl*"—At your command—came over the
phone.

"Excellent. But between ourselves *Kamerad* will do.
After all, we are all comrades in arms."

Memmers' voice came back, evidently pleased by the
flattery. "Yes, *Kamerad*."

"All I have about the man is his car number. A
Hamburg registration." The Werwolf read it slowly into
the telephone. "Got that?"

"Yes, *Kamerad*."

"I'd like you to go to Hamburg personally. I want
to know the name and address, profession, family and
dependents, social standing—you know, the normal run-
down. How long would that take you?"

"About forty-eight hours," said Memmers.

"Good, I'll call you back forty-eight hours from now.
One last thing. There is to be no approach made to
the subject. If possible it is to be done in such a way
that he does not know any inquiry has been made. Is
that clear?"

"Certainly. It's no problem."

"When you have finished, prepare your account and
give it to me over the phone when I call you. I will send
you the cash by post."

Memmers expostulated. "There will be no account,
Kamerad. Not for a matter concerning the Comradeship."

"Very well, then. I'll call you back in two days."

The Werwolf put the phone down.

Miller set off from Hamburg the same afternoon, taking the same autobahn he had traveled two weeks earlier, past Bremen, Osnabrück, and Münster toward Cologne and the Rhineland. This time his destination was Bonn, the small and boring town on the river's edge that Konrad Adenauer had chosen as the capital of the Federal Republic, because he came from it.

Just south of Bremen his Jaguar crossed Memmers' Opel speeding north to Hamburg. Oblivious of each other, the two men flashed past on their separate missions.

It was dark when he entered the single long main street of Bonn and, seeing the white-topped peaked cap of a traffic policeman, he drew up beside him.

"Can you tell me the way to the British Embassy?" he asked the policeman.

"It will be closed in an hour," said the policeman, a true Rhinelander.

"Then I'd better get there all the quicker," said Miller. "Where is it?"

The policeman pointed straight down the road toward the south. "Keep straight on down here, follow the tramlines. This street becomes Friedrich Ebert Allee. Just follow the tramlines. As you are about to leave Bonn and enter Bad Godesberg, you'll see it on your left. It's lit up and it's got the British flag flying outside it."

Miller nodded his thanks and drove on. The British Embassy was where the policeman had said, sandwiched between a building site on the Bonn side and a football field on the other, both a sea of mud in the December fog rolling up off the river behind the embassy.

It was a long, low gray concrete building, built back-to-front, referred to by British newspaper correspondents in Bonn since it was built as "the vacuum-cleaner factory." Miller swung off the road and parked in one of the slots provided for visitors.

He walked through the wooden-framed glass doors and found himself in a small foyer with a desk on his left, behind which sat a middle-aged receptionist. Beyond her was a small room inhabited by two blue-serge-suited men who bore the unmistakable stamp of former Army sergeants.

"I would like to speak with the press attaché, please," said Miller, using his halting school English.

The receptionist looked worried. "I don't know if he's still here. It is Friday afternoon, you know."

"Please try," said Miller, and proffered his press card.

The receptionist looked at it and dialed a number on her house telephone. Miller was in luck. The press attaché was just about to leave. He evidently asked for a few minutes to get his hat and coat back off again. Miller was shown into a small waiting room adorned by several Rowland Hilder prints of the Cotswolds in autumn. On a table lay several back copies of the *Tatler* and brochures depicting the onward march of British industry. Within seconds, however, he was summoned by one of the ex-sergeants and led upstairs and along a corridor and shown into a small office.

The press attaché, he was glad to see, was in his mid-thirties and seemed eager to help. "What can I do for you?" he asked.

Miller decided to go straight into the matter. "I am investigating a story for a news magazine," he lied. "It's about a former SS captain, one of the worst, a man still sought by our own authorities. I believe he was also on the wanted list of the British authorities when this part of Germany was under British administration. Can you tell me how I can check whether the British ever captured him, and if so what happened to him?"

The young diplomat was perplexed. "Good Lord, I'm sure I don't know. I mean, we handed over all our records and files to your government in nineteen forty-nine. They took over where our chaps left off. I suppose they would have all these things now."

Miller tried to avoid mentioning that the German auhorities had all declined to help. "True," he said. "Very true. However, all my inquiries so far indicate he has never been put on trial in the Federal Republic since nineteen forty-nine. That would indicate he had not been caught since nineteen forty-nine. However, the American Document Center in West Berlin reveals that a copy of the man's file was requested from them by the British in nineteen forty-seven. There must have been a reason for that, surely?"

"Yes, one would indeed suppose so," said the attaché. He had evidently taken in the reference to Miller's having procured the cooperation of the American authorities in West Berlin, and furrowed his brow in thought.

"So who on the British side would be the investigating authority during the Occupation—I mean, the administration period?"

"Well, you see, it would have been the Provost Marshal's office of the Army at that time. Apart from Nuremberg, which were the major war-crimes trials, the separate Allies were investigating individually, although obviously we cooperated with each other. Except the Russians. These investigations led to some zonal war-crimes trials—do you follow me?"

"Yes."

"The investigations were carried out by the Provost Marshal's department, that's the military police, you know, and the trials were prepared by the Legal Branch. But the files of both were handed over in nineteen forty-nine. Do you see?"

"Well, yes," said Miller, "but surely copies must have been kept by the British?"

"I suppose they were," said the attaché. "But they'd be filed away in the archives of the Army by now."

"Would it be possible to look at them?"

The attaché appeared shocked. "Oh, I very much doubt it. I don't think so. I suppose bona fide research scholars might be able to make an application to see them, but it would take a long time. And I don't think a reporter would be allowed to see them—no offense meant, you understand?"

"I understand," said Miller.

"The point is," resumed the attaché earnestly, "that, well, you're not exactly *official*, are you? And one doesn't wish to upset the German authorities, does one?"

"Certainly not."

The attaché rose. "I don't think there's really much the embassy can do to help you."

"Okay. One last thing. Was there anybody here then who is still here now?"

"On the embassy staff? Oh, dear me, no. No, they've all changed many times." He escorted Miller to the door. "Wait a minute, there's Cadbury. I think he was here then. He's been here for ages, I do know that."

"Cadbury?" said Miller.

"Anthony Cadbury. The foreign correspondent. He's the sort of senior British press chap here. Married a German girl. I think he was here after the war, just after. You might ask him."

"Fine," said Miller. "I'll try him. Where do I find him?"

"Well, it's Friday now," said the attaché. "He'll probably be at his favorite place by the bar in the Cercle Français later on. Do you know it?"

"No, I've never been here before."

"Ah, yes, well, it's a restaurant, run by the French, you know. Jolly good food, too. It's very popular. It's in Bad Godesberg, just down the road."

Miller found it, a hundred yards from the bank of the Rhine on a road called Ann Schwimmbad. The barman knew Cadbury well but had not seen him that evening. He told Miller if the doyen of the British foreign correspondents' corps in Bonn was not in that evening, he would almost certainly be there for prelunch drinks the following day.

Miller checked into the Dreesen Hotel down the road, a great turn-of-the-century edifice that had formerly been Adolf Hitler's favorite hotel in Germany, the place he had picked to meet Neville Chamberlain of Britain for their first meeting in 1938. He dined at the Cercle Français and dawdled over his coffee, hoping Cadbury would turn up. But by eleven the Englishman had not put in an appearance, so he went back to the hotel to sleep.

Cadbury walked into the bar of the Cercle Français a few minutes before twelve the following morning, greeted a few acquaintances, and seated himself on his favorite corner stool at the bar. When he had taken his first sip of his Ricard, Miller rose from his table by the window and came over.

"Mr. Cadbury?"

The Englishman turned and surveyed him. He had smooth-brushed white hair coming back from what had evidently once been a very handsome face. The skin was still healthy, with a fine tracery of tiny veins on the surface of each cheek. The eyes were bright blue under shaggy gray eyebrows. He surveyed Miller warily. "Yes."

"My name is Miller. Peter Miller. I am a reporter from Hamburg. May I talk with you a moment, please?"

Anthony Cadbury gestured to the stool beside him. "I think we had better talk in German, don't you?" he said, dropping into the language. Miller was relieved that he could go back to his own language, and it must have showed. Cadbury grinned. "What can I do for you?"

Miller glanced at the shrewd eyes and backed a hunch. Starting at the beginning, he told Cadbury the story from the moment of Tauber's death. The London man was a good listener. He did not interrupt once. When Miller had finished he gestured to the barman to fill his own Ricard and bring another beer for Miller.

"Spätenbräu, wasn't it?" he asked.

Miller nodded and poured the fresh beer to a foaming head on top of the glass.

"Cheers," said Cadbury. "Well, now, you've got quite a problem. I must say I admire your nerve."

"Nerve?" said Miller.

"It's not quite the most popular story to investigate among your countrymen in their present state of mind," said Cadbury, "as you will doubtless find out in course of time."

"I already have," said Miller.

"Mmm. I thought so," said the Englishman and

grinned suddenly. "A spot of lunch? My wife's away for the day."

Over lunch Miller asked Cadbury if he had been in Germany at the end of the war.

"Yes, I was a war correspondent. Much younger then, of course. About your age. I came in with Montgomery's army. Not to Bonn, of course. No one had heard of it then. The headquarters was at Lüneburg. Then I just sort of stayed on. Covered the end of the war, signature of the surrender and all that; then the paper asked me to remain."

"Did you cover the zonal war-crimes trials?" asked Miller.

Cadbury transferred a mouthful of fillet steak and nodded while he chewed. "Yes. All the ones held in the British Zone. We had a specialist come over for the Nuremberg Trials. That was the American Zone, of course. The star criminals in our zone were Josef Kramer and Irma Grese. Heard of them?"

"No, never."

"Well, they were called the Beast and Beastess of Belsen. I invented the titles, actually. They caught on. Did you hear about Belsen?"

"Only vaguely," said Miller. "My generation wasn't told much about all that. Nobody wanted to tell us anything."

Cadbury shot him a shrewd glance under his bushy eyebrows. "But you want to know now?"

"We have to know sooner or later. May I ask you something? Do you hate the Germans?"

Cadbury chewed for a few minutes, considering the question seriously. "Just after the discovery of Belsen, a crowd of journalists attached to the British Army went up for a look. I've never been so sickened in my life, and in war you see a few terrible things. But nothing like Belsen. I think at that moment, yes, I hated them all."

"And now?"

"No. Not any longer. Let's face it, I married a German girl in nineteen forty-eight. I still live here. I wouldn't if I still felt the way I did in nineteen forty-five. I'd have gone back to England long ago."

"What caused the change?"

"Time. The passage of time. And the realization that not all Germans were Josef Kramers. Or—what was his name, Roschmann? Or Roschmanns. Mind you, I still can't get over a sneaking sense of mistrust for people of my own generation among your nation."

"And my generation?" Miller twirled his wineglass and gazed at the light refracting through the red liquid.

"They're better," said Cadbury. "Let's face it, you have to be better."

"Will you help me with the Roschmann inquiry? Nobody else will."

"If I can," said Cadbury. "What do you want to know?"

"Do you recall him being put on trial in the British Zone?"

Cadbury shook his head. "No. Anyway, you said he was Austrian by birth. Austria was also under four-power occupation at the time. But I'm certain there was no trial against Roschmann in the British Zone of Germany. I'd remember the name if there were."

"But why would the British authorities request a photocopy of his career from the Americans in Berlin?"

Cadbury thought for a moment. "Roschmann must have come to the attention of the British in some way. At that time nobody knew about Riga. The Russians were at the height of their obstinacy in the late forties. They didn't give us any information from the east. Yet that was where the overwhelming majority of the worst crimes of mass murder took place. So we were in the odd position of having about eighty per cent of the crimes against humanity committed east of what is now the Iron Curtain, and the ones responsible for them were about ninety per cent in the three western zones. Hundreds of guilty men slipped through our hands because we knew nothing about what they had done a thousand miles to the east.

"But if an inquiry was made about Roschmann in

nineteen forty-seven, he must have come to our attention somehow."

"That's what I thought," said Miller. "Where would one start to look, among the British records?"

"Well, we can start with my own files. They're back at my house. Come on, it's a short walk."

Fortunately, Cadbury was a methodical man and had kept every one of his dispatches from the end of the war onward. His study was lined with file boxes along two walls. Besides these, there were two gray filing cabinets in one corner.

"I run the office from my home," he told Miller as they entered the study. "This is my own filing system, and I'm about the only one who understands it. Let me show you." He gestured to the filing cabinets. "One of these is stuffed with files on people, listed under the names in alphabetical order. The other concerns subjects, listed under subject headings, alphabetically. We'll start with the first one. Look under Roschmann."

It was a brief search. There was no folder with Roschmann's name on it.

"All right," said Cadbury. "Now let's try subject headings. There are four that might help. There's one called Nazis, another labeled SS. Then there's a very large section headed Justice, which has subsections, one of which contains clippings about trials that have taken place. But they're mostly criminal trials that have taken place in West Germany since nineteen forty-nine. The last one that might help is about war crimes. Let's start going through them."

Cadbury read faster than Miller, but it took them until nightfall to wade through the hundreds of clippings in all four files. Eventually Cadbury rose with a sigh, closed the War Crimes file, and replaced it in its proper place in the filing cabinet.

"I'm afraid I have to go out to dinner tonight," he said. "The only things left to look through are these." He gestured to the box files on shelves along two of the walls.

Miller closed the file he had been searching. "What are those?"

"Those," said Cadbury, "are nineteen years of dispatches from me to the paper. That's the top row. Below them are nineteen years of clippings from the paper of news stories and articles about Germany and Austria. Obviously a lot in the first set are repeated in the second. Those are my pieces that were printed. But there are other pieces in the second set that were not from me. After all, other contributors have had pieces printed in the paper as well. And some of the stuff I sent was not used.

"There are about six boxes of clippings per year. That's quite a lot to get through. Fortunately it's Sunday tomorrow, so we can use the whole day if you like."

"It's very kind of you to take so much trouble," said Miller.

Cadbury shrugged. "I had nothing else to do this weekend. Anyway, weekends in late December in Bonn are hardly full of gaiety. My wife's not due back till tomorrow evening. Meet me for a drink in the Cercle Français about eleven-thirty."

It was in the middle of Sunday afternoon that they found it. Anthony Cadbury was nearing the end of the box file labeled November–December 1947 of the set that contained his own dispatches. He suddenly shouted, "Eureka," eased back the spring clip, and took out a single sheet of paper, long since faded, typewritten and headed "December 23, 1947."

"No wonder it wasn't used in the paper," he said. "No one would have wanted to know about a captured SS man just before Christmas. Anyway, with the shortage of newsprint in those days, the Christmas Eve edition must have been tiny."

He laid the sheet on the writing desk and shone the Anglepoise lamp onto it. Miller leaned over to read it.

British Military Government, Hanover, 23rd Dec.— A former captain of the notorious SS has been arrested by British military authorities at Graz, Austria, and is being held pending further investigation, a spokesman at BMG headquarters said here today.

The man, Eduard Roschmann, was recognized on the streets of the Austrian town by a former inmate of a concentration camp, who alleged Roschmann had been the commandant of the camp in Latvia. After identification at the house to which the former camp inmate followed him, Roschmann was arrested by members of the British Field Security Service in Graz.

A request has been made to Soviet Zonal headquarters at Potsdam for further information about the concentration camp in Riga, Latvia, and a search for further witnesses is under way, the spokesman said. Meanwhile the captured man has been positively identified as Eduard Roschmann from his personal file, stored by the American authorities in their SS Index in Berlin. endit. Cadbury.

Miller read the brief dispatch four or five times. "Christ," he breathed. "You got him."

"I think this calls for a drink," said Cadbury.

When he had made the call to Memmers on Friday morning, the Werwolf had overlooked the fact that forty-eight hours later it would be Sunday. Despite this, he tried to call to Memmers' office from his home on Sunday, just as the two men in Bad Godesberg made their discovery. There was no reply.

But Memmers was in the office the following morning at nine sharp. The call from the Werwolf came through at half past.

"So glad you called, *Kamerad,*" said Memmers. "I got back from Hamburg late last night."

"You have the information?"

"Certainly. If you would like to note it?"

"Go ahead," said the voice on the phone.

In his office Memmers cleared his throat and began to read from his notes.

"The owner of the car is a freelance reporter, one Peter Miller. Description: aged twenty-nine, just under six feet tall, brown hair, brown eyes. Has a widowed mother who lives in Osdorf, just outside Hamburg. He himself lives in an apartment close to the Steindamm in central Hamburg." Memmers read off Miller's address and telephone number. "He lives there with a girl, a striptease dancer, Miss Sigrid Rahn. He works mainly for the picture magazines. Apparently does very well. Specializes in investigative journalism. Like you said, *Kamerad,* a snooper."

"Any idea who commissioned him on his latest inquiry?" asked the Werwolf.

"No, that's the funny thing. Nobody seems to know what he is doing at the moment. Or for whom he is working. I checked with the girl, claiming to be from the editorial office of a big magazine. Only by phone, you understand. She said she did not know where he was, but she expected a call from him this afternoon, before she goes to work."

"Anything else?"

"Just the car. It's very distinctive. A black Jaguar, British model, with a yellow stripe down the side. A sports car, two-seater, fixed-head coupe, called the XK one-fifty. I checked his local garage."

The Werwolf digested this. "I want to try and find out where he is now," he said at length.

"He's not in Hamburg now," said Memmers hastily. "He left on Friday about lunchtime, just as I was arriving. He spent Christmas there. Before that he was away somewhere else."

"I know," said the Werwolf.

"I could find out what story he is inquiring about," said Memmers helpfully. "I did not inquire too closely, because you said you did not want him to discover he was being asked about."

"I know what story he is working on. Exposing one of our comrades." The Werwolf thought for a minute. "Could you find out where he is now?" he asked.

"I think so," said Memmers. "I could call the girl back this afternoon, pretend I was from a big magazine and needed to contact Miller urgently. She sounded a simple girl on the phone."

"Yes, do that," said the Werwolf. "I'll call you at four this afternoon."

That Monday morning Cadbury was down in Bonn, where a ministerial press conference was scheduled. He rang Miller at the Dreesen Hotel at ten-thirty.

"Glad to get you before you left," he told the German. "I've got an idea. It might help you. Meet me at the Cercle Français this afternoon around four."

Just before lunch Miller rang Sigi and told her he was at the Dreesen.

When they met, Cadbury ordered tea. "I had an idea while not listening to that wretched conference this morning," he told Miller. "If Roschmann was captured and identified as a wanted criminal, his case would have come under the eyes of the British legal officials in our zone of Germany at the time. All files were copied and passed between the British, French, and Americans in both Germany and Austria at that time. Have you ever heard of a man called Lord Russell of Liverpool?"

"No, never," said Miller.

"He was the Legal Adviser to the British Military Governor during the occupation. Later he wrote a book called *The Scourge of the Swastika*. You can imagine what it was about. Didn't make him terribly popular in Germany, but it was quite accurate. About atrocities."

"He's a lawyer?" asked Miller.

"He was," said Cadbury. "A very brilliant one. He's retired now, lives in Wimbledon. I don't know if he'd remember me, but I could give you a letter of introduction."

"Would he remember so far back?"

"He might. He's not a young man any more, but he was reputed to have a memory like a filing cabinet. If the case of Roschmann was ever referred to him to prepare a prosecution, he'd remember every detail of it. I'm sure of that."

Miller nodded and sipped his tea. "Yes, I could fly to London to talk to him."

Cadbury reached into his pocket and produced an envelope. "I've written the letter already." He handed Miller the letter of introduction and stood up. "Good luck."

Memmers had the information for the Werwolf when the latter called just after four.

"His girl friend got a call from him," said Memmers. "He's in Bad Godesberg, staying at the Dreesen Hotel."

The Werwolf put the phone down and thumbed through an address book. Eventually he fixed on a name, picked up the phone again, and called a number in the Bonn–Bad Godesberg area.

Miller went back to the hotel to call Cologne airport and book a flight to London for the following day, Tuesday, December 31. As he reached the reception desk the girl behind the counter smiled brightly and pointed to the open seating area in the bay window overlooking the Rhine.

"There's a gentleman to see you, Herr Miller."

He glanced toward the groups of tapestry-backed chairs set around various tables in the window alcove. In one of them a middle-aged man in a black winter coat, holding a black Homburg and a rolled umbrella, sat waiting. Miller strolled over, puzzled as to who could have known he was there.

"You wanted to see me?" Miller asked.

The man sprang to his feet. "Herr Miller?"

"Yes."

"Herr Peter Miller?"

"Yes."

The man inclined his head in the short, jerky bow of old-fashioned Germans. "My name is Schmidt. Doctor Schmidt."

"What can I do for you?"

Dr. Schmidt smiled deprecatingly and gazed out of the windows where the black, bleak mass of the Rhine flowed under the fairy lights of the deserted terrace.

"I am told you are a journalist. Yes? A freelance

journalist. A very good one." He smiled brightly. "You have a reputation for being very thorough, very tenacious."

Miller remained silent, waiting for him to get to the point.

"Some friends of mine heard you are presently engaged on an inquiry into events that happened—well, let us say, a long time ago. A very long time ago."

Miller stiffened and his mind raced, trying to work out who the "friends" were and who could have told them. Then he realized he had been asking questions about Roschmann all over the country.

"An inquiry about a certain Eduard Roschmann." And he said tersely, "So?"

"Ah yes, about Captain Roschmann. I just thought I might be able to help you." The man swiveled his eyes back from the river and fixed them kindly on Miller. "Captain Roschmann is dead."

"Indeed?" said Miller. "I didn't know."

Dr. Schmidt seemed delighted. "Of course not. There's no reason why you should. But it is true nevertheless. Really, you are wasting your time."

Miller looked disappointed. "Can you tell me when he died?" he asked the doctor.

"You have not discovered the circumstances of his death?" the man asked.

"No. The last trace of him I can find was in late April nineteen forty-five. He was seen alive then."

"Ah yes, of course." Dr. Schmidt seemed happy to oblige. "He was killed, you know, shortly after that. He returned to his native Austria and was killed fighting against the Americans in early nineteen forty-five. His body was identified by several people who had known him in life."

"He must have been a remarkable man," said Miller.

Dr. Schmidt nodded in agreement. "Well, yes, some thought so. Yes indeed, some of us thought so."

"I mean," continued Miller as if the interruption had not occurred, "he must have been remarkable to be the first man since Jesus Christ to have risen from the dead.

He was captured alive by the British on December twentieth, nineteen forty-seven, at Graz in Austria."

The doctor's eyes reflected the glittering snow along the balustrade outside the window. "Miller, you are being very foolish. Very foolish indeed. Permit me to give you a word of advice, from an older man to a much, much younger one. Drop this inquiry."

Miller eyed him. "I suppose I ought to thank you," he said without gratitude.

"If you will take my advice, perhaps you ought," said the doctor.

"You misunderstand me again," said Miller. "Roschmann was also seen alive in mid-October this year in Hamburg. The second sighting was not confirmed. Now it is. You just confirmed it."

"I repeat, you are being very foolish if you do not drop this inquiry." The doctor's eyes were as cold as ever, but there was a hint of anxiety in them. There had been a time when people did not reject his orders, and he had never quite got used to the change.

Miller began to get angry, a slow glow of anger working up from his collar to his face. "You make me sick, *Herr Doktor,*" he told the older man. "You and your kind, your whole stinking gang. You have a respectable façade, but you are filth on the face of my country. So far as I am concerned, I'll go on asking questions till I find him."

He turned to go, but the elder man grabbed his arm. They stared at each other from a range of two inches.

"You're not Jewish, Miller. You're Aryan. You're one of us. What did we ever do to you, for God's sake, what did we ever do to you?"

Miller jerked his arm free. "If you don't know yet, *Herr Doktor,* you'll never understand."

"*Ach,* you people of the younger generation, you're all the same. Why can you never do what you're told?"

"Because that's the way we are. Or at least it's the way *I* am."

The older man stared at him with narrowed eyes. "You're not stupid, Miller. But you're behaving as if you were. As if you were one of these ridiculous creatures constantly governed by what they call their conscience. But I'm beginning to doubt that. It's almost as if you had something personal in this matter."

Miller turned to go. "Perhaps I have," he said and walked away across the lobby.

8

MILLER FOUND the house, in a quiet residential street off the main road of the London borough of Wimbledon, without difficulty. Lord Russell himself answered the ring at the door, a man in his late sixties wearing a woolen cardigan and a bow tie. Miller introduced himself.

"I was in Bonn yesterday," he told the peer, "lunching with Mr. Anthony Cadbury. He gave me your name and a letter of introduction to you. I hoped I might have a talk with you, sir."

Lord Russell gazed down at him from the step with perplexity. "Cadbury? Anthony Cadbury? I can't seem to remember . . ."

"A British newspaper correspondent," said Miller. "He was in Germany just after the war. He covered the war-crimes trials. Josef Kramer and the others from Belsen. You recall those trials."

"Course I do. Course I do. Yes, Cadbury, yes, newspaper chap. I remember him now. Haven't seen him in years. Well, don't let's stand here. It's cold and I'm not as young as I was. Come in, come in."

Without waiting for an answer he turned and walked back down the hall. Miller followed, closing the door on the chill wind of the last day of 1963. He hung his coat on a hook in the hall at Lord Russell's bidding and followed him through into the back of the house, where a welcoming fire burned in the sitting-room grate.

Miller held out the letter from Cadbury. Lord Russell took it, read it quickly, and raised his eyebrows.

"Humph. Help in tracking down a Nazi? Is that what you came about?" He regarded Miller from under his eyebrows. Before the German could reply, Lord Russell went on, "Well, sit down, sit down. No good standing around."

They sat in flower-print-covered armchairs on either side of the fire.

"How come a young German reporter is chasing Nazis?" asked Lord Russell without preamble. Miller found his gruff directness disconcerting.

"I'd better explain from the beginning," said Miller.

"I think you better had," said the peer, leaning forward to knock out the dottle of his pipe on the side of the grate. While Miller talked he refilled the pipe, lit it, and was puffing contentedly away when the German had finished.

"I hope my English is good enough," said Miller at last, when no reaction seemed to be coming from the retired prosecutor.

Lord Russell seemed to wake from a private reverie. "Oh, yes, yes, better than my German after all these years. One forgets, you know."

"This Roschmann business—" began Miller.

"Yes, interesting, very interesting. And you want to try and find him. Why?"

The last question was shot at Miller and he found the old man's eyes gazing keenly from under the eyebrows.

"Well, I have my reasons," he said stiffly. "I believe the man should be found and brought to trial."

"Humph. Don't we all? The question is, will he be? Will he ever be?"

Miller played it straight back. "If I can find him, he will be. You can take my word on that."

The British peer seemed unimpressed. Little smoke signals shot out of the pipe as he puffed, rising in perfect series toward the ceiling. The pause lengthened.

"The point is, my Lord, do you remember him?"

Lord Russell seemed to start. "Remember him? Oh yes, I remember him. Or at least the name. Wish I could put a face to the name. An old man's memory fades

with the years, you know. And there were so many of
them in those days."

"Your Military Police picked him up on December
twentieth, nineteen forty-seven, in Graz," Miller told
him.

He took the two photocopies of Roschmann's picture
from his breast pocket and passed them over. Lord
Russell gazed at the two pictures, full-face and profile,
rose and began to pace the sitting room, lost in thought.

"Yes," he said at last, "I've got him. I can see him
now. Yes, the file was sent on from Graz Field Security
to me in Hanover a few days later. That would be where
Cadbury got his dispatch from. Our office in Hanover."

He paused and swung around on Miller. "You say
your man Tauber last saw him on April third, nineteen
forty-five, driving west through Magdeburg in a car
with several others?"

"That's what he said in his diary."

"Mmmm. Two and a half years before we got him.
And do you know where he was?"

"No," said Miller.

"In a British prisoner-of-war camp. Cheeky. All right,
young man, I'll fill in what I can."

The car carrying Eduard Roschmann and his colleagues from the SS passed through Magdeburg and
immediately turned south toward Bavaria and Austria.
They made it as far as Munich before the end of April,
then split up. Roschmann by this time was in the uniform of a corporal of the German Army, with papers
in his own name but describing him as an Army man.

South of Munich the American army columns were
sweeping through Bavaria, mainly concerned not with
the civilian population, which had become merely an
administrative headache, but with rumors that the Nazi
hierarchy intended to shut themselves up in a mountain
fortress in the Bavarian Alps around Hitler's home at
Berchtesgaden and fight it out to the last man. The
hundreds of unarmed, wandering German soldiers were

paid scant attention as Patton's columns rolled through Bavaria.

Traveling by night across country, hiding by day in woodsmen's huts and barns, Roschmann crossed the Austrian border that had not even existed since the annexation of 1938 and headed south and onward for Graz, his home town. In and around Graz he knew people on whom he could count to shelter him.

He passed around Vienna and had almost made it when he was challenged by a British patrol on May 6. Foolishly he tried to run for it. As he dived into the undergrowth by the roadside a hail of bullets cut through the brushwood, and one passed clean through his chest, piercing one lung. After a quick search in the darkness, the British Tommies passed on, leaving him wounded and undiscovered in a thicket. From here he crawled to a farmer's house half a mile away.

Still conscious, he told the farmer the name of a doctor he knew in Graz, and the man cycled through the night and the curfew to fetch him. For three months he was tended by his friends, first at the farmer's house, later at another house in Graz itself. When he was fit enough to walk, the war was three months over and Austria under four-power occupation. Graz was in the heart of the British Zone.

All German soldiers were required to do two years in a prisoner-of-war camp, and Roschmann, deeming it the safest place to be, gave himself up. For two years, from August 1945 to August 1947, while the hunt for the worst of the wanted SS murderers went on, Roschmann remained at ease in the camp. For on giving himself up he had used another name, that of a former friend who had gone into the Army and had been killed in North Africa.

There were so many tens of thousands of German soldiers wandering about without any identity papers at all that the name given by the man himself was accepted by the Allies as genuine. They had neither the time nor the facilities to conduct a probing examination of Army corporals. In the summer of 1947 Roschmann was released and felt it safe to leave the custody of the camp. He was wrong.

One of the survivors of Riga camp, a native of Vienna, had sworn his own vendetta against Roschmann. This man haunted the streets of Graz, waiting for Roschmann to return to his home, the parents he had left in 1939, and the wife he had married while on leave in 1943, Hella Roschmann. The old man roamed from the house of the parents to the house of the wife, waiting for the SS man to return.

After release, Roschmann remained in the countryside outside Graz, working as a laborer in the fields. Then, on December 20, 1947, he went home to spend Christmas with his family. The old man was waiting. He hid behind a pillar when he saw the tall, lanky figure with the pale blond hair and cold blue eyes approach his wife's house, glance around a few times, then knock and enter.

Within an hour, led by the former inmate of the camp at Riga, two hefty British sergeants of the Field Security Service, puzzled and skeptical, arrived at the house and knocked. After a quick search Roschmann was discovered under a bed. Had he tried to brazen it out, claiming mistaken identity, he might have made the sergeants believe the old man was wrong. But hiding under a bed was the giveaway. He was led off to be interviewed by Major Hardy of the FSS, who promptly had him locked up in a cell while a request went off to Berlin and the American index of the SS.

Confirmation arrived in forty-eight hours, and the balloon went up. Even while the request was in Potsdam, asking for Russian help in establishing the dossier on Riga, the Americans asked for Roschmann to be transferred to Munich on a temporary basis, to give evidence at Dachau, where the Americans were putting on trial other SS men who had been active in the complex of camps around Riga. The British agreed.

At six in the morning of January 8, 1948, Rosch-

mann, accompanied by a sergeant of the Royal Military
Police and another from Field Security, was put on a
train at Graz, bound for Salzburg and Munich.

Lord Russell paused in his pacing, crossed to the fireplace, and knocked out his pipe.

"Then what happened?" asked Miller.

"He escaped," said Lord Russell.

"He *what?*"

"He escaped. He jumped from the lavatory window
of the moving train, after complaining the prison diet
had given him diarrhea. By the time his two escorts had
smashed in the lavatory door, he was gone into the
snow. They never found him. A search was mounted,
of course, but he had gone, evidently through the snowdrifts, to make contact with one of the organizations
prepared to help ex-Nazis escape. Sixteen months later,
in May nineteen forty-nine, your new republic was
founded, and we handed over all our files to Bonn."

Miller finished writing and laid his notebook down.
"Where does one go from here?" he asked.

Lord Russell blew out his cheeks. "Well, now, your
own people, I suppose. You have Roschmann's life
from birth to the eighth of January nineteen forty-eight.
The rest is up to the German authorities."

"Which ones?" asked Miller, fearing what the answer
would be.

"As it concerns Riga, the Hamburg Attorney General's office, I suppose," said Lord Russell.

"I've been there."

"They didn't help much?"

"Not at all."

Lord Russell grinned. "Not surprised, not surprised.
Have you tried Ludwigsburg?"

"Yes. They were nice, but not very helpful. Against
the rules," said Miller.

"Well, that exhausts the official lines of inquiry.
There's only one other man. Have you ever heard of
Simon Wiesenthal?"

"Wiesenthal? Yes, vaguely. The name rings a bell, but I can't place it."

"He lives in Vienna. Jewish chap, came from Polish Galicia originally. Spent four years in a series of concentration camps, twelve in all. Decided to spend the rest of his days tracking down wanted Nazi criminals. No rough stuff, mind you. He just keeps collating all the information about them he can get; then, when he's convinced he has found one, usually living under a false name—not always—he informs the police. If they don't act, he gives a press conference and puts them in a spot. Needless to say, he's not terribly popular with officialdom in either Germany or Austria. He reckons they are not doing enough to bring known Nazi murderers to book, let alone chase the hidden ones. The former SS hate his guts and have tried to kill him a couple of times; the bureaucrats wish he would leave them alone, and a lot of other people think he's a great chap and help him where they can."

"Yes, the name rings a bell now. Wasn't he the man who found Adolf Eichmann?" asked Miller.

Lord Russell nodded. "He identified him as Ricardo Klement, living in Buenos Aires. The Israelis took over from there. He's also traced several hundred other Nazi criminals. If anything more is known about your Eduard Roschmann, he'll know it."

"Do you know him?" asked Miller.

Lord Russell nodded. "I'd better give you a letter. He gets a lot of visitors wanting information. An introduction would help."

He went to the writing desk, swiftly wrote a few lines on a sheet of headed notepaper, folded the sheet into an envelope, and sealed it.

"Good luck, you'll need it," he said as he showed Miller out.

The following morning Miller took the BEA flight back to Cologne, picked up his car, and set off on the two-day run through Stuttgart, Munich, Salzburg, and Linz to Vienna.

He spent the night at Munich, having made slow time along the snow-encrusted autobahns frequently narrowed down to one lane while a snowplow or sanding truck tried to cope with the steadily falling snow. The following day he set off early and would have made Vienna by lunchtime had it not been for the long delay at Bad Tolz just south of Munich.

The autobahn was passing through dense pine forests when a series of SLOW signs brought the traffic to a halt. A police car, blue light spinning a warning, was parked at the edge of the road, and two white-coated patrolmen were standing across the road, holding back the traffic. In the left-hand, northbound lane the procedure was the same. To the right and left of the autobahn a drive cut into the pine forests, and two soldiers in winter clothing, each with a battery-powered illuminated baton, stood at the entrance to each, waiting to summon something hidden in the forests across the road.

Miller fumed with impatience and finally wound down his window to call to one of the policemen. "What's the matter? What's the hold-up?"

The patrolman walked slowly over and grinned. "The Army," he said shortly. "They're on maneuvers. There's a column of tanks coming across in a minute."

Fifteen minutes later the first one appeared, a long gun barrel poking out of the pine trees, like a pachyderm scenting the air for danger; then with a rumble the flat armored bulk of the tank eased out of the trees and clattered down to the road.

Top Sergeant Ulrich Frank was a happy man. At the age of thirty he had already fulfilled his life's ambition, to command his own tank. He could remember to the day when his life's ambition had been born in him. It was January 1945 when, as a small boy in the city of Mannheim, he had been taken to the cinema. The screen during the newsreels was full of the spectacle of

Hasso von Manteuffel's King Tiger tanks rolling forward to engage the Americans and British.

He stared in awe at the muffled figures of the commanders, steel-helmeted and goggled, gazing forward out of the turrets. For Ulrich Frank, eleven years old, it was a turning point. When he left the cinema he had made a vow, that one day he would command his own tank.

It took him nineteen years, but he made it. On those winter maneuvers in the forests around Bad Tolz, Top Sergeant Ulrich Frank commanded his first tank, an American-built M-48 Patton.

It was his last maneuver with the Patton. Waiting for the troop back at camp was a row of shining, brand-new French AMX-13s with which the unit was being re-equipped. Faster, more heavily armed than the Patton, the AMX would become his in another week.

He glanced down at the black cross of the new German Army on the side of the turret, and the tank's personal name stenciled beneath it, and felt a touch of regret. Though he had commanded it for only six months, it would always be his first tank, his favorite. He had named it Drachenfels, the Dragon Rock, after the rock overlooking the Rhine where Martin Luther, translating the Bible into German, had seen the Devil and hurled his inkpot at him. After the re-equipment, he supposed the Patton would go for scrap.

With a last pause on the far side of the autobahn, the Patton and its crew breasted the rise and vanished into the forest.

Miller finally made it to Vienna in midafternoon of that day, January 3. Without checking into a hotel, he drove straight into the city center and asked his way to Rudolf Square.

He found number 7 easily enough and glanced at the list of tenants. Against the third floor was a card saying DOCUMENTATION CENTER. He mounted and knocked at the cream-painted wooden door. From behind it someone looked through the peephole before he heard the lock being drawn back. A pretty blond girl stood in the doorway.

"Please?"

"My name is Miller. Peter Miller. I would like to speak with Herr Wiesenthal. I have a letter of introduction."

He produced his letter and gave it to the girl. She looked uncertainly at it, smiled briefly, and asked him to wait.

Several minutes later she reappeared at the end of the corridor onto which the door gave access, and beckoned him. "Please come this way."

Miller closed the front door behind him and followed her down the passage, around a corner, and to the end of the apartment. On the right was an open door. As he entered, a man rose to greet him.

"Please come in," said Simon Wiesenthal.

He was bigger than Miller had expected, a burly man over six feet tall, wearing a thick tweed jacket, stooping as if permanently looking for a mislaid piece of paper. He held Lord Russell's letter in his hand.

The office was small to the point of being cramped. One wall was lined from end to end and ceiling to floor in shelves, each crammed with books. The wall facing was decorated with illuminated manuscripts and testimonials from a score of organizations of former victims of the SS. The back wall contained a long sofa, also stacked with books, and to the left of the door was a small window looking down on a courtyard. The desk stood away from the window, and Miller took the visitor's chair in front of it. The Nazi-hunter of Vienna seated himself behind it and reread Lord Russell's letter.

"My friend Lord Russell tells me you are trying to hunt down a former SS killer," he began without preamble.

"Yes, that's true."

"May I have his name?"

"Roschmann. Captain Eduard Roschmann."

Simon Wiesenthal raised his eyebrows and exhaled his breath in a whistle.

"You've heard of him?" asked Miller.

"The Butcher of Riga? One of my top fifty wanted men," said Wiesenthal. "May I ask why you are interested in him?"

Miller began to explain briefly.

"I think you'd better start at the beginning," said Wiesenthal. "What's all this about a diary?"

With the man in Ludwigsburg, Cadbury, and Lord Russell, this made the fourth time Miller had had to relate the story. Each time it grew a little longer as another period had been added to his knowledge of Roschmann's life story. He began again and went through until he had described the help given by Lord Russell.

"What I have to know now," he ended, "is where did he go when he jumped from the train?"

Simeon Wiesenthal was gazing out into the court of the apartment house, watching the snowflakes dropping down the narrow shaft to the ground three floors below.

"Have you got the diary?" he asked at length. Miller reached down, took it out of his briefcase, and laid it on the desk.

Wiesenthal eyed it appreciatively. "Fascinating," he said. He looked up and smiled. "All right, I accept the story," he said.

Miller raised his eyebrows. "Was there any doubt?"

Simon Wiesenthal eyed him keenly. "There is always a little doubt, Herr Miller," he said. "Yours is a very strange story. I still cannot follow your motive for wanting to track Roschmann down."

Miller shrugged. "I'm a reporter. It's a good story."

"But not one you will ever sell to the press, I fear. And hardly worth your own money. Are you sure there's nothing personal in this?"

Miller ducked the question. "You're the second person who has suggested that. Hoffmann suggested the same at *Komet*. Why should there be? I'm only twenty-nine years old. All this was before my time."

"Of course." Wiesenthal glanced at his watch and rose. "It is five o'clock, and I like to get home to my wife these winter evenings. Would you let me read the diary over the weekend?"

"Yes, of course," said Miller.

"Good. Then please come back on Monday morning, and I will fill in what I know of the Roschmann story."

Miller arrived on Monday at ten and found Simon Wiesenthal attacking a pile of letters. He looked up as the German reporter came in and gestured him to a seat. There was silence for a while as the Nazi-hunter carefully snipped the edges off the sides of his envelopes before sliding the contents out.

"I collect the stamps," he said, "so I don't like to damage the envelopes." He worked away for a few more minutes. "I read the diary last night at home. Remarkable document."

"Were you surprised?" asked Miller.

"Surprised? No, not by the contents. We all went through much the same sort of thing. With variations, of course. But so precise. Tauber would have made a perfect witness. He noticed everything, even the small details. And noted them—at the time. That is very important to get a conviction before German or Austrian courts. And now he's dead."

Miller considered for a while. He looked up. "Herr Wiesenthal, so far as I know, you're the first Jew I have ever really had a long talk with, who went through all that. One thing Tauber said in his diary surprised me: he said there was no such thing as collective guilt. But we Germans have been told for twenty years that we are all guilty. Do you believe that?"

"No," said the Nazi-hunter flatly. "Tauber was right."

"How can you say that, if we killed fourteen million people?"

"Because you, personally, were not there. You did not kill anyone. As Tauber said, the tragedy is that the specific murderers have not been brought to justice."

"Then who," asked Miller, "really did kill those people?"

Simon Wiesenthal regarded him intently. "Do you know about the various branches of the SS? About the sections within the SS that really were responsible for killing those millions?" he asked.

"No."

"Then I'd better tell you. You've heard about the Reich Economic Administration Main Office, charged with exploiting the victims before they died?"

"Yes, I read something about it."

"Its job was in a sense the middle section of the operation," said Herr Wiesenthal. "That left the business of identifying the victims among the rest of the population, rounding them up, transporting them, and, when the economic exploitation was over, finishing them off. This was the task of the RSHA, the Reich Security Main Office, which actually killed the fourteen million already mentioned. The rather odd use of the word 'Security' in the title of this office stems from the quaint Nazi idea that the victims posed a threat to the Reich, which had to be made secure against them. Also in the functions of the RSHA were the tasks of rounding up, interrogating, and incarcerating in concentration camps other enemies of the Reich like Communists, Social Democrats, Liberals, editors, reporters, and priests who spoke out too inconveniently, resistance fighters in the occupied countries, and later Army officers like Field Marshal Erwin Rommel and Admiral Wilhelm Canaris, both murdered for suspicion of harboring anti-Hitler sentiments.

"The RSHA was divided into six departments, each called an Amt. Amt One was for administration and personnel; Amt Two was equipment and finance. Amt Three was the dreaded Security Service and Security Police, headed by Reinhardt Heydrich, assassinated in Prague in 1942, and later by Ernst Kaltenbrunner, executed by the Allies. Theirs were the teams who devised the tortures used to make suspects talk, both inside Germany and in the occupied countries.

"Amt Four was the Gestapo, headed by Heinrich Müller (still missing), whose Jewish Section, department B4, was headed by Adolf Eichmann, executed by the Israelis in Jerusalem after being kidnaped from Argentina. Amt Five was the Criminal Police, and Amt Six the Foreign Intelligence Service.

"The two successive heads of Amt Three, Heydrich and Kaltenbrunner, were also the over-all chiefs of the whole RSHA, and throughout the reigns of both men the head of Amt One was their deputy. He is Lieutenant General of the SS Bruno Streckenbach, who today has a well-paid job with a department store in Hamburg and lives in Vogelweide.

"If one is going to specify guilt, therefore, most of it rests on these two departments of the SS, and the numbers involved are thousands, not the millions who make up contemporary Germany. The theory of the collective guilt of sixty million Germans, including millions of small children, women, old-age pensioners, soldiers, sailors, and airmen, who had nothing to do with the holocaust, was originally conceived by the Allies, but has since suited the former members of the SS extremely well. The theory is the best ally they have, for they realize, as few Germans seem to do, that so long as the collective-guilt theory remains unquestioned nobody will start to look for specific murderers—at least, look hard enough. The specific murderers of the SS therefore hide even today behind the collective-guilt theory."

Miller digested what he had been told. Somehow the very size of the figures involved baffled him. It was not possible to consider fourteen million people as each and every one an individual. It was easier to think of one man, dead on a stretcher under the rain in a Hamburg street.

"The reason Tauber apparently had for killing himself," Miller asked, "do you believe it?"

Herr Wiesenthal studied a beautiful pair of African stamps on one of the envelopes. "I believe he was right in thinking no one would believe that he saw Roschmann on the steps of the Opera. If that's what he believed, then he was right."

"But he didn't even go to the police," said Miller.

Simon Wiesenthal snipped the edge off another envelope and scanned the letter inside. After a pause he replied, "No. Technically he should have. I don't think it would have done any good. Not in Hamburg, at any rate."

"What's wrong with Hamburg?"

"You went to the State Attorney General's office there?" asked Wiesenthal mildly.

"Yes, I did. They weren't terribly helpful."

Wiesenthal looked up. "I'm afraid the Attorney General's department in Hamburg has a certain reputation in this office," he said. "Take for example the man mentioned by me just now, SS General Bruno Streckenbach. Remember the name?"

"Of course," said Miller. "What about him?"

For answer Simon Wiesenthal riffled through a pile of papers on his desk, abstracted one, and gazed at it. "Here he is," he said. "Known to West German justice as Document 141 JS 747/61. Want to hear about him?"

"I have time," said Miller.

"Right. Here goes. Before the war Gestapo chief in Hamburg. Climbed rapidly from then on to a top position in the SD and SP, the Security Service and Security Police sections of the RSHA. In 1939 he led an extermination squad in Nazi-occupied Poland. At the end of 1940 he was head of the SD and SP sections of the SS for the whole of Poland, the so-called General Government, sitting in Cracow. Thousands were exterminated by SD and SP units in Poland during that period, mainly through Operation AB.

"At the start of 1941 he came back to Berlin, promoted to Chief of Personnel for the SD. That was Amt Three of the RSHA. His chief was Reinhardt Heydrich, and he became his deputy. Just before the invasion of Russia he helped to organize the extermination squads that went in behind the Army. As head of staffing he picked the personnel himself, for they were all from the SD branch.

"Then he was promoted again, this time to head of personnel for the entire six branches of the RSHA, and remained deputy chief of the RSHA under first Heydrich, who was killed by Czech partisans in Prague in 1942—that was the killing that led to the reprisal at Lidice—and then under Ernst Kaltenbrunner. As such he had all-embracing responsibility for the choice of personnel of the roving extermination squads and the fixed SD units throughout the Nazi-occupied eastern territories until the end of the war."

Miller looked stunned. "They haven't arrested him?" he asked.

"Who?"

"The police of Hamburg, of course."

For answer Simon Wiesenthal rummaged in a drawer and produced another sheet of paper. He folded it neatly down the center from top to bottom and laid it in front of Miller so that only the left side of the sheet was facing upward.

"Do you recognize those names?" he asked.

Miller scanned the list of ten names with a frown. "Of course. I've been a police reporter in Hamburg for years. These are all senior police officers of the Hamburg force. Why?"

"Spread the paper out," said Wiesenthal.

Miller did so. Fully expanded, the sheet read:

Name	Nazi Pty. No.	SS No.	Rank	Promotion Date
A.	———	455,336	Capt.	1.3.43
B.	5,451,195	429,339	1st Lt.	9.11.42
C.	———	353,004	1st Lt.	1.11.41
D.	7,039,564	421,176	Capt.	21.6.44
E.	———	421,445	1st Lt.	9.11.42
F.	7,040,308	174,902	Major	21.6.44
G.	———	426,553	Capt.	1.9.42
H.	3,138,798	311,870	Capt.	30.1.42
I.	1,867,976	424,361	1st Lt.	20.4.44
J.	5,063,331	309,825	Major	9.11.43

Miller looked up. "Christ," he said.

"Now do you begin to understand why a lieutenant general of the SS is walking around Hamburg today? They can't arrest him. He was their commanding officer once."

Miller looked at the list in disbelief. "That must have been what Brandt meant about inquiries into the former SS not being very popular in the Hamburg police."

"Probably," said Wiesenthal. "Nor is the Attorney General's office the most energetic in Germany. There's one lawyer on the staff at least who is trying, but certain interested parties have tried to have him dismissed several times."

The pretty secretary poked her head around the door. "Tea or coffee?" she asked.

After a lunchtime break, Miller returned to the office. Simon Wiesenthal had in front of him a number of sheets spread out, extracts from his own Roschmann file. Miller settled himself in front of the desk, got out his notebook, and waited.

Simon Wiesenthal began to relate the Roschmann story from January 8, 1948.

It had been agreed between the British and American authorities that after Roschmann had testified at Dachau he would be moved on to the British Zone of Germany, probably Hanover, to await his own trial and almost certain hanging. Even while in prison in Graz he had begun to plan his escape.

He had made contact with a Nazi escape organization working in Austria called the Six-Point Star, nothing to do with the Jewish symbol of the six-pointed star, but so called because the Nazi organization had its tentacles in six major Austrian cities, mainly in the British Zone.

At 6:00 a.m. on the eighth, Roschmann was awakened and taken to the train waiting at Graz station. Once he was in the compartment, an argument started between the Military Police sergeant, who wanted to keep the handcuffs on Roschmann throughout the journey, and the Field Security sergeant, who suggested taking them off.

Roschmann influenced the argument by claiming that he had diarrhea from the prison diet and wished to go to the lavatory. He was taken, the handcuffs were removed, and one of the sergeants waited outside the door until he had finished. As the train chugged through the snowbound landscape Roschmann made three requests to go to the lavatory. Apparently during this time he prized the window in the lavatory open, so that it slid easily on its runners.

Roschmann knew he had to get out before the Americans took him over at Salzburg for the last run by car to their own prison at Munich, but station after station went by, and still the train was going too fast. It stopped at Hallein, and one of the sergeants went to buy some food on the platform. Roschmann again said he wanted to go to the lavatory. It was the more easygoing FSS sergeant who accompanied him, warning him not to use the toilet while the train was stationary. As the train moved slowly out of Hallein, Roschmann jumped from the window into the snowdrifts. It was ten minutes before the sergeants beat down the door, and by then the train was running fast down the mountains toward Salzburg.

He staggered through the snow as far as a peasant's cottage and took refuge there. The following day he crossed the border from Upper Austria into Salzburg province and contacted the Six-Point Star organization. It brought him to a brick factory, where he passed as a laborer, while contact was made with the Odessa for a passage to the south and Italy.

At that time the Odessa was in close contact with the recruitment section of the French Foreign Legion, into which scores of former SS soldiers had fled. Four days after contact was made, a car with French number plates was waiting outside the town of Ostermieting and took on board Roschmann and five other Nazi escapers. The Foreign Legion driver, equipped with papers that enabled the car to cross borders without being searched, brought the six SS men over the Italian border to Merano and was paid in cash by the Odessa representative there, a hefty sum per head of his passengers.

From Merano, Roschmann was taken down to an Italian displaced-persons camp at Rimini. Here, in the camp hospital, he had the five toes of his right foot amputated, for they were rotten with frostbite he had picked up while wandering through the snow after escaping from the train. Since then he had worn an orthopedic shoe.

His wife in Graz got a letter from him in October 1948 from the camp at Rimini. For the first time he used the new name he had been given, Fritz Bernd Wegener.

Shortly afterward he was transferred to the Franciscan Monastery in Rome, and when his papers were finalized he set sail from the harbor at Naples for Buenos Aires. Throughout his stay at the monastery in the Via Sicilia he had been among scores of comrades of the SS and the Nazi Party and under the personal supervision of Bishop Alois Hudal, who ensured that they lacked nothing.

In the Argentinian capital he was received by the Odessa and lodged with a German family called Vidmar in the Calle Hipolito Irigoyen. Here he lived for months in a furnished room. Early in 1949 he was advanced the sum of 50,000 American dollars out of the Bormann funds in Switzerland and went into business as an exporter of South American hardwood timber to Western Europe. The firm was called Stemmler and Wegener, for his false papers from Rome firmly established him as Fritz Bernd Wegener, born in the South Tirol province of Italy.

He also engaged a German girl as his secretary, Irmtraud Sigrid Müller, and in early 1955 he married her, despite his wife Hella, still living in Graz. But Roschmann was becoming nervous. In July 1952 Eva Perón, the wife of the dictator of Argentina and the power behind the throne, had died of cancer. Three years later the writing was on the wall for the Perón regime, and Roschmann spotted it. If Perón fell, much of the protection accorded by him to ex-Nazis might be removed by his successors. With his new wife, Roschmann left for Egypt.

He spent three months there in the summer of 1955 and came to West Germany in the autumn. Nobody would have known a thing but for the anger of a woman betrayed. His first wife, Hella Roschmann, wrote to him from Graz, care of the Vidmar family in Buenos Aires, during that summer. The Vidmars, having no forwarding address for their former lodger, opened the letter and replied to the wife in Graz, telling her that he had gone back to Germany but had married his secretary.

Furious, the wife informed the police of his new name, Fritz Wegener, and asked for a warrant for his his arrest on a charge of bigamy.

Immediately a lookout was posted for a man calling himself Fritz Bernd Wegener in West Germany.

"Did they get him?" asked Miller.

Wiesenthal looked up and shook his head. "No, he disappeared again. Almost certainly under a new set of false papers, and almost certainly in Germany. You see, that's why I believe Tauber could have seen him. It all fits with the known facts."

"Where's the first wife, Hella Roschmann?" asked Miller.

"She still lives in Graz."

"Is it worth contacting her?"

Wiesenthal shook his head. "I doubt it. The moment she learned of the bigamy, she spilled the beans to the police as far as she knew anything. There's nothing more she knows beyond what she has said, for she now hates him like poison and wants him arrested. Needless to say, after being 'blown,' Roschmann is not likely to reveal his whereabouts to her again. Or his new name. For him it must have been quite an emergency when his identity of Wegener was exposed. He must have acquired his new papers in a devil of a hurry."

"Who would have got them for him?" asked Miller.

"The Odessa, certainly."

"Just what is the Odessa? You've mentioned it several times in the course of the Roschmann story."

"You've never heard of them?" asked Wiesenthal.

"No. Not until now."

Simon Wiesenthal glanced at his watch. "You'd better come back in the morning. I'll tell you all about them."

9

PETER MILLER returned to Simon Wiesenthal's office the following morning.

"You promised to tell me about the Odessa," he said. "I remembered something overnight that I forgot to tell you yesterday."

He recounted the incident of Dr. Schmidt, who had accosted him at the Dreesen Hotel and warned him off the Roschmann inquiry.

Wiesenthal pursed his lips and nodded. "You're up against them, all right," he said. "It's most unusual for them to take such a step as to warn a reporter in that way, particularly at such an early stage. I wonder what Roschmann is up to that could be so important."

Then for two hours the Nazi-hunter told Miller about the Odessa, from its start as an organization for getting wanted SS criminals to a place of safety to its development into an all-embracing free-masonry among those who had once worn the black-and-silver collars, their aiders and abettors.

When the Allies stormed into Germany in 1945 and found the concentration camps with their hideous contents, they not unnaturally rounded on the German people to demand who had carried out the atrocities. The answer was "The SS"—but the members of the SS were nowhere to be found.

Where had they gone? They had either gone underground inside Germany and Austria, or fled abroad. In both cases their disappearance was no spur-of-the-moment flight. What the Allies failed to realize until much later was that each had meticulously prepared his disappearance beforehand.

It casts an interesting light on the so-called patriotism of the SS that, starting at the top with Heinrich Himmler, each tried to save his own skin at the expense of the suffering German people. As early as November 1944 Heinrich Himmler tried to negotiate his own safe conduct through the offices of Count Bernadotte of the Swedish Red Cross. The Allies refused to consider letting him off the hook. While the Nazis and the SS screamed at the German people to fight on until the wonder weapons waiting around the corner were delivered, they themselves prepared for their departure to a comfortable exile elsewhere. They at least knew there were no wonder weapons, and that the destruction of the Reich and, if Hitler had anything to do with it, of the entire German nation, was inevitable.

On the Eastern Front the German Army was bullied into battle against the Russians to take unbelievable casualties, not to produce victory but to produce a delay while the SS finalized its escape plans. Behind the Army stood the SS, shooting and hanging some of the Army men who took a step backward after already taking more punishment than military flesh and blood is usually expected to stand. Thousands of officers and men of the Wehrmacht died in SS nooses in this way.

Just before the final collapse, delayed six months after the chiefs of the SS knew defeat was inevitable, the leaders of the SS disappeared. From one end of the country to the other they quit their posts, changed into civilian clothes, stuffed their beautifully (and officially) forged personal papers into their pockets, and vanished into the chaos that was Germany in May 1945. They left the old men of the Home Guard to meet the British and the Americans at the gates of the concentration camps, the exhausted Wehrmacht to go into prisoner-of-war camps, and the women and children to live or die under Allied rule in the coming bitter winter of 1945.

Those who knew they were too well known to escape detection for long fled abroad. This was where the Odessa came in. Formed just before the end of the war, it was designed to get wanted SS men out of Germany to safety. Already it had established close and friendly links with Juan Perón's Argentina, which had issued seven thousand Argentinian passports "in blank" so that the refugee merely had to fill in a false name and his own photograph, get it stamped by the ever-ready Argentine consul, and board ship for Buenos Aires or the Middle East.

Thousands of SS murderers poured southward through Austria and into the South Tirol province of Italy. They were shuttled from safe house to safe house along the route, thence mainly to the Italian port of Genoa or farther south to Rimini and Rome. A number of organizations, some supposed to be concerned with charitable work among the truly dispossessed, took it upon themselves, for reasons best known to themselves, to decide, on some evidence of their own imagining, that the SS refugees were being overharshly persecuted by the Allies.

Among the chief Scarlet Pimpernels of Rome who spirited thousands away to safety was Bishop Alois Hudal, the German Bishop in Rome. The main hiding-out station for the SS killers was the enormous Franciscan monastery in Rome, where they were hidden and boarded until papers could be arranged, along with a passage to South America. In some cases the SS men traveled on Red Cross travel documents, issued through the intervention of the Vatican, and in many cases the charitable organization Caritas paid for their tickets.

This was the first task of Odessa, and it was largely successful. Just how many thousands of SS murderers who would have died for their crimes, had they been caught by the Allies, passed to safety will never be known, but they were well over eighty per cent of those meriting the death sentence.

Having established itself comfortably on the proceeds of mass murder, transferred from the Swiss banks, the Odessa sat back and watched the deterioration of relations between the Allies of 1945. The early ideas of the quick establishment of a Fourth Reich were discarded in the course of time by the leaders of the Odessa in South America as impractical, but with the establishment in May 1949 of a new Republic of West Germany, those leaders of the Odessa set themselves five new tasks.

The first was the reinfiltration of former members of the SS into every facet of life in the new Germany. Throughout the late forties and fifties former members of the SS slipped into the civil service at every level, back into lawyers' offices, onto judges' benches, into the police forces, local government, and doctors' surgeries. From these positions, however lowly, they were able to protect each other from investigation and arrest, advance each other's interests, and generally ensure that investigation and prosecution of former comrades— they called each other *Kamerad*—went forward as slowly as possible, if at all.

The second task was to infiltrate the mechanisms of political power. Avoiding the high levels, former Nazis slipped into the grassroots organization of the ruling party at ward and constituency level. Again, there was no law to forbid a former member of the SS from joining a political party. It may be a coincidence, but unlikely, that no politician with a known record of calling for increased vigor in the investigation and prosecution of SS crimes has ever been elected in the CDU or the CSU, either at federal level or at the equally important level of the very powerful provincial parliaments. One politician expressed it with crisp simplicity: "It's a question of election mathematics. Six million dead Jews don't vote. Five million former Nazis can and do, at every election."

The main aim of both these programs was simple. It was and is to slow down, if not to stop, the investigation and prosecution of former members of the SS. In this the Odessa had one other great ally. This was the secret knowledge in the minds of hundreds of thousands that they had either helped in what was done, albeit in a

small way, or had known at the time what was going on
and had remained silent. Years later, established and
respected in their communities and professions, they
could hardly relish the idea of energetic investigation
into past events, let alone the mention of their names
in a faraway courtroom where an SS man was on trial.

The third task the Odessa set itself in postwar Germany was to reinfiltrate business, commerce, and industry. To this end certain former SS men were established
in businesses of their own in the early fifties, bankrolled
by funds from the Zurich deposits. Any reasonably well-
administered concern founded with plenty of liquidity
in the early fifties could take full advantage of the stag-
gering economic miracle of the fifties and sixties, to
become in turn a large and flourishing business. The
point of this was to use funds out of the profits from
these businesses to influence press coverage of the SS
crimes through advertising revenue, to assist financially
the crop of SS-oriented propaganda sheets that have
come and gone in postwar Germany, to keep alive some
of the ultra-Right Wing publishing houses, and to provide jobs for former *Kameraden* fallen on hard times.

The fourth task was and still is to provide the best
possible legal defense for any SS man forced to stand
trial. In every case where an SS murderer has come
before a court, his defense lawyers have been among
the most brilliant and the most expensive in Germany.
But no one ever asks who pays them when their client
is a poor man, and they would be the first to deny that
they do their work for SS men for free.

The fifth task is propaganda. This takes many forms,
from encouraging the dissemination of Right Wing
pamphlets to lobbying for a final ratification of the
Statute of Limitations, under whose terms an end would
be put to all culpability in law of the SS. Efforts are
made to assure the Germans of today that the death figures of the Jews, Russians, Poles, and others were but
a tiny fraction of those quoted by the Allies—100,000
dead Jews is the usual figure mentioned—and to point

out that the Cold War between the West and the Soviet Union in some way proves Hitler to have been right.

But the mainstay of the Odessa propaganda is to persuade the seventy million Germans of today—and with a large degree of success—that the SS men were in fact patriotic soldiers like the Wehrmacht and that solidarity among former comrades must be upheld. This is the weirdest ploy of them all.

During the war the Wehrmacht kept its distance from the SS, which it regarded with repugnance, while the SS treated the Wehrmacht with contempt. At the end, millions of young Wehrmacht men were hurled into death or captivity at Russian hands, from which only a small proportion returned, and this so that the SS men could live prosperously elsewhere. Thousands more were executed by the SS, including five thousand in the aftermath of the July 1944 plot against Adolf Hitler, in which fewer than fifty men were implicated.

How former members of the German Army, Navy, and Air Force can conceivably regard ex-SS men as meriting from them the salutation *Kamerad,* let alone their solidarity and protection from prosecution, is a mystery. Yet herein lies the real success of the Odessa.

By and large the Odessa has succeeded in its tasks of stultifying West German efforts to hunt down and bring to trial the SS murderers. It has succeeded by virtue of its own ruthlessness, occasionally against its own kind if they seem likely to make full confessions to the authorities, of Allied mistakes between 1945 and 1949, of the Cold War, and of the usual German cowardice when faced with a moral problem, in stark contrast to German courage when faced with a military task or a technical issue like the reconstruction of postwar Germany.

When Simon Wiesenthal had finished, Miller laid down the pencil with which he had made copious notes and sat back.

"I hadn't the faintest idea," he said.

"Very few Germans have," conceded Wiesenthal. "In

fact, very few people know much about the Odessa at all. The word is hardly ever mentioned in Germany and just as certain members of the American underworld will stoutly deny the existence of the Mafia, so any former member of the SS will deny the existence of the Odessa. To be perfectly frank, the term is not used as much nowadays as formerly. The new word is 'the Comradeship,' just as the Mafia in America is called *Cosa Nostra*. But what's in a name? The Odessa is still there, and will be while there is an SS criminal to protect."

"And you think these are the men I'm up against?" asked Miller.

"I'm sure of it. The warning you were given in Bad Godesberg could not have come from anyone else. Do be careful; these men can be dangerous."

Miller's mind was on something else. "When Roschmann disappeared, after his wife had given away his new name, you said he would need a fresh passport?"

"Certainly."

"Why the passport particularly?"

Simon Wiesenthal leaned back in his chair and nodded. "I can understand why you are puzzled. Let me explain. After the war in Germany, and here in Austria, there were tens of thousands wandering about with no identification papers. Some had genuinely lost them; others had thrown them away for good reason.

"To obtain new ones, it would normally be necessary to produce a birth certificate. But millions had fled from the former German territories overrun by the Russians. Who was to say if a man was, or was not, born in a small village in East Prussia, now miles behind the Iron Curtain? In other cases the buildings in which the certificates were stored had been destroyed by bombing.

"So the process was very simple. All one needed were two witnesses to swear that one was who one said, and a fresh personal ID card was issued. In the case of prisoners-of-war, they often had no papers either. On their release from camp, the British and American camp authorities would sign a release paper to the effect that Corporal Johann Schumann was certified as released from prisoner camp. These papers were then taken by the soldier to the civilian authorities, who issued an ID card in the same name. But often the man had only told the Allies his name was Johann Schumann. It could have been something else. No one checked. And so he got a new identity.

"That was all right in the immediate aftermath of the war, which was when most of the SS criminals were getting their new identities. But what happens to a man who is blown wide open in 1955, as was Roschmann? He can't go to the authorities and say he lost his papers during the war. They would be bound to ask how he had got by during the ten-year interim period. So he needs a passport."

"I understand so far," said Miller. "But why a passport? Why not a driving license or an ID card?"

"Because shortly after the founding of the republic the German authorities realized there must be hundreds or thousands wandering about under false names. There was a need for one document that was so well researched that it could act as the yardstick for all the others. They hit on the passport. Before you get a passport in Germany, you have to produce a birth certificate, several references, and a host of other documentation. These are thoroughly checked before the passport is issued.

"By contrast, once you have a passport, you can get anything else on the strength of it. Such is bureaucracy. The production of the passport convinces the civil servant that, since previous bureaucrats must have checked out the passport-holder thoroughly, no further checking is necessary. With a new passport, Roschmann could quickly build up the rest of the identity—driving license, bank accounts, credit cards. The passport is the Open Sesame to every other piece of necessary documentation in present-day Germany."

"Where would the passport come from?"

"From the Odessa. They must have a forger somewhere who can turn them out," Wiesenthal said.

Miller thought for a while. "If one could find the passport-forger, one might find the man who could identify Roschmann today?" he suggested.

Wiesenthal shrugged. "One might. But it would be a long shot. And to do that one would have to penetrate the Odessa. Only an ex-SS man could do that."

"Then where do I go from here?" said Miller.

"I should think your best bet would be to try and contact some of the survivors of Riga. I don't know whether they would be able to help you further, but they'd certainly be willing. We are all trying to find Roschmann. Look." He flicked open the diary on his desk. "There's reference here to a certain Olli Adler from Munich, who was in Roschmann's company during the war. It may be she survived and came home to Munich."

Miller nodded. "If she did, where would she register?"

"At the Jewish Community Center. It still exists. It contains the archives of the Jewish community of Munich—since the war, that is. Everything else was destroyed. I'd try there."

"Do you have the address?"

Simon Wiesenthal checked through an address book. "Reichenbachstrasse, number twenty-seven, Munich," he said. "I suppose you want the diary of Salomon Tauber back?"

"Yes, I'm afraid I do."

"Too bad. I'd like to have kept it. A remarkable diary."

He rose and escorted Miller to the front door. "Good luck," he said, "and let me know how you get on."

Miller had dinner that evening in the House of the Golden Dragon, which had been in business as a beer house and restaurant in the Steindelgasse without a break from 1566, and thought over the advice. He had little hope of finding more than a handful of survivors of

Riga still in Germany or Austria, and even less hope that any might help him track Roschmann beyond November 1955. But it was a hope, a last hope.

He left the next morning for the drive back to Munich.

10

MILLER DROVE into Munich at midmorning of January 9 and found 27 Reichenbachstrasse from a map of Munich bought at a newspaper kiosk in the outskirts. Parking down the road, he surveyed the Jewish Community Center before entering. It was a flat-fronted five-story building. The façade of the ground floor was of uncovered stone blocks; above this the façade was of gray cement over brick. The fifth and top floor was marked by a row of mansard windows set in the red tiled roof. At ground level there was a double door of glass panels at the extreme left end of the building.

The building contained a kosher restaurant, the only one in Munich, on the ground floor, the leisure rooms of the old people's home on the one above. The third floor contained the administration and records department, and the upper two housed the guest rooms and sleeping quarters of the inmates of the old people's home. At the back was a synagogue.

He went up to the third floor and presented himself at the inquiry desk. While he waited he glanced around the room. There were rows of books, all new, for the original library had long since been burned by the Nazis. Between the library shelves were portraits of some of the leaders of the Jewish community, stretching back hundreds of years, teachers and rabbis, gazing out of their frames above luxuriant beards, like the figures of the prophets he had seen in his Scripture textbooks at school. Some wore phylacteries bound to their foreheads, and all were hatted.

There was a rack of newspapers, some in German, others in Hebrew. He presumed the latter were flown in from Israel. A short dark man was scanning the front page of one of these.

"Can I help you?"

He looked around to the inquiry desk to find it now occupied by a dark-eyed woman in her mid-forties. There was a strand of hair falling over her eyes, which she nervously brushed back into place several times a minute.

Miller made his request: any trace of Olli Adler, who might have reported back to Munich after the war?

"Where would she have returned from?" asked the woman.

"From Magdeburg. Before that, Stutthof. Before that, from Riga."

"Oh dear, Riga," said the woman. "I don't think we have anyone on the lists who came back here from Riga. They all disappeared, you know. But I'll look."

She went into a back room, and Miller could see her going steadily through an index of names. It was not a big index. She returned after five minutes.

"I'm sorry. Nobody of that name reported back here after the war. It is a common name. But there is nobody listed."

Miller nodded. "I see. That looks like it, then. Sorry to have troubled you."

"You might try the International Tracing Service," said the woman. "It's really their job to find people who are missing. They have lists from all over Germany, whereas we only have the lists of those originating in Munich who came back."

"Where is the Tracing Service?" asked Miller.

"It's at Arolsen-in-Waldeck. That's just outside Hanover, Lower Saxony. It's run by the Red Cross, really."

Miller thought for a minute. "Would there be anybody else left in Munich who was at Riga? The man I'm really trying to find is the former commandant."

There was silence in the room. Miller sensed the man by the newspaper rack turn around to look at him. The woman seemed subdued.

"It might be possible there are a few left who were at Riga and now live in Munich. Before the war there were twenty-five thousand Jews in Munich. About a tenth came back. Now we are about five thousand again, half of them children born since nineteen forty-five. I might find someone who was at Riga. But I'd have to go through the whole list of survivors. The camps they were in are marked against the names. Could you come back tomorrow?"

Miller thought for a moment, debating whether to give up and go home. The chase was getting pointless.

"Yes," he said at length. "I'll come back tomorrow. Thank you."

He was back in the street, reaching for his car keys, when he felt a step behind him.

"Excuse me," said a voice. He turned. The man behind him was the one who had been reading the newspapers.

"You are inquiring about Riga?" asked the man. "About the commandant of Riga? Would that be Captain Roschmann?"

"Yes, it would," said Miller. "Why?"

"I was at Riga," said the man. "I knew Roschmann. Perhaps I can help you."

The man was short and wiry, somewhere in his mid-forties, with button-bright brown eyes and the rumpled air of a damp sparrow.

"My name is Mordecai," he said. "But people call me Motti. Shall we have coffee and talk?"

They adjourned to a nearby coffee shop. Miller, melted slightly by his companion's chirpy manner, explained his hunt so far, from the back streets of Altona to the Community Center of Munich.

The man listened quietly, nodding occasionally. "Mmmm. Quite a pilgrimage. Why should you, a German, want to track down Roschmann?"

"Does it matter? I've been asked that so many times I'm getting tired of it. What's so strange about a German being angry at what was done years ago?"

Motti shrugged. "Nothing," he said. "It's unusual for a man to go to such lengths, that's all. About Roschmann's disappearance in nineteen fifty-five. You really think this new passport must have been provided by the Odessa?"

"That's what I've been told," replied Miller. "And it seems the only way to find the man who forged it would be to penetrate the Odessa."

Motti considered the young German in front of him for some time. "What hotel are you staying at?" he asked at length.

Miller told him he had not checked into any hotel yet, as it was still early afternoon. But there was one he knew, that he had stayed in before. At Motti's request he went to the coffee-shop telephone and called the hotel for a room.

When he got back to the table, Motti had gone. There was a note under the coffee cup. It said: "Whether you get a room there or not, be in the residents' lounge at eight tonight."

Miller paid for the coffees and left.

The same afternoon, in his lawyer's office, the Werwolf read once again the written report that had come in from his colleague in Bonn, the man who had introduced himself to Miller a week earlier as Dr. Schmidt.

The Werwolf had had the report already for five days, but his natural caution had caused him to wait and reconsider before taking direct action.

The last words his superior, General Glücks, had spoken to him in Madrid in late November virtually robbed him of any freedom of action, but like most deskbound men he found comfort in delaying the inevitable. "A permanent solution" had been the way his orders were expressed, and he knew what that meant. Nor did the phraseology of "Dr. Schmidt" leave him any more room for maneuver.

"A stubborn young man, truculent and headstrong,

probably obstinate, and with an undercurrent of genuine and personal hatred in him for the *Kamerad* in question, Eduard Roschmann, for which no explanation seems to exist. Unlikely to listen to reason, even in the face of personal threat. . . ."

The Werwolf read the doctor's summing up again and sighed. He reached for the phone and asked his secretary, Hilda, for an outside line. When he had it he dialed a number in Düsseldorf.

After several rings it was answered, and a voice said simply, "Yes."

"There's a call for Herr Mackensen," said the Werwolf.

The voice from the other end said simply, "Who wants him?"

Instead of answering the question directly, the Werwolf gave the first part of the identification code. "Who was greater than Frederick the Great?"

The voice from the other end replied, "Barbarossa." There was a pause, then: "This is Mackensen," said the voice.

"Werwolf," replied the chief of the Odessa in West Germany. "The holiday is over, I'm afraid. There is work to be done. Get over here by tomorrow morning."

"When?" replied Mackensen.

"Be here at ten," said the Werwolf. "Tell my secretary your name is Keller. I will ensure you have an appointment in that name."

He put the phone down. In Düsseldorf, Mackensen rose and went into the bathroom of his flat to shower and shave. He was a big, powerful man, a former sergeant of the Das Reich division of the SS, who had learned his killing when hanging French hostages in Tulle and Limoges, back in 1944.

After the war he had driven a truck for the Odessa, running human cargoes south through Germany and Austria into the South Tirol province of Italy. In 1946, stopped by an overly suspicious American patrol, he had slain all four occupants of the jeep, two of them with his bare hands. From then on, he too was on the run.

Employed later as a bodyguard for senior men of the Odessa, he had been saddled with the nickname "Mack the Knife," although, oddly, he never used a knife, preferring the strength of his butcher's hands to strangle or break the necks of his "assignments."

Rising in the esteem of his superiors, he had become in the mid-fifties the executioner of the Odessa, the man who could be relied on to cope quietly and discreetly with those who came too close to the top men of the organization, or those from within who elected to squeal on their comrades. By January 1964 he had fulfilled twelve assignments of this kind.

The call came on the dot of eight. It was taken by the reception clerk, who put his head around the corner of the residents' lounge, where Miller sat watching television.

He recognized the voice on the end of the phone.

"Herr Miller? It's me, Motti. I think I may be able to help you. Rather, some friends may be able to. Would you like to meet them?"

"I'll meet anybody who can help me," said Miller, intrigued by the maneuvers.

"Good," said Motti. "Leave your hotel and turn left down Schillerstrasse. Two blocks down on the same side is a cake and coffee shop called Lindemann. Meet me in there."

"When? Now?" asked Miller.

"Yes. Now. I would come to the hotel, but I'm with my friends here. Come right away."

He hung up. Miller took his coat and walked out through the doors. He turned left and headed down the pavement. Half a block from the hotel something hard was jabbed into his ribs from behind, and a car slid up to the curb.

"Get into the back seat, Herr Miller," said a voice in his ear.

The door beside him swung open and with a last dig in the ribs from the man behind, Miller ducked his head and entered the car. The driver was up front; the back seat contained another man, who slid over to make room for him. He felt the man behind him enter the car also; then the door was slammed and the car slid from the curb.

Miller's heart was thumping. He glanced at the three men in the car with him, but recognized none of them.

The man to his right, who had opened the door for him to enter, spoke first. "I am going to bind your eyes," he said simply, producing a sort of black sock. "We would not want you to see where you are going."

Miller felt the sock being pulled over his head until it covered his nose. He remembered the cold blue eyes of the man in the Dreesen Hotel and recalled what the man in Vienna had told him. "Do be careful, these men can be dangerous." Then he remembered Motti and wondered how one of them could have been reading a Hebrew newspaper in the Jewish Community Center.

The car drove for twenty-five minutes, then slowed and stopped. He heard some gates being opened; the car surged forward again and stopped finally. He was eased out of the back seat, and with a man on each side he was helped across a courtyard. For a moment he felt the cold night air on his face; then he was back inside again. A door slammed behind him, and he was led down some steps into what seemed to be a cellar. But the air was warm and the chair into which he was lowered was well upholstered.

He heard a voice say, "Take off the bandage," and the sock over his head was removed. He blinked as his eyes got used to the light.

The room he was in was evidently below ground, for it had no windows. But an air extractor hummed high on one wall. It was well decorated and comfortable, evidently a form of committee room, for there was a long table with eight chairs ranged close to the far wall. The remainder of the room was an open space, fringed by five armchairs. In the center were a circular carpet and a coffee table.

Motti was standing, smiling quietly, almost apologetically, beside the committee table. The two men who had brought Miller, both well built and in early middle age, were perched on the arms of the armchairs to his left and right. Directly opposite him, across the coffee table, was a fourth man. Miller supposed the car driver had remained upstairs to lock up.

The fourth man was evidently in command. He sat at ease in his chair while his three lieutenants stood or perched around him. Miller judged him to be about sixty, lean and bony, with a hollow-cheeked, hook-nosed face. The eyes worried Miller. They were brown and deep-sunk into the sockets, but bright and piercing, the eyes of a fanatic. It was he who spoke.

"Welcome, Herr Miller. I must apologize for the strange way in which you were brought to my home. The reason for it was that if you decide you wish to turn down my proposal to you, you can be returned to your hotel and will never see any of us again.

"My friend here"—he gestured to Motti—"informs me that for reasons of your own you are hunting a certain Eduard Roschmann. And that to get closer to him you might be prepared to attempt to penetrate the Odessa. To do that you would need help. A lot of help. However, it might suit our interests to have you inside the Odessa. Therefore we might be prepared to help you. Do you follow me?"

Miller stared at him in astonishment. "Let me get one thing straight," he said at length. "Are you telling me you are not from the Odessa?"

The man raised his eyebrows. "Good heavens, you *have* got hold of the wrong end of the stick." He leaned forward and drew back the sleeve of his left wrist. On the forearm was tattooed a number in blue ink.

"Auschwitz," said the man. He pointed to the two men at Miller's sides. "Buchenwald and Dachau." He pointed at Motti. "Riga and Treblinka." He replaced his sleeve.

"Herr Miller, there are some who think the murderers of our people should be brought to trial. We do not agree. Just after the war I was talking with a British officer, and he told me something that has guided my life ever since. He said to me, 'If they had murdered six million of my people, I too would build a monument of skulls. Not the skulls of those who died in the concentration camps, but of those who put them there.' Simple logic, Herr Miller, but persuasive. I and my group are men who decided to stay on inside Germany after nineteen forty-five with one object, and one only, in mind. Revenge, revenge pure and simple. We don't arrest them, Herr Miller; we kill them like the swine they are. My name is Leon."

Leon interrogated Miller for four hours before he was satisfied of the reporter's genuineness. Like others before him, he was puzzled about the motivation but had to concede it was possible Miller's reason was the one he gave, indignation at what had been done by the SS during the war. When he had finished, Leon leaned back in his chair and surveyed the younger man for a long time.

"Are you aware how risky it is to try and penetrate the Odessa, Herr Miller?" he asked.

"I can guess," said Miller. "For one thing, I'm too young."

Leon shook his head. "There's no question of your trying to persuade former SS men you are one of them under your own name. For one thing, they have lists of former SS men, and Peter Miller is not on that list. For another, you have to age ten years at least. It can be done, but it involves a complete new identity, and a real identity. The identity of a man who really existed and was in the SS. That alone means a lot of research by us, and the expenditure of a lot of time and trouble."

"Do you think you can find such a man?" asked Miller.

Leon shrugged. "It would have to be a man whose death cannot be checked out," he said. "Before the Odessa accepts a man at all, it checks him out. You have to pass all the tests. That also means you will have to live for five or six weeks with a genuine former SS man who can teach you the folklore, the technical terms, the phraseology, the behavior patterns. Fortunately, we know such a man."

Miller was amazed. "Why should he do such a thing?"

"The man I have in mind is an odd character. He is a genuine SS captain who sincerely regretted what was done. He experienced remorse. Later he was inside the Odessa and passed information about wanted Nazis to the authorities. He would be doing so still, but he was 'shopped' and was lucky to escape with his life. Now he lives under a new name, in a house outside Bayreuth."

"What else would I have to learn?"

"Everything about your new identity. Where he was born, his date of birth, how he got into the SS, where he trained, where he served, his unit, his commanding officer, his entire history from the end of the war onward. You will also have to be vouched for by a guarantor. That will not be easy. A lot of time and trouble will have to be spent on you, Herr Miller. Once you are in, there will be no pulling back."

"What's in this for you?" asked Miller suspiciously.

Leon rose and paced the carpet. "Revenge," he said simply. "Like you, we want Roschmann. But we want more. The worst of the SS killers are living under false names. We want those names. That's what's in it for us."

"That sounds like information that might be of use to Israeli Intelligence," said Miller.

Leon glanced at him shrewdly. "It is," he said shortly. "We occasionally cooperate with them, though they do not own us."

"Have you ever tried to get your own men inside the Odessa?" asked Miller.

Leon nodded. "Twice," he said.

"What happened?"

"The first was found floating in a canal without his fingernails. The second disappeared without trace. Do you still want to go ahead?"

Miller ignored the question. "If your methods are so efficient, why were they caught?"

"They were both Jewish," said Leon shortly. "We tried to get the tattoos from the concentration camps off their arms, but they left scars. Besides, they were both circumcised. That was why, when Motti reported to me on a genuine Aryan German with a grudge against the SS, I was interested. By the way, are you circumcised?"

"Does it matter?" inquired Miller.

"Of course. If a man is circumcised it does not prove he's a Jew. Many Germans are circumcised as well. But if he is not, it more or less proves he is not a Jew."

"I'm not," said Miller shortly.

Leon nodded with pensive satisfaction. "Certainly that improves your chances. That just leaves the problem of changing your appearance and training you to play a very dangerous role."

It was long past midnight. Leon looked at his watch. "Have you eaten?" he asked Miller. The reporter shook his head.

"Motti, I think a little food for our guest."

Motti grinned and nodded. He disappeared through the door of the cellar room and went up into the house.

"You'll have to spend the night here," said Leon to Miller. "We'll bring a bedroll down to you. Don't try to leave, please. The door has three locks, and all will be shut on the far side. Give me your car keys, and I'll have your car brought around here. It will be better out of sight for the next few weeks. Your hotel bill will be paid and your luggage brought around here too. In the morning you will write letters to your mother and girl friend, explaining that you will be out of contact for several weeks, maybe months. Understood?"

Miller nodded and handed over his car keys. Leon gave them to one of the other two men, who quietly left.

"In the morning we will drive you to Bayreuth, and you will meet our SS officer. His name is Alfred Oster. He's the man you will live with. I will arrange it. Meanwhile, excuse me. I have to start looking for a new name and identity for you."

He rose and left. Motti soon returned with a plate of food and half a dozen blankets, leaving Miller to his cold chicken, potato salad, and growing doubts.

Far away to the north, in the General Hospital of Bremen, a ward orderly was patrolling his ward in the small hours of the morning. Around a bed at the end of the room was a tall screen that shut off the occupant from the rest of the ward.

The orderly, a middle-aged man called Hartstein, peered around the screen at the man in the bed. He lay very still. Above his head a dim light was burning through the night. The orderly entered the screened-off area and checked the patient's pulse. There was none.

He looked down at the ravaged face of the cancer victim, and something the man had said in delirium three days earlier caused the orderly to lift the left arm of the dead man out of the blankets. Inside the man's armpit was tattooed a number. It was the dead man's blood group, a sure sign that the patient had once been in the SS. The reason for the tattoo was that SS men were regarded in the Reich as more valuable than ordinary soldiers, so when wounded they always had first chance at any available plasma. Hence the tattooed blood group.

Orderly Hartstein covered the dead man's face and glanced into the drawer of the bedside table. He drew out the driving license that had been placed there along with the other personal possessions when the man had been brought in after collapsing in the street. It showed a man of about thirty-nine, date of birth June 18, 1925, and the name of Rolf Gunther Kolb.

The orderly slipped the driving license into the pocket of his white coat and went off to report the death to the night physician.

11

PETER MILLER wrote his letters to his mother and Sigi under the watchful eye of Motti, and finished by midmorning. His luggage had arrived from his hotel, the bill had been paid, and shortly before noon the two of them, accompanied by the driver of the previous night, set off for Bayreuth.

With a reporter's instinct he flashed a glance at the number plates of the blue Opel which had taken the place of the Mercedes that had been used the night before. Motti, at his side, noticed the glance and smiled. "Don't bother," he said. "It's a hired car, taken out in a false name."

"Well, it's nice to know one is among professionals," said Miller.

Motti shrugged. "We have to be. It's one way of staying alive when you're up against the Odessa."

The garage had two berths, and Miller noticed his own Jaguar in the second slot. Half-melted snow from the previous night had formed puddles beneath the wheels, and the sleek black bodywork gleamed in the electric light.

Once he was in the back of the Opel, the black sock was again pulled over his head, and he was pushed down to the floor as the car eased out of the garage, through the gates of the courtyard, and into the street. Motti kept the blindfold on him until they were well clear of Munich and heading north up autobahn E 6 toward Nuremberg and Bayreuth.

When Miller finally lost the blindfold he could see there had been another heavy snowfall overnight. The rolling forested countryside where Bavaria ran into Franconia was clothed in a coat of unmarked white, giving a chunky roundness to the leafless trees of the beech forests along the road. The driver was slow and careful, the windshield wipers working constantly to clear the glass of the fluttering flakes and the mush thrown up by the trucks they passed.

They lunched at a wayside inn at Ingolstadt, pressed on to skirt Nuremberg to the east, and were at Bayreuth an hour later.

Set in the heart of one of the most beautiful areas of Germany, nicknamed the Bavarian Switzerland, the small country town of Bayreuth has only one claim to fame, its annual festival of Wagner music. In earlier years the town had been proud to play host to almost the whole Nazi hierarchy as it descended in the wake of that keen Wagnerite, Adolf Hitler.

In January it is a quiet little town, blanketed by snow, the holly wreaths only a few days since removed from the door knockers of its neat and well-kept houses. They found the cottage of Alfred Oster on a quiet byroad a mile beyond the town, and there was not another car on the road as the small party went to the front door.

The former SS officer was expecting them—a big bluff man with blue eyes and a fuzz of ginger hair spreading over the top of his cranium. Despite the season, he had the healthy tan of men who spend their time in the mountains among wind and sun and unpolluted air.

Motti made the introductions and handed Oster a letter from Leon. The Bavarian read it and nodded, glancing sharply at Miller.

"Well, we can always try," he said. "How long can I have him?"

"We don't know yet," said Motti. "Obviously, until he's ready. Also, it will be necessary to devise a new identity for him. We will let you know."

A few minutes later he was gone.

Oster led Miller into the living room and drew the curtains against the descending dusk before he put on the light. "So, you want to be able to pass as a former SS man, do you?" he asked.

Miller nodded. "That's right," he said.

Oster turned on him. "Well, we'll start by getting a few basic facts rights. I don't know where you did your military service, but I suspect it was in that ill-disciplined, democratic, wet-nursing shambles that calls itself the new German Army. Here's the first fact. The new German Army would have lasted exactly ten seconds against any crack regiment of the British, Americans, or Russians during the last war. Whereas the Waffen SS, man for man, could beat the shit out of five times their own number of Allies of the last war.

"Here's the second fact. The Waffen SS were the toughest, best-trained, best-disciplined, smartest, fittest bunch of soldiers who ever went into battle in the history of this planet. Whatever they did can't change that. So SMARTEN UP, MILLER. So long as you are in this house, this is the procedure.

"When I walk into a room, you leap to attention. And I mean LEAP. When I walk past, you smack those heels together and remain at attention until I am five paces beyond you. When I say something to you that needs an answer, you reply, 'JAWOHL, *Herr Haupsturm-führer.*' And when I give an order or an instruction, you reply, 'ZU BEFEHL, *Herr Haupsturmführer.*' Is that clearly understood?"

Miller nodded in amazement.

"Heels together," roared Oster. "I want to hear the leather smack. All right, since we may not have much time, we'll press on, starting from tonight. Before supper we'll tackle the ranks, from private up to full general. You'll learn the titles, mode of address, and collar insignia of every SS rank that ever existed. Then we'll go on to the various types of uniform used, the differing branches of the SS and their different insignia, the occasions when gala uniform, full-dress uniform, walking-out uniform, combat uniform, and fatigue dress would be worn.

"After that I'll put you through the full political-ideological course that you would have undergone at Dachau SS training camp, had you been there. Then you'll learn the marching songs, the drinking songs, and the various unit songs.

"I can get you as far as your departure from training camp for your first posting. After that Leon has to tell me what unit you were supposed to have joined, where you worked, under which commanding officer, what happened to you at the end of the war, how you have passed your time since nineteen forty-five. However, the first part of the training will take from two to three weeks, and that's a crash course.

"By the way, don't think this is a joke. If you are once inside the Odessa, knowing who the top men are, and you make one slip in procedure, you'll end up in a canal. Believe me, I'm no milksop, and after betraying the Odessa, even I'm running scared of them. That's why I live here under a new name."

For the first time since he had set off on his one-man hunt for Eduard Roschmann, Miller wondered if he had not already gone too far.

Mackensen reported to the Werwolf on the dot of ten. When the door to the room where Hilda worked was safely shut, the Werwolf seated the executioner in the client's chair opposite the desk and lit a cigar.

"There is a certain person, a newspaper reporter, inquiring about the whereabouts and the new identity of one of our comrades," he began. The liquidator nodded with understanding. Several times before, he had heard one of his briefings begin in the same way.

"In the normal course of events," resumed the Werwolf, "we would be prepared to let the matter rest, either convinced that the reporter would eventually give up for lack of progress, or because the man being sought was not worth our while making an expensive and hazardous effort to save."

"But this time—it's different?" asked Mackensen softly.

The Werwolf nodded with what might have been genuine regret. "Yes. Through bad luck, ours on the grounds of the inconvenience involved, his on the grounds it will cost him his life, the reporter has unwittingly touched a nerve. For one thing, the man he is seeking is a man of vital, absolutely vital, importance to us and to our long-term planning. For another, the reporter himself seems to be an odd character—intelligent, tenacious, ingenious, and, I regret, wholly committed to extracting a sort of personal vengeance from the *Kamerad*."

"Any motive?" asked Mackensen.

The Werwolf's puzzlement showed in his frown. He tapped ash from his cigar before replying. "We cannot understand why there should be, but evidently there is," he murmured. "The man he is looking for undoubtedly has a background which might excite certain dislike among such as the Jews and their friends. He commanded a ghetto in Ostland. Some, mainly foreigners, refuse to acknowledge our justification for what was done there. The odd thing about this reporter is that he is neither foreign, nor Jewish, nor a noted Left-Winger, nor one of the well-known type of conscience-cowboy—who, in any case, seldom get beyond giving vent to a lot of piss and wind, but nothing else.

"But this man seems different. He's a young German, Aryan, son of a war hero, nothing in his background to suggest such a depth of hatred toward us, nor such an obsession with tracing one of our *Kameraden*, despite a firm and clear warning to stay off the matter. It gives me some regret to order his death. Yet he leaves me no alternative. That is what I must do!"

"Kill him?" asked Mack the Knife.

"Kill him," confirmed the Werwolf.

"Whereabouts?"

"Not known." The Werwolf flicked two sheets of foolscap paper covered with typed words across the desk. "That's the man. Peter Miller, reporter and investigator. He was last seen at the Dreesen Hotel in Bad Godesberg. He's certainly gone from there by now, but it's a good enough place to start. The other place would be his own flat, where his girl friend lives with him. You should represent yourself as a man sent by one of the major magazines for which he normally works. That way, the girl will probably talk to you, if she knows his whereabouts. He drives a noticeable car. You'll find all the details of it there."

"I'll need money," said Mackensen. The Werwolf had foreseen the request. He pushed a wad of 10,000 marks across the desk.

"And the orders?" asked the killer.

"Locate and liquidate," said the Werwolf.

It was January 13 before the news of the death in Bremen five days earlier of Rolf Günther Kolb reached Leon in Munich. The letter from his North German representative enclosed the dead man's driving license.

Leon checked the man's rank and number on his list of former SS men, checked the West German wanted list and saw that Kolb was not on it, spent some time gazing at the face on the driving license, and made his decision.

He called Motti, who was on duty at the telephone exchange where he worked, and the assistant reported to Leon when he had finished his shift.

Leon laid Kolb's driving license in front of him. "That's the man we need," he said. "He was a staff sergeant at the age of nineteen, promoted just before the war ended. They must have been very short of material. Kolb's face and Miller's don't match, even if Miller were made up, which is a procedure I don't like anyway. It's too easy to see through at close range. But the height and build fit with Miller. So we'll need a new photograph. That can wait. To cover the photograph we'll need a replica of the stamp of the Bremen Police Traffic Department. See to it."

When Motti had gone, Leon dialed a number in Bremen and gave further orders.

"All right," said Alfred Oster to his pupil. "Now we'll start on the songs. You've heard of the 'Horst Wessel Song'?"

"Of course," said Miller. "It was the Nazi marching song."

Oster hummed the first few bars.

"Oh, yes, I remember hearing it now. But I can't remember the words."

"Okay," said Oster. "I'll have to teach you about a dozen songs. Just in case you are asked. But this is the most important. You may even have to join in a singsong, when you're among the *Kameraden*. Not to know it would be a death sentence. Now, after me:

> "The flags are high,
> The ranks are tightly closed. . . ."

It was January 18.

Mackensen sat and sipped a cocktail in the bar of the Schweizerhof Hotel in Munich and considered the source of his puzzlement: Miller, the reporter whose personal details and face were etched in his mind. A thorough man, Mackensen had even contacted the main Jaguar agents for West Germany and obtained from them a series of publicity photographs of the Jaguar XK 150 sports car, so he knew what he was looking for. His trouble was he could not find it.

The trail at Bad Godesberg had quickly led to Cologne Airport and the answer that Miller had flown to London and back within thirty-six hours over the New Year. Then he and his car had vanished.

Inquiries at his flat led to a conversation with his handsome and cheerful girl friend, but she had only been able to produce a letter postmarked from Munich, saying Miller would be staying there for a while.

For a week Munich had proved a dead lead. Mackensen had checked every hotel, public and private parking space, servicing garage, and gas station. There was nothing. The man he sought had disappeared as if from the face of the earth.

Finishing his drink, Mackensen eased himself off his bar stool and went to the telephone to report to the Werwolf. Although he did not know it, he stood just twelve hundred meters from the black Jaguar with the yellow stripe, which was parked inside the walled court-yard of the antique shop and private house where Leon lived and ran his small and fanatic organization.

In Bremen General Hospital a man in a white coat strolled into the registrar's office. He had a stethoscope around his neck, almost the badge of office of a new intern.

"I need a look at the medical file on one of our patients, Rolf Günther Kolb," he told the receptionist and filing clerk.

The woman did not recognize the intern, but that meant nothing. There were scores of them working in the hospital. She ran through the names in the filing cabinet, spotted the name of Kolb on the edge of a dossier, and handed it to the intern. The phone rang, and she went to answer it.

The intern sat on one of the chairs and flicked through the dossier. It revealed simply that Kolb had collapsed in the street and been brought in by ambulance. An examination had diagnosed cancer of the intestine in a virulent and terminal form. A decision had later been made not to operate. The patient had been put on a series of drugs, without any hope, and later on pain-killers. The last sheet in the file stated simply: "Patient deceased on the night of January 8/9. Cause of death: carcinoma of the main intestine. No next of kin. Corpus delicti delivered to the municipal mortuary January 10." It was signed by the doctor in charge of the case.

The new intern eased the last sheet out of the file and inserted in its place one of his own. The new sheet read: "Despite serious condition of patient on admission, the carcinoma responded to a treatment of drugs and went into recession. Patient was adjudged fit to be transferred on January 16. At his own request he was transferred by ambulance for convalescence at the Arcadia Clinic, Delmenhorst." The signature was an illegible scrawl.

The intern gave the file back to the filing clerk, thanked her with a smile, and left. It was January 22.

Three days later Leon received a piece of information that filled in the last section of his private jigsaw puzzle. A clerk in a ticket agency in North Germany sent a message to say a certain bakery proprietor in Bremerhaven had just confirmed bookings on a winter cruise for himself and his wife. The pair would be touring the Caribbean for four weeks, leaving from Bremerhaven on Sunday, February 16. Leon knew the man to have been a colonel of the SS during the war, and a member of Odessa after it. He ordered Motti to go out and buy a book of instructions on the art of making bread.

The Werwolf was puzzled. For nearly three weeks he had had his representatives in the major cities of Germany on the lookout for a man called Miller and a black Jaguar sports car. The apartment and the garage in Hamburg had been watched, a visit had been made to a middle-aged woman in Osdorf, who had said only that she did not know where her son was. Several telephone calls had been made to a girl called Sigi, purporting to come from the editor of a major picture magazine with an urgent offer of very lucrative employment for Miller, but the girl had also said she did not know where her boy friend was.

Inquiries had been made at his bank in Hamburg, but he had not cashed any checks since November. In short, he had disappeared. It was already January 30, and against his wishes the Werwolf felt obliged to make a phone call. With regret, he lifted his receiver and made it.

Far away, high in the mountains, a man put down his telephone half an hour later and swore softly and violently for several minutes. It was a Friday evening, and he had barely returned to his weekend manor for two days of rest when the call had come through.

He walked to the window of his elegantly appointed study and looked out. The light from the window spread out across the thick carpet of snow on the lawn, the glow reaching away toward the pine trees that covered most of the estate.

He had always wanted to live like this, in a fine house on a private estate in the mountains, since, as a boy, he had seen during the Christmas vacation the houses of the rich in the mountains around Graz. Now he had it, and he liked it.

It was better than the house of a brewery worker, where he had been brought up; better than the house in Riga where he had lived for four years; better than a furnished room in Buenos Aires or a hotel room in Cairo. It was what he had always wanted.

The call he had taken disturbed him. He had told the caller there had been no one spotted near his house, no one hanging around his factory, no one asking questions about him. But he was worried. Miller? Who the hell was Miller? The assurances on the phone that the reporter would be taken care of only partly assuaged his anxiety. The seriousness with which the caller and his colleagues took the threat posed by Miller was indicated by the decision to send him a personal bodyguard the next day to act as his chauffeur and stay with him until further notice.

He drew the curtains of the study, shutting out the winter landscape. The thickly padded door cut out all sounds from the rest of the house. The only sound in the room was the crackle of fresh pine logs on the hearth; the cheerful glow was framed by the great cast-iron fireplace with its wrought vine leaves and curlicues, one of the fittings he had kept when he bought and modernized the house.

The door opened, and his wife put her head around it. "Dinner's ready," she said.

"Coming, dear," said Eduard Roschmann.

The next morning, Saturday, Oster and Miller were disturbed by the arrival of a party from Munich. The car contained Leon and Motti, the driver, and another man, who carried a black bag.

When they reached the living room, Leon said to the man with the bag, "You'd better get up to the bathroom and set out your gear."

The man nodded and went upstairs. The driver had remained in the car.

Leon sat at the table and bade Oster and Miller take their places. Motti remained by the door, a camera with flash attachment in his hand.

Leon passed a driving license over to Miller. Where the photograph had been was a blank.

"That's who you are going to become," said Leon. "Rolf Günther Kolb, born June eighteenth, nineteen twenty-five. That would make you nineteen at the end of the war, almost twenty. And thirty-eight years old now. You were born and brought up in Bremen. You joined the Hitler Youth at the age of ten in nineteen thirty-five, and the SS in January nineteen forty-four, at the age of eighteen. Both your parents are dead. They were killed in an air raid on Bremen docks in nineteen forty-four."

Miller stared down at the driving license in his hand.

"What about his career in the SS?" asked Oster. "At the moment we have reached something of a dead end."

"How is he so far?" asked Leon. Miller might as well not have been there.

"Pretty good," said Oster. "I gave him a two-hour interrogation yesterday, and he could pass. Until someone starts asking for specific details of his career. Then he knows nothing."

Leon nodded for a while, examining some papers he had taken from his attaché case. "We don't know Kolb's career with the SS," he said. "It couldn't have been very much, for he's not on any wanted list and nobody has ever heard of him. In a way that's just as well, for the chances are the Odessa has never heard of him either. But the disadvantage is, he has no reason to seek refuge and help from the Odessa unless he is being pursued. So we have invented a career for him. Here it is."

He passed the sheets over to Oster, who began to read them. When he had finished he nodded. "It's good," he said. "It all fits with the known facts. And it would be enough to get him arrested if he were exposed."

Leon grunted with satisfaction. "That's what you have to teach him. Incidentally, we have found a guarantor for him. A man in Bremerhaven, a former SS colonel, is going on a sea cruise, starting February sixteenth. The man is now a bakery-owner. When Miller presents himself, which must be after February sixteenth, he will have a letter from this man assuring the Odessa that Kolb, his employee, is genuinely a former SS man and genuinely in trouble. By that time the bakery-owner will be on the high seas and uncontactable. By the way"—he turned to Miller and passed a book across to him—"you can learn baking as well. That's what you have been since nineteen forty-five, an employee in a bakery."

He did not mention that the bakery-owner would be away for only four weeks, and that after that period Miller's life would hang by a thread.

"Now my friend the barber is going to change your appearance somewhat," Leon told Miller. "After that we'll take a new photograph for the driving license."

In the upstairs bathroom the barber gave Miller one of the shortest haircuts he had ever had. The white scalp gleamed through the stubble almost up to the crown of the head by the time he had finished. The rumpled look was gone, but he also looked older. A ruler-straight parting was scraped in the short hair on the left side of his head. His eyebrows were plucked until they almost ceased to exist.

"Bare eyebrows don't make a man look older," said the barber chattily, "but they make the age almost unguessable within six or seven years. There's one last thing. You're to grow a mustache. Just a thin one, the same width as your mouth. It adds years, you know. Can you do that in a couple of weeks?"

Miller knew the way the hair on his upper lip grew. "Sure," he said. He gazed back at his reflection. He looked in his mid-thirties. The mustache would add another four years.

When they got downstairs, Miller was stood up against a white sheet held in place by Oster and Leon, and Motti took several full-face portraits of him.

"That'll do," he said. "I'll have the driving license ready within three days."

The party left, and Oster turned to Miller. "Right, Kolb," he said, having ceased to refer to him in any other way, "you were trained at Dachau SS training camp, seconded to Flossenburg concentration camp in July nineteen forty-four, and in April nineteen forty-five you commanded the squad that executed Admiral Canaris, chief of the Abwehr. You also helped kill a number of the other Army officers suspected by the Gestapo of complicity in the July nineteen forty-four assassination attempt on Hitler. No wonder the authorities today would like to arrest you. Admiral Canaris and his men were not Jews. There can be no overlooking that. Okay, let's get down to work, Staff Sergeant."

The weekly meeting of the Mossad had reached its end when General Amit raised his hand and said, "There is just one last matter, though I regard it as of comparatively low importance. Leon has reported from Munich that he has for some time had under training a young German, an Aryan, who for some reason of his own has a grudge against the SS and is being prepared to infiltrate the Odessa."

"His motive?" asked one of the men suspiciously.

General Amit shrugged. "For reasons of his own, he wants to track down a certain former SS captain called Roschmann."

The head of the Office for the Countries of Persecution, a former Polish Jew, jerked his head up. "Eduard Roschmann? The Butcher of Riga?"

"That's the man."

"Phew. If we could get him, that would be an old score settled."

General Amit shook his head. "I have told you before, Israel is no longer in the retribution business. My orders are absolute. Even if the man finds Roschmann, there is to be no assassination. After the Ben-Gal affair, it would be the last straw on Erhard's back. The trouble now is that if any ex-Nazi dies in Germany, Israeli agents get the blame."

"So what about this young German?" asked the Shabak chief.

"I want to try and use him to identify any more Nazi scientists who might be sent out to Cairo this year. For us that is priority number one. I propose to send an agent over to Germany, simply to put the young man under surveillance. Just a watching brief, nothing else."

"You have such a man in mind?"

"Yes," said General Amit. "He's a good man, reliable. He'll just follow the German and watch him, reporting back to me personally. He can pass for a German. He's a Yekke. He came from Karlsruhe."

"What about Leon?" asked someone else. "Will he not try to settle accounts on his own?"

"Leon will do what he's told," said General Amit angrily. "There is to be no more settling of accounts."

In Bayreuth that morning, Miller was being given another grilling by Alfred Oster.

"Okay," said Oster, "what are the words engraved on the hilt of the SS dagger?"

"Blood and Honor," replied Miller.

"Right. When is the dagger presented to an SS man?"

"At his passing-out parade from training camp," replied Miller.

"Right. Repeat to me the oath of loyalty to the person of Adolf Hitler."

Miller repeated it, word for word.

"Repeat the blood oath of the SS."

Miller complied.

"What is the significance of the emblem of the death's head?"

Miller closed his eyes and repeated what he had been taught. "The sign of the death's head comes from distant Germanic mythology. It is the emblem of those groups of Teuton warriors who have sworn fealty to their leader and to each other, unto the grave and even beyond, into Valhalla. Hence the skull and the crossbones, signifying the world beyond the grave."

"Right. Were all SS men automatically members of death's-head units?"

"No."

Oster rose and stretched. "Not bad," he said. "I can't think of anything else you might be asked in general terms. Now let's get on to specifics. This is what you would have to know about Flossenburg Concentration Camp, your first and only posting. . . ."

The man who sat in the window seat of the Olympic Airways flight from Athens to Munich seemed quiet and withdrawn.

The German businessman next to him, after several attempts at conversation, took the hint and confined himself to reading *Playboy* magazine. His next-door neighbor stared out of the window as the Aegean Sea passed beneath them and the airliner left the sunny spring of the eastern Mediterranean for the snow-capped peaks of the Dolomites and the Bavarian Alps.

The businessman had at least elicited one thing from his companion. The traveler in the window seat was undoubtedly a German, his grasp of the language fluent and familiar, his knowledge of the country without fault. The businessman, traveling home after a sales mission to the Greek capital, had not the slightest doubt that he was seated next to a fellow countryman.

He could hardly have been more wrong. The man next to him had been born in Germany thirty-three years earlier, under the name of Josef Kaplan, son of a Jewish tailor, in Karlsruhe. He had been three years old when Hitler came to power, seven when his parents had been taken away in a black van; he had been hidden in an attic for another three years until, at the age of ten in 1940, he too had been discovered and taken away in a van. His early teens had been spent using the resilience and the ingenuity of youth to survive in a series of concentration camps until in 1945, with the suspicion of a wild animal burning in his eyes, he had snatched a thing called a Hershey bar from the out-stretched hand of a man who spoke to him in a foreign language through his nose, and had run away to eat the offering in a corner of the camp before it could be taken away from him.

Two years later, weighing a few pounds more, aged seventeen and hungry as a rat, with that creature's sus-picion and mistrust of everyone and everything, he had come on a ship called the *President Warfield,* alias the *Exodus,* to a new shore many miles from Karlsruhe and Dachau.

The passing years had mellowed him, matured him, taught him many things, given him a wife and two children, a commission in the army, but never eliminated the hatred he felt for the country to which he was traveling that day. He had agreed to go, to swallow his feelings, to take up again, as he had done twice before in the previous ten years, the façade of amiability and bonhomie that was necessary to effect his transformation back into a German.

The other requirements had been provided by the service: the passport in his breast pocket, the letters, cards, and documentary paraphernalia of a citizen of a West European country, the underclothes, shoes, suits, and luggage of a German commercial traveler in textiles.

As the heavy and freezing clouds of Europe engulfed the plane he reconsidered his mission, fed into him in days and nights of briefing by the quiet-spoken colonel on the kibbutz that produced so little fruit and so many Israeli agents. To follow a man, to keep an eye on him, a young German four years his junior, while that man

sought to do what several had tried and failed to do—
infiltrate the Odessa. To observe him and measure his
success, to note the persons he contacted and was passed
on to, check on his findings, ascertain if the German
could trace the recruiter of the new wave of German
scientists headed for Egypt to work on the rockets.
Never to expose himself, never to take matters into his
own hands. Then to report back with the sum total of
what the young German had found out before he was
"blown" or discovered, one of which was bound to
happen.

He would do it; he did not have to enjoy doing it,
that was not part of the requirement. Fortunately, no
one required that he like becoming a German again.
No one asked him to enjoy mixing with Germans, speaking their language, smiling and joking with them. Had
this been asked, he would have refused the job. For he
hated them all, the young reporter he was ordered to follow included. Nothing, he was certain, would ever change
that.

The following day Oster and Miller had their last
visit from Leon. Apart from Leon and Motti, there was
a new man, sun-tanned and fit-looking, much younger
than the others. Miller adjudged the new man to be in
his mid-thirties. He was introduced simply as Josef.
He said nothing throughout.

"By the way," Motti told Miller, "I drove your car
up here today. I've left it in a public parking lot down
in the town, by the market square."

He tossed Miller the keys, adding, "Don't use it
when you go to meet the Odessa. For one thing, it's too
noticeable; for another, you're supposed to be a bakery
worker on the run after being spotted and identified as
a former camp guard. Such a man would not have a
Jaguar. When you go, travel by rail."

Miller nodded his agreement, but privately he regretted being separated from his beloved Jaguar.

"Right. Here is your driving license, complete with

your photograph as you now look. You can tell anyone who asks that you drive a Volkswagen but you have left it in Bremen, as the number could identify you to the police."

Miller scanned the driving license. It showed himself with his short hair but no mustache. The one he now had could simply be explained as a precaution, grown since he was identified.

"The man who, unknown to him, is your guarantor, left from Bremerhaven on a cruise ship on the morning tide. This is the former SS colonel, now a bakery-owner and your former employer. His name is Joachim Eberhardt. Here is a letter from him to the man you are going to see. The paper is genuine, taken from his office. The signature is a perfect forgery. The letter tells its recipient that you are a good former SS man, reliable, now fallen on misfortune after being recognized, and it asks the recipient to help you acquire a new set of papers and a new identity."

Leon passed the letter across to Miller. He read it and put it back in its envelope.

"Now seal it," said Leon.

Miller did so. "Who's the man I have to present myself to?" he asked.

Leon held out a sheet of paper with a name and address on it. "This is the man," he said. "He lives in Nuremberg. We're not certain what he was in the war, for he almost certainly has a new name. However, of one thing we are quite certain. He is very high up in the Odessa. He may have met Eberhardt, who is a big wheel in the Odessa in North Germany. So here is a photograph of Eberhardt the baker. Study it, in case your man asks for a description of him from you. Got that?"

Miller looked at Eberhardt's photograph and nodded.

"When you are ready, I suggest a wait of a few days until Eberhardt's ship is beyond the reach of ship-to-shore radio-telephone. We don't want the man you will see to get through a telephone call to Eberhardt while the ship is still off the German coast. Wait till it's in mid-Atlantic. I think you should probably present yourself on next Thursday morning."

Miller nodded.

"All right. Thursday it is."

"Two last things," said Leon. "Apart from trying to trace Roschmann, which is your desire, we also would like some information. We want to know who is now recruiting scientists to go to Egypt and develop Nasser's rockets for him. The recruiting is being done by the Odessa, here in Germany. We need to know specifically who the new chief recruiting officer is. Secondly, stay in touch. Use public telephones and phone this number." He passed a piece of paper across to Miller. "The number will always be manned, even if I am not there. Report in whenever you get anything."

Twenty minutes later, the group was gone.

In the back seat of the car on their way back to Munich, Leon and Josef sat side by side, the Israeli agent hunched in his corner and silent. As they left the twinkling lights of Bayreuth behind them Leon nudged Josef with his elbow. "Why so gloomy?" he asked. "Everything is going fine."

Josef glanced at him. "How reliable do you reckon this man Miller?" he asked.

"Reliable? he's the best chance we have ever had for penetrating the Odessa. You heard Oster. He can pass for a former SS man in any company, provided he keeps his head."

Josef retained his doubts. "My brief was to watch him at all times," he grumbled. "I ought to be sticking to him when he moves, keeping an eye on him, reporting back on the men he is introduced to and their position in the Odessa. I wish I'd never agreed to let him go off alone and check in by phone when he sees fit. Supposing he doesn't check in?"

Leon's anger was barely controlled. It was evident they had been through this argument before. "Now, listen one more time. This man is my discovery. His infiltration into the Odessa was my idea. He's my agent. I've waited years to get someone where he is now—a non-Jew. I'm not having him exposed by someone tagging along behind him."

"He's an amateur. I'm a pro," growled the agent.

"He's also an Aryan," riposted Leon. "By the time he's outlived his usefulness, I hope he'll have given us the names of the top ten Odessa men in Germany. Then we go to work on them one by one. Among them, one must be the recruiter of the rocket scientists. Don't worry, we'll find him, and the names of the scientists he intends to send to Cairo."

Back in Bayreuth, Miller stared out of the window at the falling snow. Privately he had no intention of checking in by phone, for he had no interest in tracing recruited rocket scientists. He still had only one objective—Eduard Roschmann.

12

IT WAS actually on the evening of Wednesday, February 19, that Peter Miller finally bade farewell to Alfred Oster in his cottage in Bayreuth and headed for Nuremberg.

The former SS officer shook him by the hand on the doorstep. "Best of luck, Kolb. I've taught you everything I know. Let me give you a last word of advice. I don't know how long your cover can hold. Probably not long. If you ever spot anyone who you think has seen through the cover, don't argue. Get out and revert to your real name."

As the young reporter walked down the drive, Oster muttered to himself, "Craziest idea I ever heard," shut the door, and went back to his hearth.

Miller walked the mile to the railway station, going steadily downhill and passing the public parking lot. At the small station, with its Bavarian eaves and gables, he bought a single ticket to Nuremberg.

It was only as he passed through the ticket barrier toward the windswept platform that the collector told him, "I'm afraid you'll have quite a wait, sir. The Nuremberg train will be late tonight."

Miller was surprised. German railroads make a point of honor of running on time. "What's happened?" he asked.

The ticket collector nodded up the line, where the track disappeared into close folds of hills and valleys heavy-hung with fresh snow. "There's been a large snowfall down the track. Now we've just heard the snow plow's gone on the blink. The engineers are working on it."

Years in journalism had given Miller a deep loathing of waiting rooms. He had spent too long in them, cold, tired, and uncomfortable. In the small station café he sipped a cup of coffee and looked at his ticket. It had already been clipped. His mind went back to his car parked up the hill.

Surely, if he parked it on the other side of Nuremberg, several miles from the address he had been given . . . ? If, after the interview, they sent him on somewhere else by another means of transport, he would leave the Jaguar in Munich. He could even park it in a garage, out of sight. No one would ever find it. Not before the job was done. Besides, he reasoned, it wouldn't be a bad thing to have another way of getting out fast if the occasion required. There was no reason for him to think anyone in Bavaria had ever heard of him or his car.

He thought of Motti's warning about its being too noticeable, but then he recalled Oster's tip an hour earlier about getting out in a hurry. To use it was a risk, of course, but then so was to be stranded on foot. He gave the prospect another five minutes, then left his coffee, walked out of the station and back up the hill. Within ten minutes he was behind the wheel of the Jaguar and heading out of town.

It was a short trip to Nuremberg. When he arrived, Miller checked into a small hotel near the main station, parked his car in a side street two blocks away, and walked through the King's Gate into the old walled medieval city of Albrecht Dürer.

It was already dark, but the lights from the streets and windows lit up the quaint pointed roofs and decorated gables of the walled town. It was almost possible to think oneself back in the Middle Ages, when the Kings of Franconia had ruled over Nuremberg, one of the richest merchant cities of the Germanic states. It was hard to recall that almost every brick and stone of what he saw around him had been built since 1945, meticulously reconstructed from the actual architects' plans of the original town, which had been reduced with its cobbled streets and timbered houses to ashes and rubble by the Allied bombs of 1943.

He found the house he was looking for two streets from the square of the main market, almost under the twin spires of Saint Sebald's Church. The name on the doorplate checked with the one typed on the letter he carried, the forged introduction supposedly from former SS Colonel Joachim Eberhardt of Bremen. As he had never met Eberhardt, he could only hope the man in the house in Nuremberg had not met him either.

He walked back to the market square, looking for a place to have supper. After strolling past two or three traditional Franconian eating houses, he noticed smoke curling up into the frosty night sky from the red-tiled roof of the small sausage house in the corner of the square, in front of the doors of Saint Sebald's. It was a pretty little place, fronted by a terrace fringed with boxes of purple heather, from which a careful owner had brushed the morning's snow.

Inside, the warmth and good cheer hit him like a wave. The wooden tables were almost all occupied, but a couple from a corner table were leaving, so he took it, bobbing and smiling back as the couple, on their way out, wished him a good appetite. He ordered the specialty of the house, the small spiced Nuremberg sausages, a dozen on one plate, and treated himself to a bottle of the local wine to wash them down.

After his meal he sat back and dawdled over his coffee and chased the black liquid home with two Asbachs. He didn't feel like bed, and it was pleasant to sit and gaze at the logs flickering in the open fire, to listen to the crowd in the corner roaring out a Franconian drinking song, locking arms and swinging from side to side to the music, voices and wine tumblers raised high each time they reached the end of a stanza.

For a long time he wondered why he should bother to risk his life in the quest for a man who had committed crimes twenty years before. He almost decided to let the matter drop, to shave off his mustache, grow his hair again, go back to Hamburg and the bed warmed by Sigi.

The waiter came over, bowed, deposited the bill on the table with a cheerful *"Bitte schön."*

He reached into his pocket for his wallet, and his fingers touched a photograph. He pulled it out and gazed at it for a while. The pale red-rimmed eyes and the rattrap mouth stared back at him above the collar with the black tabs and the silver lightning symbols. After a while he muttered, "You shit," and held the corner of the photograph above the candle on his table. When the picture had been reduced to ashes he crumpled them in the copper tray. He would not need it again. He could recognize the face when he saw it.

Peter Miller paid for his meal, buttoned his coat about him, and walked back to his hotel.

Mackensen was confronting an angry and baffled Werwolf at about the same time.

"How the hell *can* he be missing?" snapped the Odessa chief. "He can't vanish off the face of the earth, he can't disappear into thin air. His car must be one of the most distinctive in Germany, visible half a mile off. Six weeks of searching, and all you can tell me is that he hasn't been seen. . . ."

Mackensen waited until the outburst of frustration had spent itself. "Nevertheless, it's true," he pointed out at length. "I've had his apartment in Hamburg checked out, his girl friend and mother interviewed by supposed friends of Miller, his colleagues contacted. They all know nothing. His car must have been in a garage somewhere all this time. He must have gone to ground. Since he was traced leaving the airport parking lot in Cologne, after returning from London, and driving south, he has gone."

"We have to find him," repeated the Werwolf. "He must not get near this *Kamerad*. It would be a disaster."

"He'll show up," said Mackensen with conviction. "Sooner or later he has to break cover. Then we'll have him."

The Werwolf considered the patience and logic of

the professional hunter. He nodded slowly. "Very well. Then I want you to stay close to me. Check into a hotel here in town, and we'll wait it out. If you're nearby, I can get you easily."

"Right, sir. I'll get into a hotel downtown and call you to let you know. You can get me there any time." He bade his superior good night and left.

It was just before nine the following morning that Miller presented himself at the house and rang the brilliantly polished bell. He wanted to get the man before he left for work. The door was opened by a maid, who showed him into the living room and went to fetch her employer.

The man who entered the room ten minutes later was in his mid-fifties with medium-brown hair and silver tufts at each temple, self-possessed and elegant. The furniture and decor of his room also spelled elegance and a substantial income.

He gazed at his unexpected visitor without curiosity assessing at a glance the inexpensive trousers and jacket of a working-class man. "And what can I do for you?" he inquired calmly.

The visitor was plainly embarrassed and ill at ease among the opulent surroundings of the room. "Well, *Herr Doktor,* I was hoping you might be able to help me."

"Come now," said the Odessa man, "I'm sure you know my office is not far from here. Perhaps you should go there and ask my secretary for an appointment."

"Well, it's not actually professional help I need," said Miller. He had dropped into the vernacular of the Hamburg and Bremen area, the language of working people. He was obviously embarrassed. At a loss for words, he produced a letter from his inside pocket and held it out. "I brought a letter of introduction from the man who suggested I come to you, sir."

The Odessa man took the letter without a word, slit it open, and cast his eyes quickly down it. He stiffened slightly and gazed narrowly across the sheet of paper at Miller. "I see, Herr Kolb. Perhaps you had better sit down."

He gestured toward an upright chair, while he himself took an easy chair. He spent several minutes looking speculatively at his guest, a frown on his face. Suddenly he snapped, "What did you say your name was?"

"Kolb, sir."

"First names?"

"Rolf Günther, sir."

"Do you have any identification on you?"

Miller looked nonplused. "Only my driving license."

"Let me see it, please."

The lawyer—for that was his profession—stretched out a hand, forcing Miller to rise from his seat and place the driving license in the outstretched palm. The man took it, flicked it open, and digested the details inside. He glanced over it at Miller, comparing the photograph and the face. They matched.

"What is your date of birth?" he snapped suddenly.

"My birthday? Oh—er—June eighteenth, sir."

"The year, Kolb?"

"Nineteen twenty-five, sir."

The lawyer considered the driving license for another few minutes. "Wait here," he said suddenly, got up, and left.

He traversed the house and entered the rear portion of it, an area that served as his office and was reached by clients from a street at the back. He went straight into the office and opened the wall safe. From it he took a thick book and thumbed through it.

By chance he knew the name of Joachim Eberhardt but had never met the man. He was not completely certain of Eberhardt's last rank in the SS. The book confirmed the letter. Joachim Eberhardt, promoted colonel of the Waffen SS on January 10, 1945. He flicked over several more pages and checked against Kolb. There were seven such names, but only one Rolf Günther. Staff Sergeant as of April 1945. Date of birth

18/6/25. He closed the book, replaced it, and locked the safe. Then he returned through the house to the living room. His guest was still sitting awkwardly on the upright chair.

He settled himself again. "It may not be possible for me to help you. You realize that, don't you?"

Miller bit his lip and nodded. "I've nowhere else to go, sir. I went to Herr Eberhardt for help when they started looking for me, and he gave me the letter and suggested I come to you. He said if you couldn't help me no one could."

The lawyer leaned back in his chair and gazed at the ceiling. "I wonder why he didn't call me if he wanted to talk to me," he mused. Then he evidently waited for an answer.

"Maybe he didn't want to use the phone on a matter like this," Miller suggested hopefully.

The lawyer shot him a scornful look. "It's possible," he said shortly. "You'd better tell me how you got into this mess in the first place."

"Oh, yes. Well, sir—I mean I was recognized by this man, and then they said they were coming to arrest me. So I got out, didn't I? I mean, I had to."

The lawyer sighed. "Start at the beginning," he said wearily. "Who recognized you, and as what?"

Miller drew a deep breath. "Well, sir, I was in Bremen. I live there, and I work—well, I worked, until this happened, for Herr Eberhardt. In the bakery. Well, I was walking in the street one day about four months back, and I suddenly got very sick. I felt terribly ill, with stomach pains. Anyway, I must have passed out. I fainted on the pavement. So they took me away to the hospital."

"Which hospital?"

"Bremen General, sir. They did some tests and they said I had cancer. In the intestine. I thought that was it, see?"

"It usually is it," observed the lawyer dryly.

"Well, that's what I thought, sir. Only apparently it

was caught at an early stage. Anyway, they put me on a course of drugs instead of operating, and after some time the cancer went into a remission."

"So far as I can see, you're a lucky man. What's all this about being recognized?"

"Yes, well, it was this hospital orderly, see? He was Jewish, and he kept staring at me. Every time he was on duty he kept staring at me. It was a funny sort of look, see? And it got me worried. The way he kept looking at me. With a sort of 'I know you' look on his face. I didn't recognize him, but I got the impression he knew me."

"Go on." The lawyer was showing increasing interest.

"So about a month ago they said I was ready to be transferred, and I was taken away and put in a convalescent clinic. It was the employees' insurance plan at the bakery that paid for it. Well, before I left the Bremen General, I remembered him. The Jew-boy I mean. It took me weeks; then I got it. He was an inmate at Flossenburg."

The lawyer jackknifed upright. "You were at Flossenburg?"

"Yes, I was getting around to telling you that, wasn't I? I mean, sir. And I remembered this hospital orderly from then. I got his name in the Bremen hospital. But at Flossenburg he had been in the party of Jewish inmates that we used to burn the bodies of Admiral Canaris and the other officers we hanged for their part in the assassination attempt on the Führer."

The lawyer stared at him again. "You were one of those who executed Canaris and the others?" he asked.

Miller shrugged. "I commanded the execution squad," he said simply. "Well, they were traitors, weren't they? They tried to kill the Führer."

The lawyer smiled. "My dear fellow, I'm not reproaching you. Of course they were traitors. Canaris had even been passing information to the Allies. They were all traitors, those Army swine, from the generals down. I just never thought to meet the man who killed them."

Miller grinned weakly. "The point is, the police would like to get their hands on me for that. I mean, knocking off Jews is one thing, but now there's a lot of them saying Canaris and that crowd—saying they were sort of heroes."

The lawyer nodded. "Yes, certainly that would get you into bad trouble with the present authorities in Germany. Go on with your story."

"I was transferred to this clinic, and I didn't see the Jewish orderly again. Then last Friday I got a telephone call at the convalescent clinic. I thought it must be the bakery calling, but the man wouldn't give his name. He just said he was in a position to know what was going on, and that a certain person had informed those swine at Ludwigsburg who I was, and there was a warrant being prepared for my arrest. I didn't know who the man could be, but he sounded as if he knew what he was talking about. Sort of official-sounding voice, if you know what I mean, sir?"

The lawyer nodded understandingly. "Probably a friend on the police force of Bremen. What did you do?"

Miller looked surprised. "Well, I got out, didn't I? I discharged myself. I didn't know what to do. I didn't go home in case they were waiting for me there. I didn't even go and pick up my Volkswagen, which was still parked in front of my house. I slept out Friday night; then on Saturday I had an idea. I went to see the boss, Herr Eberhardt, at his house. He was in the telephone book. He was real nice to me. He said he was leaving with Frau Eberhardt for a winter cruise the next morning, but he'd try and see that I was all right. So he gave me the letter and told me to come to you."

"What made you suspect Herr Eberhardt would help you?"

"Well, you see I didn't know what he had been in the war. But he was always real nice to me at the bakery. Then about two years back we were having the staff party. We all got a little drunk, and I went to the men's room. There was Herr Eberhardt washing his hands. And singing. He was singing the 'Horst Wessel Song.'

So I joined in. There we were, singing it in the men's room. Then he clapped me on the back, and said, 'Not a word, Kolb,' and went out. I didn't think any more about it till I got into trouble. Then I thought—well, he might have been in the SS like me. So I went to him for help."

"And he sent you to me?"

Miller nodded.

"What was the name of this Jewish orderly?"

"Hartstein, sir."

"And the convalescent clinic you were sent to?"

"The Arcadia Clinic, at Delmenhorst, just outside Bremen."

The lawyer nodded again, made a few notes on a sheet of paper taken from a desk, and rose. "Stay here," he said and left again.

He crossed the passage and entered his study. From the telephone information operator he elicited the numbers of the Eberhardt Bakery, the Bremen General Hospital, and the Arcadia Clinic at Delmenhorst. He called the bakery first.

Eberhardt's secretary was most helpful. "I'm afraid Herr Eberhardt is away, sir. No, he can't be contacted, he has taken his usual winter cruise to the Caribbean with Frau Eberhardt. He'll be back in four weeks. Can I be of any assistance?"

The lawyer assured her she could not and hung up. Next he dialed the Bremen General and asked for Personnel and Staff.

"This is the Department of Social Security, Pensions Section," he said smoothly. "I just wanted to confirm that you have a ward orderly on the staff by the name of Hartstein."

There was a pause while the girl at the other end went through the staff file. "Yes, we do," she said. "David Hartstein."

"Thank you," said the lawyer in Nuremberg and hung up. He dialed the same number again and asked for the registrar's office.

"This is the secretary of the Eberhardt Baking Company," he said. "I just wanted to check on the progress of one of our staff who has been in your hospital with a tumor in the intestine. Can you tell me of his progress? Rolf Günther Kolb."

There was another pause. The girl filing clerk got out the file on Rolf Günther Kolb and glanced at the last page.

"He's been discharged," she told the caller. "His condition improved to a point where he could be transferred to a convalescent clinic."

"Excellent," said the lawyer. "I've been away on my annual skiing vacation, so I haven't caught up yet. Can you tell me which clinic?"

"The Arcadia, at Delmenhorst," said the girl.

The lawyer hung up again and dialed the Arcadia Clinic. A girl answered. After listening to the request, she turned to the doctor by her side. She covered the mouthpiece. "There's a question about that man you mentioned to me, Kolb," she said.

The doctor took the telephone. "Yes," he said. "This is the Chief of the Clinic. I am Doctor Braun. Can I help you?"

At the name of Braun the secretary shot a puzzled glance at her employer. Without batting an eyelid, he listened to the voice from Nuremburg and replied smoothly, "I'm afraid Herr Kolb discharged himself last Friday afternoon. Most irregular, but there was nothing I could do to prevent him. Yes, that's right, he was transferred here from the Bremen General. A tumor, well on the way to recovery."

He listened for a moment, then said, "Not at all. Glad I could be of help to you."

The doctor, whose real name was Rosemayer, hung up and then dialed a Munich number. Without preamble he said, "Someone's been on the phone asking about Kolb. The checking up has started."

Back in Nuremberg, the lawyer replaced the phone and returned to the living room. "Right, Kolb, you evidently are who you say you are."

Miller stared at him in astonishment.

"However, I'd like to ask you a few more questions. You don't mind?"

Still amazed, the visitor shook his head. "No, sir."

"Good. Are you circumcised?"

Miller stared back blankly. "No, I'm not," he said dumbly.

"Show me," said the lawyer calmly. Miller just sat in his chair and stared at him.

"Show me, Staff Sergeant," snapped the lawyer.

Miller shot out of his chair, ramrodding to attention. *"Zu Befehl,"* he responded, quivering at attention. He held the attention position, thumbs down the seams of his trousers, for three seconds, then unzipped his fly. The lawyer glanced at him briefly, then nodded that he could zip his fly up again.

"Well, at least you're not Jewish," he said amiably.

Back in his chair Miller stared at him, open-mouthed. "Of course I'm not Jewish," he blurted.

The lawyer smiled. "Nevertheless, there have been cases of Jews trying to pass themselves off as one of the *Kameraden.* They don't last long. Now you'd better tell me your story, and I'm going to shoot questions at you. Just checking up, you understand. Where were you born?"

"Bremen, sir."

"Right. Place of birth is in your SS records. I just checked. Were you in the Hitler Youth?"

"Yes, sir. Entered at the age of ten in nineteen thirty-five, sir."

"Your parents were good National Socialists?"

"Yessir, both of them."

"What happened to them?"

"They were killed in the great bombing of Bremen."

"When were you inducted into the SS?"

"Spring nineteen forty-four, sir. Age eighteen."

"Where did you train?"

"Dachau SS training camp, sir."

"You had your blood group tattooed under your right armpit?"

"No, sir. And it would have been the left armpit."

"Why weren't you tattooed?"

"Well, sir, we were due to pass out of training camp in August nineteen forty-four and go to our first posting in a unit of the Waffen SS. Then in July a large group of officers involved in the plot against the Führer was sent down to Flossenburg camp. Flossenburg asked for immediate troops from Dachau training camp to increase the staff at Flossenburg. I and about a dozen others were singled out as cases of special aptitude and sent straight there. We missed our tattooing and the formal passing-out parade of our draft. The commandant said the blood group was not necessary, as we would never get to the front, sir."

The lawyer nodded. No doubt the commandant had also been aware in July 1944 that, with the Allies well into France, the war was drawing to a close.

"Did you get your dagger?"

"Yes, sir. From the hands of the commandant."

"What are the words on it?"

"Blood and Honor, sir."

"What kind of training did you get at Dachau?"

"Complete military training, sir, and political-ideological training to supplement that of the Hitler Youth."

"Did you learn the songs?"

"Yessir."

"What was the book of marching songs from which the 'Horst Wessel Song' was drawn?"

"The album *Time of Struggle for the Nation,* sir."

"Where was Dachau training camp?"

"Ten miles north of Munich, sir. Three miles from the concentration camp of the same name."

"What was your uniform?"

"Gray-green tunic and breeches, jackboots, black collar lapels, rank on the left one, black leather belt, and gunmetal buckle."

"The motto on the buckle?"

"A swastika in the center, ringed with the words 'My honor is loyalty,' sir."

The lawyer rose and stretched. He lit up a cigar and strolled to the window. "Now you'll tell me about

Flossenburg Camp, Staff Sergeant Kolb. Where was it?"

"On the border of Bavaria and Thuringia, sir."

"When was it opened?"

"In nineteen thirty-four, sir. One of the first for the pigs who opposed the Führer."

"How large was it?"

"When I was there, sir, three hundred meters by three hundred. It was ringed by nineteen watchtowers with heavy and light machine guns mounted. It had a roll-call square one-twenty meters by one-forty. God, we had some fun there with them Yids—"

"Stick to the point," snapped the lawyer. "What were the accommodations?"

"Twenty-four barracks, a kitchen for the inmates, a washhouse, a sanatorium, and various workshops."

"And for the SS guards?"

"Two barracks, a shop, and a bordello."

"How were the bodies of those who died disposed of?"

"There was a small crematorium outside the wire. It was reached from inside the camp by an underground passage."

"What was the main kind of work done?"

"Stone-breaking in the quarry, sir. The quarry was also outside the wire, surrounded by barbed wire and watchtowers of its own."

"What was the population in late nineteen forty-four?"

"Oh, about sixteen thousand inmates, sir."

"Where was the commandant's office?"

"Outside the wire, sir, halfway up a slope overlooking the camp."

"Who were the successive commandants?"

"Two were before I got there, sir. The first was SS Major Karl Kunstler. His successor was SS Captain Karl Fritsch. The last one was SS Lieutenant Colonel Max Kögel."

"Which was the number of the political department?"

"Department Two, sir."

"Where was it?"

"In the commandant's block."

"What were its duties?"

"To ensure that requirements from Berlin that certain prisoners received special treatment were carried out."

"Canaris and the other plotters were so indicated?"

"Yes, sir. They were all designated for special treatment."

"When was this carried out?"

"April twentieth, nineteen forty-five, sir. The Americans were moving up through Bavaria, so the orders came to finish them off. A group of us was designated to do the job. I was then a newly promoted staff sergeant, although I had arrived at the camp as a private. I headed the detail for Canaris and five others. Then we had a burial party of Jews bury the bodies. Hartstein was one of them, damn his eyes. After that we burned the camp documents. Some time later we were ordered to march the prisoners northward. On the way we heard the Führer had killed himself. Well, sir, the officers left us then. The prisoners started running off into the woods. We shot a few, us sergeants, but there didn't seem much point in marching on. I mean the Yanks were all over the place."

"One last question about the camp, Staff Sergeant. When you looked up, from anywhere in the camp, what did you see?"

Miller looked puzzled. "The sky," he said.

"Fool, I mean what dominated the horizon?"

"Oh, you mean the hill with the ruined castle keep on it?"

The lawyer nodded and smiled. "Fourteenth century, actually," he said. "All right, Kolb, you were at Flossenburg. Now, how did you get away?"

"Well, sir, it was on the march. We all broke up. I found an Army private wandering around, so I hit him on the head and took his uniform. The Yanks caught me two days later. I did two years in a prisoner-of-war camp, but just told them I was an Army private. Well, you know how it was, sir, there were rumors floating about that the Yanks were shooting SS men out of hand. So I said I was in the Army."

The lawyer exhaled a draft of cigar smoke. "You weren't alone in that. Did you change your name?"

"No, sir. I threw my papers away, because they identified me as SS. But I didn't think to change the name. I didn't think anyone would look for a staff sergeant. At the time the business with Canaris didn't seem very important. It was only much later people started to make a fuss over those Army officers, and made a shrine of the place in Berlin where they hanged the ringleaders. But then I had papers from the Federal Republic in the name of Kolb. Anyway, nothing would have happened if that orderly hadn't spotted me, and after that it wouldn't have mattered what I called myself."

"True. Right, now we'll go on to a little of the things you were taught. Start by repeating to me the oath of loyalty to the Führer," said the lawyer.

It went on for another three hours. Miller was sweating, but was able to say he had left the hospital prematurely and had not eaten all day. It was past lunchtime when at last the lawyer professed himself satisfied.

"Just what do you want?" he asked Miller.

"Well, the thing is, sir, with them all looking for me, I'm going to need a set of papers showing I am not Rolf Günther Kolb. I can change my appearance, grow my hair, let the mustache grow longer, and get a job in Bavaria or somewhere. I mean, I'm a skilled baker, and people need bread, don't they?"

For the first time in the interview the lawyer threw back his head and laughed. "Yes, my good Kolb, people need bread. Very well. Listen. Normally people of your standing in life hardly merit a lot of expensive time and trouble being spent on them. But as you are evidently in trouble through no fault of your own, obviously a good and loyal German, I'll do what I can. There's no point in your getting simply a new driving license. That would not enable you to get a social-security card without producing a birth certificate, which you haven't got. But a new passport would get you all these things. Have you got any money?"

"No, sir. I'm dead broke. I've been hitchhiking south for the past three days."

The lawyer gave him a hundred-mark note. "You can't stay here, and it will take at least a week before your new passport comes through. I'll send you to a friend of mine who will acquire the passport for you. He lives in Stuttgart. You'd better check into a commercial hotel and go and see him. I'll tell him you're coming, and he'll be expecting you."

The lawyer wrote on a piece of paper. "He's called Franz Bayer, and here's his address. You'd better take the train to Stuttgart, find a hotel, and go straight to him. If you need a little more money, he'll help you out. But don't go spending a lot. Stay under cover and wait until Bayer can fix you up with a new passport. Then we'll find you a job in southern Germany, and no one will ever trace you."

Miller took the hundred marks and the address of Bayer with embarrassed thanks. "Oh, thank you, *Herr Doktor,* you're a real gentleman."

The maid showed him out, and he walked back toward the station, his hotel, and his parked car. An hour later he was speeding toward Stuttgart, while the lawyer rang Bayer and told him to expect Rolf Günther Kolb, refugee from the police, in the early evening.

There was no autobahn between Nuremberg and Stuttgart in those days, and on a bright sunny day the road leading across the lush plain of Franconia and into the wooded hills and valleys of Württemberg would have been picturesque. On a bitter February afternoon, with ice glittering in the dips of the road surface and mist forming in the valleys, the twisting ribbon of tarmac between Ansbach and Crailsheim was murderous. Twice the heavy Jaguar almost slithered into a ditch, and twice Miller had to tell himself there was no hurry. Bayer, the man who knew how to get false passports, would still be there.

He arrived after dark and found a small hotel in the outer city that nevertheless had a night porter for those who preferred to stay out late, and a garage at the back for the car. From the hall porter he got a town plan and found Bayer's street in the suburb of Ostheim, a well-set-up area not far from the Villa Berg, in whose gardens the Princes of Württemberg and their ladies had once disported themselves on summer nights.

Following the map, he drove the car down into the bowl of hills that frames the center of Stuttgart, along which the vineyards come up to the outskirts of the city, and parked his car a quarter of a mile from Bayer's house. As he stooped to lock the driver's-side door, he failed to notice a middle-aged lady coming home from her weekly meeting of the Hospital Visitors Committee at the nearby Villa Hospital.

It was at eight that evening that the lawyer in Nuremberg thought he had better ring Bayer and make sure the refugee Kolb had arrived safely. It was Bayer's wife who answered.

"Oh, yes, the young man. He and my husband have gone out to dinner somewhere."

"I just rang to make sure he had arrived safe and sound," said the lawyer smoothly.

"Such a nice young man," burbled Frau Bayer cheerfully. "I passed him as he was parking his car. I was just on my way home from the Hospital Visitors Committee meeting. But miles away from the house. He must have lost his way. It's very easy, you know, in Stuttgart, so many dead ends and one-way streets—"

"Excuse me, Frau Bayer," the lawyer cut in. "The man did not have his Volkswagen with him. He came by train."

"No, no," said Frau Bayer, happy to be able to show superior knowledge. "He came by car. Such a nice young man, and such a lovely car. I'm sure he's a success with all the girls with a—"

"Frau Bayer, listen to me. Carefully, now. What kind of a car was it?"

"Well, I don't know the make, of course. But a sports

car. A long black one, with a yellow stripe down the side—"

The lawyer slammed down the phone, then raised it and dialed a number in Nuremberg. He was sweating slightly. When he got the hotel he wanted he asked for a room number. The phone extension was lifted, and a familiar voice said, "Hello."

"Mackensen," barked the Werwolf, "get over here fast. We've found Miller."

13

FRANZ BAYER was as fat and round and jolly as his wife. Alerted by the Werwolf to expect the fugitive from the police, he welcomed Miller on his doorstep when he presented himself just before eight o'clock.

Miller was introduced briefly to his wife in the hallway before she bustled off to the kitchen.

"Well, now," said Bayer, "have you ever been in Württemberg before, my dear Kolb?"

"No, I confess I haven't."

"Ha, well, we pride ourselves here on being a very hospitable people. No doubt you'd like some food. Have you eaten yet today?"

Miller told him he had had neither breakfast nor lunch, having been on the train all afternoon.

Bayer seemed most distressed. "Good heavens, how awful. You must eat. Tell you what, we'll go into town and have a really good dinner. . . . Nonsense, my boy, the least I can do for you."

He waddled off into the back of the house to tell his wife he was taking their guest out for a meal in downtown Stuttgart, and ten minutes later they were heading in Bayer's car toward the city center.

It is at least a two-hour drive from Nuremberg to Stuttgart along the old E12 highroad, even if one pushes the car hard. And Mackensen pushed his car that night. Half an hour after he received the Werwolf's call, fully briefed and armed with Bayer's address, he was on the road. He arrived at half past ten and went straight to Bayer's house.

Frau Bayer, alerted by another call from the Werwolf that the man calling himself Kolb was not what he seemed to be and might indeed be a police informer, was a trembling and frightened woman when Mackensen arrived. His terse manner was hardly calculated to put her at her ease.

"When did they leave?"

"About a quarter to eight," she quavered.

"Did they say where they were going?"

"No. Franz just said the young man had not eaten all day and he was taking him into town for a meal at a restaurant. I said I could make something here at home, but Franz just loves dining out. Any excuse will do——"

"This man Kolb. You said you saw him parking his car. Where was this?"

She described the street where the Jaguar was parked, and how to get to it from her house.

Mackensen thought deeply for a moment. "Have you any idea which restaurant your husband might have taken him to?" he asked.

She thought for a while. "Well, his favorite eating place is the Three Moors restaurant on Friedrich-strasse," she said. "He usually tries there first."

Mackensen left the house and drove the half-mile to the parked Jaguar. He examined it closely, certain that he would recognize it again whenever he saw it. He was of two minds whether to stay with it and wait for Miller's return. But the Werwolf's orders were to trace Miller and Bayer, warn the Odessa man and send him home, then take care of Miller. For that reason he had not telephoned the Three Moors. To warn Bayer now would be to alert Miller to the fact that he had been uncovered, giving him the chance to disappear again.

Mackensen glanced at his watch. It was ten to eleven. He climbed back into his Mercedes and headed for the center of town.

In a small and obscure hotel in the back streets of Munich, Josef was lying awake on his bed when a call came from the reception desk to say a cable had arrived for him. He went downstairs and brought it back to his room.

Seated at the rickety table, he slit the buff envelope and scanned the lengthy contents. It began:

Celery: 481 marks, 53 pfennigs.
Melons: 362 marks, 17 pfennigs.
Oranges: 627 marks, 24 pfennigs.
Grapefruit: 313 marks, 88 pfennigs. . . .

The list of fruit and vegetables was long, but all the articles were those habitually exported by Israel, and the cable read like the response to an inquiry by the German-based representative of an export company for price quotations. Using the public international cable network was not secure, but so many commercial cables pass through Western Europe in a day that checking them all would need an army of men.

Ignoring the words, Josef wrote down the figures in a long line. The five-figure groups into which the marks and pfennigs were divided disappeared. When he had them all in a line, he split them up into groups of six figures. From each six-figure group he subtracted the date, February 20, 1964, which he wrote as 20264. In each case the result was another six-figure group.

It was a simple book code, based on the paperback edition of Webster's New World Dictionary as published by Popular Library of New York. The first three figures in the group represented the page in the dictionary; the fourth figure could be anything from one to nine. An odd number meant column one, an even number column two. The last two figures indicated the number of words down the column from the top. He worked steadily for half an hour, then read the message through and slowly held his head in his hands.

Thirty minutes later he was with Leon in the latter's house. The revenge-group leader read the message and swore. "I'm sorry," he said at last. "I couldn't have known."

Unknown to either man, three tiny fragments of

information had come into the possession of the Mossad in the previous six days. One was from the resident Israeli agent in Buenos Aires to the effect that someone had authorized the payment of a sum equivalent to one million German marks to a figure called Vulkan "to enable him to complete the next stage of his research project."

The second was from a Jewish employee of a Swiss bank known habitually to handle currency transfers from secret Nazi funds elsewhere to pay off Odessa men in Western Europe; it was to the effect that one million marks had been transferred to the bank from Beirut and collected in cash by a man operating an account at the bank for the previous ten years in the name of Fritz Wegener.

The third was from an Egyptian colonel in a senior position in the security apparat around Factory 333, who, for a substantial consideration in money to help him prepare a comfortable retirement, had talked with a man from the Mossad for several hours in a Rome hotel. What the man had to say was that the rocket project was lacking only the provision of a reliable tele-guidance system, which was being researched and con-structed in a factory in West Germany, and that the project was costing the Odessa millions of marks.

The three fragments, among thousands of others, had been processed in the computer banks of Professor Youvel Neeman, the Israeli genius who had first har-nessed science in the form of the computer to intelli-gence analysis, and who later went on to become the father of the Israeli atomic bomb. Where a human memory might have failed, the whirring microcircuits had linked the three items, recalled that up to his ex-posure by his wife in 1955 Roschmann had used the name of Fritz Wegener, and reported accordingly.

Josef rounded on Leon in their underground head-quarters. "I'm staying here from now on. I'm not moving out of range of that telephone. Get me a powerful motor-cycle and protective clothing. Have both ready within the hour. If and when your precious Miller checks in, I'll have to get to him fast."

"If he's exposed, you won't get there fast enough," said Leon.

"No wonder they warned him to stay away. They'll kill him if he gets within a mile of his man."

As Leon left the cellar Josef ran his eye over the cable from Tel Aviv once again. It said:

RED ALERT NEW INFORMATION INDICATES VITAL KEY
ROCKET SUCCESS GERMAN INDUSTRIALIST OPERAT(ING)
YOUR TERRITORY STOP CODE NAME VULCAN STOP
PROBABLE IDENTIFICATION ROSH MAN STOP USE MILLER
INSTANTLY STOP TRACE AND ELIMINATE STOP
CORMORANT

Josef sat at the table and meticulously began to clean and arm his Walther PPK automatic. From time to time he glanced at the silent telephone.

Over dinner Bayer had been the genial host, roaring with laughter in great gusts as he told his own favorite jokes. Miller tried several times to get the talk around to the question of a new passport for himself.

Each time Bayer clapped him soundly on the back, told him not to worry, and added, "Leave it to me, old boy, leave it to old Franz Bayer."

He tapped the right-hand side of his nose with his forefinger, winked broadly, and dissolved into gales of merriment.

One thing Miller had inherited from eight years as a reporter was the ability to drink and keep a clear head. He was not used to the white wine of which copious drafts were used to wash down the meal. But white wine has one advantage if one is trying to get another man drunk. It comes in buckets of ice and cold water, to keep it chilled, and three times Miller was able to tip his entire glass into the ice bucket when Bayer was looking the other way.

By the dessert course they had demolished two bottles

of excellent cold hock, and Bayer, squeezed into his tight horn-buttoned jacket, was perspiring in torrents. The effect was to enhance his thirst, and he called for a third bottle of wine.

Miller feigned to be worried that it would prove impossible to obtain a new passport for him, and that he would be arrested for his part in the events at Flossenburg in 1945.

"You'll need some photographs of me, won't you?" he asked with concern.

Bayer guffawed. "Yes, a couple of photographs. No problem. You can get them taken in one of the automatic booths at the station. Wait till your hair's a little longer, and the mustache a little fuller, and no one will ever know it's the same man."

"What happens then?" asked Miller, agog.

Bayer leaned over and placed a fat arm around his shoulders. Miller smelled the stench of wine as the fat man chuckled in his ear. "Then I send them away to a friend of mine, and a week later back comes the passport. With the passport we get you a driving license—you'll have to pass the test, of course—and a social-security card. So far as the authorities are concerned, you've just arrived back home after fifteen years abroad. No problem, old chap, stop worrying."

Although Bayer was getting drunk, he was still in command of his tongue. He declined to say more, and Miller was afraid to push him too far in case he suspected something was amiss with his young guest and closed up completely.

Although he was dying for coffee, Miller declined, in case the coffee should begin to sober up Franz Bayer. The fat man paid for the meal from a well-stuffed wallet, and they headed for the coat-check counter. It was half past ten.

"It's been a wonderful evening, Herr Bayer. Thank you very much."

"Franz, Franz," wheezed the fat man as he struggled into his coat.

"I suppose that's the end of what Stuttgart has to offer in the way of night life," observed Miller as he slipped into his own.

"Ha, silly boy. That's all you know. We have a great little city here, you know. Half a dozen good cabarets. You'd like to go on to one?"

"You mean there are cabarets, with stripteases and everything?" asked Miller, pop-eyed.

Bayer wheezed with mirth. "Are you kidding? I wouldn't be against the idea of watching some of the little ladies take their clothes off." Bayer tipped the coat-check girl handsomely and waddled outside.

"What nightclubs are there in Stuttgart?" asked Miller innocently.

"Well, now, let's see. There's the Moulin Rouge, the Balzac, the Imperial, and the Sayonara. Then there's the Madeleine in Eberhardtstrasse—"

"Eberhardt? Good Lord, what a coincidence. That was my boss in Bremen, the man who got me out of this mess and passed me on to the lawyer in Nuremberg," exclaimed Miller.

"Good. Good. Excellent. Let's go there, then," said Bayer and led the way to his car.

Mackensen reached the Three Moors at quarter past eleven. He inquired of the headwaiter, who was supervising the departure of the last guests.

"Herr Bayer? Yes, he was here tonight. Left about half an hour ago."

"He had a guest with him? A tall man with short brown hair and a mustache."

"That's right. I remember them. Sitting at the corner table over there."

Mackensen slipped a twenty-mark note into the man's hand without difficulty. "It's vitally important that I find him. It's an emergency. His wife, you know, a sudden collapse . . ."

The headwaiter's face puckered with concern. "Oh dear, how terrible!"

"Do you know where they went from here?"

"I confess I don't," said the headwaiter. He called to one of the junior waiters. "Hans, you served Herr Bayer and his guest at the corner table. Did they mention if they were going on anywhere?"

"No," said Hans. "I didn't hear them say anything about going on anywhere."

"You could try the hat-check girl," suggested the headwaiter. "She might have heard them say something."

Mackensen asked the girl. Then he asked for a copy of the tourist booklet, *What's Going on in Stuttgart*. In the section for cabarets were half a dozen names. In the middle pages of the booklet was a street map of the city center. He walked back to his car and headed for the first name on the list of cabarets.

Miller and Bayer sat at a table for two in the Madeleine nightclub. Bayer, on his second large tumbler of whisky, stared with pop eyes at a generously endowed young woman gyrating her hips in the center of the floor while her fingers unhooked the fasteners of her brassière. When it finally came off, Bayer jabbed Miller in the ribs with his elbow. He was quivering with mirth.

"What a pair, eh, lad, what a pair?" He chuckled. It was well after midnight, and he was becoming very drunk.

"Look, Herr Bayer, I'm worried," whispered Miller. "I mean, it's me who's on the run. How soon can you make this passport for me?"

Bayer draped his arm around Miller's shoulders. "Look, Rolf, old buddy, I've told you. You don't have to worry, see? Just leave it to old Franz." He winked broadly. "Anyway, I don't make the passports. I just send off the photographs to the chap who makes them, and a week later, back they come. No problem. Now, have a drink with old pal Franz." He raised a pudgy hand and flapped it in the air. "Waiter, another round."

Miller leaned back and considered. If he had to wait

until his hair grew before the passport photographs
could be taken, he might wait weeks. Nor was he going
to get the name and address of the Odessa passport-
maker from Bayer by guile. Drunk the man might be,
but not so drunk he would give away his contact in the
forging business by a slip of the tongue.

He could not get the fat Odessa man away from
the club before the end of the first floor show. When
they finally made it back to the cold night air outside,
it was after one in the morning. Bayer was unsteady on
his feet, one arm slung around Miller's shoulders, and
the sudden shock of the cold air made him worse.

"I'd better drive you home," Miller told him as they
approached the car parked by the curb. He took the car
keys from Bayer's coat pocket and helped the unpro-
testing fat man into the passenger seat. After slamming
the door on him, he walked around to the driver's side
and climbed in. At that moment a gray Mercedes
slewed around the corner behind them and jammed on
its brakes to stop twenty yards up the road.

Behind the windshield Mackensen, who had already
visited five nightclubs, stared at the number plate of
the car moving away from the curb outside the Madeleine. It was the number Frau Bayer had given him.
Her husband's car. Letting in the clutch, he followed it.

Miller drove carefully, fighting his own alcohol level.
The last thing he wanted was to be stopped by a patrol
car and tested for drunkenness. He drove not back to
Bayer's house, but to his own hotel. On the way Bayer
dozed, his head nodding forward, spreading out his
multiple chins into an apron of fat over his collar and
tie.

Outside the hotel, Miller nudged him awake. "Come
on," he said, "come on, Franz, old pal, let's have a
nightcap."

The fat man stared about him. "Must get home,"
he mumbled. "Wife waiting."

"Come on, just a little drink to finish the evening. We

can have a noggin in my room and talk about the old times."

Bayer grinned drunkenly. "Talk about the old times. Great times we had in those days, Rolf."

Miller climbed out and came around to the passenger door to help the fat man to the pavement.

"Great times," he said as he helped Bayer across the pavement and through the door. "Come and have a chat about old times."

Down the street the Mercedes had doused its lights and merged with the gray shadows of the street.

Miller had kept his room key in his pocket. Behind his desk the night porter dozed. Bayer started to mumble.

"Ssssh," said Miller, "got to be quiet."

"Got to be quiet," repeated Bayer, tiptoeing like an elephant toward the stairs. He giggled at his own play-acting. Fortunately for Miller, his room was on the second floor, or Bayer would never have made it. He eased open the door, flicked on the light, and helped Bayer into the only armchair in the room, a hard upright affair with wooden arms.

Outside in the street, Mackensen stood across from the hotel and watched the blacked-out façade. At two in the morning there were no lights burning. When Miller's light came on, he noted it was on the second floor, to the right of the hotel as he faced it.

He debated whether to go straight up and hit Miller as he opened his bedroom door. Two things decided him against it. Through the glass door of the lobby he could see that the night porter, waked by the heavy tread of Bayer past his desk, was puttering around the inside of the foyer. He would undoubtedly notice a nonresident heading up the stairs at two in the morning, and later give a good description to the police. The other thing that dissuaded him was Bayer's condition. He had watched the fat man being helped across the pavement, and knew he could never get him out of the hotel in a hurry after killing Miller. If the police got Bayer, there would be trouble with the Werwolf. Despite appearances, Bayer was a much-wanted man under his real name, and important inside the Odessa.

One last factor persuaded Mackensen to go for a window-shot. Across from the hotel was a building halfway through construction. The frame and the floors were in place, with a rough concrete stairway leading up to the second and third floors. He could wait; Miller was not going anywhere. He walked purposefully back to his car and the hunting rifle locked in the trunk.

Bayer was taken completely by surprise when the blow came. His reactions, slowed by drink, gave him no chance to duck in time. Miller, pretending to search for his bottle of whisky, opened the wardrobe door and took out his spare tie. The only other one he had was around his neck. He took this off too.

He had never had occasion to use the blows he and his fellow rookies had practiced in the gymnasium of their Army training camp ten years before and was not entirely certain how effective they were. The vast bulk of Bayer's neck, like a pink mountain when seen from behind as the man sat in the chair muttering, "Good old times, great old times . . ." caused him to hit as hard as he could.

It was not even a knockout blow, for the edge of his hand was soft and inexperienced, and Bayer's neck was insulated by layers of fat. But it was enough. By the time the Odessa contact man had cleared the dizziness from his brain, both his wrists were lashed tightly to the arms of the wooden chair.

"What the shit?" he growled thickly, shaking his head to clear the muzziness. His own tie came off and secured his left ankle to the foot of the chair, and the telephone cord secured the right one.

He looked up owlishly at Miller as comprehension began to dawn in his button eyes. Like all of his kind, Bayer had one nightmare that never quite left him.

"You can't get me away from here," he said. "You'll

never get me to Tel Aviv. You can't prove anything. I
never touched you people—"

The words were cut off as a rolled-up pair of socks
was stuffed in his mouth and a woolen scarf, a present
to Miller from his ever-solicitous mother, was wound
around his face. From above the patterned knitting his
eyes glared balefully out.

Miller drew up the other chair in the room, reversed
it, and sat astride, his face two feet away from that
of his prisoner.

"Listen, you fat slug. For one thing, I'm not an
Israeli agent. For another, you're not going anywhere.
You're staying right here, and you're going to talk right
here. Understand?"

For answer Franz Bayer stared back above the scarf.
The eyes no longer twinkled with merriment. They were
red-tinged, like those of an angry boar in a thicket.

"What I want, and what I'm going to have before
this night is through, is the name and address of the man
who makes the passports for the Odessa."

Miller looked around, spotted the lamp on the bedside
table, unhooked the wall socket, and brought it over.

"Now, Bayer, or whatever your name is, I'm going
to take the gag off. You are going to talk. If you attempt
to yell, you get this right across the head. I don't really
care if I crack your head or not. Got it?"

Miller was not telling the truth. He had never killed
a man before and had no desire to start now.

Slowly he eased off the scarf and pulled the rolled
socks out of Bayer's mouth, keeping the lamp poised in
his right hand, high over the fat man's head.

"You bastard," whispered Bayer. "You're a spy.
You'll get nothing out of me."

He hardly got the words out before the socks went
back into his bulging cheeks. The scarf was replaced.

"No?" said Miller. "We'll see. I'll start on your fingers
and see how you like it."

He took the little finger and ring finger of Bayer's
right hand and bent them backward until they were

almost vertical. Bayer threw himself about in the chair so that it almost fell over. Miller steadied it and eased the pressure on the fingers.

He took off the gag again. "I can break every finger on both your hands, Bayer," he whispered. "After that I'll take the bulb out of the table lamp, switch it on, and stuff your prick down the socket."

Bayer closed his eyes, and sweat rolled in torrents off his face. "No, not the electrodes. No, not the electrodes. Not there," he mumbled.

"You know what it's like, don't you?" said Miller, his mouth a few inches from Bayer's ear.

Bayer closed his eyes and moaned softly. He knew what it was like. Twenty years before, he had been one of the men who had pounded the White Rabbit, Wing Commander Yeo-Thomas, to a maimed pulp in the cellars beneath Fresnes Jail in Paris. He knew too well what it was like, but not on the receiving end.

"Talk," whispered Miller. "The forger, his name and address."

Bayer slowly shook his head. "I can't," he whispered. "They'll kill me."

Miller replaced the gag. He took Bayer's little finger, closed his eyes, and jerked once. The bone snapped at the knuckle. Bayer heaved in his chair and vomited into the gag.

Miller whipped it off before he could drown. The fat man's head jerked forward, and the evening's highly expensive meal, accompanied by two bottles of wine and several double Scotches, poured down his chest into his lap.

"Talk," said Miller. "You've got seven more fingers to go."

Bayer swallowed, eyes closed. "Winzer," he said.

"Who?"

"Winzer. Klaus Winzer. He makes the passports."

"He's a professional forger?"

"He's a printer."

"Where? Which town?"

"They'll kill me."

"I'll kill you if you don't tell me. Which town?"

"Osnabrück," whispered Bayer.

Miller replaced the gag across Bayer's mouth and thought. Klaus Winzer, a printer in Osnabrück. He went to his attaché case, which contained the diary of Salomon Tauber and various maps, and took out a road map of Germany.

The autobahn to Osnabrück, far away to the north in Nord Rhine/Westphalia, led through Mannheim, Frankfurt, Dortmund, and Münster. It was a four- to five-hour drive, depending on road conditions. It was already nearly three in the morning of February 21.

Across the road Mackensen shivered in his niche on the third floor of the half-completed building. The light still shone in the room over the road, the second-floor front. He flicked his eyes constantly from the illuminated window to the front door. If only Bayer would come out, he thought, he could take Miller alone. Or if Miller came out, he could take him farther down the street. Or if someone opened the window for a breath of fresh air. . . . He shivered again and clasped the heavy Remington .300 rifle. At a range of thirty yards there would be no problems with such a gun. Mackensen could wait; he was a patient man.

In his room Miller quietly packed his things. He needed Bayer to remain quiescent for at least six hours. Perhaps the man would be too terrified to warn his chiefs that he had given away the secret of the forger. But Miller couldn't count on it.

He spent a last few minutes tightening the bonds and the gag that held Bayer immobile and silent, then eased the chair onto its side so the fat man could not raise an alarm by rolling the chair over with a crash. The telephone cord was already ripped out. He took a last look around the room and left, locking the door behind him.

He was almost at the top of the stairs when a thought came to him. The night porter might have seen them both mount the stairs. What would he think if only one came down, paid his bill, and left? Miller retreated and headed toward the back of the hotel. At the end of the corridor was a window looking out onto the fire-escape. He slipped the catch and stepped out onto the escape ladder. A few seconds later he was in the rear courtyard, where the garage was situated. A back entrance led to a small alley behind the hotel.

Two minutes later he was striding the three miles to where he had parked his Jaguar, half a mile from Bayer's house. The effect of the drink and the night's activities combined to make him feel desperately tired. He needed sleep badly but realized he had to reach Winzer before the alarm was raised.

It was almost four in the morning when he climbed into the Jaguar, and half past the hour before he had made his way back to the autobahn leading north for Heilbronn and Mannheim.

Almost as soon as he had gone, Bayer, by now completely sober, began to struggle to get free. He tried to lean his head forward far enough to use his teeth, through the sock and the scarf, on the knots of the ties that bound his wrists to the chair. But his fatness prevented his head from getting low enough, and the sock in his mouth forced his teeth apart. Every few minutes he had to pause to take deep breaths through his nose.

He tugged and pulled at his ankle bonds, but they held. Finally, despite the pain from his broken and swelling little finger, he decided to wriggle his wrists free.

When this did not work, he spotted the table lamp lying on the floor. The bulb was still in it, but a crushed light bulb leaves enough slivers of glass to cut a single necktie.

It took him an hour to inch the overturned chair across the floor and crush the light bulb.

It may sound easy, but it isn't, to use a piece of broken glass to cut wrist-bonds. It takes hours to get through a single strand of cloth. Bayer's wrists poured sweat, dampening the cloth of the neckties and making them even tighter around his fat wrists. It was seven in the morning, and light was beginning to filter over the roofs of the town, before the first strands binding his left wrist parted from the effects of being rubbed on a piece of broken glass. It was nearly eight when his left wrist came free.

By that time Miller's Jaguar was boring around the Cologne Ring to the east of the city with another hundred miles before Osnabrück. It had started to rain, an evil sleet running in curtains across the slippery autobahn, and the mesmeric effect of the windshield wipers almost sent him to sleep.

He slowed down to a steady cruise at eighty m.p.h., rather than risk running off the road into the muddy fields on either side.

With his left hand free, Bayer took only a few minutes to rip off his gag, then lay for several minutes, whooping in great gulps of air. The smell in the room was appalling, a mixture of sweat, fear, vomit, and whisky. He unpicked the knots on his right wrist, wincing as the pain from the snapped finger shot up his arm, then released his feet.

His first thought was the door, but it was locked. He tried the telephone, lumbering about on feet long since devoid of feeling from the tightness of the bindings. Finally he staggered to the window, ripped back the curtains, and jerked the windows inward and open.

In his shooting niche across the road, Mackensen was almost dozing despite the cold, when he saw the curtains of Miller's room pulled back. Snapping the Remington up into the aiming position, he waited until the figure behind the net curtains jerked the windows inward, then fired straight into the face of the figure.

The bullet hit Bayer in the base of the throat, and he was dead before his reeling bulk tumbled backward to

the floor. The crash of the rifle might be put down to a
car backfiring for a minute, but not longer. Within less
than a minute, even at that hour of the morning,
Mackensen knew someone would investigate.

Without waiting to cast a second look into the room
across the road, he was out of the third floor and
running down the concrete steps of the building toward
the ground. He left by the back, dodging two cement-
mixers and a pile of gravel in the rear yard. He regained
his car within sixty seconds of firing, stowed the gun
in the trunk, and drove off.

He knew as he sat at the wheel and inserted the
ignition key that all was not right. He suspected he had
made a mistake. The man the Werwolf had briefed him
to kill was tall and lean. The mind's-eye impression of
the figure at the window was of a fat man. From what
he had seen the previous evening, he was sure it was
Bayer he had hit.

Not that it was too serious a problem. Seeing Bayer
dead on his carpet, Miller would be bound to flee as
fast as his legs would carry him. Therefore he would
return to his Jaguar, parked three miles away. Mackensen headed the Mercedes back to where he had last
seen the Jaguar. He only began to worry badly when
he saw the space between the Opel and the Benz truck
where the Jaguar had stood the previous evening in the
quiet residential street.

Mackensen would not have been the chief executioner
for the Odessa if he had been the sort who panics
easily. He had been in too many tight spots before. He
sat at the wheel of his car for several minutes before he
reacted to the prospect of Miller's now being hundreds
of miles away.

If Miller had left Bayer alive, he reasoned, it could
only be because he had got nothing from him or he had
got something. In the first case, there was no harm done;
he could take Miller later. There was no hurry. If Miller
had got something from Bayer, it could only be information. The Werwolf alone would know what kind of

information Miller had been seeking, that Bayer had to give. Therefore, despite his fear of the Werwolf's rage, he would telephone him.

It took him ten minutes to find a public telephone. He always kept a pocketful of one-mark pieces for long-distance calls.

When he took the call in Nuremberg and heard the news, the Werwolf went into a transport of rage, mouthing abuse down the line at his hired killer. It took several seconds before he could calm down. "You'd better find him, you oaf, and quickly. God knows where he's gone now."

Mackensen explained to his chief he needed to know what kind of information Bayer could have supplied to Miller before he died.

At the other end of the line the Werwolf thought for a while. "Dear God," he breathed, "the forger. He's got the name of the forger."

"What forger, Chief?" asked Mackensen.

The Werwolf pulled himself together. "I'll get on to the man and warn him," he said crisply. "This is where Miller has gone." He dictated an address to Mackensen and added, "You get the hell up to Osnabrück like you've never moved before. You'll find Miller at that address, or somewhere in the town. If he's not at the house, keep searching the town for the Jaguar. And this time, don't leave the Jaguar. It's the one place he always returns."

He slammed down the phone, then picked it up again and asked for Information. When he had the number he sought, he dialed a number in Osnabrück.

In Stuttgart, Mackensen was left holding a buzzing receiver. With a shrug he replaced it and went back to his car, facing the prospect of a long, wearying drive followed by another "job." He was almost as tired as Miller, by then twenty miles short of Osnabrück. Neither man had slept for twenty-four hours, and Mackensen had not even eaten since the previous lunch.

Chilled to the marrow from his night's vigil, longing for piping-hot coffee and a Steinhäger to chase it, he got back into the Mercedes and headed it north on the road to Westphalia.

14

To LOOK at him, there was nothing about Klaus Winzer to suggest he had ever been in the SS. For one thing, he was well below the required height of six feet; for another, he was nearsighted. At the age of forty, he was plump and pale, with fuzzy blond hair and a diffident manner.

In fact he had had one of the strangest careers of any man to have worn the uniform of the SS. Born in 1924, he was the son of a certain Johann Winzer, a pork butcher of Wiesbaden, a large, boisterous man who from the early twenties onward was a trusting follower of Adolf Hitler and the Nazi Party. From his earliest days Klaus could remember his father coming home from street battles with the Communists and Socialists.

Klaus took after his mother, and to his father's disgust grew up small, weak, shortsighted, and peaceful. He hated violence, sports, and belonging to the Hitler Youth. At only one thing did he excel: from his early teens he fell completely in love with the art of handwriting and the preparation of illuminated manuscripts, an activity his disgusted father regarded as an occupation for sissies.

With the coming of the Nazis, the pork butcher flourished, obtaining as a reward for his earlier services to the Party the exclusive contract to supply meat to the local SS barracks. He mightily admired the strutting SS youths and devoutly hoped he might one day see his own son wearing the black and silver of the *Schutzstaffel*.

Klaus showed no such inclination, preferring to spend his time poring over his manuscripts, experimenting with colored inks and beautiful lettering.

The war came, and in the spring of 1942 Klaus

turned eighteen, the draft age. In contrast to his ham-
fisted, brawling, Jew-hating father, he was small, pallid,
and shy. Failing even to pass the medical then required
for a desk job with the Army, Klaus was sent home
from the draft board. For his father it was the last straw.

Johann Winzer took the train to Berlin to see an old
friend from his street-fighting days who had since risen
high in the ranks of the SS, in the hopes the man might
intercede for his son and obtain an entry into some
branch of service to the Reich. The man was as helpful
as he could be, which was not much, and asked if there
was anything the young Klaus could do well. Shamefacedly his father admitted he could write illuminated
manuscripts.

The man promised he would do what he could, but
meanwhile he asked if Klaus would prepare an illuminated address on parchment in honor of a certain SS
Major Fritz Suhren.

Back in Wiesbaden, the young Klaus did as he was
asked, and at a ceremony in Berlin a week later this
manuscript was presented to Suhren by his colleagues.
Suhren, then the commandant of Sachsenhausen concentration camp, was being sent to take over command
of the even more notorious Ravensbrück.

Suhren was executed by the French in 1945.

At the handing-over ceremony in the RSHA headquarters in Berlin, everyone admired the beautifully
prepared manuscript, and not least a certain SS Lieutenant Alfred Naujocks. This was the man who had
carried out the mock attack on Gleiwitz radio station on
the German-Polish border in August 1939, leaving the
bodies of concentration-camp inmates in German Army
uniforms as "proof" of the Polish attack on Germany,
Hitler's excuse for invading Poland the following week.

Naujocks asked who had done the manuscript, and,
on being told, he requested the young Klaus Winzer be
brought to Berlin.

Before he knew what was happening, Klaus Winzer
was inducted into the SS, without any formal training
period, made to swear the oath of loyalty and another

oath of secrecy, and told he would be transferred to a
top-secret Reich project. The butcher of Wiesbaden,
bewildered, was in seventh heaven.

The project involved was then being carried out
under the auspices of the RSHA, Amt Six, Section F, in
a workshop in Delbrückstrasse, Berlin. Basically it was
quite simple. The SS was trying to forge hundreds of
thousands of British £5 notes and American $100
bills. The paper was being made in the Reich banknote-
paper factory at Spechthausen, outside Berlin, and the
job of the workshop in Delbrückstrasse was to try and
get the right watermarks for British and American
currency. It was for his knowledge of papers and inks
that they wanted Klaus Winzer.

The idea was to flood Britain and America with
phony money, thus ruining the economies of both
countries. In early 1943, when the watermark for the
British fivers had been achieved, the project of making
the printing plates was transferred to Block 19, Sachsenhausen concentration camp, where Jewish and non-
Jewish graphologists and graphic artists worked under
the direction of the SS. The job of Winzer was quality
control, for the SS did not trust its prisoners not to make
a deliberate error in their work.

Within two years Klaus Winzer had been taught by
his charges everything they knew, and that was enough
to make him a forger extraordinary. Toward the end
of 1944 the project in Block 19 was also being used
to prepare forged identity cards for the SS officers to
use after the collapse of Germany.

In the early spring of 1945 the private little world,
happy in its way when contrasted with the devastation
then overtaking Germany, was brought to an end.

The whole operation, commanded by a certain SS
Captain Bernhard Krüger, was ordered to leave Sachsenhausen and transfer itself into the remote mountains of
Austria and continue the good work. The group drove
south and set up the forgery again in the deserted
brewery of Redl-Zipf in Upper Austria. A few days
before the end of the war, a brokenhearted Klaus

Winzer stood weeping on the edge of a lake as millions
of pounds and billions of dollars in his beautiful forged
currency were dumped into the lake.

He went back to Wiesbaden and home. To his
astonishment, having never lacked for a meal in the SS,
he found the German civilians almost starving in that
summer of 1945. The Americans now occupied Wiesbaden, and although they had plenty to eat, the Germans
were nibbling at crusts. His father, by now a lifelong
anti-Nazi, had come down in the world. Where once his
shop had been stocked with hams, only a single string
of sausages hung from the rows of gleaming hooks.

Klaus's mother explained to him that all food had to
be bought on ration cards issued by the Americans. In
amazement Klaus looked at the ration cards, noted they
were locally printed on fairly cheap paper, took a handful, and retired to his room for a few days. When he
emerged, it was to hand over to his astonished mother
sheets of American ration cards, enough to feed them
all for six months.

"But they're forged," gasped his mother.

Klaus explained patiently what by then he sincerely
believed: they were not forged, just printed on a different machine.

His father backed Klaus. "Are you saying, foolish
woman, that our son's ration cards are inferior to the
Yankee ration cards?"

The argument was unanswerable, the more so when
they sat down to a four-course meal that night.

A month later Klaus Winzer met Otto Klops, flashy,
self-assured, the king of the black market of Wiesbaden,
and they were in business. Winzer turned out endless
quantities of ration cards, gasoline coupons, zonal
border passes, driving licenses, United States military
passes, PX cards; Klops used them to buy food, gasoline, truck tires, nylon stockings, soap, cosmetics, and
clothing, keeping a part of the booty to enable him and
the Winzers to live well, selling the rest at black-market
prices. Within thirty months, by the summer of 1948,

Klaus Winzer was a rich man. In his bank account reposed five million Reichsmarks.

To his horrified mother he explained his simple philosophy. "A document is not either genuine or forged; it is either efficient or inefficient. If a pass is supposed to get you past a checkpoint, and it gets you past the checkpoint, it is a good document."

In October 1948 came the second dirty trick played on Klaus Winzer. The authorities reformed the currency, substituting the new Deutschmark for the old Reichsmark. But instead of giving one for one, they simply abolished the Reichsmark and gave everyone the flat sum of 1000 new marks. He was ruined. Once again his fortune was mere useless paper.

The populace, no longer needing the black-marketeers as goods came on the open market, denounced Klops, and Winzer had to flee. Taking one of his own zonal passes, he drove to the headquarters of the British Zone at Hanover and applied for a job in the passport office of the British Military Government.

His references from the United States authorities at Wiesbaden, signed by a full colonel of the USAF, were excellent. They should have been; he had written them himself. The British major who interviewed him for the job put down his cup of tea and told the applicant, "I do hope you realize the importance of people having proper documentation on them at all times."

With complete sincerity Winzer assured the major that he did indeed. Two months later came his lucky break. He was alone in a beer hall, sipping a beer, when a man got into conversation with him. The man's name was Herbert Molders. He confided to Winzer he was being sought by the British for war crimes and needed to get out of Germany. But only the British could supply passports to Germans, and he dared not apply. Winzer murmured that it might be arranged but would cost money.

To his amazement, Molders produced a genuine diamond necklace. He explained that he had been in a concentration camp, and one of the Jewish inmates had tried to buy his freedom with the family jewelry. Molders had taken the jewelry, ensured that the Jew was in the first party to the gas chambers, and against orders had kept the booty.

A week later, armed with a photograph of Molders, Winzer prepared the passport. He did not even forge it. He did not need to.

The system at the passport office was simple. In Section One, applicants turned up with all their documentation and filled out forms. Then they went away, leaving their documents for study. Section Two examined the birth certificates, ID cards, driving licenses, etc., for possible forgery, checked the war criminals wanted list, and, if the application was approved, passed the documents, accompanied by a signed approval from Head of Department, to Section Three. Section Three, on receipt of the note of approval from Section Two, took a blank passport from the safe where it was stored, filled it out, stuck in the applicant's photograph, and gave the passport to the applicant, who presented himself a week later.

Winzer got himself transferred to Section Three. Quite simply, he filled out an application form for Molders in a new name, wrote out an "Application Approved" slip from the head of Section Two, and forged that British officer's signature.

He walked through into Section Two and picked up the nineteen application forms and approval slips waiting for collection, slipped the Molders application form and approval slip among them, and took the sheaf to Major Johnstone. Johnstone checked that there were twenty approval slips, went to his safe, took out twenty blank passports, and handed them to Winzer. Winzer duly filled them out, gave them the official stamp, and handed nineteen to the waiting nineteen happy applicants. The twentieth went into his pocket. Into the filing cabinet went twenty application forms to match the twenty issued passports.

That evening he handed Molders his new passport

and took the diamond necklace. He had found his new métier.

In May 1949 West Germany was founded, and the passport office was handed over to the state government of Lower Saxony, capital city Hanover. Winzer stayed on. He did not have any more clients. He did not need them. Each week, armed with a full-face portrait of some nonentity bought from a studio photographer, Winzer carefully filled out a passport-application form, attached the photograph to the form, forged an approval slip with the signature of the head of Section Two (by now a German), and went to see the head of Section Three with a sheaf of application forms and approval slips. So long as the numbers tallied, he got a bunch of blank passports in return. All but one went to the genuine applicants. The last blank passport went into his pocket. Apart from that, all he needed was the official stamp. To steal it would have aroused suspicion. He took it for one night and by morning had a casting of the stamp of the passport office of the state government of Lower Saxony.

In sixty weeks he had sixty blank passports. He resigned his job, blushingly acknowledged the praise of his superiors for his careful, meticulous work as a clerk in their employ, left Hanover, sold the diamond necklace in Antwerp, and started a nice little printing business in Osnabrück, at a time when gold and dollars could buy anything well below market price.

He would never have got involved with the Odessa if Molders had kept his mouth shut. But once arrived in Madrid and among friends, Molders boasted of his contact who could provide genuine West German passports in a false name to anyone who asked.

In late 1950 a "friend" came to see Winzer, who had just started work as a printer in Osnabrück. There was nothing Winzer could do but agree. From then on, whenever an Odessa man was in trouble, Winzer supplied the new passport.

The system was perfectly safe. All Winzer needed was a photograph of the man and his age. He had kept a copy of the personal details written into each of the application forms by then reposing in the archive in Hanover. He would take a blank passport and fill in the personal details already written on one of those application forms from 1949. The name was usually a common one, the place of birth usually by then far behind the Iron Curtain, where no one would check, the date of birth would almost correspond to the real age of the SS applicant, and then he would stamp it with the stamp of Lower Saxony. The recipient would sign his new passport in his own handwriting with his new name when he received it.

Renewals were easy. After five years the wanted SS man would simply apply for renewal at the state capital of any state other than Lower Saxony. The clerk in Bavaria, for example, would check with Hanover: "Did you issue a passport number so-and-so in nineteen fifty to one Walter Schumann, place of birth such and date of birth such?" In Hanover another clerk would check the records in the files and reply, "Yes." The Bavarian clerk, reassured by his Hanoverian colleague that the original passport was genuine, would issue a new one, stamped by Bavaria.

So long as the face on the application form in Hanover was not compared with the face in the passport presented in Munich, there could be no problem. And comparison of faces never took place. Clerks rely on forms correctly filled in, correctly approved, and passport numbers, not faces.

Only after 1955, more than five years after the original issuing of the Hanover passport, would immediate renewal be necessary for the holder of a Winzer passport. Once the passport was obtained, the wanted SS man could acquire a fresh driving license, social-security card, bank account, credit card, in short an entire new identity.

By the spring of 1964 Winzer had supplied forty-two passports out of his stock of sixty originals.

But the cunning little man had taken one precaution. It occurred to him that one day the Odessa might wish to dispose of his services, and of him. So he kept a record. He never knew the real names of his clients; to make out a false passport in a new name, it was not necessary. The point was immaterial. He took a copy of every photograph sent to him, pasted the original in the passport he was sending back, and kept the copy. Each photograph was pasted onto a sheet of cartridge paper. Beside it was typed the new name, the address (addresses are required on German passports), and the new passport number.

These sheets were kept in a file. The file was his life insurance. There was one in his house, and a copy with a lawyer in Zurich. If his life were ever threatened by the Odessa, he would tell them about the file and warn them that if anything happened to him the lawyer in Zurich would send the copy to the German authorities.

The West Germans, armed with a photograph, would soon compare it with their rogues' gallery of wanted Nazis. The passport number alone, checked quickly with each of the sixteen state capitals, would reveal the domicile of the holder. Exposure would take no more than a week. It was a foolproof scheme to ensure that Klaus Winzer stayed alive and in good health.

This, then, was the man who sat quietly munching his toast and jam, sipping his coffee, and glancing through the front page of the Osnabrück *Zeitung* over breakfast at half past eight that Friday morning, when the phone rang. The voice at the other end was first peremptory, then reassuring.

"There is no question of your being in any trouble with us at all," the Werwolf assured him. "It's just this damn reporter. We have a tip that he's coming to see you. It's perfectly all right. We have one of our men coming up behind him, and the whole affair will be taken care of within the day. But you must get out of there within ten minutes. Now here's what I want you to do. . . ."

Thirty minutes later a very flustered Klaus Winzer had a small bag packed, cast an undecided glance in the direction of the safe where the file was kept, came to the conclusion he would not need it, and explained to a startled housemaid, Barbara, that he would not be going to the printing plant that morning. On the contrary, he had decided to take a brief vacation in the Austrian Alps. A breath of fresh air—nothing like it to tone up the system.

Barbara stood on the doorstep open-mouthed as Winzer's Kadett shot backward down the drive, swung out into the residential road in front of his house, and drove off. Ten minutes after nine o'clock he had reached the cloverleaf four miles west of the town, where the road climbed up to join the autobahn. As the Kadett shot up the incline to the motorway on one side, a black Jaguar was coming down the other side, heading into Osnabrück.

Miller found a filling station at the Saar Platz at the western entrance to the town. He pulled up by the pumps and climbed wearily out. His muscles ached and his neck felt as if it were locked solid. The wine he had drunk the evening before gave his mouth a taste like parrot droppings.

"Fill her up. Super," he told the attendant. "Have you got a pay phone?"

"In the corner," said the boy.

On the way over, Miller noticed a coffee machine and took a steaming cup into the phone booth with him. He flicked through the phone book for Osnabrück. There were several Winzers, but only one Klaus. The name was repeated twice. Against the first entry was the word "Printer." The second Klaus Winzer had the abbreviation "res." for residence against it. It was nine-twenty. Working hours. He rang the printing plant.

The man who answered was evidently the foreman. "I'm sorry, he's not in yet," said the voice. "Usually he's here at nine sharp. He'll no doubt be along soon. Call back in half an hour."

Miller thanked him and considered dialing the house. Better not. If Winzer was at home, Miller wanted him personally. He noted the address and left the booth.

"Where's Westerberg?" he asked the pump attendant as he paid for the gas, noting that he had only 500 marks left of his savings. The boy nodded across to the north side of the road.

"That's it. The posh suburb. Where all the rich people live."

Miller bought a town plan as well and traced the street he wanted. It was barely ten minutes away.

The house was obviously prosperous, and the whole area spoke of well-to-do professional people living in comfortable surroundings. He left the Jaguar at the end of the drive and walked to the front door.

The maid who answered it was in her late teens and very pretty. She smiled brightly at him.

"Good morning. I've come to see Herr Winzer," he told her.

"Oooh, he's left, sir. You just missed him by about twenty minutes."

Miller recovered. Doubtless Winzer was on his way to the printing plant and had been held up.

"Oh, what a pity. I'd hoped to catch him before he went to work," he said.

"He hasn't gone to work, sir. Not this morning. He's gone off on vacation," replied the girl helpfully.

Miller fought down a rising feeling of panic. "Vacation? That's odd at this time of year. Besides"—he invented quickly—"we had an appointment this morning. He asked me to come here especially."

"Oh, what a shame," said the girl, evidently distressed. "He went off very suddenly. He got this phone call in the library; then he went upstairs. 'Barbara,' he said —that's my name—'Barbara, I'm going on a vacation in Austria. Just for a week,' he said. Well, I hadn't heard any plans for a vacation. He told me to call the plant and say he's not coming in for a week. Then off he went. That's not like Herr Winzer at all. He's usually so quiet."

Inside Miller, the hope began to die. "Did he say where he was going?" he asked.

"No. Nothing. Just said he was going to the Austrian Alps."

"No forwarding address? No way of getting in touch with him?"

"No, that's what's so strange. I mean, what about the printing plant? I just called them before you came. They were very surprised, with all the orders they had to be completed."

Miller calculated fast. Winzer had a half-hour's start on him. Driving at eighty miles an hour, he would have covered forty miles. Miller could keep up a hundred, overtaking at twenty miles an hour. That would mean two hours before he saw the tail of Winzer's car. Too long. Winzer could be anywhere in two hours. Besides, there was no proof he was heading south to Austria.

"Then could I speak to Frau Winzer, please?" he asked.

Barbara giggled and looked at him archly. "There isn't any Frau Winzer," she said. "Don't you know Herr Winzer at all?"

"No, I never met him."

"Well, he's not the marrying kind, really. I mean very nice, but not really interested in women, if you know what I mean."

"So he lives here alone, then?"

"Well, except for me, I mean, I live in. It's quite safe. From that point of view." She giggled.

"I see. Thank you," said Miller and turned to go.

"You're welcome," said the girl, and watched him go down the drive and climb into the Jaguar, which had already caught her attention. What with Herr Winzer being away, she wondered if she might be able to ask a nice young man home for the night before her employer got back. She watched the Jaguar drive away with a roar of exhaust, sighed for what might have been, and closed the door.

Miller felt the weariness creeping over him, accentuated by the last and, so far as he was concerned, final disappointment. He surmised Bayer had wriggled free from his bonds and used the hotel telephone in Stuttgart to call Winzer and warn him. He had got so close, fifteen minutes from his target, and almost made it. Now he felt only the need for sleep.

He drove past the medieval wall of the old city, followed the map to the Theodor Heuss Platz, parked the Jaguar in front of the station, and checked into the Hohenzollern Hotel across the square.

He was lucky; they had a room available at once, so he went upstairs, undressed, and lay on the bed. There was something nagging in the back of his mind, some point he had not covered, some tiny detail of a question he had left unasked. It was still unsolved when he fell asleep at half past ten.

Mackensen made it to the center of Osnabrück at half past one. On the way into town he had checked the house in Westerberg, but there was no sign of a Jaguar. He wanted to call the Werwolf before he went there, in case there was more news.

By chance the post office in Osnabrück flanks one side of the Theodor Heuss Platz. A whole corner and one side of the square is taken up by the main railway station, and a third side is occupied by the Hohenzollern Hotel. As Mackensen parked by the post office, his face split in a grin. The Jaguar he sought was in front of the station.

The Werwolf was in a better mood. "It's all right. Panic over for the moment," he told the killer. "I reached the forger in time, and he got out of town. I just phoned his house again. It must have been the maid who answered. She told me her employer had left barely twenty minutes before a young man with a black sports car came inquiring after him."

"I've got some news too," said Mackensen. "The Jaguar is parked right here on the square in front of me. Chances are he's sleeping it off in the hotel. I can take him right here in the hotel room. I'll use the silencer."

"Hold it, don't be in too much of a hurry," warned the Werwolf. "I've been thinking. For one thing, he must not get it inside Osnabrück town. The maid has seen him and his car. She would probably report to the police. That would bring attention to our forger, and he's the panicking kind. I can't have him involved. The maid's testimony would cast a lot of suspicion on him. First he gets a phone call, then he dashes out and vanishes, then a young man calls to see him, then the man is shot in a hotel room. It's too much."

Mackensen's brow was furrowed. "You're right," he said at length. "I'll have to take him when he leaves."

"He'll probably stick around for a few hours, checking for a lead on the forger. He won't get one. There's one other thing. Does Miller carry a document case?"

"Yes," said Mackensen. "He had it with him as he left the cabaret last night. And took it with him when he went back to his hotel room."

"So why not leave it locked in the trunk of his car? Why not in his hotel room? Because it's important to him. You follow me?"

"Yes," said Mackensen.

"The point is," said the Werwolf, "he has now seen me and knows my name and address. He knows of the connection with Bayer and the forger. And reporters write things down. That document case is now vital. Even if Miller dies, the case must not fall into the hands of the police."

"I've got you. You want the case as well?"

"Either get it or destroy it," said the voice from Nuremberg.

Mackensen thought for a moment. "The best way to do both would be for me to plant a bomb in the car. Linked to the suspension, so it will detonate when he hits a bump at high speed on the autobahn."

"Excellent," said the Werwolf. "Will the case be destroyed?"

"With the bomb I have in mind, the car, Miller, and the case will go up in flames and be completely gutted. Moreover, at high speed it looks like an accident. The gas tank exploded, the witnesses will say. What a pity."

"Can you do it?" asked the Werwolf.

Mackensen grinned. The killing kit in the trunk of his car was an assassin's dream. It included nearly a pound of plastic explosive and two electric detonators.

"Sure," he growled, "no problem. But to get at the car I'll have to wait until dark."

He stopped talking, gazed out of the window of the post office, and barked into the phone, "Call you back."

He called back in five minutes. "Sorry about that. I just saw Miller, attaché case in hand, climbing into his car. He drove off. I checked the hotel, and he's registered there all right. He's left his traveling bags, so he'll be back. No panic, I'll get on with the bomb and plant it tonight."

Miller had waked up just before one, feeling refreshed and somewhat elated. In sleeping he had remembered what was troubling him. He drove back to Winzer's house.

The maid was plainly pleased to see him. "Hello. You again?" She beamed.

"I was just passing on my way back home," said Miller, "and I wondered, how long have you been in service here?"

"Oh, about ten months. Why?"

"Well, with Herr Winzer not being the marrying kind, and you being so young, who looked after him before you came?"

"Oh, I see what you mean. His housekeeper, Fräulein Wendel."

"Where is she now?"

"Oh, in the hospital. I'm afraid she's dying. Cancer of the breast, you know. Terrible thing. That's what makes it so funny that Herr Winzer dashed off like that. He goes to visit her every day. He's devoted to her. Not that they ever—well, you know—did anything, but she was with him for a long time, since nineteen fifty, I think, and he thinks the world of her. He's always saying to me, 'Fräulein Wendel did it this way,' and so on."

"What hospital is she in?" asked Miller.

"I forget now. No, wait a minute. It's on the telephone notepad. I'll get it."

She was back in two minutes and gave him the name of the clinic, an exclusive private sanatorium just beyond the outskirts of the town.

Finding his way by the map, Miller presented himself at the clinic just after three in the afternoon.

Mackensen spent the early afternoon buying the ingredients for his bomb. "The secret of sabotage," his instructor had once told him, "is to keep the requirements simple. The sort of thing you can buy in any shop."

From a hardware store he bought a soldering iron and a small stick of solder; a roll of black insulating tape; a yard of thin wire and a pair of cutters; a one-foot hacksaw blade and a tube of instant glue. In an electrician's he acquired a nine-volt transistor battery; a small bulb, one inch in diameter; and two lengths of fine single-strand, five-amp plastic-coated wire, each three yards long, one colored red and the other blue. He was a neat man and liked to keep positive and negative terminals distinct. A stationer's supplied him with five erasers of the large kind, one inch wide, two inches long, and a quarter of an inch thick. In a drugstore he bought two packages of condoms, each containing three rubber sheaths, and from a high-class grocer he got a canister of fine tea. It was a 250-gram can with a tight-fitting lid. As a good workman, he hated the idea of his explosive getting wet, and the tea can's lid would keep out the air, let alone the moisture.

With his purchases made, he took a room in the Hohenzollern Hotel overlooking the square, so that he could keep an eye on the parking area, to which he was certain Miller would return, while he worked.

Before entering the hotel, he took from his trunk half a pound of the plastic explosive, squashy stuff like children's plasticene, and one of the electric detonators.

Seated at the table in front of the window, keeping

half an eye on the square, with a pot of strong black coffee to stave off his tiredness, he went to work.

It was a simple bomb he made. First he emptied the tea down the toilet and kept the can only. In the lid he jabbed a hole with the handle of the wire clippers. He took the nine-foot length of red wire and cut a ten-inch length off it.

One end of this short length of red-coated wire he spot-soldered to the positive terminal of the battery. To the negative terminal he soldered one end of the long, blue-colored wire. To ensure that these wires never touched each other, he drew one down each side of the battery and whipped both wires and battery together with insulating tape.

The other end of the short red wire was twirled around the contact point on the detonator. To the same contact point was fixed one end of the other, eight-foot piece of red wire.

He deposited the battery and its wires in the base of the square tea can, embedded the detonator deep into the plastic explosive, and smoothed the explosive into the can on top of the battery until the can was full.

A near-circuit had now been set up. A wire went from the battery to the detonator. Another went from the detonator to nowhere, its bare end in space. From the battery, another wire went to nowhere, its bare end in space. But when these two exposed ends, one of the eight-foot-long red wire, the other of the blue wire, touched each other, the circuit would be complete. The charge from the battery would fire the detonator, which would explode with a sharp crack. But the crack would be lost in the roar as the plastic went off, enough to demolish two or three of the hotel's bedrooms.

The remaining device was the trigger mechanism. For this he wrapped his hands in handkerchiefs and bent the hacksaw blade until it snapped in the middle, leaving him with two six-inch lengths, each one perforated at one end by the small hole that usually fixes a hacksaw blade to its frame.

He piled the five erasers one on top of another so that together they made a block of rubber. Using this to separate the halves of the blade, he bound them along the upper and lower side of the block of rubber, so that the six-inch lengths of steel stuck out, parallel to each other and one and a quarter inches apart. In outline they looked rather like the jaws of a crocodile. The rubber block was at one end of the lengths of steel, so four inches of the blades were separated only by air. To make sure there was a little more resistance than air to prevent their touching, Mackensen lodged the light bulb between the open jaws, fixing it in place with a generous blob of glue. Glass does not conduct electricity.

He was almost ready. He threaded the two lengths of wire, one red and one blue, which protruded from the can of explosive through the hole in the lid and re-placed the lid on the can, pushing it firmly back into place. Of the two pieces of wire, he soldered the end of one to the upper hacksaw blade, the other to the lower blade. The bomb was now live.

Should the trigger ever be trodden on, or subjected to sudden pressure, the bulb would shatter, the two lengths of sprung steel would close together, and the electric circuit from the battery would be complete. There was one last precaution. To prevent the exposed hacksaw blades from ever touching the same piece of metal at the same time, which would also complete the circuit, he smoothed all six condoms over the trigger, one on top of another, until the device was protected from outside detonation by six layers of thin but insulating rubber. That at least would prevent accidental detonation.

His bomb complete, he stowed it in the bottom of the wardrobe, along with the binding wire, the clippers and the rest of the sticky tape, which he would need to fix it to Miller's car. Then he ordered more coffee to stay awake, and settled down at the window to wait for Miller's return to the parking lot in the center of the square.

He did not know where Miller had gone, nor did he

care. The Werwolf had assured him there were no leads he could pick up to give him the whereabouts of the forger, and that was that. As a good technician, Mackensen was prepared to do his job and leave the rest to those in charge. He was prepared to be patient. He knew Miller would return sooner or later.

15

THE DOCTOR glanced with little favor at the visitor. Miller, who hated collars and ties and avoided wearing them whenever he could, had on a white nylon turtle-necked sweater and over it a black pullover with a crew neck. Over the two pullovers he wore a black blazer. For hospital-visiting, the doctor's expression clearly said, a collar and tie would be more appropriate.

"Her nephew?" he repeated with surprise. "Strange, I had no idea Fräulein Wendel had a nephew."

"I believe I am her sole surviving relative," said Miller. "Obviously I would have come far sooner, had I known of my aunt's condition, but Herr Winzer only called me this morning to inform me, and asked me to visit her."

"Herr Winzer is usually here himself about this hour," observed the doctor.

"I understand he's been called away," said Miller blandly. "At least, that was what he told me on the phone this morning. He said he would not be back for some days, and asked me to visit in his stead."

"Gone away? How extraordinary. How very odd." The doctor paused for a moment, irresolute, and then added, "Would you excuse me?"

Miller saw him go back from the entrance hall where they had been talking to a small office to one side. From the open door he heard snatches of conversation as the clinic doctor rang Winzer's house.

"He has indeed gone away? . . . This morning? . . . Several days? . . . Oh, no, thank you, Fräulein, I just wanted to confirm that he will not be visiting this afternoon."

The doctor hung up and came back to the hall. "Strange," he murmured. "Herr Winzer has been here, as regular as clockwork, since Fräulein Wendel was brought in. Evidently a most devoted man. Well, he had better be quick if he wishes to see her again. She is very far gone, you know."

Miller looked sad. "So he told me on the phone," he lied. "Poor Auntie."

"As her relative, of course you may spend a short time with her. But I must warn you, she is hardly coherent, so I must ask you to be as brief as you can. Come this way."

The doctor led Miller down several passages of what had evidently once been a large private house, now converted into a clinic, and stopped at a bedroom door.

"She's in here," he said and showed Miller in, closing the door after him. Miller heard his footsteps retreating down the passage.

The room was in semi-darkness and until his eyes had become accustomed to the dull light from the wintry afternoon that came through the gap in the slightly parted curtains, he failed to distinguish the shriveled form of the woman in the bed. She was raised on several pillows under her head and shoulders, but so pale was her nightgown and the face above it that she almost merged with the bedclothes. Her eyes were closed. Miller had few hopes of obtaining from her the likely bolt-hole of the vanished forger.

He whispered, "Fräulein Wendel," and the eyelids fluttered and opened.

She stared at him without a trace of expression in the eyes, and Miller doubted if she could even see him. She closed her eyes again and began to mutter incoherently. He leaned closer to catch the phrases coming in a monotonous jumble from the gray lips.

They meant very little. There was something about Rosenheim, which he knew to be a small village in Bavaria, perhaps the place she had been born. Something else about "all dressed in white, so pretty, so very pretty." Then there was another jumble of words that meant nothing.

Miller leaned closer. "Fräulein Wendel, can you hear me?"

The dying woman was still muttering. Miller caught the words ". . . each carrying a prayer book and a posy, all in white, so innocent then."

Miller frowned in thought before he understood. In delirium she was trying to recall her First Communion. Like himself, she had once been a practicing Roman Catholic.

"Can you hear me, Fräulein Wendel?" he repeated, without any hope of getting through. She opened her eyes again and stared at him, taking in the white band around his neck, the black material over his chest, and the black jacket. To his astonishment she closed her eyes again, and her flat torso heaved in spasm. Miller was worried. He thought he had better call the doctor. Then two tears, one from each closed eye, rolled down the parchment cheeks.

On the coverlet one of her hands crawled slowly toward his wrist, where he had supported himself on the bed while leaning over her. With surprising strength, or simply desperation, her hand gripped his wrist possessively. Miller was about to detach himself and go, convinced she could tell him nothing about Klaus Winzer, when she said quite distinctly, "Bless me, Father, for I have sinned."

For a few seconds Miller failed to understand, then a glance at his own chest-front made him realize the mistake the woman had made in the dim light. He debated for two minutes whether to leave her and go back to Hamburg, or whether to risk his soul and have one last try at locating Eduard Roschmann through the forger.

He leaned forward again. "My child, I am prepared to hear your confession."

Then she began to talk. In a tired, dull monotone, her life story came out. Once she had been a girl, born and brought up amid the fields and forests of Bavaria. Born in 1910, she remembered her father going away to the First War and returning three years later after the

Armistice of 1918, angry and bitter against the men in Berlin who had capitulated.

She remembered the political turmoil of the early twenties and the attempted *Putsch* in nearby Munich when a crowd of men headed by a streetcorner rabble-rouser called Adolf Hitler had tried to overthrow the government. Her father had later joined the man and his party, and by the time she was twenty-three the rabble-rouser and his party had become the government of Germany. There were the summer outings of the Union of German Maidens, the secretarial job with the Gauleiter of Bavaria, and the dances with the handsome blond young men in their black uniforms.

But she had grown up ugly, tall, bony, and angular, with a face like a horse and hair along her upper lip. Her mousy hair tied back in a bun, in heavy clothes and sensible shoes, she had realized in her late twenties there would be no marriage for her, as for the other girls in the village. By 1939 she had been posted, an embittered and hate-filled woman, as a wardress in a camp called Ravensbrück.

She told of the people she had beaten and clubbed, the days of power and cruelty in the camp in Brandenburg, the tears rolling quietly down her cheeks, her fingers gripping Miller's wrist lest he should depart in disgust before she had done.

"And after the war?" he asked softly.

There had been years of wandering—abandoned by the SS, hunted by the Allies, working in kitchens as a scullery maid, washing dishes and sleeping in Salvation Army hostels. Then in 1950 she met Winzer staying in a hotel in Osnabrück while he looked for a house to buy. She had been a waitress. He bought his house, the little neuter man, and suggested she come and keep house for him.

"Is that all?" asked Miller when she stopped.

"Yes, Father."

"My child, you know I cannot give you absolution if you have not confessed all your sins."

"That is all, Father."

Miller drew a deep breath. "And what about the forged passports? The ones he made for the SS men on the run?"

She was silent for a while, and he feared she had passed into unconsciousness.

"You know about that, Father?"

"I know about it."

"I did not make them," she said.

"But you knew about them, about the work Klaus Winzer did."

"Yes." The word was a low whisper.

"He has gone now. He has gone away," said Miller.

"No. Not gone. Not Klaus. He would not leave me. He will come back."

"Do you know where he has gone?"

"No, Father."

"Are you sure? Think, my child. He has been forced to run away. Where would he go?"

The emaciated head shook slowly against the pillow. "I don't know, Father. If they threaten him, he will use the file. He told me he would."

Miller started. He looked down at the woman, her eyes now closed as if in sleep. "What file, my child?"

They talked for another five minutes. Then there was a soft tap on the door. Miller eased the woman's hand off his wrist and rose to go.

"Father . . ." The voice was plaintive, pleading. He turned. She was staring at him, her eyes wide open. "Bless me, Father."

The tone was imploring. Miller sighed. It was a mortal sin. He hoped somebody somewhere would understand. He raised his right hand and made the sign of the cross.

"*In nomine Patris, et Filii, et Spiritus Sancti, ego te absolvo a peccatis tuis.*"

The woman sighed deeply, closed her eyes, and passed into unconsciousness.

Outside in the passage, the doctor was waiting. "I really think that is long enough," he said.

Miller nodded. "Yes, she is sleeping," he said, and,

after a glance around the door, the doctor escorted him back to the entrance hall.

"How long do you think she has?" asked Miller.

"Very difficult to say. Two days, maybe three. Not more. I'm very sorry."

"Yes, well, thank you for letting me see her," said Miller. The doctor held open the front door for him. "Oh, there is one last thing, Doctor. We are all Catholics in our family. She asked me for a priest. The last rites, you understand?"

"Yes, of course."

"Will you see to it?"

"Certainly," said the doctor. "I didn't know. I'll see to it this afternoon. Thank you for telling me. Good-by."

It was late afternoon and dusk was turning into night when Miller drove back into the Theodor Heuss Platz and parked the Jaguar twenty yards from the hotel. He crossed the road and went up to his room. Two floors above, Mackensen had watched his arrival. Taking his bomb in his suitcase, he descended to the foyer, paid his bill for the coming night, explaining that he would be leaving very early in the morning, and went out to his car. He maneuvered it into a place where he could watch the hotel entrance and the Jaguar, and settled down to another wait.

There were still too many people in the area for him to go to work on the Jaguar, and Miller might come out of the hotel any second. If he drove off before the bomb could be planted, Mackensen would take him on the open highway, several miles from Osnabrück, and steal the document case. If Miller slept in the hotel, Mackensen would plant the bomb in the small hours, when no one was about.

In his room, Miller was racking his brains for a name. He could see the man's face, but the name still escaped him.

It had been just before Christmas 1961. He had been in the press box in the Hamburg provincial court, waiting for a case in which he was interested. He had caught the tail end of the preceding case. There was a little ferret of a man standing in the dock, and defending counsel was asking for leniency, pointing out that it was just before the Christmas period and his client had a wife and five children.

Miller remembered glancing at the well of the court, and noting the tired, harassed face of the convicted man's wife. She had covered her face with her hands in utter despair when the judge, explaining the sentence would have been longer but for the defending counsel's plea for leniency, sentenced the man to eighteen months in jail. The prosecution had described the prisoner as one of the most skillfull safecrackers in Hamburg.

Two weeks later, Miller had been in a bar not two hundred yards from the Reeperbahn, having a Christmas drink with some of his underworld contacts. He was flush with money, having been paid for a big picture feature that day. There was a woman scrubbing the floor at the far end. He had recognized the worried face of the wife of the cracksman who had been sentenced two weeks earlier. In a fit of generosity which he regretted the next morning, he had pushed a 100-mark note into her apron pocket and left.

In January he had got a letter from Hamburg Jail. It was hardly literate. The woman must have asked the barman for his name and told her husband. The letter had been sent to a magazine for which he sometimes worked. They had passed it on to him.

Dear Herr Miller,
    My wife wrote me about what you done just before Christmas. I never met you, and I don't know why you done it, but I want to thank you very much. You are a real good guy. The money helped Marta and the kids have a real good time over Christmas and the New Year. If ever I can do you a good turn back, just let me know. Yours with respects . . .

But what was the name on the bottom of that letter? Koppel. That was it. Viktor Koppel. Praying that he had not got himself back inside prison again, Miller took out his little book of contacts' names and telephone numbers, dragged the hotel telephone onto his knees, and started calling friends in the underworld of Hamburg.

He found Koppel at half past seven. As it was a Friday evening, he was in a bar with a crowd of friends, and Miller could hear the jukebox in the background. It was playing the Beatles' "I Want to Hold Your Hand," which had almost driven him mad that winter, so frequently had it been played.

With a little prompting, Koppel remembered him, and the present he had given to Marta two years earlier. Koppel had evidently had a few drinks.

"Very nice of you that was, Herr Miller, very nice thing to do."

"Look, you wrote me from prison saying if there was ever anything you could do for me, you'd do it. Remember?"

Koppel's voice was wary. "Yeah, I remember."

"Well, I need a bit of help. Not much. Can you help me out?" said Miller.

The man in Hamburg was still wary. "I ain't got much on me, Herr Miller."

"I don't want a loan," said Miller. "I want to pay you for a job. Just a small one."

Koppel's voice was full of relief. "Oh, I see, yes, sure. Where are you?"

Miller gave him his instructions. "Just get down to Hamburg station and grab the first train to Osnabrück. I'll meet you at the station. One last thing: bring your working tools with you."

"Now look, Herr Miller, I don't work off my turf. I don't know about Osnabrück."

Miller dropped into the Hamburg slang. "It's a walkover, Koppel. Empty, owner gone away, and a load of gear inside. I've cased it, and there's no problem. You can be back in Hamburg for breakfast, with a bagful of loot and no questions asked. The man will be away for a week. You can unload the stuff before he's back, and the cops down here will think it was a local job."

"What about my train fare?" asked Koppel.

"I'll give it to you when you get here. There's a train at nine out of Hamburg. You've got an hour. So get moving."

Koppel sighed deeply. "All right, I'll be on the train."

Miller hung up, asked the hotel switchboard operator to call him at eleven, and dozed off.

Outside, Mackensen continued his lonely vigil. He decided to start on the Jaguar at midnight if Miller had not emerged.

But Miller walked out of the hotel at quarter past eleven, crossed the square, and entered the station. Mackensen was surprised. He climbed out of the Mercedes and went to look through the entrance hall. Miller was on the platform, standing waiting for a train.

"What's the next train from this platform?" Mackensen asked a porter.

"Eleven thirty-three to Münster," said the porter.

Mackensen wondered idly why Miller should want to take a train when he had a car. Still puzzled, he returned to his Mercedes and resumed his wait.

At eleven thirty-five his problem was solved. Miller came back out of the station, accompanied by a small, shabby man carrying a black leather bag. They were in deep conversation. Mackensen swore. The last thing he wanted was for Miller to drive off in the Jaguar with company. That would complicate the killing to come. To his relief, the pair approached a waiting taxi, climbed in, and drove off. He decided to give them twenty minutes and then start on the Jaguar, still parked twenty yards away from him.

At midnight the square was almost empty. Mackensen slipped out of his car, carrying a pencil-flashlight and three small tools, crossed to the Jaguar, cast a glance around, and slid underneath it.

Amid the mud and snow-slush of the square, his suit, he knew, would be wet and filthy within seconds. That was the least of his worries. Using the flashlight beneath the front end of the Jaguar, he located the locking switch for the hood. It took him twenty minutes to ease it free. The hood jumped upward an inch when the catch was

released. Simple pressure from on top would relock it
when he had finished. At least he had no need to break
into the car to release the catch from inside.

He went back to the Mercedes and brought the bomb
over to the sports car. A man working under the hood
of a car attracts little or no attention. Passers-by assume
he is tinkering with his own car.

Using the binding wire and the pliers, he lashed the
explosive charge to the inside of the engine compartment, fixing it to the wall directly in front of the driving
position. It would be barely three feet from Miller's
chest when it went off. The trigger mechanism, connected to the main charge by two wires eight feet long,
he lowered through the engine area to the ground beneath.

Sliding back under the car, he examined the front
suspension by the light of his flashlight. He found the
place he needed within five minutes and tightly wired
the rear end of the trigger to a handy bracing-bar. The
open jaws of the trigger, sheathed in rubber and held
apart by the glass bulb, he jammed between two of the
coils of the stout spring that formed the front near-
side suspension.

When it was firmly in place, unable to be shaken
free by normal jolting, he came back out from under.
He estimated the first time the car hit a bump or a
normal pothole at speed, the retracting suspension on
the front near-side wheel would force the open jaws of
the trigger together, crushing the frail glass bulb that
separated them and make contact between the two
lengths of electrically charged hacksaw blade. When
that happened, Miller and his incriminating documents
would be blown to pieces.

Finally Mackensen gathered up the slack in the wires
connecting the charge and the trigger, made a neat loop
of them, and taped them out of the way at the side of
the engine compartment, so they would not trail on the
ground and be rubbed through by abrasion against the
road surface. This done, he closed the hood and snapped
it shut. Then he returned to the back seat of the Mer-

cedes, curled up, and dozed. He had done, he thought, a good night's work.

Miller ordered the taxi-driver to take them to the Saarplatz, paid him, and dismissed him. Koppel had had the good sense to keep his mouth shut during the ride, and it was only when the taxi was disappearing back into town that he opened it again.

"I hope you know what you're doing, Herr Miller. I mean, it's strange you being on a caper like this, you being a reporter."

"Koppel, there's no need to worry. What I'm after is a bunch of documents kept in a safe inside the house. I'll take them. You get anything else there is on hand. Okay?"

"Well, since it's you, all right. Let's get it over with."

"There's one last thing. The place has a live-in maid," said Miller.

"You said it was empty," protested Koppel. "If she comes down, I'll split. I don't want no part of violence."

"We'll wait until two in the morning. She'll be fast asleep."

They walked the mile to Winzer's house, cast a quick look up and down the road, and darted through the gate. To avoid the gravel, both men walked up the grass edge along the driveway, then crossed the lawn to hide in the rhododendron bushes facing the windows of what looked like the study.

Koppel, moving like a furtive little animal through the undergrowth, made a tour of the house, leaving Miller to watch the bag of tools. When he came back he whispered, "The maid's still got her light on. Window at the back under the eaves."

Not daring to smoke, they sat for an hour, shivering beneath the fat evergreen leaves of the bushes. At one in the morning Koppel made another tour and reported the girl's bedroom light was out.

They sat for another ninety minutes before Koppel squeezed Miller's wrist, took his bag, and padded across the stretch of moonlight on the lawn toward the study windows. Somewhere down the road a dog barked, and farther away a car tire squealed as a motorist headed home.

Fortunately for them, the area beneath the study windows was in shadow, the moon not having come around the side of the house. Koppel flicked on a pencil-flashlight and ran it around the window frame, then along the bar dividing the upper and lower sections. There was a good burglar-proof window catch but no alarm system. He opened his bag and bent over it for a second, straightening up with a roll of sticky tape, a suction pad on a stick, a diamond-tipped glass-cutter like a fountain pen, and a rubber hammer.

With remarkable skill he cut a perfect circle on the surface of the glass just below the window catch. For double insurance he taped two lengths of sticky tape across the disk, with the ends of each tape pressed to the uncut section of window. Between the tapes he pressed the sucker, well licked, so that a small area of glass was visible on either side of it.

Using the rubber hammer, holding the stick from the sucker in his left hand, he gave the exposed area of the cut circle of window pane a sharp tap.

At the second tap there was a crack, and the disk fell inward toward the room. They both paused and waited for reaction, but no one had heard the sound. Still gripping the end of the sucker, to which the glass disk was attached inside the window, Koppel ripped away the two pieces of sticky tape. Glancing through the window, he spotted a thick rug five feet away, and with a flick of the wrist tossed the disk of glass and the sucker inward, so they fell soundlessly on the rug.

Reaching through the hole, he unscrewed the burglar catch and eased up the lower window. He was over it as nimbly as a fly, and Miller followed more cautiously. The room was pitch-black by contrast with the moonlight on the lawn, but Koppel seemed to be able to see perfectly well.

He whispered, "Keep still," to Miller, who froze, while the burglar quietly closed the window and drew the curtains across it. He drifted through the room, avoiding the furniture by instinct, closed the door that led to the passage, and only then flicked on his flashlight.

It swept around the room, picking out a desk, a telephone, a wall of bookshelves, and a deep armchair, and finally settled on a handsome fireplace with a large surround of red brick.

He materialized at Miller's side. "This must be the study. There can't be two rooms like this, and two brick fireplaces, in one house. Where's the lever that opens the brickwork?"

"I don't know," muttered Miller back, imitating the low murmur of the burglar, who had learned the hard way that a murmur is far more difficult to detect than a whisper. "You'll have to find it."

"God. It could take ages," said Koppel.

He sat Miller in the chair, warning him to keep his string-backed driving gloves on at all times. Taking his bag, Koppel went over to the fireplace, slipped a headband around his head, and fixed the flashlight into a bracket so that it pointed forward. Inch by inch, he went over the brickwork, feeling with sensitive fingers for bumps or lugs, indentations or hollow areas. Abandoning this when he had covered it all, he started again with a palette knife probing for cracks. He found it at half past three.

The knife blade slipped into a crack between two bricks, and there was a low click. A section of bricks, two feet by two feet in size, swung an inch outward. So skillfully had the work been done that no naked eye could spot the square area among the rest of the surround.

Koppel eased the door open; it was hinged on the left side by silent steel hinges. The four-square-foot area of brickwork was set in a steel tray that formed a door. Behind the door, the thin beam of Koppel's headlamp picked out the front of a small wall safe.

He kept the light on but slipped a stethoscope around his neck and fitted the earpieces. After five minutes spent gazing at the four-disk combination lock, he held the listening end where he judged the tumblers would be and began to ease the first ring through its combinations.

Miller, from his seat ten feet away, gazed at the work and became increasingly nervous. Koppel, by contrast, was completely calm, absorbed in his work. Apart from this, he knew that both men were unlikely to cause anyone to investigate the study so long as they remained completely immobile. The entry, the moving about, and the exit were the danger periods.

It took him forty minutes until the last tumbler fell over. Gently he eased the safe door back and turned to Miller, the beam from his head darting over a table containing a pair of silver candlesticks and a heavy old snuffbox.

Without a word, Miller rose and went to join Koppel by the safe. He reached up, took the light from Koppel's head bracket, and used it to probe the interior. There were several bundles of banknotes, which he pulled out and passed to the grateful burglar, who uttered a low whistle that carried no more than several feet.

The upper shelf in the safe contained only one object, a buff manila folder. Miller pulled it out, flicked it open, and riffled through the sheets inside. There were about forty of them. Each contained a photograph and several lines of type. At the eighteenth he paused and said out loud, "Good God."

"Quiet," muttered Koppel with urgency.

Miller closed the file, handed the flashlight back to Koppel, and said, "Close it."

Koppel slid the door back into place and twirled the dial not merely until the door was locked, but until the figures were in the same order in which he had found them. When he was done he eased the brickwork across the area and pressed it firmly home. It gave another soft click and locked into place.

He had stuffed the banknotes in his pocket, the cash proceeds of Winzer's last four passports, and he remained only to lay the candlesticks and snuffbox gently into his black leather bag.

After switching off his light, he led Miller by the arm

to the window, slipped the curtains back to right and left, and took a good look out through the glass. The lawn was deserted, and the moon had gone behind cloud. Koppel eased up the window, hopped over it, bag and all, and waited for Miller to join him. He pulled the window down and headed for the shrubbery, followed by the reporter, who had stuffed the file inside his polo-necked sweater.

They kept to the bushes until close to the gate, then emerged onto the road. Miller had an urge to run.

"Walk slowly," said Koppel in his normal talking voice. "Just walk and talk like we were coming home from a party."

It was three miles back to the railway station, and already it was close to five o'clock. The streets were not wholly deserted, although it was Saturday, for the German working man rises early to go about his business. They made it to the station without being stopped and questioned.

There was no train to Hamburg before seven, but Koppel said he would be glad to wait in the café and warm himself with coffee and a double whisky.

"A very nice little job, Herr Miller," he said. "I hope you got what you wanted."

"Oh, yes, I got it all right," said Miller.

"Well, mum's the word. By-by, Herr Miller."

The little burglar nodded and strolled toward the station café. Miller turned back and crossed the square to the hotel, unaware of the red-rimmed eyes that watched him from the back of a parked Mercedes.

It was too early to make the inquiries Miller needed to make, so he allowed himself three hours of sleep and asked to be waked at nine-thirty.

The phone shrilled at the exact hour, and he ordered coffee and rolls, which arrived just as he had finished a piping-hot shower. Over coffee he sat and studied the file of papers, recognizing about half a dozen of the faces but none of the names. The names, he had to tell himself, were meaningless.

Sheet eighteen was the one he came back to. The man

was older, the hair longer, a sporting mustache covered the upper lip. But the ears were the same—the part of a face that is more individual to each owner than any other feature, yet which are always overlooked. The narrow nostrils were the same, the tilt of the head, the pale eyes.

The name was a common one; what fixed his attention was the address. From the postal district, it had to be the center of the city, and that would probably mean an apartment.

Just before ten o'clock he called the telephone Information department of the city named on the sheet of paper. He asked for the number of the superintendent for the apartment house at that address. It was a gamble, and it came off. It *was* an apartment house, and an expensive one.

He called the superintendent and explained that he had repeatedly called one of the tenants but could get no reply, which was odd because he had specifically been asked to call the man at that hour. Could the superintendent help him? Was the phone out of order?

The man at the other end was most helpful. The *Herr Direktor* would probably be at the factory, or perhaps at his weekend house in the country.

What factory was that? Why, his own, of course. The radio factory. Oh, yes, of course, how stupid of me, said Miller and rang off. Information gave him the number of the factory. The girl who answered passed him to the boss's secretary, who told the caller the *Herr Direktor* was spending the weekend at his country house and would be back on Monday morning. The private house number was not to be divulged from the factory. A question of privacy. Miller thanked her and hung up.

The man who finally gave him the private number and address of the owner of the radio factory was an old contact, the industrial and business affairs correspondent of a large newspaper in Hamburg. He had the man's address in his private address book.

Miller sat and stared at the face of Roschmann, the new name, and the private address scribbled in his notebook. Now he remembered hearing of the man before,

an industrialist from the Ruhr; he had even seen the
radios in the stores. He took out his map of Germany
and located the country villa on its private estate, or at
least the area of villages where it was situated.

It was past twelve o'clock when he packed his bags,
descended to the hall, and settled his bill. He was
famished, so he went into the hotel dining room, taking
only his document case, and treated himself to a large
steak.

Over his meal he decided to drive the last section of
the chase that afternoon and confront his target the next
morning. He still had the slip of paper with the private
telephone number of the lawyer with the Z Commission
in Ludwigsburg. He could have called him then, but
he wanted, was determined, to face Roschmann first.
He feared if he tried that evening, the lawyer might not
be at home when he called him to ask for a squad of
policemen within thirty minutes. Sunday morning would
be fine, just fine.

It was nearly two when he finally emerged, stowed his
suitcase in the trunk of the Jaguar, tossed the document
case onto the passenger seat, and climbed behind the
wheel.

He failed to notice the Mercedes that tailed him to
the edge of Osnabrück. The car behind him came onto
the main autobahn after him, paused for a few seconds
as the Jaguar accelerated fast down the southbound
lane, then left the main road twenty yards farther on
and drove back into town.

From a telephone booth by the roadside, Mackensen
phoned the Werwolf in Nuremberg.

"He's on his way," he told his superior. "I just left
him going down the southbound lane like a bat out of
hell."

"Is your device accompanying him?"

Mackensen grinned. "Right. Fixed to the front near-
side suspension. Within fifty miles he'll be in pieces
you couldn't identify."

"Excellent," purred the man in Nuremberg. "You

must be tired, my dear *Kamerad*. Go back into town and get some sleep."

Mackensen needed no second bidding. He had not slept a full night since Wednesday.

Miller made those fifty miles, and another hundred. For Mackensen had overlooked one thing. His trigger device would certainly have detonated quickly if it had been jammed into the cushion suspension system of a Continental saloon car. But the Jaguar was a British sports car, with a far harder suspension system. As it tore down the autobahn toward Frankfurt, the bumping caused the heavy springs above the front wheels to retract slightly, crushing the small bulb between the jaws of the bomb trigger to fragments of glass. But the electrically charged lengths of steel failed to touch each other. On the hard bumps they flickered to within a millimeter of each other before springing apart.

Unaware of how close to death he was, Miller made the trip past Münster, Dortmund, Wetzlar, and Bad Homburg to Frankfurt in just under three hours, then turned off the ring road toward Königstein and the wild, snow-thick forests of the Taunus Mountains.

16

IT WAS already dark when the Jaguar slid into the small spa town in the eastern foothills of the mountain range. A glance at his map told Miller he was less than twenty miles from the private estate he sought. He decided to go no farther that night, but to seek a hotel and wait till morning.

To the north lay the mountains, straddled by the road to Limburg, lying quiet and white under the thick carpet of snow that muffled the rocks and shrouded the miles and miles of pine forest. There were lights twinkling down the main street of the small town, and the glow of them picked out the skeletal frame of the ruined castle brooding on its hill, once the fortress home of the Lords of Falkenstein. The sky was clear, but an icy wind gave promise of more snow to come during the night.

At the corner of Hauptstrasse and Frankfurtstrasse he found a hotel, the Park, and asked for a room. In a spa town in February the cold-water cure has hardly the same charm as in the summer months. There was plenty of room.

The porter directed him to put his car in the small lot at the back of the hotel, fringed by trees and bushes. He had a bath and went out for supper, picking the Grüne Baum hostelry in the Hauptstrasse, one of the dozen old, beamed eating houses the town had to offer.

It was over his meal that the nervousness set in. He noticed his hands were shaking as he raised his wine-glass. Part of the condition was exhaustion, the lack of sleep in the past four days, the catnapping for one and two hours at a time.

Part was delayed reaction from the tension of the

break-in with Koppel, and part the sense of astonishment at the luck that had rewarded his instinct to go
back to Winzer's house after the first visit and ask the
maid who had looked after the bachelor forger all these
years.

But most, he knew, was the sense of the impending
end of the chase, the confrontation with the man he
hated and had sought through so many unknown byways
of inquiry, coupled with the fear that something might
still go wrong.

He thought back to the anonymous doctor in the
hotel in Bad Godesberg who had warned him to stay
away from the men of the Comradeship; and the Jewish
Nazi-hunter of Vienna who had told him, "Be careful;
these men can be dangerous." Thinking back, he wondered why they had not struck at him yet. They knew
his name as Miller—the Dreesen Hotel visit proved that;
and as Kolb—the beating of Bayer in Stuttgart would
have blown that cover. Yet he had seen no one. One
thing they could not know, he was sure, was that he
had got as far as he had. Perhaps they had lost him,
or decided to leave him alone, convinced, with the forger
in hiding, he would end up by going in circles.

And yet he had the file, Winzer's secret and explosive
evidence, and with it the greatest news story of the
decade in West Germany. He grinned to himself, and
the passing waitress thought it was for her. She swung
her bottom as she passed his table next time, and he
thought of Sigi. He had not called her since Vienna, and
the letter he wrote in early January was the last she had
had, six weeks back. He felt now that he needed her as
he never had before.

Funny, he thought, how men always need women
more when they are afraid. He had to admit he *was*
frightened, partly of what he had done, partly of the
mass-murderer who waited, unknowing, for him in
the mountains.

He shook his head to shake off the mood and ordered
another half-bottle of wine. This was no time for melan-

choly; he had pulled off the greatest journalistic coup he had ever heard of and was about to settle a score as well.

He ran over his plan as he drank the second portion of wine. A simple confrontation, a telephone call to the lawyer at Ludwigsburg, the arrival thirty minutes later of a police van to take the man away for imprisonment, trial, and a life sentence. If Miller had been a harder man, he would have wanted to kill the SS captain himself.

He thought it over and realized he was unarmed. Supposing Roschmann had a bodyguard? Would he really be alone, confident his new name would protect him from discovery? Or would there be a strong-arm retainer in case of trouble?

During Miller's military service, one of his friends, spending a night in the guardroom for being late back into camp, had stolen a pair of handcuffs from the Military Police. Later he had become worried by the thought they might be found in his kitbag and had given them to Miller. The reporter had kept them, simply as a trophy of a wild night in the Army. They were at the bottom of a trunk in his Hamburg flat.

He also had a gun, a small Sauer automatic, bought quite legally when he had been covering an exposé of Hamburg's vice rackets in 1960 and had been threatened by Little Pauli's mobsters. That was locked in a desk drawer, also in Hamburg.

Feeling slightly dizzy from the effects of his wine, a double brandy, and tiredness, he rose, paid his bill, and went back to the hotel. He was just about to enter to make his phone call, when he saw two public booths almost at the hotel door. Safer to use these.

It was nearly ten o'clock, and he found Sigi at the club where she worked. Above the clamor of the band in the background, he had to shout to make her hear him.

Miller cut short her stream of questions about where he had been, why he had not got in touch, where he was now, and told her what he wanted. She protested she couldn't get away, but something in his voice stopped her.

"Are you all right?" she shouted over the line.

"Yes, I'm fine. But I need your help. Please, darling, don't let me down. Not now, not tonight."

There was a pause; then she said simply, "I'll come. I'll tell them it's an emergency. Close family or something."

"Do you have enough to rent a car?"

"I think so. I can borrow something off one of the girls."

He told her the address of an all-night car-rental firm he had used before, and stressed she should mention his name, as he knew the proprietor.

"How far is it?" she asked.

"From Hamburg, five hundred kilometers. You can make it in five hours. Say six hours from now. You'll arrive about five in the morning. And don't forget to bring the things."

"All right, you can expect me then." There was a pause, then: "Peter darling . . ."

"What?"

"Are you afraid of something?"

The time signal started, and he had no more one-mark pieces.

"Yes," he said and put down the receiver as they were cut off.

In the foyer of the hotel he asked the night porter if he could have a large envelope, and after some hunting beneath the counter the man obligingly produced a stiff brown one large enough to take a quarto-sized sheet of paper. Miller also bought enough stamps to cover the cost of sending the envelopes by first-class mail with a lot of contents, emptying the porter's stock of stamps, which were usually needed only when a guest wished to send a postcard.

Back in his room he took his document case, which he had carried throughout the evening, laid it on the bed, and took out Salomon Tauber's diary, the sheaf of papers from Winzer's safe, and two photographs. He read again the two pages in the diary that had originally sent him on this hunt for a man he had never heard of, and studied the two photographs side by side.

Finally he took a sheet of plain paper from his case and wrote on it a brief but clear message, explaining to any reader what the sheaf of documents enclosed really was. The note, along with the file from Winzer's safe and one of the photographs, he placed inside the envelope, addressed it, and stuck on all the stamps he had bought.

The other photograph he put into the breast pocket of his jacket. The sealed envelope and the diary went back into his attaché case, which he slid under the bed.

He carried a small flask of brandy in his suitcase, and he poured a measure into the glass above the wash-basin. He noticed his hands were trembling, but the fiery liquid relaxed him. He lay down on the bed, his head spinning slightly, and dozed off.

In the underground room in Munich, Josef paced the floor, angry and impatient. At the table, Leon and Motti gazed at their hands. It was forty-eight hours since the cable had come from Tel Aviv.

Their own attempts to trace Miller had brought no result. At their request by telephone, Alfred Oster had been to the parking lot in Bayreuth and later called back to tell them the car was gone.

"If they spot that car, they'll know he can't be a bakery worker from Bremen," growled Josef when he heard the news, "even if they don't know the car-owner is Peter Miller."

Later a friend in Stuttgart had informed Leon the local police were looking for a young man in connection with the murder in a hotel room of a citizen called Bayer. The description fitted Miller in his disguise as Kolb too well for it to be any other man, but fortunately the name from the hotel register was neither Kolb nor Miller, and there was no mention of a black sports car.

"At least he had the sense to register in a false name," said Leon.

"That would be in character with Kolb," Motti pointed out. "Kolb was supposed to be on the run from the Bremen police for war crimes."

But it was scant comfort. If the Stuttgart police could not find Miller, neither could the Leon group, and the latter could only fear the Odessa would by now be closer than either.

"He must have known, after killing Bayer, that he had blown his cover, and therefore reverted to the name of Miller," reasoned Leon. "So he has to abandon the search for Roschmann, unless he got something out of Bayer that took him to Roschmann."

"Then why the hell doesn't he check in?" snapped Josef. "Does the fool think he can take Roschmann on his own?"

Motti coughed quietly. "He doesn't know Roschmann has any real importance to the Odessa," he pointed out.

"Well, if he gets close enough, he'll find out," said Leon.

"And by then he'll be a dead man, and we'll all be back to square one," snapped Josef. "Why doesn't the idiot call in?"

But the phone lines were busy elsewhere that night, for Klaus Winzer had called the Werwolf from a small mountain chalet in the Regensburg region. The news he got was reassuring.

"Yes, I think it's safe for you to return home," the Odessa chief had answered in reply to the forger's question. "The man who was trying to interview you has by now certainly been taken care of."

The forger had thanked him, settled his overnight bill, and set off through the darkness for the north and the familiar comfort of his large bed at home in Westerberg, Osnabrück. He expected to arrive in time for a hearty breakfast, a bath, and a long sleep. By Monday morning he would be back in his printing plant, supervising the handling of the business.

Miller was waked by a knock at the bedroom door. He blinked, realizing the light was still on, and opened. The night porter stood there, Sigi behind him.

Miller quieted his fears by explaining the lady was his wife, who had brought him some important papers from home for a business meeting the following morning. The porter, a simple country lad with an indecipherable Hessian accent, took his tip and left.

Sigi threw her arms around him as he kicked the door shut. "Where have you been? What are you doing here?"

He shut off the questions in the simplest way, and by the time they parted Sigi's cold cheeks were flushed and burning and Miller was feeling like a fighting rooster.

He took her coat and hung it on the hook behind the door. She started to ask more questions.

"First things first," he said and pulled her down onto the bed, still warm under the thick feather cushion, where he had lain dozing.

She giggled. "You haven't changed."

She was still wearing her hostess dress from the cabaret, low-cut at the front, with a skimpy sling-bra beneath it. He unzipped the dress down the back and eased the thin shoulder-straps off.

"Have you?" he asked quietly.

She took a deep breath and lay back as he bent over her, pushing herself toward his face. She smiled. "No," she murmured, "not at all. You know what I like."

"And you know what I like," muttered Miller indistinctly.

She squealed. "Me first. I've missed you more than you've missed me."

There was no reply, only silence disturbed by Sigi's rising sighs and groans.

It was an hour before they paused, panting and happy, and Miller filled the glass with brandy and water.

Sigi sipped a little, for she was not a heavy drinker, despite her job, and Miller took the rest.

"So," said Sigi teasingly, "first things having been dealt with—"

"For a while," interjected Miller.

She giggled. "For a while. Would you mind telling me why the mysterious letter, why the six-week absence, why that awful skin-head haircut, and why this small room in an obscure hotel in Hesse?"

Miller grew serious. At length he rose, still naked, crossed the room, and came back with his document case. He seated himself on the edge of the bed.

"You're going to learn pretty soon what I've been up to," he said. "So I may as well tell you now."

He talked for nearly an hour, starting with the discovery of the diary, which he showed her, and ending with the break into the forger's house. As he talked, she grew more and more horrified.

"You're mad," she said when he had finished. "You're stark, staring, raving mad. You could have got yourself killed or imprisoned or a hundred things."

"I had to do it," he said, bereft of an explanation for things that now seemed to him to have been crazy.

"All this for a rotten old Nazi? You're nuts. It's over, Peter, all that is over. What do you want to waste your time on them for?" She was staring at him in bewilderment.

"Well, I have," he said defiantly.

She sighed heavily and shook her head to indicate her failure to understand. "All right," she said, "so now it's done. You know who he is and where he is. You just come back to Hamburg, pick up the phone, and call the police. They'll do the rest. That's what they're paid for."

Miller did not know how to answer her. "It's not that simple," he said at last. "I'm going up there later this morning."

"Going up where?"

He jerked his thumb toward the window and the still-dark range of mountains beyond it. "To his house."

"To his house? What for?" Her eyes widened in horror. "You're not going in to see him?"

"Yes. Don't ask me why, because I can't tell you. It's just something I have to do."

Her reaction startled him. She sat up with a jerk, turned onto her knees, and glared down at where he lay smoking, his head propped up by a pillow.

"That's what you wanted the gun for," she threw at him, her breasts rising and falling in her growing anger. "You're going to kill him—"

"I'm not going to kill him—"

"Well, then, he'll kill you. And you're going up there alone with a gun against him and his mob. You bastard, you rotten, stinking, horrible—"

Miller was staring at her in amazement. "What have you got so het up for? Over Roschmann?"

"I'm not het up about that horrid old Nazi. I'm talking about me. About me and you, you stupid dumb oaf. You're going to risk getting yourself killed up there, all to prove some silly point and make a story for your idiotic magazine readers. You don't even think for a minute about me."

She had started crying as she talked, the tears making tracks of mascara down each cheek like black railway lines.

"Look at me—just damn well look at me. What do you think I am, just another good screw? You really think I want to give myself every night to some randy reporter so he can feel pleased with himself when he goes off to chase some idiot story that could get him killed? You really think that? Listen, you moron, I want to get married. I want to be Frau Miller. I want to have babies. And you're going to get yourself killed. Oh, God . . ."

She jumped off the bed, ran into the bathroom, slammed the door behind her, and locked it.

Miller lay on the bed, open-mouthed, the cigarette burning down to his fingers. He had never seen her so angry, and it had shocked him. He thought over what she had said as he listened to the tap running in the bathroom.

Stubbing out the cigarette, he crossed the room to the bathroom door.

"Sigi."

There was no answer.

"Sigi."

The tap was turned off. "Go away."

"Sigi, please open the door. I want to talk to you."

There was a pause; then the door was unlocked. She stood there, naked and looking sulky. She had washed the mascara streaks off her face.

"What do you want?" she asked.

"Come over to the bed. I want to talk to you. We'll freeze standing here."

"No, you just want to start making love again."

"I won't. Honestly. I promise you I won't. I just want to talk."

He took her hand and led her back to the bed and the warmth it offered.

Her face looked up warily from the pillow. "What do you want to talk about?" she asked suspiciously.

He climbed in beside her and put his face close to her ear. "Sigrid Rahn, will you marry me?"

She turned to face him. "Do you mean it?" she asked.

"Yes, I do. I never really thought of it before. But then, you never got angry before."

"Gosh." She sounded as if she couldn't believe her ears. "I'll have to get angry more often."

"Do I get an answer?" he asked.

"Oh yes, Peter, I will. We'll be so good together."

He began caressing her again, becoming aroused as he did so.

"You said you weren't going to start that again," she accused him.

"Well, just this once. After that I promise I'll leave you strictly alone for the rest of time."

She swung her thigh across him and slid her hips on

top of his lower belly. Looking down at him, she said, "Peter Miller, don't you dare."

Miller reached up and pulled the toggle that extinguished the light, as she started to make love to him. . . .

Outside in the snow there was a dim light breaking over the eastern horizon. Had Miller glanced at his watch, it would have told him the time was ten minutes before seven on the morning of Sunday, February 23. But he was already asleep.

Half an hour later Klaus Winzer rolled up the drive of his house, stopped before the closed garage door, and climbed out. He was stiff and tired, but glad to be home.

Barbara was not yet up, taking advantage of her employer's absence to sleep longer than usual. When she did appear, after Winzer had let himself in and called from the hallway, it was in a nightgown that would have set another man's pulses bounding. Instead, Winzer required fried eggs, toast and jam, a pot of coffee, and a bath. He got none of them.

She told him, instead, of her discovery on Saturday morning, on entering the study to dust, of the broken window and the missing silverware. She had called the police, and they had been positive the neat circular hole was the work of a professional burglar. She had had to tell them the house-owner was away, and they said they wanted to know when he returned, just for routine questions about the missing items.

Winzer listened in absolute quiet to the girl's chatter, his face paling, a single vein throbbing steadily in his temple. He dismissed her to the kitchen to prepare coffee, went into his study, and locked the door. It took him thirty seconds and frantic scratching inside the empty safe to convince himself that the file of forty Odessa criminals was gone.

As he turned away from the safe, the phone rang. It was the doctor from the clinic to inform him Fräulein Wendel had died during the night.

For two hours Winzer sat in his chair before the unlit

fire, oblivious of the cold seeping in through the news-
paper-stuffed hole in the window, aware only of the cold
fingers worming around inside himself as he tried to
think what to do. Barbara's repeated calls from outside
the locked door that breakfast was ready went unheeded.
Through the keyhole she could hear him muttering occasionally, "Not my fault, not my fault at all."

Miller had forgotten to cancel the morning call he had
ordered the previous evening. The bedside phone shrilled
at nine. Bleary-eyed, he answered it, grunted his thanks,
and climbed out of bed. He knew if he did not, he would
fall asleep again. Sigi was still fast asleep, exhausted by
her drive from Hamburg, their lovemaking, and the con-
tentment of being engaged at last.

Miller showered, finishing off with several minutes under the ice-cold spray, rubbed himself briskly with the
towel he had left over the radiator all night, and felt like
a million dollars. The depression and anxiety of the night
before had vanished. He felt fit and confident.

He dressed in ankle boots and slacks, a thick roll-neck
pullover, and his double-breasted blue duffel overjacket,
a German winter garment called a *Joppe,* halfway between a jacket and a coat. It had deep slit pockets at
each side, capable of taking the gun and the handcuffs,
and an inside breast pocket for the photograph. He took
the handcuffs from Sigi's bag and examined them. There
was no key, and the manacles were self-locking, which
made them useless for anything other than locking a
man up until he was released by the police or a hacksaw
blade.

The gun he opened and examined. He had never
fired it, and it still had the maker's grease on the interior.
The magazine was full; he kept it that way. To familiar-
ize himself with it once again, he worked the breech
several times, made sure he knew which positions of the
safety catch were the "On" and "Fire," smacked the
magazine into the grip, pushed a round into the chamber, and set the safety catch to "On." He stuffed the

telephone number of the lawyer in Ludwigsburg into his trouser pocket.

He took his attaché case out from under the bed, and on a plain sheet from it wrote a message for Sigi to read when she awoke. It said: "My darling. I am going now to see the man I have been hunting. I have a reason for wanting to look into his face and be present when the police take him away in handcuffs. It is a good one, and by this afternoon I will be able to tell you. But just in case, here is what I want you to do. . . ."

The instructions were precise and to the point. He wrote down the telephone number in Munich she was to call, and the message she was to give the man at the other end. He ended: "Do not under any circumstances follow me up the mountain. You could only make matters worse, whatever the situation. So if I am not back by noon, or have not called you in this room by then, call that number, give that message, check out of the hotel, mail the envelope at any box in Frankfurt, then drive back to Hamburg. Don't get engaged to anyone else in the meantime. All my love, Peter."

He propped the note on the bedside table by the telephone, along with the large envelope containing the Odessa file, and three 50-mark bills. Tucking Salomon Tauber's diary under his arm, he slipped out of the bedroom and headed downstairs. Passing the reception desk, he ordered the porter to give his room another morning call at eleven-thirty.

He came out of the hotel doorway at nine-thirty and was surprised at the amount of snow that had fallen during the night.

Miller walked around to the back, climbed into the Jaguar, gave full choke, and pressed the starter. It took several minutes before the engine caught. While it was warming up he took a hand-brush from the trunk and brushed the thick carpet of snow off the hood, roof, and windshield.

Back behind the wheel, he slipped into gear and drove out onto the main road. The thick layer of snow over everything acted as a sort of cushion, and he could hear it crunching under the wheels. After a glance at the ordnance survey map he had bought the previous evening just before closing time, he set off down the road toward Limburg.

17

THE MORNING had turned out gray and overcast after a brief and brilliant dawn which he had not seen. Beneath the clouds the snow glittered under the trees and a wind keened off the mountains.

The road led upward, winding out of town and immediately becoming lost in the sea of trees that make up the Romberg Forest. After he had cleared town, the carpet of snow along the road was almost virgin, only one set of tracks running parallel through it, where an early-morning visitor to Königstein for church service had headed an hour before.

Miller took the branch-off toward Glashütten, skirted the flanks of the towering Feldberg mountain, and took a road signposted as leading to the village of Schmitten. On the flanks of the mountain the wind howled through the pines, its pitch rising to a near-scream among the snow-clogged boughs.

Although Miller had never bothered to think about it, it was once out of these and other oceans of pine and beech that the old Germanic tribes had swarmed to be checked by Caesar at the Rhine. Later, converted to Christianity, they had paid lip service by day to the Prince of Peace, dreaming only in the dark hours of the ancient gods of strength and lust and power. It was this ancient atavism, the worship in the dark of the private gods of screaming endless trees, that Hitler had ignited with a magic touch.

After another twenty minutes of careful driving, Miller checked his map again and began to look for a gateway off the road onto a private estate. When he found it, it was a barred gate held in place by a steel catch, with a notice board to one side saying: PRIVATE PROPERTY, KEEP OUT.

Leaving the engine running, he climbed out and swung the gate inward.

Miller entered the estate and headed up the driveway. The snow was untouched, and he kept in low gear, for there was only frozen sand beneath the snow.

Two hundred yards up the track, a branch from a massive oak tree had come down in the night, overladen with half a ton of snow. The branch had crashed into the undergrowth to the right, and some of its twigs lay on the track. It had also brought down a thin black pole that had stood beneath it, and this lay square across the drive.

Rather than get out and move it, he drove carefully forward, feeling the bump as the pole passed under the front and then the rear wheels.

Clear of the obstruction, he moved on toward the house and emerged into a clearing, which contained the villa and its gardens, fronted by a circular area of gravel. He halted the car in front of the main door, climbed out, and rang the bell.

While Miller was climbing out of his car, Klaus Winzer made his decision and called the Werwolf. The Odessa chief was brusque and irritable, for it was long past the time he should have heard on the news of a sports car being blown to pieces, apparently by an exploding gas tank, on the autobahn south of Osnabrück. But as he listened to the man on the other end of the telephone, his mouth tightened in a thin, hard line.

"You did what? You fool, you unbelievable, stupid little cretin. Do you know what's going to happen to you if that file is not recovered? . . ."

Alone in his study in Osnabrück, Klaus Winzer replaced the receiver after the last sentences from the Werwolf came over the wire, and went back to his desk. He was quite calm. Twice already life had played him the worst of tricks: first the destruction of his war work in the lakes; then the ruin of his paper fortune in 1948. And now this. Taking an old but serviceable Luger from the bottom drawer, he placed the end in his mouth and

shot himself. The lead slug that tore his head apart was
not a forgery.

The Werwolf sat and gazed in something close to horror at the silent telephone. He thought of the men for
whom it had been necessary to obtain passports through
Klaus Winzer, and the fact that each of them was a
wanted man on the list of those destined for arrest and
trial if caught. The exposure of the dossier would lead
to a welter of prosecutions that could only jerk the
population out of its growing apathy toward the question
of continuing pursuit of wanted SS men, regalvanize the
hunting agencies. . . . The prospect was appalling.

But his first priority was the protection of Roschmann,
one of those he knew to be on the list taken from Winzer. Three times he dialed the Frankfurt area code, followed by the private number of the house on the hill,
and three times he got a busy signal. Finally he tried
through the operator, who told him the line must be out
of order.

Instead, he rang the Hohenzollern Hotel in Osnabrück
and caught Mackensen about to leave. In a few sentences he told the killer of the latest disaster, and where
Roschmann lived.

"It looks as if your bomb hasn't worked," he told
him. "Get down there faster than you've ever driven,"
he said. "Hide your car and stick close to Roschmann.
There's a bodyguard called Oskar as well. If Miller goes
straight to the police with what he's got, we've all had it.
But if he comes to Roschmann, take him alive and make
him talk. We must know what he's done with those papers before he dies."

Mackensen glanced at his road map inside the phone
booth and estimated the distance.

"I'll be there at one o'clock," he said.

The door opened at the second ring, and a gust of
warm air flowed out of the hall. The man who stood in
front of Miller had evidently come from his study, the

door of which Miller could see standing open and leading off the hallway.

Years of good living had put weight on the once lanky
SS officer. His face had a flush, either from drinking or
from the country air, and his hair was gray at the sides.
He looked the picture of middle-aged, upper-middle-
class, prosperous good health. But although different in
detail, the face was the same Tauber had seen and described.

The man surveyed Miller without enthusiasm. "Yes?"
he said.

It took Miller another ten seconds before he could
speak. What he had rehearsed just went out of his head.

"My name is Miller," he said, "and yours is Eduard
Roschmann."

At the mention of both names, something flickered
through the eyes of the man in front of him, but iron
control kept his face muscles straight. "This is prepos-
terous," he said at length. "I've never heard of the man
you are talking about."

Behind the façade of calm, the former SS officer's
mind was racing. Several times in his life since 1945 he
had survived through sharp thinking in a crisis. He recognized the name of Miller well enough and recalled
his conversation with the Werwolf weeks before. His
first instinct was to shut the door in Miller's face, but
he overcame it.

"Are you alone in the house?" asked Miller.

"Yes," said Roschmann truthfully.

"We'll go into your study," said Miller flatly.

Roschmann made no objection, for he realized he
was now forced to keep Miller on the premises and stall
for time, until . . .

He turned on his heel and strode back across the hallway. Miller slammed the front door after him and was at
Roschmann's heels as they entered the study. It was a
comfortable room, with a thick, padded door, which
Miller closed behind him, and a log fire burning in the
grate.

Roschmann stopped in the center of the room and turned to face Miller.

"Is your wife here?" asked Miller.

Roschmann shook his head. "She has gone away for the weekend to visit relatives," he said. This much was true. She had been called away the previous evening at a moment's notice and had taken the second car. The first car owned by the pair was, by ill luck, in the garage for repairs. She was due back that evening.

What Roschmann did not mention, but what occupied his racing mind, was that his bulky, shaven-headed chauffeur-bodyguard, Oskar, had bicycled down to the village half an hour earlier to report that the telephone was out of order. He knew he had to keep Miller talking until the man returned.

When he turned to face Miller, the young reporter's right hand held an automatic pointed straight at his belly.

Roschmann was frightened but covered it with bluster. "You threaten me with a gun in my own house?"

"Then call the police," said Miller, nodding at the telephone on the writing desk. Roschmann made no move toward it.

"I see you still limp a little," remarked Miller. "The orthopedic shoe almost disguises it, but not quite. The missing toes, lost in an operation in Rimini camp. The frostbite you got wandering through the fields of Austria caused that, didn't it?"

Roschmann's eyes narrowed slightly, but he said nothing.

"You see, if the police come, they'll identify you, *Herr Direktor*. The face is still the same, the bullet wound in the chest, the scar under the left armpit where you tried to remove the Waffen SS blood-group tattoo, no doubt. Do you really want to call the police?"

Roschmann let out the air in his lungs in a long sigh. "What do you want, Miller?"

"Sit down," said the reporter. "Not at the desk, there in the armchair, where I can see you. And keep your hands on the armrests. Don't give me an excuse to shoot, because, believe me, I'd dearly love to."

Roschmann sat in the armchair, his eyes on the gun.

Miller perched on the edge of the desk, facing him. "So now we talk," he said.

"About what?"

"About Riga. About eighty thousand people, men, women, and children, whom you had slaughtered up there."

Seeing he did not intend to use the gun, Roschmann began to regain his confidence. Some of the color returned to his face. He switched his gaze to the face of the younger man in front of him.

"That's a lie. There were never eighty thousand disposed of in Riga."

"Seventy thousand? Sixty?" asked Miller. "Do you really think it matters precisely how many thousand you killed."

"That's the point," said Roschmann eagerly. "It doesn't matter—not now, not then. Look, young man, I don't know why you've come after me. But I can guess. Someone's been filling your head with a lot of sentimental claptrap about so-called war crimes and suchlike. It's all nonsense. Absolute nonsense. How old are you?"

"Twenty-nine."

"Then you were in the Army for military service?"

"Yes. One of the first national servicemen of the postwar army. Two years in uniform."

"Well, then, you know what the Army is like. A man's given orders; he obeys those orders. He doesn't ask whether they are right or wrong. You know that as well as I do. All I did was to obey my orders."

"Firstly, you weren't a soldier," said Miller quietly. "You were an executioner. Put more bluntly, a murderer, and a mass-murderer. So don't compare yourself with a soldier."

"Nonsense," said Roschmann earnestly. "It's all nonsense. We were soldiers just like the rest. We obeyed our orders just like the rest. You young Germans are all the same. You don't want to understand what it was like then."

"So tell me, what was it like?"

Roschmann, who had leaned forward to make his point, leaned back in the chair, almost at ease, the immediate danger past.

"What was it like? It was like ruling the world. Because we did rule the world, the Germans. We had beaten every army they could throw at us. For years they had looked down on us, we poor Germans, and we had shown them, yes, all of them, that we were a great people. You youngsters today don't realize what it is to be proud of being a German.

"It lights a fire inside you. When the drums beat and the bands played, when the flags were waving and the whole nation was united behind one man, we could have marched to the ends of the world. That is greatness, young Miller, greatness your generation has never known and never will know. And we of the SS were the elite, still are the elite. Of course they hunt us down now, first the Allies and then the wishy-washy old women of Bonn. Of course they want to crush us. Because they want to crush the greatness of Germany, which we represented and still do.

"They say a lot of stupid things about what happened then in a few camps a sensible world would long since have forgotten about. They make a big fuss because we had to clean up Europe from the pollution of this Jewish filth that impregnated every facet of German life and kept us down in the mud with them. We had to do it, I tell you. It was a mere sideshow in the great design of a Germany and a German people, pure in blood and ideals, ruling the world as is their right, *our* right, Miller, *our* right and our destiny, if those hell-damned Britishers and the eternally stupid Americans had not stuck their prissy noses in. For make no bones about it, you may point that thing at me, but we are on the same side, young man, a generation between us, but still on the same side. For we are Germans, the greatest people in the world. And you would let your judgment of all this, of the greatness that once was Germany's—and will be again one day—of the essential unity of us, all of us, the German people, you will let your judgment of all this be affected by what happened to a few miserable Jews? Can't you see, you poor misled young fool, that we are on the same side, you and me, the same side, the same people, the same destiny?"

Despite the gun, he rose from his chair and paced the carpet between the desk and the window.

"You want proof of our greatness? Look at Germany today. Smashed to rubble in nineteen forty-five, utterly destroyed and prey to the barbarians from the east and the fools in the west. And now? Germany is rising again, slowly and surely, still lacking the essential discipline that we were able to give her, but increasing each year in her industrial and economic power. Yes, and military power. One day, when the last vestiges of the influence of the Allies of nineteen forty-five have been shaken off, we will be as mighty again as we ever were. It will take time, and a new leader, but the ideals will be the same, and the glory—yes, that will be the same too.

"And you know what brings this about? I will tell you, yes, I will tell you, young man. It's discipline and management. Harsh discipline, the harsher the better, and management, *our* management, the most brilliant quality after courage that we possess. For we can manage things; we have shown that. Look at all this—you see all this? This house, this estate, the factory down in the Ruhr, mine and thousands like it, tens, hundreds of thousands, churning out power and strength each day, with each turn of the wheel another ounce of might to make Germany mighty once again.

"And who do you think did all this? You think people prepared to spend time mouthing platitudes over a few miserable Yids did all this? You think cowards and traitors trying to persecute good honest, patriotic German soldiers did all this? *We* did this, we brought this prosperity back to Germany, the same men as we had twenty, thirty years ago."

He turned from the window and faced Miller, his eyes

alight. But he also measured the distance from the far-thest point of his pacing along the carpet to the heavy iron poker by the fire. Miller had noticed the glances.

"Now, you come here, a representative of the young generation, full of your idealism and your concern, and point a gun at me. Why not be idealistic for Germany, your own country, your own people? You think you represent the people, coming to hunt me down? You think that's what they want, the people of Germany?"

Miller shook his head. "No, I don't," he said shortly.

"Well, there you are, then. If you call the police and turn me in to them, they might make a trial out of it—I say only 'might' because even that is not certain, so long afterward, with all the witnesses scattered or dead. So put your gun away and go home. Go home and read the true history of those days, learn that Germany's greatness then and her prosperity today stem from pa-triotic Germans like me."

Miller had sat through the tirade mute, observing with bewilderment and rising disgust the man who paced the carpet in front of him, seeking to convert him to the old ideology. He had wanted to say a hundred, a thou-sand things about the people he knew and the millions beyond them who did not want or see the necessity of purchasing glory at the price of slaughtering millions of other human beings. But the words did not come. They never do when one needs them. So he just sat and stared until Roschmann had finished.

After some seconds of silence Miller asked, "Have you ever heard of a man called Tauber?"

"Who?"

"Salomon Tauber. He was a German too. Jewish. He was in Riga from the beginning to the end."

Roschmann shrugged. "I can't remember him. It was a long time ago. Who was he?"

"Sit down," said Miller. "And this time stay seated."

Roschmann shrugged impatiently and went back to the armchair. With his rising conviction that Miller would not shoot, his mind was concerned with the problem of trapping him before he could get away, rather than with an obscure and long-dead Jew.

"Tauber died in Hamburg on November twenty-second last year. He gassed himself. Are you listening?"

"Yes. If I must."

"He left behind a diary. It was an account of his story, what happened to him, what you and others did to him, in Riga and elsewhere. But mainly in Riga. But he survived, he came back to Hamburg, and he lived for eighteen years, because he was convinced you were alive and would never stand trial. I got hold of his diary. It was my starting point in finding you today, here, under your new name."

"The diary of a dead man's not evidence," growled Roschmann.

"Not for a court, but enough for me."

"And you really came here to confront me over the diary of a dead Jew?"

"No, not at all. There's a page of that diary I want you to read."

Miller opened the diary at a certain page and pushed it into Roschmann's lap. "Pick it up," he ordered, "and read it—aloud."

Roschmann unfolded the sheet and began to read it. It was the passage in which Tauber described the murder by Roschmann of an unnamed German Army officer wearing the Knight's Cross with Oak Leaf Cluster.

Roschmann reached the end of the passage and looked up. "So what?" he said, puzzled. "The man struck me. He disobeyed orders. I had the right to commandeer that ship to bring the prisoners back."

Miller tossed a photograph onto Roschmann's lap. "Is that the man you killed?"

Roschmann looked at it and shrugged. "How should I know? It was twenty years ago."

There was a slow *ker-lick* as Miller thumbed the hammer back and pointed the gun at Roschmann's face. "Was that the man?"

Roschmann looked at the photograph again. "All right. So that was the man. So what?"

"That was my father," said Miller.

The color drained out of Roschmann's face as if a plug had been pulled. His mouth dropped open; his gaze dropped to the gun barrel two feet from his face, and the steady hand behind it.

"Oh, dear God," he whispered, "you didn't come about the Jews at all."

"No. I'm sorry for them, but not that sorry."

"But how could you know, how could you possibly know from that diary that the man was your father? I never knew his name. This Jew who wrote the diary never knew. How did you know?"

"My father was killed on October eleventh, nineteen forty-four, in Ostland," said Miller. "For twenty years that was all I knew. Then I read the diary. It was the same day, the same area, the two men had the same rank. Above all, both men wore the Knight's Cross with Oak Leaf Cluster, the highest award for bravery in the field. There weren't all that many of those awarded, and very few to mere Army captains. It would have been millions to one against two similar officers dying in the same area on the same day."

Roschmann knew he was up against a man whom no argument could influence. He stared, as if mesmerized, at the gun. "You're going to kill me. You mustn't do that, not in cold blood. You wouldn't do that. Please, Miller, I don't want to die."

Miller leaned forward and began to talk. "Listen to me, you repulsive piece of dogshit. I've listened to you and your twisted mouthings till I'm sick to my guts. Now you're going to listen to me while I make up my mind whether you die here or rot in some jail for the rest of your days.

"You had the nerve, the damned crass nerve, to tell me that you, you of all people, were a patriotic German. I'll tell you what you are. You and your kind were and are the filthiest crap that was ever elevated from the gutters of this country to positions of power. And in twelve years you smeared my country with your dirt in a way that has never happened throughout our history.

"What you did sickened and revolted the whole of civilized mankind and left my generation a heritage of shame to live down that's going to take us all the rest of our lives. You spat on Germany throughout your lives. You bastards used Germany and the German people until they could not be used any more, and then you quit while the going was good. You brought us so low it would have been inconceivable before your crew came along—and I don't mean in terms of bomb damage.

"You weren't even brave. You were the most sickening cowards ever produced in Germany or Austria. You murdered millions for your own profit and in the name of your maniac power-lust, and then you got out and left the rest of us in the shit. You ran away from the Russians, hanged and shot Army men to keep them fighting, and then disappeared and left me to carry the can back.

"Even if there could be any oblivion about what you did to the Jews and the others, there can never be any forgetting that your bunch ran and hid like the dogs you are. You talk of patriotism; you don't even know the meaning of the word. And as for daring to call Army soldiers and others who fought, really fought, for Germany, *Kamerad*, it's a damned obscenity.

"I'll tell you one other thing, as a young German of the generation you so plainly despise. This prosperity we have today—it's got nothing to do with you. It's got a lot to do with millions who do a hard day's work and never murdered anyone in their lives. And as for murderers like you who may still be among us, as far as I and my generation are concerned, we would put up with a little less prosperity if we could be sure scum like you were not still around. Which, incidentally, you are not going to be for very long."

"You're going to kill me," mumbled Roschmann.

"As a matter of fact, I'm not." Miller reached behind him and pulled the telephone over toward where he sat on the desk. He kept his eyes on Roschmann and the gun pointed. He took the receiver off the cradle, slid it onto the desk, and dialed. When he had finished, he picked up the receiver.

"There's a man in Ludwigsburg who wants to have a chat with you," he said and put the telephone to his ear. It was dead.

He laid it back in the cradle, took it off again, and listened for the dial tone. There was none.

"Have you cut this off?" he asked.

Roschmann shook his head.

"Listen, if you've pulled the connection out, I'll drill you here and now."

"I haven't. I haven't touched the phone this morning. Honestly."

Miller remembered the fallen branch of the oak tree and the pole lying across the track to the house. He swore softly.

Roschmann gave a small smile. "The lines must be down," he said. "You'll have to go into the village. What are you going to do now?"

"I'm going to put a bullet through you unless you do as you're told," Miller snapped back. He dragged the handcuffs he had thought to use on a bodyguard out of his pocket.

He tossed the bracelets over to Roschmann. "Walk over to the fireplace," he ordered and followed the man across the room.

"What are you going to do?"

"I'm going to handcuff you to the fireplace, then go and phone from the village," said Miller.

He was scanning the wrought-iron scrollwork that composed the surround of the fireplace when Roschmann dropped the handcuffs at his feet. The SS man bent to pick them up, and Miller was almost caught unawares when Roschmann instead gripped a heavy poker and swung it viciously at Miller's kneecaps. The reporter stepped back in time, the poker swished past, and Roschmann was off balance.

Miller stepped in, whipped the barrel of the pistol across the bent head, and stepped back. "Try that again, and I'll kill you," he said.

Roschmann straightened up, wincing from the blow to the head.

"Clip one of the bracelets around your right wrist," Miller commanded, and Roschmann did as he was told. "You see that vine-leaf ornament in front of you? At head height? There's a branch next to it that comes out of the metalwork and rejoins it again. Lock the other bracelet onto that."

When Roschmann had snapped the second link home, Miller walked over and kicked the fire-tongs and poker out of reach. Keeping his gun against Roschmann's jacket, he frisked him and cleared the area around the chained man of all objects which he could throw to break the window.

Outside in the driveway, the man called Oskar pedaled toward the door, his errand to report the broken phone line accomplished. He paused in surprise on seeing the Jaguar, for his employer had assured him before he went that no one was expected.

He leaned the bicycle against the side of the house and quietly let himself in by the front door. In the hallway he stood irresolute, hearing nothing through the padded door to the study and not being heard himself by those inside.

Miller took a last look around and was satisfied. "Incidentally," he told the glaring Roschmann, "it wouldn't have done you any good if you had managed to hit me. It's eleven o'clock now, and I left the complete dossier of evidence on you in the hands of my accomplice, to drop into the mailbox, addressed to the right authorities, if I have not returned or phoned by noon. As it is, I'm going to phone from the village. I'll be back in twenty minutes. You won't be out of there in twenty minutes, even with a hacksaw. When I get back, the police will be thirty minutes behind me."

As he talked, Roschmann's hopes began to flicker. He knew he had only one chance left—for the returning Oskar to take Miller alive so that he could be forced to make the phone call from a phone in the village at their demand and keep the documents from reaching the mailbox.

Miller swung open the door at the other side of the

room and walked through it. He found himself staring at the roll-neck pullover worn by a man a full head taller than he was. From his place by the fire Roschmann recognized Oskar and screamed, *"Hold him."*

Miller stepped back into the room and jerked up the gun he had been replacing in his pocket. He was too slow. A swinging left backhander from Oskar's paw swept the automatic out of his grasp, and it flew across the room. At the same time Oskar thought his employer cried, *"Hit him."* He crashed a right hand into Miller's jaw. The reporter weighed 170 pounds, but the blow lifted him off his feet and threw him backward. His feet caught in a low newspaper rack, and as he went over, his head slammed into the corner of a mahogany bookcase. Crumpling like a rag doll, his body slid to the carpet and rolled onto one side.

For several seconds there was silence as Oskar took in the spectacle of his employer manacled to the fire-place, and Roschmann stared at the inert figure of Miller, from the back of whose head a trickle of blood flowed onto the floor.

"You fool," yelled Roschmann when he had taken in what had happened. Oskar looked baffled. "Get over here."

The giant lumbered across the room and stood wait-ing for orders.

Roschmann thought fast. "Try and get me out of these handcuffs," he commanded. "Use the fire-irons."

But the fire-irons had been made in an age when craftsmen intended their handiwork to last for a long time. The result of Oskar's efforts was a curly poker and a pair of wriggly tongs.

"Bring him over here," he told Oskar at last. While Oskar held Miller up, Roschmann looked under the re-porter's eyelids and felt his pulse. "He's still alive, but out cold," he said. "He'll need a doctor to come around in less than an hour. Bring me a pencil and paper."

Writing with his left hand, he scribbled two phone numbers on the paper while Oskar brought a hacksaw blade from the tool chest under the stairs. When he returned, Roschmann gave him the sheet of paper.

"Get down to the village as fast as you can," he told Oskar. "Ring this Nuremberg number and tell the man who answers it what has happened. Ring this local number and get the doctor up here immediately. You understand? Tell him it's an emergency. Now hurry."

As Oskar ran from the room, Roschmann glanced at the clock again. Ten-fifty. If Oskar could make the village by eleven, and he and the doctor could be back by eleven-fifteen, they might bring Miller around in time to get to a phone and delay the accomplice, even if the doctor would only work at gunpoint. Urgently, Roschmann began to saw at his handcuffs.

In front of the door Oskar grabbed his bicycle, then paused and glanced at the parked Jaguar. He peered through the driver's window and saw the key in the ignition. His master had told him to hurry, so he dropped the bicycle, climbed behind the wheel of the car, gunned it into life, and spurted gravel in a wide arc as he slid the sports car out of the forecourt into the driveway.

He had got up into third gear and was boring down the slippery track as fast as he could take it when he hit the snow-covered telegraph pole lying across the road.

Roschmann was still sawing at the chain linking the two bracelets when the shattering roar in the pine forest stopped him. Straining to one side, he could peer through the French windows, and although the car and the driveway were out of sight, the plume of smoke drifting across the sky told him at least that the car had been destroyed by an explosion. He recalled the assurance he had been given that Miller would be taken care of. But Miller was on the carpet a few feet away from him, his bodyguard was certainly dead, and time was running out without hope of reprieve. He leaned his head against the chill metal of the fire-surround and closed his eyes.

"Then it's over," he murmured quietly. After several

minutes he continued sawing. It was over an hour before the specially hardened steel of the military handcuffs parted to the now blunt hacksaw. As he stepped free, with only a bracelet around his right wrist, the clock chimed twelve.

If he had had time, he might have paused to kick the body on the carpet, but he was a man in a hurry. From the wall safe he took a passport and several fat bundles of new, high-denomination banknotes. Twenty minutes later, with these and a few clothes in a bag, he was bicycling down the track, around the shattered hulk of the Jaguar and the still-smoldering body lying face down in the snow, past the scorched and broken pines, toward the village.

From there he called a taxi and ordered it to take him to Frankfurt international airport. He walked to the flight-information desk and inquired. "What time is the next flight out of here for Argentina—preferably within an hour? Failing that, for Madrid."

18

IT WAS ten past one when Mackensen's Mercedes turned off the country road into the gate of the estate. Halfway up the drive to the house he found the way blocked.

The Jaguar had evidently been blown apart from inside, but its wheels had not left the road. It was still upright, slewed slantwise across the drive. The forward and rear sections were recognizable as those of a car, still held together by the tough steel girders that formed the chassis. But the center section, including the cockpit, was missing from floor to roof. Bits of this section were scattered in an area around the wreckage.

Mackensen surveyed the skeleton with a grim smile and walked over to the bundle of scorched clothes and their contents on the ground twenty feet away. Something about the size of the corpse caught his attention, and he stooped over it for several minutes. Then he straightened and ran at an easy lope up the rest of the drive toward the house.

He avoided ringing the front doorbell but tried the handle. The door opened, and he went into the hallway. For several seconds he listened, poised like a carnivorous animal by a water hole, sensing the atmosphere for danger. There was no sound. He reached under his left armpit and brought out a long-barreled Luger automatic, flicked off the safety catch, and started to open the doors leading off the hall.

The first was to the dining room, the second to the study. Although he saw the body on the hearthrug at once, he did not move from the half-open door before he had covered the rest of the room. He had known two men to fall for that trick—the obvious bait and the hidden ambush. Before entering, he glanced through the crack between the door's hinges to make sure no one waited behind it, then entered.

Miller was lying on his back with his head turned to one side. For several seconds Mackensen stared down into the chalky white face, then bent to listen to the shallow breathing. The matted blood on the back of the head told him roughly what had happened.

He spent ten minutes scouring the house, noting the open drawers in the master bedroom, the missing shaving gear from the bathroom. Back in the study, he glanced into the yawning and empty wall safe, then sat himself at the desk and picked up the telephone.

He sat listening for several seconds, swore under his breath, and replaced the receiver. There was no difficulty in finding the tool chest under the stairs, for the cupboard door was still open. He took what he needed and went back down the drive, passing through the study to check on Miller and leaving by the French windows.

It took him almost an hour to find the parted strands of the telephone line, sort them out from the entangling undergrowth, and splice them back together. When he was satisfied with his handiwork he walked back to the house, sat at the desk, and tried the phone. He got the dial tone and called his chief in Nuremberg.

He had expected the Werwolf to be eager to hear from him, but the man's voice coming down the wire sounded tired and only half-interested. Like a good sergeant, he reported what he had found: the car, the corpse of the bodyguard, the half-handcuff still linked to the scrollwork by the fire, the blunt hacksaw blade on the carpet, Miller unconscious on the floor. He finished with the absent owner.

"He hasn't taken much, Chief. Overnight things, probably money from the open safe. I can clear up here; he can come back if he wants to."

"No, he won't come back," the Werwolf told him. "Just before you called, I put the phone down. He called me from Frankfurt airport. He's got a reservation on a flight to Madrid, leaving in ten minutes. Connection this evening to Buenos Aires—"

"But there's no need," protested Mackensen. "I'll make Miller talk, we can find where he left his papers. There was no document case in the wreckage of the car, and nothing on him, except a sort of diary lying on the study floor. But the rest of his stuff must be somewhere not far away."

"Far enough," replied the Werwolf. "In a mailbox."

Wearily he told Mackensen what Miller had stolen from the forger, and what Roschmann had just told him on the phone from Frankfurt. "Those papers will be in the hands of the authorities in the morning, or Tuesday at the latest. After that everyone on that list is on borrowed time. That includes Roschmann, the owner of the house you're in, and me. I've spent the whole morning trying to warn everyone concerned to get out of the country inside twenty-four hours."

"So where do we go from here?" asked Mackensen.

"You get lost," replied his chief. "You're not on that list. I am, so I have to get out. Go back to your flat and wait until my successor contacts you. For the rest, it's over. Vulkan has fled and won't come back. With his departure his whole operation is going to fall apart unless someone new can come in and take over the project."

"What Vulkan? What project?"

"Since it's over, you might as well know. Vulkan was the name of Roschmann, the man you were supposed to protect from Miller. . . ." In a few sentences the Werwolf told the executioner why Roschmann had been so important, why his place in the project and the project itself were irreplaceable.

When he had finished, Mackensen uttered a low whistle and stared across the room at the form of Peter Miller. "That little boy sure fucked things up for everyone," he said.

The Werwolf seemed to pull himself together, and some of his old authority returned to his voice. "Ka-

merad, you must clear up the mess over there. You remember that disposal squad you used once before?"

"Yes, I know where to get them. They're not far from here."

"Call them up, bring them over. Have them leave the place without a trace of what happened. The man's wife must be coming back late tonight; she must never know what happened. Understand?"

"It'll be done," said Mackensen.

"Then make yourself scarce. One last thing. Before you go, finish that bastard Miller. Once and for all."

Mackensen looked across at the unconscious reporter with narrowed eyes. "It'll be a pleasure," he grated.

"Then good-by and good luck."

The phone went dead. Mackensen replaced it, took out an address book, thumbed through it, and dialed a number. He introduced himself to the man who answered and reminded him of the previous favor the man had done for the Comradeship. He told him where to come and what he would find.

"The car and the body beside it have to go into a deep gorge off a mountain road. Plenty of gasoline over it, a real big blaze. Nothing identifiable about the man— go through his pockets and take everything, including his watch."

"Got it," said the voice on the phone. "I'll bring a trailer and winch."

"There's one last thing. In the study of the house you'll find another stiff on the floor and a bloodstained hearthrug. Get rid of them. Not in the car—a long, cold drop to the bottom of a long, cold lake. Well weighted. No traces. Okay?"

"No problem. We'll be there by five and gone by seven. I don't like to move that kind of cargo in daylight."

"Fine," said Mackensen. "I'll be gone before you get here. But you'll find things like I said."

He hung up, slid off the desk, and walked over to

Miller. He pulled out his Luger and automatically checked the breech, although he knew it was loaded.

"You little shit," he told the body and held the gun at arm's length pointing downward, lined up on the forehead.

Years of living like a predatory animal and surviving where others, victims and colleagues, had ended on a pathologist's slab had given Mackensen the senses of a leopard. He didn't see the shadow that fell onto the carpet from the open French window; he felt it and spun around, ready to fire. But the man was unarmed.

"Who the hell are you?" growled Mackensen, keeping him covered.

The man stood in the French window, dressed in the black leather leggings and jacket of a motorcyclist. In his left hand he carried his crash helmet, gripped by the short peak and held across his stomach. The man flicked a glance at the body at Mackensen's feet and the gun in his hand.

"I was sent for," he said innocently.

"Who by?" said Mackensen.

"Vulkan," replied the man. "My *Kamerad,* Roschmann."

Mackensen grunted and lowered the gun. "Well, he's gone."

"Gone?"

"Fucked off. Heading for South America. The whole project's off. And all thanks to this little bastard reporter." He jerked the gun barrel toward Miller.

"You going to finish him?" asked the man.

"Sure. He screwed up the project. Identified Roschmann and mailed the information to the police, along with a pile of other stuff. If you're in that file, you'd better get out too."

"What file?"

"The Odessa file."

"I'm not in it," said the man.

"Neither am I," growled Mackensen. "But the Werwolf is, and his orders are to finish this one off before we quit."

"The Werwolf?"

Something began to sound a small alarm inside Mackensen. He had just been told that in Germany no one apart from the Werwolf and himself knew about the Vulkan project. The others were in South America, from where he assumed the new arrival had come. But such a man would know about the Werwolf. His eyes narrowed slightly.

"You're from Buenos Aires?" he asked.

"No."

"Where from, then?"

"Jerusalem."

It took half a second before the meaning of the name made sense to Mackensen. Then he swung up his Luger to fire. Half a second is a long time, long enough to die.

The foam rubber inside the crash helmet was scorched when the Walther went off. But the nine-millimeter parabellum slug came through the fiberglass without a pause and took Mackensen high in the breastbone with the force of a kicking mule. The helmet dropped to the ground to reveal the agent's right hand, and from inside the cloud of blue smoke the PPK fired again.

Mackensen was a big man and a strong one. Despite the bullet in the chest he would have fired, but the second slug, entering his head two finger-widths above the right eyebrow, spoiled his aim. It also killed him.

Miller awoke on Monday afternoon in a private ward in Frankfurt General Hospital. He lay for half an hour, becoming slowly aware that his head was swathed in bandages and contained a pair of energetic artillery units. He found a buzzer and pressed it, but the nurse who came told him to lie quietly because he had severe concussion.

So he lay and, piece by piece, recollected the events of the previous day until the middle of the morning. After that there was nothing. He dozed off and when he woke it was dark outside and a man was sitting by his bed. The man smiled.

Miller stared at him. "I don't know you," he said.

"Well, I know you," said the visitor.

Miller thought. "I've seen you," he said at length. "You were in Oster's house. With Leon and Motti."

"That's right. What else do you remember?"

"Almost everything. It's coming back."

"Roschmann?"

"Yes. I talked with him. I was going for the police."

"Roschmann's gone. Fled back to South America. The whole affair's over. Complete. Finished. Do you understand?"

Miller slowly shook his head. "Not quite. I've got one hell of a story. And I'm going to write it."

The visitor's smile faded. He leaned forward. "Listen, Miller. You're a lousy amateur, and you're lucky to be alive. You're going to write nothing. For one thing, you've got nothing to write. I've got Tauber's diary, and it's going back home with me, where it belongs. I read it last night. There was a photograph of an Army captain in your jacket pocket. Your father?"

Miller nodded.

"So that was what it was really all about?" asked the agent.

"Yes."

"Well, in a way I'm sorry. About your father, I mean. I never thought I'd say that to a German. Now about the file. What was it?"

Miller told him.

"Then why the hell couldn't you let us have it? You're an ungrateful man. We took a lot of trouble getting you in there, and when you get something you hand it over to your own people. We could have used that information to best advantage."

"I had to send it to someone, through Sigi. That meant by mail. You're so clever, you never let me have Leon's address."

Josef nodded. "All right. But either way, you have

no story to tell. You have no evidence. The diary's gone, the file is gone. All that remains is your personal word. If you insist on talking, nobody will believe you except the Odessa, and they'll come for you. Or rather, they'll probably hit Sigi or your mother. They play rough, remember?"

Miller thought for a while. "What about my car?"

"You don't know about that. I forgot."

Josef told Miller about the bomb in it, and the way it went off. "I told you they play rough. The car has been found gutted by fire in a ravine. The body in it is unidentified, but not yours. Your story is that you were flagged down by a hitchhiker, he hit you with an iron bar and went off in it. The hospital will confirm you were brought in by a passing motorcyclist who called an ambulance when he saw you by the roadside. They won't recognize me again; I was in a helmet and goggles at the time. That's the official version, and it will stay. To make sure, I rang the German press agency two hours ago, claiming to be the hospital, and gave them the same story. You were the victim of a hitchhiker who later crashed and killed himself."

Josef stood up and prepared to leave. He looked down at Miller. "You're a lucky bastard, though you don't seem to realize it. I got the message your girl friend passed me, presumably on your instructions, at noon yesterday, and by riding like a maniac I made it from Munich to the house on the hill in two and a half hours dead. Which was what you almost were—dead. They had a guy who was going to kill you. I managed to interrupt him in time."

He turned, hand on the doorknob. "Take a word of advice. Claim the insurance on your car, get a Volkswagen, go back to Hamburg, marry Sigi, have kids, and stick to reporting. Don't tangle with professionals again."

Half an hour after he had gone, the nurse came back. "There's a phone call for you," she said.

It was Sigi, crying and laughing on the line. She had

received an anonymous call telling her Peter was in Frankfurt General. "I'm on my way down right this minute," she said and hung up.

The phone rang again. "Miller? This is Hoffmann. I just saw a piece on the agency tapes. You got a bang on the head. Are you all right?"

"I'm fine, Herr Hoffmann," said Miller.

"Great. When are you going to be fit?"

"In a few days. Why?"

"I've got a story that's right up your alley. A lot of daughters of wealthy papas in Germany are going down to the ski slopes and getting screwed by these handsome young ski-instructors. There's a clinic in Bavaria that gets them back out of trouble—for a fat fee and no word to Daddy about it. Seems some of the young studs take a rake-off from the clinic. A great little story. Sex amid the Snow, Orgies in Oberland. When can you start?"

Miller thought. "Next week."

"Excellent. By the way, that thing you were on. Nazi-hunting. Did you get the man? Is there a story at all?"

"No, Herr Hoffmann," said Miller slowly. "No story."

"Didn't think so. Hurry up and get well. See you in Hamburg."

Josef's plane from Frankfurt via London came into Lod Airport, Tel Aviv, as dusk was setting on Tuesday evening. He was met by two men in a car and taken to headquarters for debriefing by the colonel who had signed the cable from Cormorant. They talked until almost two in the morning, a stenographer noting it all down. When it was over, the colonel leaned back, smiled, and offered his agent a cigarette.

"Well done," he said simply. "We've checked on the factory and tipped off the authorities—anonymously, of course. The research section will be dismantled. We'll see to that, even if the German authorities don't. But they will. The scientists apparently didn't know whom they were working for. We'll approach them all privately, and most will agree to destroy their records. They know, if the story broke, the weight of opinion in Germany today is pro-Israeli. They'll get other jobs in industry and keep their mouths shut. So will Bonn, and so will we. What about Miller?"

"He'll do the same. What about those rockets?"

The colonel blew a column of smoke and gazed at the stars in the night sky outside. "I have a feeling they'll never fly now. Nasser has to be ready by the summer of 'sixty-seven at the latest, and if the research work in that Vulkan factory is destroyed, they'll never mount another operation in time to fit the guidance systems to the rockets before the summer of 'sixty-seven."

"Then the danger's over," said the agent.

The colonel smiled. "The danger's never over. It just changes shape. This particular danger may be over. The big one goes on. We're going to have to fight again, and maybe after that, before it's over. Anyway, you must be tired. You can go home now."

He reached into a drawer and produced a polyethylene bag of personal effects, while the agent deposited on the desk his false German passport, money, wallet, and keys. In a side room he changed clothes, leaving the German clothes with his superior.

At the door the colonel looked the figure up and down with approval and shook hands. "Welcome home, Major Uri Ben-Shaul."

The agent felt better back in his own identity, the one he had taken in 1947 when he first came to Israel and enlisted in the Palmach. He took a taxi back home to his flat in the suburbs and let himself in with the key that had just been returned to him with his other effects.

In the darkened bedroom he could make out the sleeping form of Rivka, his wife, the light blanket rising and falling with her breathing. He peeked into the children's room and looked down at their two boys: Shlomo, who was six, and the two-year-old baby, Dov.

He wanted badly to climb into bed beside his wife

and sleep for several days, but there was one more job to be done. He set down his case and quietly undressed, taking off even the underclothes and socks. He dressed in fresh ones taken from the clothes chest, and Rivka slept on, undisturbed.

From the closet he took his uniform trousers, cleaned and pressed as they always were when he came home, and laced up the gleaming black calf-boots over them. His khaki shirts and ties were where they always were, with razor-sharp creases down the shirt where the hot iron had pressed. Over them he slipped his battle jacket, adorned only with the glinting steel wings of a paratroop officer and the five campaign ribbons he had earned in Sinai and in raids across the borders.

The final article was his red beret. When he had dressed he took several articles and stuffed them into a small bag. There was already a dim glint in the east when he got back outside and found his small car still parked where he had left it a month before in front of the apartment house.

Although it was only February 26, three days before the end of the last month of winter, the air was mild again and gave promise of a brilliant spring.

He drove eastward out of Tel Aviv and took the road to Jerusalem. There was a stillness about the dawn that he loved, a peace and a cleanness that never ceased to cause him wonder. He had seen it a thousand times on patrol in the desert, the phenomenon of a sunrise, cool and beautiful, before the onset of a day of blistering heat and sometimes of combat and death. It was the best time of the day.

The road led across the flat, fertile countryside of the littoral plain toward the ocher hills of Judea, through the waking village of Ramleh. After Ramleh there was in those days a detour around the Latroun Salient, five miles to skirt the front positions of the Jordanian forces. To his left he could see the morning breakfast fires of the Arab Legion sending up thin plumes of blue smoke.

There were a few Arabs awake in the village of Abu

Gosh, and when he had climbed up the last hills to Jerusalem the sun had cleared the eastern horizon and glinted off the Dome of the Rock in the Arab section of the divided city.

He parked his car a quarter of a mile from his destination, the mausoleum of Yad Vashem, and walked the rest, down the avenue flanked by trees planted in memory of the gentiles who had tried to help, and to the great bronze doors that guard the shrine to six million of his fellow Jews who had died in the holocaust.

The old gatekeeper told him it was not open so early in the morning, but he explained what he wanted, and the man let him in. He passed through into the Hall of Remembrance and glanced about him. He had been there before to pray for his own family, and still the massive gray granite blocks of which the hall was built overawed him.

He walked forward to the rail and gazed at the names written in black on the gray stone floor, in Hebrew and Roman letters. There was no light in the sepulcher but that from the Eternal Flame, flickering above the shallow black bowl from which it sprang.

By its light he could see the names across the floor, score upon score: Auschwitz, Treblinka, Belsen, Ravensbrück, Buchenwald. . . . There were too many to count, but he found the one he sought. Riga.

He did not need a yarmulka to cover himself, for he still wore his red beret, which would suffice. From his bag he took a fringed silk shawl, the tallith, the same kind of shawl Miller had found among the effects of the old man in Altona and had not understood. This he draped around his shoulders.

He took a prayer book from his bag and opened it at the right page. He advanced to the brass rail that separates the hall into two parts, gripped it with one hand, and gazed across it at the flame in front of him. Because he was not a religious man, he had to consult his prayer book frequently, as he recited the prayer already five thousand years old.

> *"Yitgaddal,*
> *Veyitkaddash,*
> *Shemay rabbah . . ."*

And so it was that, twenty-one years after it had died in Riga, a major of paratroops of the Army of Israel, standing on a hill in the Promised Land, finally said Kaddish for the soul of Salomon Tauber.

It would be agreeable if things in this world always finished with all the ends neatly tied up. That is very seldom the case. People go on, to live and die in their own appointed time and place. So far as it has been possible to establish, this is what happened to the main characters.

Peter Miller went home, married, and stuck to reporting the sort of things that people want to read over breakfast and in the hairdresser's. By the summer of 1970 Sigi was carrying their third child.

The men of the Odessa scattered. Eduard Roschmann's wife returned home and later received a cable from her husband telling her he was in Argentina. She refused to follow him. In the summer of 1965 she wrote to him at their old address, the Villa Jerbal, to ask him for a divorce before the Argentinian courts.

The letter was forwarded to his new address, and she got a reply consenting to her request, but stipulating the German courts, and enclosing a legal document agreeing to a divorce. She was awarded this in 1966. She still lives in Germany but has retaken her maiden name of Müller, of which there are tens of thousands in Germany. The man's first wife, Hella, still lives in Austria.

The Werwolf finally made his peace with his furious superiors in Argentina and settled on a small estate he bought with the money realized from the sale of his effects, on the Spanish island of Formenteria.

The radio factory went into liquidation. The scientists working on the guidance systems for the rockets of Helwan all found jobs in industry or the academic world. The project on which they had unwittingly been working for Roschmann, however, collapsed.

The rockets at Helwan never flew. The fuselages were ready, along with the rocket fuel. The warheads were under production. Those who may doubt the authenticity of those warheads should examine the evidence of Professor Otto Yoklek, given at the trial of Yossef ben Gal, June 10 to June 26, 1963, Basel Provincial Court, Switzerland. The forty preproduction rockets, helpless for want of the electronic systems necessary to guide them to their targets in Israel, were still standing in the deserted factory at Helwan when they were destroyed by bombers during the Six-day War. Before that the German scientists had disconsolately returned to Germany.

The exposure to the authorities of Klaus Winzer's file upset a lot of Odessa applecarts. The year which began so well ended for them disastrously. So much so that years later a lawyer and investigator of the Z Commission in Ludwigsburg was able to say, "Nineteen sixty-four was a good year for us, yes, a very good year."

At the end of 1964 Chancellor Erhard, shaken by the exposures, issued a nationwide and international appeal for all those having knowledge of the whereabouts of wanted SS criminals to come forward and tell the authorities. The response was considerable, and the work of the men of Ludwigsburg received an enormous boost which continued for several more years.

Of the politicans behind the arms deal between Germany and Israel, Chancellor Adenauer of Germany lived in his villa at Rhöndorf, above his beloved Rhine and close to Bonn, and died there on April 19, 1967. The Israeli Premier David Ben-Gurion stayed on as a member of the Knesset (Parliament) until 1970, then finally retired to his home on the kibbutz of Sede Boker, in the heart of the brown hills of the Negev, on the road from Beersheba to Eilat. He likes to receive visitors and talks with animation about many things, but not about the rockets of Helwan and the reprisal campaign against the German scientists who worked on them.

Of the secret-service men in the story, General Amit remained Controller until September 1968, and on his shoulders fell the massive responsibility of ensuring that his country was provided with pinpoint information in time for the Six-Day War. As history records, he succeeded brilliantly.

On his retirement he became chairman and managing director of the labor-owned Koor Industries of Israel. He still lives very modestly, and his charming wife, Yona, refuses, as ever, to employ a maid, preferring to do all her own housework.

His successor, who still holds the post, is General Zvi Zamir.

Major Uri Ben-Shaul was killed on Wednesday, June 7, 1967, at the head of a company of paratroops fighting their way into Old Jerusalem. He took a bullet in the head from an Arab Legionary and went down four hundred yards east of the Mandelbaum Gate.

Simon Wiesenthal still lives and works in Vienna, gathering a fact here, a tip there, slowly tracking down the whereabouts of wanted SS murderers, and each month and year brings him a crop of successes.

Leon died in Munich in 1968, and after his death the group of men he had led on his personal crusade of vengeance lost heart and split up.

And last, Top Sergeant Ulrich Frank, the tank commander who crossed Miller's path on the road to Vienna. He was wrong about the fate of his tank, the Dragon Rock. It did not go to the scrap heap. It was taken away on a low-loader, and he never saw it again. Forty months later he would not have recognized it anyway.

The steel-gray of its body had been painted out and covered with paint the color of dust-brown to merge with the landscape of the desert. The black cross of the German Army was gone from the turret and replaced by the pale blue six-pointed Star of David. The name he had given it was gone too, and it had been renamed *The Spirit of Masada*.

It was still commanded by a top sergeant, a hawk-nosed, black-bearded man called Nathan Levy. On June 5, 1967, the M-48 began its first and only week of combat since it had rolled from the workshops of Detroit, Michigan, ten years before. It was one of those tanks that General Israel Tal hurled into the battle for the Mitla Pass two days later, and at noon on Saturday, June 10, caked with dust and oil, scored by bullets, its tracks worn to wafers by the rocks of Sinai, the old Patton rolled to a stop on the eastern bank of the Suez Canal.

ABOUT THE AUTHOR

Written in hotels in Austria and Germany during the fall of 1971, *THE ODESSA FILE*—like the phenomenally successful *The Day of the Jackal* before it—is based on FREDERICK FORSYTH's life experiences as a Reuters man reporting from London, Paris and East Berlin in the early 1960's. Mr. Forsyth is currently at work on a third novel, *The Dogs of War,* which he has set among mercenaries in Africa and in which he has included details of gun-running from Europe he uncovered while researching his nonfiction book, *The Biafra Story,* and while serving as the BBC's television correspondent in Biafra during the Nigerian civil war.

HOW MUCH DO YOU REALLY KNOW ABOUT YOUR CONGRESSMEN?

Get To Know Who's Who In Congress And What They Do *Between* Elections

Aside from their names and their political affiliations, what else do you know about the congressmen who represent you? Probably not too much. At least not enough.

The Ralph Nader Congress Project has turned out the most thorough and most informative biographical study of members of Congress ever assembled—Individual Profiles are currently available on *every* Senator and Representative in the current 93rd Congress —except those elected for the first time in November 1972.

Each Profile reports on a member's background, politics and performance and tells how he got where he is, who helped him, how he voted, what he promised . . . and much, much more!

The Profiles run 20 to 40 magazine-size pages and contain such information as:

- **POSITIONS ON AS MANY AS 85 KEY VOTES ON A VARIETY OF ISSUES**
- **FINANCIAL INTERESTS AND CAMPAIGN CONTRIBUTIONS**
- **LEGISLATIVE INTERESTS**
- **SUPPORTERS IN WASHINGTON —AND ELSEWHERE**
- **PERSONAL AND POLITICAL BIOGRAPHY**

Individual Profiles cost $1.00 each, postage paid.

Libraries and other groups interested in obtaining the complete bound set may purchase the complete set of 484 Profiles in 9 volumes at $450.00, including shipping.

To order while the supply lasts send the names of the members whose Profiles you wish and $1.00 check or money order for each Profile to:

**Ralph Nader Congress Project,
Grossman Publishers, Dept. BB,
P.O. Box 19281, Washington, D.C. 20036**
RN1-10/73

HOW MUCH DO YOU REALLY KNOW ABOUT CONGRESS?

It's amazing how much there is to know about Congress and how little is actually known.

TV, radio, newspapers and magazines cover our national legislature, but that's not nearly enough. So a little more than a year ago Ralph Nader (and members of his Congress Project) mobilized a "citizen's army" of more than 1,000 people and tackled the awesome job of *uncovering* Congress—both inside and out!

The result is WHO RUNS CONGRESS?—a fascinating and thoroughly documented study of the highly esteemed but little understood branch of government.

WHO RUNS CONGRESS? reveals the real functions, failures and successes on Capitol Hill. What's more, it will also help you learn:

- **HOW AFTER A 1970 LAW TO MAKE COMMITTEE SESSIONS PUBLIC, 36% WERE STILL BEING HELD BEHIND CLOSED DOORS**
- **HOW THE U.S. IS BOUND BY 4,000 "TREATIES" WHICH CONGRESS NEVER APPROVED**
- **HOW BILLIONS OF DOLLARS APPROPRIATED BY CONGRESS TO SOLVE SOCIAL PROBLEMS WERE BLOCKED BECAUSE OF PRESIDENTIAL POLITICS**
- **HOW NONCONFORMISTS GET VETOED FROM MAJOR COMMITTEE ASSIGNMENTS**

WHO RUNS CONGRESS? pulls no punches—it names names of congressmen involved in payoffs, influence peddling, tax dodges, committee cover-ups and much, much more!

WHO RUNS CONGRESS? (7701—$1.95) is one of the most useful and important books you will ever own. To get your copy (or copies) simply send your order to:

Bantam Books, Inc.
414 East Golf Road
Des Plaines, Illinois 60016

RN2-10/73

RELAX!
SIT DOWN
and Catch Up On Your Reading!